Alfred N. Palmer

A History of the Older Nonconformity of Wrexham

And its neighbourhood

Alfred N. Palmer

A History of the Older Nonconformity of Wrexham
And its neighbourhood

ISBN/EAN: 9783337369163

Printed in Europe, USA, Canada, Australia, Japan

Cover: Foto ©Andreas Hilbeck / pixelio.de

More available books at **www.hansebooks.com**

A HISTORY

OF THE

Older Nonconformity of Wrexham and its Neighbourhood,

*Being the Third Part of "A History of the Town and
Parish of Wrexham."*

BY

ALFRED NEOBARD PALMER, F.C.S.,

AUTHOR OF

*"Town, Fields, and Folk of Wrexham in the Time of
James the First."*

WREXHAM:

WOODALL MINSHALL, AND THOMAS.

PREFACE.

NO one undertaking to deal in a complete and systematic way with *The History of the Town and Parish of Wrexham* could avoid a full treatment of the history of the " Older Nonconformity " of the district. That history begins at so early a date, includes so much picturesque incident, involves so many distinguished names, and is so mixed up with the general history of the town and parish as to make some knowledge of it indispensable to all who are really interested in our local annals. Some knowledge of it will also probably be found of importance to others. For "The History of the Older Nonconformity of Wrexham" is not merely closely connected with the history of the earlier Nonconformity of other parts of North Wales, but also touches at many points various problems of more general interest.

I hope, at any rate, that the general reader will find something attractive in the account here given of the Welsh mystic—Morgan Lloyd o Wynedd—and of the translated selections from his " Llyfr y tri Aderyn," here introduced to English readers in a printed form for the first time.

It is only the history of the *older* Nonconformity of the town and district with which I have here undertaken to deal, so that no reference will be found in this book to local Methodism, which belongs wholly to modern times and with the history of which I could not here deal without swelling this book to a ruinous bulk.

I have felt the necessity of treating my subject on the one hand with sympathy and on the other with impartiality, and I hope it will be found that I have been successful in doing so.

I must acknowledge my obligations to the ministers and deacons of the three oldest congregations in Wrexham for allowing me free access to the books and documents belonging to them. I am under the like obligation to the minister of Matthew Henry's Chapel, Chester, and to John Dymond Crosfield, Esq., and the trustees of the Hardshaw West Monthly Meeting. Llewelyn Kenrick, Esq., of Wynne Hall, and Thomas Minshall, Esq., of Oswestry, have placed me under obligation by permitting me to examine the family papers in their charge. And I wish particularly to thank Francis Smith, Esq., of Brighouse, who, through Wm. Darby, Esq., of Liverpool, has supplied me with pertinent extracts from the books of the Nantwich Monthly Meeting. Finally, I have to acknowledge the important information I have received from Simon Jones, Esq., of Wrexham, W. M. Myddelton, Esq., of Stoke Newington, Peter Swinton Boult, Esq., of Liverpool, Joseph Boult, Esq., of Liverpool, and Edward Evans, Esq., of Manchester.

ALFRED NEOBARD PALMER.

WREXHAM,
    September, 1888.

CORRECTION.—I wish to withdraw the suggestion made on page 104, that the Rev. David Jones, of Chester Street, was *perhaps* the author of the *Histori Nicodemus* printed in Wrexham in the year 1745: the real author was Dafydd Jones, of Trefriew, afterwards well known as a Welsh printer.

CONTENTS.

LIST OF ILLUSTRATIONS.

INDEX.

A HISTORY OF THE OLDER NONCONFORMITY OF WREXHAM.

CHAPTER I.

Morgan Lloyd and the Puritanism of Wrexham and its Neighbourhood during the period preceding the Restoration.

1. Although the statement is erroneous which is often made, that Walter Cradock, curate of the parish, founded in 1635 the first Nonconforming Church in Wrexham, there is a sense in which Nonconformity in this town may with truth be said to be due to his preaching. He it was who here first presented the doctrines of Puritanism in a form in which they could take hold of the imagination and conscience of the people, and so produce the fruits of righteousness in those who received them. Morgan Lloyd, of Cynfael, then a lad at school in the town, afterwards the actual founder of Nonconformity in Wrexham, derived, it would appear, his first religious impulses from Mr. Cradock's preaching in this place. So also did, it is said, David ap Hugh[1], who is afterwards described as "an eminent saint and famous preacher." Many others, doubtless, fellow labourers of Morgan Lloyd, dated all that was best in them from the influences of that Pentecostal year in which Walter Cradock preached here. But to say this is a very different thing from saying that Mr. Cradock founded the first Nonconforming Church in Wrexham. He inspired some of the men who afterwards founded it. But he himself still desired to approve himself a faithful minister of the Church of England, and when, after eleven months of fruitful labour[2], the Vicar was induced to dismiss him, or the Bishop to cancel his licence, he quietly departed, making no attempt to retain, in an unauthorised way, the oversight of those whose hearts he had lightened, and whose wills he had enlisted in the service of what to him was highest and best.

---

1 The authority for these statements is Edmund Jones' *Life of Evan Williams*, a work published in 1750, which work, however, I only know at second-hand.

2 Mr. Cradock's stay in Wrexham, lasted from about October, 1634, to September, 1635. In my *History of the Parish Church of Wrexham*, (pp. 71-75,) I have given a long account of this eminent man, and of such incidents belonging to his work here as have been recorded.

B

2. Mr. Cradock was succeeded as curate by Mr. William Powell (see *Hist. Par. Ch. of Wrexham*, p. 75), a man who belonged, doubtless, to another school of theological thought, and who continued in Wrexham until the beginning of 1645. It was in January, 164⅚, at any rate, that the entries in the parish register in Mr. Powell's handwriting come suddenly to an end. Nor were there, it would appear, any churchwardens, sidesmen, overseers of the poor, or surveyors of highways elected, according to custom, on the Easter Monday following. Fourteen months before (in November, 1643) the soldiers of the Parliament, under Sir William Brereton (fresh from their engagement with Lord Capel, at Lee Bridge, on his retreat towards Shrewsbury), had made an incursion across Holt Bridge, destroying the famous organs of Wrexham[3], and defacing at least one monument there which they treated as savouring too much of "the times of idolatry." And the register itself, among its latest entries, gives significant hints of the struggle going on in the country around in the record it contains of the burial at different times of five soldiers, three of whom were "unknown."[4] These "miles ignoti" ("unknown soldiers") had, doubtless, fallen in some obscure tussles in the neighbourhood and here had been brought for burial.

3. Mr. Robert Lloyd, who was the vicar during Mr. Cradock's curacy, continued to fill that office until his death in March, 1640, and was succeeded by Mr. Rowland Owen Mr. Owen was deposed, we know, when the Puritans became triumphant in this town, but at what precise date his deposition took place is not certain. It was probably *formally* effected (having already probably been effected *actually* a year before) at the beginning of 1646, when, by the capture of Holt and Chester, the Puritan generals had wholly reduced the district to the obedience of the Parliament. If Mr. Owen managed to retain his vicarage a little longer it must, in any case, have been "sequestred," in accordance with an ordinance of Parliament, published on the 22nd of July following.[5] Beyond a statement, made 138 years afterwards, by Mr. Joshua Thomas, that Mr. Owen was removed

---

3 These soldiers thus anticipated by about six months the ordinance of the Lords and Commons published in May, 1644, by which it was provided "that all old organs and the frames or cases wherein they stand in all churches and chapels aforesaid shall be taken away, and utterly defaced and none other thereafter set up in their places."

4 The following are the entries in the parish register above referred to :—
Edwardus Head, miles, 4ᵒ, Aprilis, 164⅔, ⎫
Gulielmus quidem, miles ignotus, 9ᵒ Augusti, 1644, ⎪
Guilielmus Eborarius, miles ignotus, 29ᵒ d[i]e Augusti, 1664. ⎬ Sepulti fuere.
Thomas Banes, 2ᵒ Septembris [1644], miles, ⎪
Robertus — — —, miles ignotus, 27ᵒ Decembris, 1644. ⎭

5 "Resolved that Mr. Recorder do prepare and bring in an ordinance for the better establishing the affairs of North Wales, for putting the ordinances of Parliament in execution, and for settling a preaching ministry there; and for taking care of providing maintenance for them; and for sending down ministers that may be able to preach in the Welsh tongue; and for appointing a standing committee to take notice of and overview the actions of the several committees of those counties," etc.

"on account of his unfitness" ("am ei anghymhwysder"), I have been able to find no record of the ground of his ejectment, which must have been the work either of the Committee of Sequestration for North Wales (nominated by the Parliament), or of "the Committee for Plundered Ministers"[6] in London.

4. Before we now proceed to deal with the histo y of the Commonwealth Epoch in this town it may be well to put on record some particulars relating to the great drama of civil strife which here, as elsewhere, ended in the (temporary) triumph of the Puritan party. The main features and general results of the various sieges, occupations, battles and skirmishes which took place in this neighbourhood between the years 1643 and 1647 are already well known. But although the cause of the Parliament was stronger in Wrexham and its neighbourhood than perhaps anywhere else in North Wales, the names of only two or three of the local Parliamentary leaders have hitherto been recorded. In my various researches, however, innumerable curious particulars, relating to the history of the Commonwealth Epoch in this district, have come to light. What I now propose, therefore, to do is to give the names and brief notices of the chief persons —locally connected—who, as soldiers, were strong on the side of the Parliament during the great Civil War, and during the period of Puritan supremacy which succeeded it.

5. A much larger number of gentlemen and freeholders of the hundred of Bromfield either fought or served in the armies of the Parliament than is generally supposed.

6. The chief of these, Sir Thomas Myddelton, Knight, Major-General for the Parliament in North Wales, who belonged rather to Chirkland than Bromfield, need only be named.

7. The rest will be enumerated in the order of their military rank :—

(1) MAJOR JOHN MANLEY, a younger son of Cornelius Manley, gentleman, of Erbistock, and brother of Major Francis Manley, of Erbistock, who fought on the side of the King, and of Captain Roger Manley, both of whom were afterwards knighted. He was member for the borough of Denbigh in the Parliament of 1658, and lived at that time at Bryn-y-ffynnon, Wrexham, where he was still living in 1674. He and his wife were presented at the great Sessions held at Wrexham, October, 1663, for not going to church. He married Margaret, daughter of Isaac Dorislaus, Judge Advocate in the time of the Commonwealth, who was assassinated at the Hague by certain Royalists for his share in the trial of Charles I. He was the ancestor of the Manleys of Manley Hall, Staffordshire.

6 " The Committee for Plundered Ministers " was originally formed to provide for Puritan ministers who, at the breaking out of the Civil War, had been displaced and ill-treated by the king's party, but subsequently assumed, or became invested with, the charge of arranging for the supply of suitable ministers to parishes in all parts of the kingdom, and of deposing ministers that were esteemed unworthy.

(2) MAJOR JOHN SADLER, a commissioner under the Act of 16$\frac{49}{50}$ *for the better Propagation and Preaching of the Gospel in Wales.* I believe him to have been the father of the three children of John and Margaret Sadler, whose baptism is recorded (between the years 1624 and 1650) in the parish registers of Wrexham. His daughter Martha was the wife of Thomas Edgworth, son of Roger Edgworth, gentleman, of Holt, and an ancestor of the Edgworths, formerly of Wrexham and Marchwiel. In 1647 Major Sadler is described as Governor of Holt. The closing years of his life were spent in poverty, and on the 4th of October, 1659, he came before the Justices of the Peace sitting in Wrexham at Quarter Sessions, and told a pitiful tale, relating how he had served in the late wars for the space of ten years, and received several wounds, and how he had since become decayed in his estate, and was not now able to subsist without relief. The Justices thereupon ordered a pension of £8 a-year out of " the maimed soldiers' mize " to be paid him, but of this in the year following, after the restoration of the monarchy, he was deprived, and I cannot afterwards find him so much as named.

(3) CAPTAIN THOMAS CRITCHLEV appears to have either preceded or followed Mr. Edwards of Cilhendref as Governor of Wrexham. In 1649 I find him described as steward of the lordship of Bromfield and Yale. He was doubtless of the same family as Ralph Critchley, gentleman, of Wrexham, who was a Commissioner under the Act of 16$\frac{49}{50}$ before-named, and the father of the Joseph Critchley to whom there is a brass in Wrexham Church. (See my *Hist. Par. Ch., Wrexham*, pp. 90 and 210.) In 1670 Captain Critchley was still alive, residing within the township of Burton, and apparently at Burton Hall.

(4) CAPTAIN GERALD BARBOUR was a draper in Wrexham. I have already given a sufficient account of him in my *History of the Parish Church of Wrexham* (see p. 131) where, however, his name is wrongly spelled, as his beautiful signature, which I have since seen, shows.

(5) CAPTAIN HUGH PRICHARD had freehold estates in Broughton and Brymbo (his estate in the former township being, I am nearly sure, that called " Gatewen," and was at one time also, I believe, a tanner in Wrexham. He was alive at the time of the Restoration, but died shortly afterwards. His wife, Mrs. Eleanor Prichard, survived him.

(6) CAPTAIN EDWARD TAYLOR was a Commissioner under the Act of 16$\frac{49}{50}$ *for the better Propagation and Preaching of the Gospel in Wales*, and a member in 1651 (see sec. 58) of the Independent Church at Wrexham. He was, we may be pretty confident, the Captain Taylor to whom the Parliament voted £200 for special bravery in the action at Llandegai in June, 1648. He was serving under Colonel Carter, who, marching to relieve Carnarvon Castle, at that time besieged by the Royalist Commander, Sir John

Owen, of Cleneneu, was met near Bangor by the besiegers, who thus boldly anticipated his attack. "Captain Taylor [thereupon] singly encountering Sir John Owen, after he had broken his sword upon his head, closed with him dismounted him, and took him prisoner, and his party imm-diately fled." Of Captain Edward Taylor, Philip Henry in his diary often speaks. He lived in the township of Pickhill at a house which the diarist calls "Plas Dio, ' a name which should probably be read either "Plas Deio " ("Deio's Hall ") or "Plas Du" ("Black Hall,") but no such name is now known. The Mr. Edward Taylor " of Bedwell " [in Pickhill], who in 1664 was elected one of the churchwardens for the parish of Bangor-is-y-coed, was either the same Captain Taylor or his son Edward Taylor, junior⁷ whom I find described not long afterwards as living at Parkey (Parcau—The Parks) in the same township. Mrs Katherine Taylor, Captain Taylor's wife, was buried at Marchwiel, August 1, 1672, and there also he was himself buried January 1, 167⅔. I copy the following entries from Philip Henry's Diary relating to one or other of this worthy pair :—

"July 31, 1661. A sweet day of prayer at Captain Taylor's: We were but few, but ye Lord was one with us."

"January 11, 166-½. I was at Whitchurch . . . . . . In my way home with Captain Taylor and John Wright, Mr. Pul Roger Puleston, Esq., of Emral, Philip Henry's former pupil] overtook us and drew his sword and would needs fight, saying we were all Traytours, swearing desperately."

"June 12, 1664. Mr. Taylor and many more about Wrexham bound over to appear at Quarter Sessions for a private meeting at which yei were deprehended."

"June 2, 1672. At Captain Taylor's, a Sac . . . the good gentle-woman there ill. I am afraid not like to be long in the land of the living."

"August 1, 1672. At Marchwiel at the buryal of my dear and precious friend, Mrs. Kath. Taylor, of Plas Dio who sleepeth in Jesus. A great miss like to bee of her both in house and neighbourhood, help, Lord." (Note 8.)

(7) CAPTAIN DAVID MAURICE was also a Commissioner under the Act of 16⁴⁹⁄₅₀, and a member in 1651 (see sec. 58) of the Independent Church at Wrexham. He was not the David Maurice of Pen-y-bont and Lloran, who was sheriff of the county in 1676 and a fierce persecutor of Nonconformists, but the David Maurice

7 Edward Taylor junr., married Elizabeth, daughter of the Rev. Joseph Hanmer D.D. (who was curate of Whitewell, during the latter part of the Interregnun, but after-wards conformed and was from 1668 to 1691, Rector of Marchwiel,) and had by her a son John (baptised at Marchwiel, February 12th, 1687,) whom we shall afterwards have occasion to mention. (See ch. iii., sec. 22.)

8 Since the above was written I have seen among the papers of Chas. S. Mainwaring, Esq., of Galltfaenan, a large number of deeds relating to Captain Edward Taylor. He was, it appears, the second son of Thomas Taylor, yeoman, of Dutton Diffaeth, near Holt, and married, about the year 1632, Katherine, daughter of Richard Presland, yeoman, of Ridley, near Holt, whose widow became afterwards the second wife of the Edward Thomas who is mentioned in Note 26. Richard Presland had a lease for three lives of the house and lands in Pickhill which Captain Taylor afterwards occupied, and this lease was transferred to the latter as the marriage portion of his wife.

of Llangedwyn, who married Elizabeth, daughter of Matthew Trevor, Esq., of Trevor Hall. By his wife he had Llwyn Howel and other property in Ruabon, and it was in Ruabon I fancy that he at this time generally lived. His brother-in-law, Captain Thomas Trevor, of Trevor, who lies buried in Wrexham Church (see *Hist. Par. Ch. of Wrexham*, page 213) was engaged on the opposite side in the Civil War. One of his two daughters was the wife of Mr. John Bell, apothecary, of Wrexham.

(8) CAPTAIN THOMAS BALL, of Ball's Wood, Burton, a Commissioner under the Act of $16\frac{49}{50}$ before named, Sheriff of the county in 1652, and most assiduous in his attendance at Quarter Sessions during the Parliamentary Epoch. He appears to have served at the siege of Chester. He was originally of Boughton, near Chester, but was already settled at Burton in the year 1647. He married Margaret, daughter and eventual heir of Robert Santhy, gentleman, of Burton ; his own sister, Elizabeth, being the wife of Captain Samuel Santhy, the eldest son of the aforesaid Mr. Robert Santhy. He had four sons and six daughters, whereof two sons (Nathaniel and Jonathan) and four daughters survived him. He was buried at Gresford, March 7th, $168\frac{7}{8}$, aged 68. From his daughter, Sarah, who married Benjamin Smith, of Ashton-on-Mersey, Major Lawson-Lowe is descended. His son, Jonathan Ball, gentleman, was still living in 1713, being then unmarried.

(9) CAPTAIN SAMUEL SANTHY. All that I know of this gentleman has already been given in the last paragraph. He appears to have lived in that part of Burton which formerly constituted the hamlet of "Hunkley." "Santhy" is a corruption of the old Welsh personal name "Sanddef."

(10) CAPTAIN WILLIAM WYNNE, of Cristionydd, afterwards of Wynne Hall Ruabon, son of Hugh Wynne, gentleman, of Evenechtyd, in the township of Cymo, parish of Llandysilio yn Ial. He is said to have built Wynne Hall, and was the ancestor of the Kenricks of that place (see ch. iii., sec. 22). He was a Commissioner under the Act of $16\frac{49}{50}$, and a deacon in 1673 of the Independent Church in Wrexham. The story is told of him which is told of others, that a Bible, which he carried in his pocket, once received the impact of a nearly spent ball, and so saved his life. During the Civil Wars, while the Royalists held Denbigh Castle, he was for a while imprisoned there. Born June 4th, 1615, he died October 6th, 1692, and was buried in the Dissenters' grave yard, Wrexham, where his tombstone may still be seen.

(11) CAPTAIN ROGER SONTLEY, of the family of Sontley, of Sontley and Brondeg. He was a Commissioner under the Act of $16\frac{49}{50}$ before-named, and a strong anti-Royalist until the very eve of the Restoration. His kinsman, Colonel Robert Sontley, of Plas Sontley, was engaged on the other side. I am

nearly certain that Captain Sontley lived in the township of Broughton-in-Bromfield, although he seems to have also had a house within the liberties of Holt.

(12) CAPTAIN ANDREW ELLICE, of Althrey, in the parish of Bangor-is-y-Coed, although living just outside the hundred had much property within it, and so may here be mentioned. He was a Commissioner under the Act of 16$\frac{49}{50}$, and a Justice of the Peace who sometimes attended the Quarter Sessions for the county of Denbigh during the period of the Commonwealth.

(13) LIEUTENANT RALPH WELD, a Presbyterian, who appears to have been favourable to the Restoration, and who, I think, was at one time a mercer in High-street. He was a Church-warden in 1659. Further particulars relating to him will be found in note 16, page 87, of my *History of the Parish Church of Wrexham*.

8. The name of [THOMAS ?] EDWARDS, Esq., of Cilhendref, in the township of Dudleston, Salop, who was Governor of Wrexham in the year 1647, should also be here mentioned.

9. So also should be mentioned the name of CAPTAIN WILLIAM WENLOCKE, who was registrar, under the Act of August 24th, 1653, for marriages, births, and burials within the parishes of Wrexham, Ruabon, and Erbistock, for all of which the parish church of Wrexham was ordered to be the place of publication. Captain Wenlocke lived afterwards at Colemere, in the parish of Ellesmere. His last will was dated September, 1691. Either he or his widow—Mrs. Katherine Wenlocke—left bequests to the churchwardens of Ellesmere, Northop, Holywell, and Ner-quis. I believe Mrs. Wenlocke belonged to the family of Parry, of Hendre in Treiddyn and of Chester. I find her name among the contributors to the building of Matthew Henry's meeting-place at Chester.

10. And along with these should be named the famous COLONEL JOHN JONES, of Maes-y-Garnedd, the Regicide. He was, it is true, a Merionethshire rather than a Denbighshire man, but his first wife, Margaret, was a daughter of Mr. John Edwards, of Stansty, near Wrexham[8a]; his son appears to have lived (probably as a pupil) for a time with Mr. Morgan Lloyd, and his troop was partly recruited in this neighbourhood. At the Resto-ration Colonel Jones was sheltered for a while at Cilhendref—

8a. In a letter to Mr. Morgan Lloyd, written from Dublin, 19th Nov., 1651, Col. Jones speaks of his dearest yokefellow being upon the point of finishing her course, and ready to be gathered to the bosom of the father, and adds: "Yors that came by the last Packet, being four in number, much refreshed her spirit, and raised a conceit in her (upon yor expres-sion of dead Lazarus), that shee should Recover, saying she had faith enough to be healed, and pressing earnestly (when she was not able to turn herself in her bedd) to be carried into Wales to see the saints at Wrexham, who had soe many prayers at the Trone of grace in her behalfe, but now she perceives that her Redemption draweth nigh wherein she doeth much Rejoice, desiring to be dissolved and to be with Xt." She died a few days after the dispatch of this letter. Extracts from other letters from Col. Jones to Mr. Morgan Lloyd will be given hereafter.

the house of the Mr. Edwards mentioned in a previous paragraph[9].

11. To the names of those gentlemen of the district who maintained the cause of the Parliament on the field of battle may be added the names of some who supported it with more or less staunchness in other ways :—

(1) JOHN KYNASTON, ESQ., of Plas Kynaston (before called Cefn-y-Carneddau) in the township of Cristionydd Kenrick and the parish of Ruabon.

(2) JOHN PECKE, ESQ., of Cornish Hall, in the parish of Holt. He appears, however, at this time, not to have lived at his own house, but at Trefalun Hall, which he rented from Sir John Trevor. He was a Commissioner under the Act of $16\frac{49}{50}$[10]. He was the first of the Peckes of Cornish, and was buried at Gresford, 16 March, 166— aged 57.

(3) THOMAS RAVENSCROFT, ESQ., of Old Pickhill Hall, of the family of Ravenscroft of Bretton, in the parish of Hawarden. His wife, Margaret, was a daughter of Sir Thomas Williams, of

9 Although in this book I propose to deal solely with the history of the Puritanism of the district, it seems desirable to give at least the names and residences of those gentry in the hundred of Bromfield, who either actually drew their swords on the side of the King, or who actively and openly sympathised with that side. The following is as complete a list of these as I can make,:—

Sir Richard Lloyd, Knight, of Esclus Hall. (See ch. viii. sec. 9, *Hist. Par. Ch. of Wrexham.*)
Col. Robert Ellice, of Croes Newydd. (See ch. v., note 75.   „   „
Col. John Robinson, of Upper Gwersyllt.
Major Francis Manley, of Manley Hall, Erbistock. (See ch. v., note 35, *Hist. of Par. Ch. of Wrexham.*)
Major Hugh Roberts, of Hafod-y-bwch. (See ch. v., note 20.   „   „
Captain Ellis Sutton, of Lower Gwersyllt.
Captain John Lloyd, of Plas Madoc.
Captain Nanney Lloyd, of Wrexham. (See ch. v., note 22, *Hist. of Par. Ch of Wrexham.*)
Captain Thomas Baker, of Wrexham. (See ch. v., note 18,   „   „
Captain William Broughton, of Bersham, a younger brother of the first Sir Edward Broughton, of Marchwiel.

I find the following officers (who were probably Royalists) also mentioned in the record of the time :—

Major Samuel Powell and Captain Thomas Powell, both of the Gyffynys, Brymbo Captain Edward Jeffreys, of Acton, afterwards of Gatewen. (See ch. v. note 58 *Hist. Par. Ch. of Wrexham.*)

The names above given may fitly be supplemented by a list of those gentlemen of the hundred (some of them already named) who compounded for their estates by the payment of a fine to the Parliament:—

William Broughton, of Bersham	...	...	...	...	...	£90	0 0
Richard Dutton, of Ty'n-y-wern, Esq.	...	...	...	...	...	£185	0 0
Robert Ellice, Esq. ...	...	...	...	...	...	£150	0 0
Gerrard Eyton and Kenrick Eyton, his son, of Lower Eyton, gentlemen	...	...	...	...	...	£457	0 0
Humphrey Lloyd, of Berse, gentn. (See ch. v., note 21, *Hist. of Par. Ch. of Wrexham*) ...	...	...	...	...	...	£130	0 0
Francis Manley, of Erbistock, gentn.	...	...	...	...	£ 75	0 0
John Madocks, of Wrexham, gentn.	...	...	...	...	£ 96	0 0
Francis Pickering, of Holt, gentn.	...	...	...	...	£222	0 0
Thos. Pulford, of Wrexham, gentn. (See ch. v., note 6, *Hist. of Par. Ch. of Wrexham* ...	...	...	...	...	£ 69	0 0
John Roydon, of Roydon's Hall, Sutton Isycoed, gentn.	...	...	£ 90	0 0
Ellis Sutton, of Gwersyllt, gentn.	...	...	...	...	£ 75	0 0

10 It will have been noted how large number of the Commissioners under the *Act for the Better Propagation and Preaching of the Gospel in Wales* lived in Wrexham or near it. It is not surprising, therefore, that the Commissioners for North Wales held always their meetings in this town.

Vaenol. He was sheriff of the county of Denbigh in 1649. He died, February 18th, 1681. There is a tablet to his memory in Holy Trinity Church, Chester.

12. The three above-named, and especially the first two, were fairly constant in their attendance as Justices at Quarter Sessions during the period of Puritan ascendancy, and associated themselves with the measures of the party then predominant, but only the first of them, so far as I can discover connected himself afterwards in any way with the Nonconformists.

13. Sir John Trevor, Knight, of Plas Teg and Trefalun Hall, appears also to have rendered a general support to the Puritan cause, and after the Restoration did honour to himself by sheltering the Rev. William Jones, who was ejected under *the Act of Uniformity* from Denbigh, and settling on him land, the annual income from which sufficed to keep him from want.[11]

14. Having thus given a brief account of the gentlemen of the district who served in the levies of the Parliament, some notices which I possess[12] of various private soldiers who adventured their lives in the same cause ought not, I think, to be withheld.

(1) John Burton, of Stansty, was slain in the service of the Parliament. He was of the same family as the late Mr. John Burton, of the Yspytty, and was probably a direct ancestor of the present Mr. Thomas Painter. The Justices allowed his widow, Mary Burton, an annuity of £4 for the support of herself and four children.

(2) John Lewis, of Gwersyllt, served under Major Sadler [see sec. 7 (2)], and "lost the use of his hands at the leaguer before Holt Castle." A pension of sixty shillings a-year was allowed him.

(3). Of Hugh Roberts, of Wrexham, who received in 1649 a pension of £4 a-year it was then recorded that he "hath many years continued in the service of the Parliament, and hath received a wound at the siege of Wem, that thereby he hath lost the use thereof."

(4) Another pensioner of this date Lawrence Cooke, tobacconist, of the Green, was rather a shifty customer[13]. He appears to have at first answered to the King's Commission of Array, but afterwards joined the Parliament levies, and was present at the siege of Holt, where he lost a thumb. For this a

---

11 As the tombstone of this Mr. Jones in Hope Churchyard seems now to have perished, it may be worth while to print the inscription (preserved in Calamy) which was formerly upon it:—" Hic exuvias reliquit mortales Gulielmus Jones, assiduus Verbi Divini præco felici concionum fructu et pio exemplo ad huc loquitur." It may be of interest to say that this Mr. Jones married a daughter of Richard Parry, Esq., of Coedmarchan.

12 Most of these notices have been taken from a book containing " Records of Quarter Sessions of County Denbigh " (1641-1662), a summary of which has been lent me by Mr. W· M. Myddelton, of Stoke Newington.

13 Lawrence Cooke issued a token which Mr. Jas. W. Lloyd, of Kington, thus describes :—[Ob] LAWRENCE COOKE—a roll of tobacco. [Re] IN WREXHAM, 1666 L.E.C. 1d."

pension was bestowed upon him, of which he was afterwards deprived, but which he subsequently managed to recover. In 1674 he was elected churchwarden, but being imprisoned for some offence soon after his election "became thereby incapacitated for further discharging the duties of his office." (*Hist. Par. Ch. of Wrexham.*)

(5) JOHN SIMON, of Wrexham, served in the troop of Colonel John Jones, and died of his wounds received in Scotland. A pension of £3 a-year was allowed to his widow, Joan Simon.

(6) GEORGE PLATT, of Wrexham, served the Parliament in England and Ireland, where he died of his wounds. A pension of £3 a-year was allowed to his widow, Jane Platt, for the maintenance of herself and her three small children.

(7) VALENTINE TILSTON, of Wrexham, "served the Parliament at bewmarres under the command of Mr. Hugh Courtney, went on from thence into Ireland into the Parliament service, and there was slaine by the rebells." He was probably the son of the Valentine Tilston, gentleman, of TyMawr, Wrexham, who is mentioned in Norden's Survey of A.D. 1620. Valentine Tilston, the elder, was the son of John Tilston, gentleman, of Wrexham, and married Ellen, sister of Robert Puleston, Esq., of Hafod-y-wern, and had much property in Wrexham. But in the time of the second Valentine Tilston this property must have been alienated, and the Justices granted Elizabeth Tilston, his widow, a pension of fifty shillings a-year, afterwards raised to sixty shillings, for the support of herself and two children.

(8) JOHN POWELL, yeoman, of Holt, fought also in the Parliamentary armies, and at his death in 1644 left his sword to his eldest son Joseph. He was the son of Henry Powell, of Holt, whose father, John Powell, of Holt, was brother of the first Thomas Powell, Esq., of Horsley Hall[14]. 'Of John Powell's son, Alexander, and of his grandson, John, I shall hereafter speak.

15. Having now dealt, as fully as is necessary, with the military side of the Puritan movement in this town and neighbourhood, we are now able to give our full attention to its main manifestation, to the religious side, namely, of that movement. And we will, first of all, taking up the thread dropped at section 3, treat of the vicarship or official pastorate of the parish during the interregnum. The former vicar being ejected, a preaching minister of Puritan principles was installed in his place. It is nearly certain that it was the famous Morgan Lloyd, who now became vicar of the parish. We know, at any rate, that for some time before 1647, and until the end of his life, Mr. Morgan Lloyd was a settled minister in this town, and he is described not so very long after his death, as the predecessor of Mr. Ambrose

14 These particulars have been for the most part supplied me by Mr. Ellison Powell, of 44, Coleman Street, London.

Mostyn, who we know was actually the Puritan vicar of Wrexham. It is probable, however, that during the latter part of his life, and at the time of his death, Mr. Lloyd was a Dissenter from the ecclesiastical arrangements then established— spite of the fact that those arrangements, as to doctrine, favoured the faith of Puritanism, and, as to church order, were based upon the rejection of Episcopacy. The Dissenters' grave-yard in Rhosddu Road dates from before the Restoration, and Mr. Lloyd, who died in 1659, was buried in it. And although this fact is not perhaps so conclusive as it seems, there are other considerations which make me suspect that towards the close of his life (and probably before 1657) Mr. Lloyd resigned the vicarship. Even if he continued to the end of his life vicar of the parish he must have been *at the same time* a member of " the congregated church " here, with which, indeed, he is known to have been connected as early as the year 1651. In any case, therefore, he is to be regarded as the first Congregational minister in Wrexham, if not the actual founder of Nonconformity in the town. For this reason, and on account of the peculiar fascination which the personality of this singular man has had for me, it has seemed fitting to treat of his life and opinions with some amplitude.

16. Morgan Lloyd came of a family of small gentry, long settled on an estate called " Cynfal," or " Cynfael," in the parish of Maentwrog, Merionethshire. To this family, which, towards the end of the 16th century, adopted the surname of " Lloyd," belonged the famous Huw Llwyd (in English spelling, " Hugh Lloyd "), bard, scholar, and soldier[15]. There appear to have been two Hugh Lloyds of Cynfael, uncle and nephew (the first the son of Hywel ap Rhys, and the other the son of Dafydd Llwyd ap Hywel ap Rhys), and it has never yet been settled which of these two was Hugh Lloyd the bard. Equally unsettled is the relationship between Hugh Lloyd the bard, and Morgan Lloyd the preacher, the former being variously described as the grandfather, father, and uncle of the latter. The one can hardly, however, have been *father* of the other, if Morgan Lloyd was born in 1619, and Hugh died the year following, being then more than 80 years of age. Morgan, in his letters to his mother, mentions his sisters Dorothy and Elizabeth. Whether he had brothers we do not know.

17. I do not deem the foregoing remarks as to the preacher's family out of place, although Mr. Lloyd himself poured contempt

---

15 Huw Llwyd was regarded by many of his contemporaries as a magician, and all sorts of stories wherein he figures under this character are still current in the parishes of Ffestiniog and Maentwrog. In some of these stories he is associated with the famous Edmund Prys, rector of Ffestiniog, Archdeacon of Merioneth, and author of the metrical version of the Psalms still in use. A tall column of rock rising sheer from the river Cynfael goes even now by the name of " Pulpud Huw Llwyd " (" Hugh Lloyd's Pulpit "), and his "pastwn " or " club " is preserved in a farmhouse of the neighbourhood. Of his poems, the " Cywydd i'r Llwynog " (" Poem to the Fox ") is best known, and among the Peniarth MSS. is a transcript of a medical work written by him. He served in the army, and fought abroad for many years. He is said to have died at Cynfael in the year 1620.

on all distinctions of birth, and said that "family pedigrees were but a web woven by nature in which the spider of pride lurked."

18. The tradition is probably to be trusted which relates that young Morgan was sent to school at Wrexham, and while there received from the preaching of Walter Cradock (see sec. 1) that impulse which gave a new direction to his life. He himself says, in a poem which the late Rev. John Peter ("Ioan Pedr") discovered, that it was in Maelor[16] that he awoke out of spiritual sleep (*Ar Maelawr y dihunais*). As Mr. Cradock was curate of Wrexham in 1634 and 1635, Morgan Lloyd must have been 15 or 16 years of age when this turning point in his life came. The way had been doubtless prepared for it by the training which he had received from his mother, who was a pious woman of the Puritan type, as her son's letters to her show. Of Morgan Lloyd's history between the date of his conversion and the time when, at the age of 26 or 27, he became minister of Wrexham, little is known. We know, however, that during this period he married. We know, also, that a little later, the Civil War having now broken out, he was engaged, probably as chaplain, with the Parliamentary troops in England. Once we find him at Gloucester[17]. Nor was Gloucester, I suppose, the only place wherein he for a time tarried. And wherever he went, he preached, or had other opportunities of showing what was in him. So people in authority, as well in England as in Wales, came to be aware of his power and promise. Here was evidently a man of purest life and most fervent piety, ready to spend and be spent, finely touched to fine issues. Thus it came about that when "the settlement" of Wales took place in 1646, Mr. Morgan Lloyd was put, although so young, over the wide and wealthy parish of Wrexham. And it soon appeared that he was not merely a most searching and eloquent preacher, but also a fresh and original thinker, having something new to say, and saying nothing that he was not ready to seal with his blood. Many regarded him as one of the old prophets again standing on the earth, a man that knew the things of God at first hand, and had no need of the doctors or the schools. Even the power of seeing things to come was ascribed to him, an ascription, however, which was partly based

---

16 Maelor Gymraeg, that part of the country of Powys which now forms the hundred of Bromfield, and of which the chief town is Wrexham.

17 The letter which he wrote to his mother from Gloucester is perhaps worth translating. It is dated August 24th, but the year is not given. It runs thus:—"My dear honoured mother,—I have had no opportunity since I came out of Wales to write more than a little to anyone, this last pursuit being so swift and the waylaying of me so continual, that I could get no time. I long to hear whether or not the enemy is yet come to Wales. If he is come, we know the worst of man with his breath in his nostrils. They must needs have a little fillip before dying, for they are not yet high enough to fall, nor we low enough to mount. But, 'before the end of the harvest in Wales,' says a man of God, 'they will be taken in the snare.' We have been in peril, but God, of His grace, keeps us and we are well, and our delight is in the Lord. Be not sad on our account, for great joy is near. Spite of men and devils, God will keep His word and His children. Mary has chosen the better part which shall not be taken away from her. I long to hear how are my family and those that love me. I think it likely that before long I shall return. So I commend you to the Lord. —Your obedient son, M. Ll."

upon his mystical and mistaken interpretation of certain
Scriptures. Of course, the preacher's theology is, in many of its
points, now discredited. That the preacher himself was often
narrow and unpractical, we can also at this time plainly see.
That he could find no good in those who lived in another plane
of thought, and did not occupy his own standpoint, must be
admitted. But it is very probable that Morgan Lloyd without
his special failings would have been without his special excel-
lences. And in any case, they were failings to which we can
well afford to be now a little blind.

19. Mr. Lloyd's birthplace was in Gwynedd, and he probably
spoke the dialect of that region, a dialect differing in some
respects from the Welsh spoken in Northern Powys, the region
within which Wrexham stands. In this latter region, therefore,
it probably was that he came to be called "Morgan Llwyd o
Wynedd" ("Morgan Lloyd from Gwynedd"). Many writers,
wrongly supposing that all North Wales belongs to the land of
Gwynedd, have assumed that this name was given to him in
South Wales, and that he must, therefore, have made long
preaching journeys in that country. But there is no reason to
suppose these long journeys, and the name may as well have
been given to him here as there.

20. That Mr. Lloyd did nevertheless undertake occasional tours
of evangelisation in different parts of Wales and the Borders is
likely enough. We hear of him, in fact, preaching at Bala, at
Pwllheli, at Machynlleth, and at Whitewell, in Cheshire. But at
Bala he would stop on his regular journeys to and from Cynfael
—his mother's house, and from Cynfael, Pwllheli and Machynlleth are not very far distant, nor are Whitewell and Wrexham
many miles apart. Doubtless he preached elsewhere than in the
places above-named, but I am inclined to believe that the wide
reputation which Mr. Lloyd had in the Wales of his day was
much more due to his writings than to the sermons he preached
up and down the land.

21. Of Mr. Lloyd's writings, just indicated, something must now
be said. In 1653 were printed his *Llyfr y tri Aderyn* ("Book of
the Three Birds"), his *Gwaedd yn Nghymru yn wyneb pob Cydwybod
Euog* ("Cry in Wales in the face of every Guilty Conscience"), and
his "*Llythyr i'r Cymry Cariadus*" ("Letter to the Beloved
Welsh") These were followed in 1656 by his *Gair o'r Gair, neu
Sôn am Swn, Y Lleferydd Anfarwol* ("A word from the The Word,
or Sound for Noise, the Immortal Voice"); while in 1657
appeared, bound together, his *Ymroddiad* ("Self Resignation");
his *Dysgybl a'i Athraw o Newydd,* ("The Disciple and his
Teacher, Anew"), his *Cyfarwyddyd i'r Cymro* ("The Welshman's
Directory"); and his *Gwyddor Uchod* (see sec.26) He is said to have
written also a book in English, called "*A Dialogue between
Martha and Lazarus.*" All his Welsh books went through

several editions, either during his own lifetime or in the century following his death, and one of them, " *Gair o'r Gair*," was translated into English, but they are all, even the latest editions of them, now so scarce as to be almost unattainable.

22. Mr. Howel Wm. Lloyd, M.A., has given in part 1, vol. III. of *Y Cymmrodor* an account of four of Morgan Lloyd's works—those four that appeared in 1657 bound together in one volume, and from this account all my knowledge of them is derived.

23. The full title of the first of the four, as it is given in the second edition, is : *Yr Ymroddiad ; neu Bapuryn a gyfieithwyd i helpu'r Cymry allan o'r Hunan a'r Drygioni*[18] (" Self Resignation, or a Paper translated to help the Welsh out of Self and Evil "). Although the tract is acknowledged, in the title of it, to be a translation of some other work, the translator (or was he rather an *adapter* ?) nowhere states what the name of this other work was, nor who was its author. But there is some reason to believe, as Mr. Howel W. Lloyd has pointed out, that the *Ymroddiad* is " partly derived from an ascetic treatise by some Catholic divine." " The object of the tract is explained in the Preface (Rhagymadrodd), viz.: To bring the spirit of man into entire submission to God by subduing the natural self (Hunan) to the spiritual self."

24. The second tract—*The Disciple and his Teacher, Anew,*—" appears, although separate, to be intended for a continuation of the first," and is paged continuously with it. It seems to me, in fact, very probable that this tract is itself also a translation. It is certain, at any rate, that *The Disciple and his Master* contains one sentence[19] which is absolutely inconsistent with Morgan Lloyd's scheme of doctrine, as he had already set it forth in *The Book of the Three Birds,* · and which he could only therefore have written as a translation of another writer's words. The extracts from *The Disciple and his Teacher* given in *The Cymmrodor* seem to me also to lack that picturesqueness which is the note of nearly all that Morgan Lloyd wrote. The latter, perhaps, translated these first two tracts, and wrote the third (*The Welshman's Directory*) as a sequel to them, presenting thus their teaching in his own language, and in a form which harmonized with his own general convictions, or he may have translated (or adapted) these two to form a suitable introduction to his own tract already written. As to the title which Morgan Lloyd adopted for the second tract, he tells us that *The Disciple and his Teacher* was the name of a work already known, and implies that this was why he called his own work (or translation) " The Disciple and his Teacher—*Anew*." The contents of this

18 In the *Cambrian Bibliography* by the Rev. Wm. Rowlands (edition of Rev. D. Silvan Evans, 1869) the title of what is probably the first edition is given thus :—Y'r *Ymroddiad neu Bapuryn a gyfeithwyd ddi.cyiwaith i helpu y Cymry unwaith Allan o'r Hunan a'r Drygioni*.

19 The following is the sentence above referred to :—" Christ dwells in us through the communication of Himself to us in the Holy Sacrament."

book seem to be in the main an answer to the question :
" Whither does the soul go when the body is dead?" And the
answer is that "it is unnecessary for the soul to go forth," for at
death " only the mortal life and the body outside it separate
themselves from the soul," that " heaven or hell are in the soul
already ; " and that " these are everywhere present, and con-
sist in nothing else than the turning of the will either to God's
love or His wrath." "When the root of the will gives itself up
to God, it sinks down away from itself beyond all place and
abyss. There alone God works and wills in it, and man is
nothing since it is God that works and wills in him. The love of
God pervades his whole being, as fire pervades iron, and gives it
a new life by the presence of its light within him. In a similar
manner, the *wrath* of God works in the damned soul, which in
this life has never consented to go outside of itself, and so it
cannot enter the heavenly rest because the wrath of God is manifest in it. Then begin its everlasting sadness and helplessness,
and it is ashamed and powerless to enter into God's presence.
It is in bondage to the wrath engendered in itself, and bears
about its own hell within itself, being unable to see the light of
God, and is its own hell in whatsoever place it may be." At death
through the drawing of the veil of the flesh, each will in part
see the realities of his own condition, and at the day of doom,
through the destruction of the material world, this process
will be fully completed, and the real world, now invisible, will
stand out clear. " Christ will manifest his kingdom in the
place where the world now is, and will separate from himself
all that does not belong to Him. Hell will be everywhere in lieu
of this world, but hidden from the kingdom of heaven as the
night is in the day-time : ' the light will shine for ever in the
darkness, but the darkness will not comprehend it.' " *The Disciple and his Teacher* contains, in fact, a fuller and more systematic
statement, *with certain differences*, of certain doctrines which
Morgan Lloyd had himself already set forth in his *Book of the
Three Birds*, and which will hereafter be given in his own words.

25. Of the doctrine of the third tract of Morgan Lloyd's
(*Cyfarwyddyd i'r Cymro*,—The Welshman's Directory), published
in 1657, Mr. Howel W. Lloyd gives the following summary :—
" Regeneration is the new birth of the soul, or rather spirit . .
resulting from its perfect union with Christ which is the effect of
absolute renunciation of self (*Hunan*) and conformity to the will of
God . . . . Whatever be their religious opinions, none will be
saved except through faith in Christ; none have the right faith
except those who please God ; and none please God save those
who are like him, having been made again (*hail-wneuthur*) in the
likeness and image of God himself. None will be cast into hell
save those who are unlike the Lord."

26. The fourth of Morgan Lloyd's tracts, published in 1657 and bound together, is in verse, and entitled *Gwyddor Uchod*, a title which may be paraphrased rather than translated as *The Higher Astrology*. It is a curious and fantastic, but still an exceedingly interesting, production. "Man," he says, "is the centre-piece (*canolfa*) of the world, being created of all things: his bones are like rocks, his veins like streams, his flesh like earth, his appetite like shadows; his hair grows like grass; the wind blows from his nostrils, within and without him are fire and water" (H. W. Lloyd). He is thus the great world in little, but this great world, according to the "carnal astronomers" is ruled by "the seven planets" (the Sun, the Moon, Mercury, Venus, Mars, Jupiter. and Saturn,) and the temperaments of men, these astronomers say, are determined by the particular planet under whose ascendancy they are born. But in the world of man there are also seven planets—the seats of the several temperaments; and, apart from the grace of God, a man is what he is according as one or other of these habitudes predominates in him. And with these temperaments certain bodily conditions always go. Each of them also, according to the belief of the author's contemporaries, has its seat in, or is represented by, a special organ of the body. To these organs, Morgan Lloyd transfers, accordingly, the names of the several planets. The heart is the Sun, and the brain the Moon; the lungs he calls Mercury; the kidneys Venus; the gall is Mars; the liver Jupiter, and the bile Saturn. Those that are ruled by the heart are, therefore, "the children of the Sun." And "the children of the Sun," quoting from Mr. Howel Lloyd's summary, "are high-minded, ambitious, patriotic, true, wise, steadfast. When bad they are thankless, extravagant, foolish, drunken. Their hair is yellow; they soon grow bald; they are bearded, stout, deep of purpose, darting like the lion or the ram, or glittering like the moth; loving respect, like the peacock, eagle or swan. Such must stoop to humility if they would be saved. For this they must endure to be care-worn and broken-hearted." Thus our author goes on, describing in the language of popular astrology, in which he only in part believed,[20] the children of the other planets, and winding up his description in each case by saying that the regenerating grace of God could set straight what was crooked in character, and put all things right.

27. The only one of Morgan Lloyd's books that I have myself seen is his *Llyfr y tri Aderyn* or *Book of the Three Birds*. But this

---

20. Four years earlier Morgan Lloyd's opinion on this subject seems to have been that while the planets may possibly rule the natural man, the spiritual man is wholly exempt from their influence. Thus he says:—"The planets rule the animal fleshly mind until it come out of the body from under the sun. But the earnest spiritual man is already above the planets in his mind, although his body is as an animal still. To the froward man there is no hour that is auspicious, nor to the heavenly man one that is evil."

is the largest, and is acknowledged to be the most characteristic of his writings, that on which he has left most deeply the impress of his mind. It has certainly been the most popular of them. Spite of this, it is a book which is at the present time very little known No translation of it into English has ever been published. And in this fact will be found, I hope, a sufficient justification of me for offering my own translation of the passages from this remarkable book which I have selected for quotation.

28. The following is the full title of the 1826 edition of this work, the only edition which I have myself seen: "Llyfr y tri Aderyn; neu Ddirgelwch i rai i'wddeall, ac eraill i'w watwor, sef, Tri Aderyn yn ymddiddan, sef, yr Eryr, y Golomen, a'r Gigfran; neu Arwydd i annerch y Cymry," that is, "Book of the Three Birds; a mystery for some to understand and others to deride, being a discourse between the Eagle, the Dove, and the Raven, A Sign to address the Welsh."[20a]

29. The form into which the book is cast—that of a conversation between three birds—is, of course, very artificial. Opportunity is nevertheless thereby afforded for remarks for which a form more natural would give less occasion, and the incongruities are neither so glaring nor so numerous as might be supposed. The Dove stands for God's people, that is, for the Puritan portion of them, and the Raven for the Godless, while the Eagle, who asks questions, directs the conversation, and preserves the peace, is no other than Oliver Cromwell himself.

30. The chief burden of the conversation falls upon the Dove, who, while meant to represent the people of God generally, really gives utterance to Morgan Lloyd's own beliefs, opinions, and aspirations, which were far from being representative in all points of those entertained by the Puritan part even of God's people. But for this very reason we may treat the Dove's deliverances as giving authoritative utterance to Mr. Lloyd's sentiments. These are also presented in a way which inevitably suggests the form and method of the preacher's eloquence. In the following paragraph, for example, put into the Dove's mouth, we have clearly an echo of one of Mr. Lloyd's pulpit appeals:—

" Do not suppose that the door of mercy has been closed against you

---

20a. Since the above was written I have seen the 1778 edition of *Llyfr y tri Aderyn*, printed in Wrexham. The title of this edition differs from that above given by the addition of the words, "Am y flwyddyn 666," so that the latter part of the title would read, " Arwydd i annerch y Cymry am y flwyddyn 666."—" A sign to address the Welsh concerning the year 666." This title is varied at the top of the first page so as to read thus when translated:— "A sign to address the Welsh in the year 1653 before the coming of 666." The number 666 is, of course, " the number of the beast " (Rev. xiii. 18). Mr. Lloyd much exercised himself with speculations as to the last days. He said the great deluge happened in the year 1656 from the creation of the world, and appears to have suggested that the second destruction of the world, the fiery deluge, would take place in the 1656th year from the new creation effected by Christ. He concluded also that the people of his time were living in the sixth day of the week of the world's history, a thousand years being reckoned as one day (2 Pet. iii. 8), and that the seventh day, or eternal Sabbath, was about to dawn. " Sion," said he, " moves in her mountain, and the great last wheel has begun already to turn in the world."

while you have breath, and the will to return. But you still follow the flesh
sing carols to arouse your lusts, read filthy obscene books, and poison the
pure root, following taverns, and tables, and oaths, and cursing, and scoffing,
and scorning, loving the playhouses of the devil (like hell's cattle), despising
the poor, living gaily on the dunghill of wantonness, scoffing at sobriety, in the
dark hidden fire, in the bed of the harlot, in feastings and gluttony, in darkness
and laughter, cohabiting with shame, in envy and discontent, in presump-
tion and craftiness, in woe and the horrible pit. Awake ! arise ! thou art
still welcome. The heavenly feast stays for thee. There is bread enough in
thy Father's house. Why will ye die, O children of men? Why will ye lose
your souls for ever? "

81. In the following passages again, we hear the preacher
encouraging those who are afraid the day of their salvation is
gone, and therewith warning them lest after all they let it
pass :—

" While the birds sing and the mill turns, and the wind blows, and iron
heats, and the hour that now is lasts, and the mind strives, and the conscience
warns—before the breath fails, or the gate of the city is shut, or the soul
takes its flight, or the thread is broken, or the tree falls—before the will is
hardened, or the conscience seared, or the candle put out—before judgment
is passed, or to-day ended, or the present moment gone by, return, O children
of men ! How long will ye delay to receive life? This is the time for
thee to lift thyself to the heights and flee from the enemy by running beneath
the Cross of Christ. This is the day to break through all, this is the hour to
be blessed. O that everyone knew his hour, and made ready against the
night and the winter that is coming! The swallow and the woodcock know
their season, and the ox his owner, but man is foolisher than the wild asses.'

32. And now let us listen to one of the preacher's denuncia-
tions : —

" Woe, ye lawyers, there is a law that shall consume you ! Woe, ye mur-
derous and presumptuous ones ! many a moan has gone to the other shore
[to witness] against you ! Woe, ye froward, swallowing riches ! needs must
ye spue them all up with your own blood ! Woe, ye men in high places, evil
of example, haling the poor after you to destruction ! How shall ye render
an account for your poor tenants ? What will come of you when every high
thing shall be broken and burned? Woe, every great tree and every little
tree that brings not forth good fruit ! The fire has been kindled in Wales.
The door of thy forest, O country of the Britons, is open to the scorching fire,
and the axe is laid also at thy root. If thou do not now bring forth good
fruit thou shalt be cut off from being a people. And woe, you vain ones,
spending your time, and your health, and your money, and your everlasting
thoughts in vanity ! Woe to thee, thou ignorant labourer ! All thy work is
to dig the earth and till it, and turn the cattle on the mountains ; and these
submit to be turned by thee—witnesses are they, therefore, against thee.
Woe, thou cunningly evil reader, that searches books to discover —— or
faults ! The truth shall find fault with thee and judge thee. Woe, thou
hypocrite, that fearest the sight of man ! thou art not afraid to sin secretly :
thou shalt be judged openly. Woe, thou sturdy and idle beggar, that will not
work for any one's good ! good thou seekest not : good shall thou lose. Woe,
thou sleepy conscience, that like a dumb dog betrayest thy owner ! long the
time is for thee to howl. Woe to you that resort to the crowd, eager of
spirit, eating the sugar of the lust of the flesh in the pathway of the devil,
and carousing your souls ! shortly there shall not be for thee a drop of water,
to cool the point of thy tongue ! Woe, ye evil gentry, licking the sweat of the
poor, making your tenants groan, and breaking their bones ! the time of your
tribulation hastens and delays not. Woe, ye dumb priests, loving foxes,

hounding the sheep, blind dogs, bitter, proud, slothful, greedy, snarling, sleepy, filthy, lewd (llydlyd), stinking! Ye shall all be turned out of the church. And woe, all ye ancient people of Wales that are still unrenewed !"

33. There is one very long passage in *Llyfr y tri Aderyn* which is evidently autobiographical, and for a part of which, therefore, I must here find place. "By nature," says Morgan Lloyd, "I was dead, and when I saw this I sought to live, but could not, until everything within and about me had died to *me*. And then the creature lost its hold on me, and at that moment I got hold upon the Creator, or rather, *He* laid hold on *me*. Before, I heard sermons, but did not listen ; I said prayers, but did not pray ; I sang psalms, but my heart was dumb ; I ' sacramented,' (*mi sacramentais*) but saw not the body of the Lord. I talked and said many a thing that was not truly from my heart, until *the Rose brake forth in me* [by "the Rose" he means, of course, the new nature]. And the stir all over, need was to make an end of the end before beginning, and to die before the grain of wheat could grow through my earth." Then he speaks of himself as "born among rocks, nourished in opinions, ensnared for a time, set free in a time acceptable, loved before time's beginning, and Him I will ever love that loved me, and fully love Him when time shall end. For I am under the love of God, though I be under the reproof of all. Vile in the land, grey with the sea [" Llwyd gan mor"—the writer here playing on his own name], abounding in temptations, but joyful in hope of the heavenly glory . . . . and praying God to give heavenly peace and fulness of truth to the kindly Welsh nation, to feed them with knowledge and spiritual understanding, and to fill them with all the fulness of God, and for me, to have a share of the heavenly portion among those that are disciplined in godliness, and to hasten the time when there shall be no war anywhere save in the gates of Satan and his angels, and that war shall I see." Morgan Lloyd then describes how the devil sought to "obstruct his mind, to seal his lips, and stay his hand," saying to him: "It is self that is setting thee to work. Thou writest too obscurely ; none can understand thee until thy fog lifts itself, nor dost thou understand thyself. Be at peace. Men have knowledge enough, if they would only act according to it. There are too many books in the world already. All thy reward will be to be left as an owl in the wilderness. . . . Best for thee to be silent and leave off writing. Let everybody be quiet, and thy own conscience at ease. Be joyful. Eat thy food with a hale heart. Go : take thy pleasure as thou seest nearly all do, and then shall thy days be lengthened upon the earth." "And if," adds our author, "the Serpent had got his will, neither should I have written, nor thou have read or heard this." But the Dove, he tells us, spake to him, saying, "Go forward. Every servant must use his talent (whatever man may say), and if he

do not, woe to that servant. It is not self that urges thee, but a true love to God, and next, a faithful affection to the Welsh people. . . . Yea, although thy flesh understands not what the Holy Spirit within thee writes, the spiritual part perceives it. Nor are there, either, many Welsh books in Wales since the papers of the Britons in former times were burnt. And (says God) my people in Wales perish for lack of knowledge. And for thyself it matters not what disrespect thou gettest in the flesh." And so *The Book of the Three Birds* came to be written.

34. Mr. Lloyd made no effort, I am sure, to give perfection of form to that which he wrote, nor in any way dallied over it. He appears to have written with ease, and to have made few alterations in what he had once set down. He cared only to deliver his message, and was content if that message was understood. His style, therefore, is unequal, and a noble passage is often followed by one that is inorganic, untunable, or marred by defects of taste. Nevertheless he had the instinct of a poet, and whenever he found in his theme the necessary stimulus was sure to break out into eloquence, or stumble at least into some felicity of expression. There are few pages of this *Book of the Three Birds* which do not contain certain choice sentences, sentences over which one lingers, tit-bits full of meat and delicately served. But if Mr. Lloyd's sayings lack sometimes elegance and propriety, they are seldom without grit or a kernel of thought, and many of them are as pithy as the proverbs of the ancients. Here, for example, are a few of them :—

"It is for many too late to-morrow, because it is to-day, too soon."
"A knock or two is not enough at God's door."
"The custom of the world is the open gate to destruction."
"The lips of the righteous feed many."
"The spirit of blood is the cloud of the mind."
"He that climbs not above himself shall never sit down in the heavens."
"The time of a man is his fortune : woe to him if he spend it vainly."
"Feed thy desire and it shall slay thee."
"Abide in the tents of God until there be built the palace of the New Jerusalem."
"The lusts of the flesh are horses of war: come down from them and delay not."
"When a godly man leaves this world, he does but leave his garment, as Joseph did, in the hands of Potiphar's wife—the earth."
"Every man has cleverness enough to deceive himself."
"Beware of hardening thy conscience by often heating and chilling it."
"A man, an oak, and a day are difficult to know."
"The gimlet of instruction must be used before the hammer of discipline ; else the wood will be split or the nail bent."
"Be quiet within, and thou shalt understand everything without."
"The flesh is like black sackcloth on the windows of the mind."

35. On the duty of quietness of spirit and abstinence from unnecessary speech, Mr. Lloyd often insists. "There are many voices," he says, "in the heart of man." Desires, imaginations, and fears—"the ebb and flow of flesh and blood"—keep up in the heart a perpetual clamour, making it like a lodging of

drunkards, or the streets of a town at the time of a great fair or
market. And thus it comes that "a man knows not half his own
thoughts, nor rightly hears what his own heart speaks." It is
to this innermost voice, so easily drowned by clamour, yet expressing man's deepest want, that the heart must listen if it will
attain real blessedness. And this is the voice of the true
Shepherd of man. "And when the true Shepherd speaks, and
man listens, the heart burns within, and the flesh trembles, and
the thoughts lighten like a candle, and the conscience works like
wine in a vessel, and the will inclines to the truth." Again, the
restless thoughts, going out through the senses to the outer world,
or gazing within upon the forms and images of things seen or
remembered, are likened to Lot going out of his house to reason
with the Sodomites and putting himself in peril, till the Divine
Spirit snatched him in to have speech with God in the chamber
of the heart. The mind is also compared to the world at the
deluge, everything drowned with the flood of waters, so that
nothing can spring, and no sprout appear, but when the Heavenly
Spirit comes in "it stills and abates the water of the deluge in
thy heart, and then thou seest the tops of the hills, and the dear
everlasting thoughts appear." Our duty, then, is to still the
tumult in our minds, and keep the thoughts from restlessly
ranging over all the earth. So shall we be able to hear the
voice of the Highest speaking to us, and have leisure to attend
to the deepest needs of our nature. Not less careful must we
be to bridle our tongue, and refrain from heedless and needless
speech, for "the spirit of a talkative man is a horse for the
devil," and "such as talk much among man hear little of God
and Paradise." Therefore must we seek to be restful and quiet,
and "keep the true Sabbath within and without.

36. When the spirit is at rest the lines that indicate doubt,
weariness, and irritation will also disappear from the face. This
is the ground on which our author urges his readers, not merely to
have "a mind always sober, cheerful, thankful, pleasant, seemly,
and innocent," but also "a countenance not surly, sour, cloudy,"
but rather "the countenance as of a wise angel, resolute, silent,
composed."

37. This is Morgan Lloyd's doctrine of quietism. Quietism,
however, does not save the soul, though it often supplies the
necessary condition of salvation. The soul is saved, he says,
when God Himself comes into it, abiding there, permeating the
man's nature, and becoming in him the spring of a new life.
And here, as elsewhere, God manifests Himself under a threefold
form—as Will, Word, and Power. "The Will is in the Word,
and the Word in the Power, and the Power, and the Word, and
the Heavenly Will are in the heart of every man that is saved."
Surely, says our author, "if men knew who abide in them, want
and sin should not hinder them from coming into the mansion of
the heart where the heavenly nobility sup."

38. Will, Word, and Power, or, as we elsewhere read, Will, *Love*, and Power, compose, according to Mr. Lloyd's conception, the Divine Trinity. But answering to this Trinity, and in opposition to it, is another Trinity, a Trinity of *Wrong*—the Lust of the Flesh, the Lust of the Eye, and the Pride of Life, or " a cruel Will, a filthy Delight, and a wicked Power."

89. There is one consideration to which Morgan Lloyd often recurs —the doctrine that " the heavenly nature " is itself " Paradise," and the carnal nature, in which Self is uncrucified, is itself Hell. " Paradise is not far from thee, but in every place where the love of God reveals itself. . . . And on the other hand, hell and the fire, and the wailing and the darkness are in the hearts of many while they here walk the earth." Even the dead, the lost and the blest, are here with us, though the curtain of the flesh hinders us from seeing them. Our author insists, also, that what-ever a man thinks or purposes leaves its record. " Of one out of a thousand things " that a man does or designs, that he says or thinks, " he cannot give any account, though for all of them he will be called to reckoning." Nevertheless, everything in itself is clear already. It is but flesh and time and earthly measure that hinder each from knowing every other's thoughts, and when these are dissolved every one will see the stirrings within, and then shall each have glory or shame from the lips of God." Morgan Lloyd sums up his convictions as to these matters in the following curious paragraph :—

" Whither goes [the light of] a candle when it is put out but to its own natural fiery firmament ? Or whither go the fire and warmth of the hot iron when it is plunged into water ? Not through the lips does the spirit of a man go out of its earthen house ; and not through the lips did the soul enter the body at the first. All pure, lively, swift is the spirit of the mind of man, per-vading every body, without moving or stirring anything. O ye blind, open your eyes, and see that the spirit of every one, in breaking out of the body, stays in the nature in which it lived. If corrupt were its thoughts, everlast-ing corruption is its lodging. The nature of everlasting love or wrath holds all its own children within it, and lays hold, as a flame upon fat, of every spirit according to its nature. But man sees not his [own] home while his flesh is upon him. Men, I say, are as the birds singing in the tree that know not the root that is in them. The holy souls that slept in God are quiet in the silent light everywhere before his face and outside the spirit of the world, awaiting the moving of the body, through the stirring of the root of nature. But the lost spirits have cut the thread of life, in darkness of mind and of the wrath of God, roaring and groaning. Nevertheless, the world hears them not. Wherefore ? Because there is not with *them* in hell voice of tongue to speak, nor with most of *us* spiritual ears to hear or hearts to consider, although they are in the same nature as we."

40 Mr, Lloyd insists that God and the spirit are the only " substances," the only things that are real. " Substance is every spirit, and the seen world is but a shadow of the unseen which pervades it ; and the body also is but a shadow, and like as the clothes-horse of the spirit, or the sheath of the sword, which shall endure for ever."

41. But if the universe is the shadow of God, or " the glass in which His shadow may be seen," as Morgan Lloyd said it was, if it is pervaded by His presence, and filled with His glory, it cannot surely be wholly unvenerable. Yet, for this lordly spectacle of nature, Mr. Lloyd has no good word to say. It was for him merely the husk of the kernel, the rind of the real. It was at best but a passing show. It was the scene of sin's dominion, and all who lived in it lived in vexation and vanity. He could not therefore spend his thoughts or lavish his love on it. He did, indeed, speak lovingly of the rainbow, spiritualizing it after his manner, but this was only because "the bow in the cloud" was made in *Genesis*, the sign of something spiritual. Of course, the pageant of the material world did, in reality, immensely influence him—giving to his speech that glow and beauty and picturesqueness which we find in it. But he was affected by it in this way apart from his will, and almost unconsciously. And if you had asked him what he thought of this world, whose spaces we tread, and in whose airs we are bathed, he would have given a very bad account of it.

42. Nor could he see anything worthy of respect in the faculties, affections, and propensities of man. It is not merely, according to him, that all these are evil when they work against good, but they are evil in themselves, always and everywhere evil, and evil only. As to the bodily appetites, he borrows of them, in denouncing them, some of their own coarseness and heedlessness. Even the reason of man, his best endowment, has meted out to it condemnation not less unmeasured and unqualified. "The sense of the world, the wisdom of the flesh, the natural reason" are compared to a "coiled serpent spitting out poison against the truth." "The sense of man," we are told, " is a thief within, locking the door of every mind against the breath of the Holy Spirit. This is Ahitophel, and the Judas that betrays a man into the devil's hands. . . . This is the bow of Lucifer, and enemy of Noah, the mother of wars, the nurse of vanity, the child of hell, the Diana of the world, the castle of sin, the smoke of the pit, the advocate for evil, the spring of every misfortune, and the evil beast." Our author extends also the meaning of the word flesh, so as to make it include everything that is not consciously inclined to God's law :—

"The flesh is everything under the sun that is outside the man within. Whatever is perishable and not eternal is flesh. The sense of men and the delight of the world are flesh. Flesh is the sport of young and old. Flesh are the food and the offspring of man. Time is flesh, and everything that ends in it. Flesh are the will and the secret of man. Many prayers and sermons are flesh. The honours of great men and the height of little men are flesh. Flesh is everything that a natural man sees and hears, and gets and has. And 'all flesh is grass.' Behold, how it withers! It is not the same for a minute. The breath of Emmanuel blows upon this flower,

as upon a herb of the garden, which moulders between thy fingers. The
flesh is called 'The Old Man,' because it is crafty to deceive, easy to
remember, difficult to know, habituated to man, dear to him, near to him,
part of him, growing in him, and perishing with him. This flesh is God's
enemy, man's poison, hell's livery, the image of the beast, the sinner's
shame, the hiding-place of the hypocrite, the spider's web, the merchant of
souls, the home of the lost, the dung-hill of devils."

43. Mr. Lloyd was very fond of spiritualizing Scripture ; and
he has freighted many a Biblical phrase with a new meaning.
Nor can we in general quarrel with him if the meanings with which
he has thus charged so many passages are not those which were
at first intended. But he sometimes carries, it must be admitted,
this practice of spiritualizing to a point at which it becomes
grotesque and ridiculous. His treatment of *the Ark* especially,
is an extraordinary instance of the letter spiritualized and
transfigured until it has lost all fixed and natural meaning. The
Ark, he says, is Emmanuel, and Noah, who dwelt in it, is the
Divine Trinity. Others may have divined in the Ark and its
inhabitants this mystic significance, but no one else has developed
that significance so as to make it the foundation of a system of
thought, and a key wherewith to unlock the mysteries of nature
and grace.

44. All this finds in part its explanation in the fact that
Morgan Lloyd was " a mystic," one who believed himself to be in
possession of a divine " secret," of a mystery capable of unlock-
ing deeper mysteries, and who did violence to words in using
them to express it, making them a vehicle for a meaning they
were not fitted to carry.

45. The mystic, doubtless, his eyes blinded with seeing, goes
sometimes astray, when the dull man, his feet always in the ruts,
keeps his path ; but over the untrodden spaces, and when the
ruts lead to the wrong goal, who is the better guide then ? and
which is the likelier to help us in picking out a path for ourselves ?

46. We are not going, therefore, to forswear the companion-
ship of our mystic, because we do not find him infallible or
indefectible. It is enough if his counsels make in any way
faith or duty easier to us. Nay, it is enough if what he says
does but interest us ; for the interest that is so excited in us is
the homage we unconsciously render when we find a need of our
nature somehow answered. My readers will be glad then, perhaps, to have presented to them from *The Book of the Three
Birds*, the following stately passage, in which the writer essays
to justify to the reason the doctrine of the Trinity, and to
reconcile God's predestination with His universal love. It is the
Dove that speaks, and the Eagle that is spoken to :—

"There are in eternity three in one, namely, Will, Love, and Power, and
from everlasting these reach forth together, and each feeds upon and per-
petuates itself in the others for ever (Prov. viii.) If it were not that it is an

eternal delight to satisfy the Infinite Will, there would not be any saved. And if the agitation of the primal Will were not a consuming fire, there would not be any lost. And if the three did not thus work together, there would be neither man, nor angel, nor beast, nor anything else made. Some have been from the beginning brought to birth within the Love by the prompting of the Will, which scatters them as sparks out of itself and tempers them in the water of pleasantness (which is The Ark.) The root of the three is but love itself hating none. But in this active Will there is a prompting which concentrates that which is of its essence and leaves behind (as a tree its leaves or a man his spittle) that which is not one with the spirit of the heart. Behold, the ravens know not the touch of this string in the heavenly harp ! But do thou understand, O Eagle ; and the doves understand this more and more. For this is the root of the matter and the source of all things. This is the stock of the oak of all this visible world. This is the everlasting stirring that is the cause of every movement among all the creatures. But the birds in the branches of the tree do not consider how its root sustains their nature nor how they are in it. The primal Will is the root of every-thing as the spark comes forth of the stone, and it betakes itself always to the bosom of the Son, and quiets itself there in the Love. But some of the sparks refuse so to cool their heat, and fly with Lucifer against the light into the eternal darkness, and abide in the fiery agitation, never attaining rest because seeking it not by coming out of their own nature. There is power in the will to move, but there is no will that has the power to return, as the raven, in part speaking the truth, before said. Therefore, many reject them-selves, and accuse Noah. And although His bosom covets them, their own fiery bosom holds them in their own kingdom. But, O Eagle, if thou remem-ber to enquire further concerning this when we are by ourselves in the silence, I will show thee more at large the root of every mystery."

47. Enough has now been said of Morgan Lloyd as a writer, and it is time to speak of him as a preacher and as a man. And I do not know that I can do better than preface what I have to say on this matter by quoting an account which one of his con-temporaries (defending him from an attack made upon his memory by Richard Baxter) has given of him[21] :—

" He was extraordinary for his love to his countrymen, to whose soul-service he was entirely devoted, for which he was eminently qualified, being the deepest, truest Welshman, and the most absolute British orator, perhaps, that ever was in the ministerial function, and this without any hindrance to his English fluency. He was extraordinary for the pregnancy of his fancy, the tenaciousness of his memory, and the early matureness of his parts, being but forty when he died ; extraordinary for his charity, which was universal, not at all confined to parties and persuasions ; for the holiness of his life, diligence in his studies, unwearied meditation, spiritualizing of all things, and for his very impartial and unprejudiced searches after truth ; extraordinary also for his humility, meekness, moderation, his great seriousness, and always ready bounty to the poor, which, like the sun, shone upon the bad as well as the good. He was very exemplary for his strict education of his children ; for his gravity, which was neither starched nor supercilious, but real and obliging, whereby he awed all companies he came into ; and for a strange and unusual majesty which he wore in the pulpit, not forced nor affected, but natural, yet very heavenly and spiritual ; in a word, there was no good thing ordinary in him, but all by way of eminency. Such a person was this Mr. Morgan

<hr>

21. In a pamphlet, published in 1685, entitled *A Winding Sheet for Mr Baxter's Dead ; or those whom he hath killed in his " Catholic Communion" secretly embalmed and decently buried again: being an Apology for several ministers—viz., Mr. Erbery, Mr. Cradock, Mr. Vavasor Powell, and Mr. Morgan Lloyd.* This passage is quoted from Rees' *History of Protestant Nonconformity in Wales.*

Lloyd, and surely such an one could not be so dangerous a man as Mr. Baxter traduceth him. No; he was many ways beneficial to the world, but never prejudiced nor traduced it at all, except in one thing, and that he could not help, which was that he left it too soon."

48. In the foregoing account Morgan Lloyd's *children* are mentioned. Of these, the name of only one has been preserved ; that of a daughter—Elizabeth, whose birth in 1657 he thus announces to his mother :—"You have here a little granddaughter, and her name is Elizabeth Lloyd,—a candle kindled by the blessed Father of Spirits."

49. The author of *The Winding Sheet for Mr. Baxter's Dead* speaks of Morgan Lloyd's "very impartial and unprejudiced searches after truth." And it is precisely as a seeker after truth that this man presents himself to us, not less in his own books and letters, than in the accounts of him which others have handed down to us. For, although he had no notion of goodness except in connection with certain conceptions held by him to be fundamental, yet within the limits of those conceptions, no one took a freer range than he did, or laid less stress on what could be regarded as non-essential. Many instances might be given of the keen spirit of enquiry and wide-embracing tolerance that characterized him.

50. When, for example, the teaching of George Fox began to be everywhere discussed, Morgan Lloyd dispatched to the North two members of his congregation (see ch. vii, sec. 1), who were instructed to bring him a full and true account of the new teacher and of his doctrines. Morgan Lloyd's own doctrine of quietism was so closely allied to the doctrine of the indwelling spirit preached by George Fox, that he naturally took an interest in the latter, and was glad to befriend his followers. Thus, when Richard Baxter denounced the Quakers, Mr. Lloyd gently remonstrated with him :—"You condemne," wrote he, "the generation of the Quakers. If I were more intimate with you, I might better aske, why?" Still, although probably a good deal influenced by the Friends, both in his opinions and practices,[22] he never became one of them. "They have the truth," wrote he to his mother, "but not the whole truth." But his supposed leanings towards them did not recommend him to the more steady-going of his Puritan parishioners ; while George Fox, who distrusted him because having gone part of the way with him he did not go the whole, speaks of him in his *Journal* (on the two occasions he mentions him) with scorn.

51. The same humility and willingness to learn of whomsoever had anything to teach him, are shown in Morgan Lloyd's

22. Thus we see from the earliest letter of Mr. Morgan Lloyd that has been preserved that about the year 1643 or 1644 he still called the months by their common and accustomed names, while in and after 1655 he never names them other than by their order in the year, after the fashion of the Friends.

letter to Mr. William Erbery.[23]   In the phrase of one of
his contemporaries, Mr. Erbery was, in the latter part of his life,
"ill of his whimsies," and was led to the statement of various
strange doctrines.   Morgan Lloyd, who knew the man to be
honest and had already been in correspondence with him, was
pained by the rumours that reached him of Mr. Erbery's heresies,
and straightway wrote to him.   "I dare not believe," said he,
"what I hear of you," and "though it is no matter what flesh
without truth speaketh, yet love would be satisfied." Then, after
speaking of the world as "the devil's street in which his coaches
trundle," and assuring his correspondent that "the sweetness of
the Father's love in you is very pleasant to my taste," he goes on,
as a learner, and not as calling his friend to account, to inquire of
certain matters, points of mysticism and the like, concerning
which he desired fuller knowledge.

52. In Morgan Lloyd's two letters to Richard Baxter, the attitude of the disciple is perhaps less discernible than the eager-
ness of the seeker and the confidence of the seer. But they show
that the author of them could write as forcefully in English as in
Welsh. These letters, in Morgan Lloyd's own beautiful handwriting, may be seen at Dr. Daniel Williams' library.

FAC-SIMILE OF MORGAN LLOYD'S HANDWRITING.

The first of them, dated from Wrexham in the third month of
1656, begins thus :—"Here is a word from a friend in Wales
that hath eyed you and the spirit arising and working in you (as
your printings unfold you). You are, I perceave, digging at the
root of trueth, and your fainted spirit hath knowen in itselfe that
the fountain is deepe, and that no man can draw up the waters
of life, or unseale the booke of God." The following sentences
show the drift of the letter, which was merely to get an expres-
sion of Mr. Baxter's opinion on certain points hinted at :—" I
salute you in love and respect, though I must not now write at
large. Only I desire one private line of the upshott of your
manifold thoughts. . . . . This is a salutation, I hope not
in vaine. If you show your face in earnest in the glass Salomon
speaks of, it may be answerably reflected further by Mor. Lloyd,

    ·ₙ 23. Printed in full in the third volume of Benjamin Brooks' *Lives of the Puritans*.
This letter is said to have been written about the year 1652.

who is affected to see you in your writings so earnestly groping for the true inward doore which many inward men (I fear) mistake also."[24]

53. Although this appeal brought a " loving letter " from Mr. Baxter, the latter afterwards made a strong attack upon Morgan Lloyd's memory, and was answered, as we have seen by *The Winding Sheet for Mr. Baxter's Dead.*

54. One would like to see the letters of Morgan Lloyd to Colonel John Jones (see sec. 10); the letters of Colonel Jones to the former are still preserved (published by Mr. Joseph Mayer in the 1861 volume of the *Lancashire and Cheshire Historical Society's Transactions*), and are very interesting. I have already quoted in Note 8a from one of these letters; extracts from three others which, from the point of view of this book, are of special personal or local interest, will now be given. The first is dated from Dublin, " 9 d 8 m 1651," and invites Morgan Lloyd and [Vavasour] Powell over to Ireland:—[Here is worke for you and dear Mr. Powell and some more of our British Nuntios to divulge the bridegroom's message,"] and playfully chides the former for his apparent neglect of his native country :—

" What becomes of poor Merionethshire ? Is that countrey denied the tender of gospel mercies ? Is there no prophet nor messenger of Xt yt will make Duffryn Ardidwey in his way ? Where is Mr. Powell, M. Lloyd, &c., that once thought it a mercy and a high priviledge to be accompted worthy of being driven to the mountaynes and desolate places that they might have liberty to preach the Gospel there. Yor office and duty is to encoûnter with sinn and the power of the prince of the ayre, and where is there more sinn to encounter with ? where more ignorance ? where more hatred to the people of God ? where the word saint more scorned than in Merionethshire ? "

The second letter is dated from Drogheda, August 23, 1652. Herein the writer makes special enquiry as to what the things were "that are printed against the Saints at Wrexham, unto whom" he says :—

"I hope, the Lord hath given a Speritt of Sobriety as well as of Xtian zeal, not to affect empty vaine speculations which hath deceaved many into a contempt of the Ordinances of Christ and His written word, and at length (like him that believed himself to be that great Star which he looked upon and pointed at), believe that themselves are God and Christ, that noe Act of theires is sinfull, that Cheques of Conscience against the Committall of any Act, be it ever so sinfull or monstrous, proceeds from the want of that perfection which *they* have acquired and professedly Act in, as the enjoyment of that liberty and Priviledge which the[ir] Perfection entitles them unto. . . . . I would have beene glad to have seen what is in printe; question-

24. In the second letter to Mr. Baxter, written seven months after the first, Morga, Lloyd speaks of the age in which he lived as " bookish, partiall, formall, fierce, factious and animositous." The following sentences may also be quoted :—" One cause of our present wofull babilonish contention is the want of right apprehensions of the Godhead in his Christ and spirit. Neither shall man agree in God till the fleshly mind (that perks up in man's heart to judge of God's mind) bee mortifyed. And in that the Quakers say well as I think. And because the foundations of present churches (however called), since the Apostacy from the true, cleare, chrystall, primitive knowledge, were not layd deepe and large enough in an eternall interest, therefore they fall and crumble, one after another, in hostile partyes."

less, it may be guessed from what speritt and from what hand it proceeded : lett Patience work, and you shall see that shame will be the reward of the Authors and promoters of these lyes. The Lord reward you for your great love and kindness to my boy, and give strength to my dear friend your wife. . . . . I wish Mr. Powell would leave his disputeing, and that he and you would come over to Ireland for some time. Many gratious hearts and heddes here conceave that disputes produce neither grace nor knowledg, but ad-minster and ingender striffe : pray remember my dear love to Mr. Powell and Mr. Mostin [see sec. 69] when you write, and to all our friends."

In the third letter, written from Dublin, 30th Sept., 1658, Col. Jones says :—

"I intend to send you herewith one or more coppyes of your paper printed [Could this be the *Llyfr y tri Aderyn*; printed in 1653 ?]. . . . I intend to send the bookes to Major Swift ; from thence you may order the disposall of them as you please. I confess the discourse is exceedingly good and spirituall according to my understanding, yet myselfe and many other sober wise Christians heere conceive that if it had been penned in a language or still lesse parabolicall and in more plane Scripture expressions, it would be more usefull. Babes must be fed with milk. There was one of my family with you lately, whose report and a paper sent him from my boy makes some of our friends heere feare that you in Wales have layed aside all gospell ordi-nances, and particularly that of prayer. I know the reporter's temper (and the paper having neither the gravity, sobriety, and meeke temper of yor spirit in ye language of it, but, like Jobe's friends, too quick in sensuring what could not be in ye cognizance of ye penman), I esteeme not as an evidence in this matter honerd. I desire you to send me an account of ye state and condition of ye Sts and Church of God in Wales, and especially with you, and wt your p'sent practice is, that the mouth of the adversary may be stopped, and yt thei yt feare ye Lord may rejoice with you and for you, and may glorifie our father wch is in heaven."

55. It is quite certain that the charge of Antinomianism hinted at in two of the letters just given, was, so far at least as Morgan Lloyd was concerned, wholly false. No one was more absorbed than he in well-doing, or submitted himself more entirely to the obligations of duty. But his poetical language and his beautiful charity were misunderstood by the dunder-headed and coarse-natured.

56. It was, in fact, precisely some of Morgan Lloyd's finest qualities—his open-mindedness, unconventionality, and fidelity to conviction—which aroused distrust in many of his contem-poraries, and hindered his popularity.

57. There was another fact which stood greatly in the way of Mr. Lloyd's *general* acceptance in the place of his ministry. While he was at first, as seems likely, the authorized minister of the parish, many of the leading Puritans of the place being Presby-terians, *he was himself a decided Independent.* It is certain he was a *member* of the Independent Church, which as early as 1651 was already constituted in the town. It does not, however, follow that there was in Wrexham at that time an Independent *congregation* of which Mr. Lloyd was pastor. On the contrary, it seems probable that while the members of the church named met regularly together for breaking of bread, for prayer, and for

confirming each other in faith and good works, they joined, at first, for common worship with the Presbyterians and the rest of the parishioners at the Parish Church, there waiting upon the ministry of Mr. Lloyd who, amongst themselves, was no more than a private member.

58. We know of the existence in 1651 of the Independent Church just mentioned, through an address of congratulation presented to Oliver Cromwell after the battle of Worcester (Sept. 3, 1651). This address purports to proceed " from the Church of Christ at Wrexham," and is signed by six members of it, namely : — " Daniel Lloyd, Mor. Lloyd, John Browne, Edw. Taylor, An. Maddockes, Dav. Maurice." It contains the following sentence :— " Christ has revealed His own arm, and broke the arm of the mighty once and again, and now lately at Worcester, so that to conclude (in Ezekiel's phrase) there will be found no roller to bind the late king's arm to hold a sword again."[25] In signing his name second instead of first, Mr. Morgan Lloyd showed his desire to avoid any assumption of primacy among his fellows. I conclude " the Church of Christ at Wrexham " to have been Independent rather than Presbyterian, or of mixed constitution, because no Presbyterian could rejoice in a victory, gained over Presbyterians, by one who was mainly responsible for the death of the late king, and whose triumph shattered for ever the hope of establishing the Presbyterian order and discipline throughout the land.

59. The signatures to the address of congratulation mentioned in the last paragraph are interesting as giving us the names of the more prominent members of the early Independent Church in Wrexham.

60. " Daniel Lloyd " was doubtless the same " Daniel Lloyd, gentleman," who was nominated in 1649 a commissioner under the "Act for the Better Propagation and Preaching of the Gospel in Wales." He was satirized as " a sequestrating saint " in a scurrilous local ballad dated 1647, a copy of which I possess. This epithet leaves us in no doubt that he was a member of the Committee of Sequestration for North Wales. From the pleadings in a certain suit held in the year 1655, it would appear that he was also the receiver in this district of estates that

---

25. Printed in *The Diurnall* of November 10, 1651; see also *Count Grammont's Memoirs*, Bohn's Edition, page 516. There has also been preserved an address from " The Church at Wrexham to that noble brigade under the command of Major-General Harrison." This address is undated, but it was probably forwarded, in August, 1651, to the general while he was watching the southward movements of the Scotch army and covenanted king, that was to end so disastrously at Worcester. The address begins thus :—" Dear brethren,—Your quickening letter was received with joy and thankfulness. Seasonably it came to us, two days before a meeting of our church appointed and kept yesterday, in which our weak forces on the hills were mightily encouraged by the presence of our great Lord, who is the God of the hills and of the vallies." The following sentence from the address may also be quoted :—" If the Lord call for us by you, here we are, awaiting the sound of the trumpet." Unfortunately, the names of those who signed this letter (for a knowledge of which I am indebted to Mr. E. G. Salisbury) have not been preserved.

had been forfeited "to the use of the state."²⁶ There is a letter in existence to Mr. Daniel Lloyd from Colonel John Jones (see sec. 54), in which the writer says :—" I thank you for the accounte you gave me of the Sts' Church of God with you, and blessed be our Lord that preserves you from being entangled with ye snares of the Serpent, and leads you with so much zeale and fervency to avoid contentions and strife, and to provoke the people of God to unity and love, which are the bonds of peace and p'fection." Mr. Lloyd died in the year 1655, and was buried, doubtless by his own desire, in a field opposite the front of Pen-y-bryn farmhouse in Abenbury. Here his gravestone, now prostrate and broken in two, may still be seen ; it bears the following inscription :—" Here is asleep Daniel Lloyd, Servant of Jesus Christ, interred November 19th, 1655."

61. "John Browne, gentleman," was another of the Commissioners nominated under the above-named Act. He is, I suppose, the same Mr. John Browne who is mentioned in 1673 as a deacon of the Independent Church, Wrexham, but to what family he belonged, and where he lived, I have not yet been able to discover.

62. Of Edward Taylor and David Maurice, two other of the signators to the address of congratulation, enough has been already [sec 7 (6) and (7)] said. I have two or three times seen the signature of " Andrewe Maddockes," the last of the six, but know little more about him than that he appears to have lived in Acton, and that the baptism of several of his children by his wife Anne is recorded in the parish registers. He was dead in 1661.

63. It may conduce to the better understanding of several points in Mr. Lloyd's history if something is now said of the relations to one another of the Independents and Presbyterians of his time. The Presbyterians were the Whigs of the Interregnum. Most of them were at first merely Evangelical churchmen, and either actually preferred Episcopacy or were willing to submit to it. But when they saw the bishops definitely setting themselves to root Puritanism out of the land, they naturally drifted into Presbyterianism. At last the crisis came, and they threw bishops and prayer book—now become the symbols of despotism—out of

26. Another person who was connected with the collection of subsidies and dues during the period of the Commonwealth was Edward Thomas, corviser, of Beast-Market Street. His house was that nearest the Beast Market on the south side of Charles Street and is still in existence. In the ballad above mentioned he is described as "Judas," and as bearing "the bag the saints have made." Lady Puleston, of Emral, on the other hand, described him as her " friend," as " an ancient professor of Godliness in these parts and one of approved integrity." He married, as his second wife, Margaret Presland, widow Captain Edward Taylor's mother-in-law (see note 8.) By his first wife, Sara, he had two sons, who, according to the Welsh custom, took their surname from their father's christian name. The elder of these, Jonathan (baptized at the parish church Jan. 4, 164½), became afterwards famous as Dr. Jonathan Edwards, Vice-Chancellor of the University of Oxford, and author of a work against Socinianism. The younger son. Samuel Edwards (baptd. March 4, 164¾) become a friend of Philip Henry, and is often mentioned in his diary. Edward Thomas died about the time of the Restoration.

doors. But when the Presbyterians had done this, and purged
the church of what they held (in many cases, no doubt, quite
wrongly) to be mere remnants of Popery, they were content that
everything else should go on as before. They retained the
parochial system, proposing, however, certain reforms of it which
have since been carried out with general applause. They still
called the incumbents by the old names of "rector," "vicar," or
"curate," as well as by the newer name of "minister." Churchwardens continued to be yearly elected, and vestry meetings to
be regularly held. The rights of patrons were still recognised,
the patrons' nominees being required nevertheless to be accepted
by the congregations, tried by a body of ministers, and installed
by the authority of the State. The Presbyterians of the Commonwealth period were also strongly convinced of the desirability
of a national church-establishment, which should be committed
to a definite scheme of doctrine, and conform everywhere in
respect of its order and government to the same model. Of
course, however, this scheme of doctrine was intended to be
Evangelical and Calvinistic, and this model to be Presbyterian.
And by an ordinance of Parliament, which passed the House of
Lords, June 6th, 1644. Presbyterianism was specifically declared
to be the religion of the State. Spite of this, Presbyterianism
was never, except in London, Lancashire, and Essex, actually
and fully established in the country. Synods or provincial assemblies were indeed held in nearly every county, but they were
merely voluntary associations that had no authority to enforce
their discipline by civil penalties. This failure to secure the
definite and universal establishment of the Presbyterian system
was due to the action of the Independents, who were now rapidly
growing in numbers and influence, and who were apprehensive
lest the legal supremacy of Presbyterianism should involve the
harassing, and perhaps the suppression, of their own congregations.
This apprehension was undoubtedly well grounded, for the leaders
of the Presbyterians, or most of them, had not yet reached the
stage at which toleration had ceased to appear sinful, and they
were, moreover, at this time particularly incensed against the Independents who, when at last "a settlement in religion" was
almost in sight, were standing out, and preventing the provisional
arrangement already attained from becoming a final and complete one.

64. The Independents were all agreed in regarding the faithful
of every congregation duly joined together "in Gospel order" as
composing a true and scriptural church. Such a church, it was
maintained, was fully competent to determine the conditions of
its own activity, and exemption was therefore claimed for it from
all external interference. This *independence* of each religious
society or congregation of every other was then, as now, the

central principle of Independency (now called "Congregational-
ism"), the principle which distinguished it, considered as a form
of church order, from both Presbyterianism and Episcopacy.
From the Presbyterian and Episcopalian standpoints the name
"church" was properly applicable not to the separate congregations, but to the larger organisations of which they formed a
part. Under these last-named systems, therefore, the amount of
self-government belonging to the single congregations is restricted,
the determination of all the larger issues affecting them being
left, in the case of the Presbyterians, to the synods or provincial
assemblies, and in the case of the Episcopalians, to the bishop or
his officials. Many of the Independents of the Commonwealth
time considered their opinions as to church order quite consistent
with the recognition and support of religion by the State ; and
most of the parish ministers who had adopted Congregational
principles denied, for this reason, their obligation to relinquish
their livings, and thus many of them were at the same time, as
already has been explained, incumbents of parishes and pastors
(or merely members) of Congregational (Independent or Baptist)
churches. There were, however, great differences among the Independents in this respect, and large numbers of them were opposed to the maintenance of a State church of any sort, paid no
respect to the old parochial system, denied the right to levy com-
pulsory tithes, and looked with suspicion upon the existence of a
special ministerial class. I fancy Morgan Lloyd, in his later
days, to have been one of these Independents. Speaking broadly,
the Independents of this extreme type were stricter Calvinists
and more rigid disciplinarians than the Presbyterians, and they
perceived that it was only as voluntary societies, free from external control, that they could preserve that purity of doctrine
and strictness of discipline which they so much prized. They
were thus led by the very strictness with which they interpreted
their religious obligations to look upon the principle of toleration
with complacency, while the definite advocacy of that principle
was at last forced upon them by the necessities of their position
as a sect conspicuously outnumbered by the predominant Presbyterians. It was in this way that the Independents became the
zealous advocates of religious liberty, while some of them went
on to be the champions of civil liberty also. Large numbers of
them were avowed Republicans, and this was why they at first
strongly supported Cromwell in his measures and afterwards as
strongly opposed him.

65. In speaking, as we have just done, of the Republicanism
of many of the Independents, we have touched the main cause
of the quarrel which the Presbyterians had with them. The
differences as to church government which existed between these
two parties were by no means incapable of adjustment, and were
at one time in a fair way to being settled on the two principles of

D

a fairly comprehensive national church and a certain toleration for those who could not be comprehended in the latter. But the Presbyterians could never forgive those who had been responsible for cutting off the king's head. It is true the Presbyterians had themselves borne arms against the king, but, according to their own contention, they were only fighting to rescue him from the hands of evil advisers. Their wars were levied, by a convenient fiction, in the name of the " king *and* Parliament," and they swore in their *Solemn League and Covenant* to maintain the authority of the one as well as the rights and liberties of the other. They were in fact fighting for the establishment of a limited monarchy such as that which was afterwards actually constituted.[27] It was difficult, however, for the Presbyterians to play consistently their part as Constitutional Royalists while they were actually fighting against the king, and were continually being reminded in their negociations with him that they were dealing with one on whose plighted word they could not rely. But when the king was dead, executed in the teeth of their protests, their thoughts turned warmly to the young Prince, who was in no way responsible for his father's misdeeds, and whom, having taken the covenant, the Scots were now welcoming as their king. Suddenly, at the head of 14,000 men the Prince marched into England, expecting his friends to rally to him. But the feud between the English Presbyterians was still too recent to allow them to act together ; each distrusted the other ; there was no time to settle terms of accommodation ; and the expedition ended (September 3rd, 1651) ingloriously at Worcester, leaving Cromwell supreme. The Independents of Wrexham who had watched anxiously (see note 25) the southward march of Charles's army gave utterance to their delight at its overthrow by forwarding to Oliver Cromwell an address of congratulation. The Presbyterians, on the other hand, who, spite of Morgan Lloyd's influence, were very numerous in Wrexham, heard, we may be sure, the news of Worcester battle with very different feelings.

66. In the light of what has just been said, it becomes possible to discuss more fully and formally than we have hitherto been able to do the question of Morgan Lloyd's ministerial status in Wrexham. All the contemporary accounts of him that we have appear to suggest the conclusion that he was at first the official minister, or vicar of the parish. Nor does the fact that he was at the same time a member of the Congregational Church at Wrexham in any way make against this conclusion. The only thing known to me that does make against it is the fact that the vicarage-house of

---

27. If their ecclesiastical aims did not also get ultimately realized, this was because they wholly missed the true solution of the difficulty, which would have been found in a policy of toleration and comprehension, and only sought to set up one form of absolutism instead of another.

1333884

the parish is returned in 1649, and again in 1651, as unoccupied.
On the other hand there are several considerations which make
us suspect that, during the last years of his life, Morgan Lloyd
was no longer the vicar of the parish, but merely minister of the
Congregational Church of Wrexham. His strained relations with
the dominant Presbyterians of the parish, or his own scruples
against the forced levying of tithes, may have led to this result.
The considerations which suggest the conclusion just indicated,
the conclusion, namely, that at the time of his death Morgan
Lloyd had no connection with the parish church, are mainly
three:—first, the tradition of the local Independents in the middle
of last century seems to point in that direction; secondly, Mr.
Philip Henry was invited to become vicar of Wrexham in March,
165°, three months before Mr. Lloyd's death, a fact which shows
that the vicarship was then vacant; and, lastly Mr. Lloyd was
buried, it seems certain, in what was afterwards known as the
Dissenters' Grave-yard. But, as to this last-mentioned fact, it is
not impossible that the grave-yard in question was intended
originally for the parishioners in general; and I am far from
thinking the two considerations first named absolutely decisive.
It is extraordinary that so much obscurity should exist as to the
specific status of one so often mentioned by his contemporaries.

67. And now nothing more remains to be said of Morgan Lloyd
than that he died June 3rd, 1659, aged 40 years, his finely
wrought organism fretted away before its due time. Yet herein
was his death happy that he so escaped the fury of the
Restoration. How much he thus escaped is suggested by the
story told by "one who then inhabited Wrexham," that when
the Restoration came a soldier sought out Mr. Lloyd's grave (in
the Rhosddu Lane Burying Ground), and "in great rage and
malice thrust down his sword into it as far as it would go."

68. What became of Mr. Lloyd's wife and children after his
death I do not know. They probably withdrew to Cynfael where
his mother still lived. His mother I take to be the Mary Lloyd
of Cynfael, who, when in 1672 Charles the Second issued his
Declaration of Indulgence, registered her house for Congregational
worship. She appears, from inquiries I have made, to have sold
the estate of Cynfael in the year 1688, a certain Samuel Lloyd
(probably her son) being also mentioned in the deed of sale.

69. Whatever doubt there may be as to the exact ministerial
status of Mr. Morgan Lloyd, there is no such doubt as to the
status of the *Mr. Ambrose Mostyn, M.A.*, who not long after Mr.
Lloyd's death is described as his successor. He was, beyond
question, the duly recognised Presbyterian Vicar of Wrexham.
And whether he was Mr. Lloyd's successor or not, his appointment must be taken as a sign of the predominance of the Presbyterians in the district in the last year of the Commonwealth era.

70. I do not know that I can do better than quote here the account of Mr. Ambrose Mostyn that I have already given in my *History of the Parish Church of Wrexham* :—'' Mr. Mostyn is said to have been a son of Dr. Henry Mostyn, of Calcot (or Caldicot), in the parish of Holywell,[28] and to have been born in 1610. ' He matriculated at Brazenose College, Oxford, on the 15th of January, 1629. Immediately after completing his course in the University, he settled in South Wales *(Dr. Thos. Rees)*, but in what capacity is not known. I find, however, that in 1642 the parishioners of ' Pennard ' in a petition to the House of Commons, prayed for the nomination of this Mr. Mostyn as ' lecturer' to them, describing him as a man ' of godly sort' and one who ' could preach in the Welsh and English tongues.' '' He exercised the functions of an '' Approver'' under the provisions of the Act of 1650 '' For the better Propagation and Preaching of the Gospel in Wales.'' Before he settled in Wrexham, he resided for some time in Holt, acting, doubtless, as curate there. He was twice married, but had no children. His first wife was buried in the graveyard at Sweeney Park, near Oswestry.[29] His second wife is said to have been a daughter of the first Sir Edward Broughton, of Marchwiel.'' '' Mr. Mostyn was a man very different from his predecessor. It was not merely that Mr. Lloyd exhibited Congregational tendencies, while Mr. Mostyn was a decided Presbyterian. Mr. Lloyd, if somewhat narrow, was at least no copy of another man ; released from the bondage of tradition, and surrendering himself absolutely to what he believed to be the voice of heaven in his heart, he was apt to entertain new and ' inconvenient' notions of duty; and he was used always to champion with the fervour of his nature, and with the resources of a singular eloquence, whatever opinions he had come to espouse. It is easy to understand, therefore, that his career was attended by the enthusiastic love of his friends, and the suspicion or hatred of those whom he was unable to win. Mr. Mostyn was less original, more moderate, conventional, mediocre, and being withal a man of character, refinement, and ability, was doubtless more generally acceptable than his predecessor. The bodily sufferings he endured tended also to make him less aggressive, and to win for him the sympathy of those who knew him, while his family connections recommended him to many whom his Presbyterianism would repel.''

71. Mr. Ambrose Mostyn was assisted by Mr. Ambrose Lewis, who is described as a '' candidate for the ministry.'' He was of the stock of the Lewises of Presaddfed, in Anglesey, and probably the fourth son of Robert Lewis, Esq., of Cemlyn in the aforesaid

---

28. See Note 8 page 64 of my *History of the Parish Church of Wrexham.*

29. The inscription on her tombstone ran thus :—'' Here lyeth the body of a blessed saint exercised all her days in mortification and self-denial, strong loves to God and the most spiritual saints, zeal to his glory and the most tender (affection) to her husband, honest Jane, ye wife of Ambrose Mostin, deceased, July 26, 1651.''

county. He was an active, intelligent, and pious young Puritan. The first mention I can find of him is in Philip Henry's Diary, under date January 13th, 165?, when he preached at Worthenbury, as he continued to do once a month until "The Restoration" (*History of Parish Church of Wrexham*.) After that event, like most of the Presbyterians, he conformed, all his children being afterwards baptised in the parish church. Dr. Griffith. bishop of the diocese, who was his friend, was thus enabled to licence him as schoolmaster (master, it is said, of the Wrexham Grammar School). In Dec., 1663, Philip Henry writes of him that the bishop was keeping him "in salvâ conscientiâ." In 1678 he is still described as "schoolmaster." Not long after this latter date (in 1681), a letter of his was intercepted wherein he communicated to a friend a design, in which many godly people had concurred, to spend a portion of every Monday evening in prayer for the Church and nation, labouring under the special difficulties of the time. This harmless design was thereupon magnified into a plot, and the writer was presented at the forthcoming assizes. Sir George Jeffreys (afterwards the notorious Lord Jeffreys), was at that time Chief Justice of Chester, and it was before him, accordingly, that Mr. Lewis was brought. Sir George is said (with what truth I know not) to have been a pupil of the latter. However this may have been, the Chief Justice in his charge to the grand jury, "rallied against Mr. Lewis particularly . . . for keeping conventicler in the school; 'by which means,' saith he, ' your children get the twang of fanaticism in their noses when they are young, and they will never leave it.'" (Matthew Henry's *Life of Philip Henry*). Mr. Ambrose Lewis married Catherine, one of the two daughters and co-heiresses of Mr. Roger Davies of Erlas Hall, the last of the Davieses of that place. He had much property in Wrexham and the neighbourhood, and lived for many years in one of the large houses at the top of Hope Street, opposite to Bryn-y-ffynnon. We shall meet with him again (see ch. II. sec. 31).

72. It is now necessary to say something of the Restoration and of the political events immediately preceding and following it.

73. While Oliver Cromwell lived, all attempts to restore the monarchy were foredoomed to failure. Cromwell was, it is true, disliked by most of the Presbyterians as having cut off the king's head, and (ultimately) by many of the Independents as having upset the Republic, but he was strong in the attachment of the army, and in the support of thousands of influential people who believed before all things in a strong ruler, and were well satisfied so long as order was everywhere maintained, and the affairs of the country effectively and economically administered at home, and firmly and successfully handled abroad. But when

the great Protector was dead, and Richard Cromwell had
shown that he had neither the abilities nor the ambition of his
father, the Royalists began to prepare everywhere to make a
demonstration of their strength. It was the Puritans who made
the first move. Sir George Booth, of Dunham Massey, the
leader of the Cheshire and Lancashire Presbyterians, entered into
negociations with the chief men of his own party, and with the
leading cavaliers of the neighbourhood. Sir Thomas Myddelton,
of Chirk, co-operated, and many gentlemen of Wrexham and the
neighbourhood readily entered into the movement. Among
these were Sir Thomas Powell, of Horsley, Captain Thos.
Baker, of Wrexham, and Colonel Broughton, who must have
been either Sir Edward Broughton, of Marchwiel or his kinsman,
the Captain William Broughton, of Bersham, who has been
already mentioned (see note 9.) It was agreed to muster at
Warrington on the 2nd of August, 1659, upon the pretext of
suppressing a rising of the Quakers, seize Chester, and make a
demand for a free Parliament. The Presbyterians mustered on
the appointed day in great strength, and many cavaliers also
came, but most of the latter " failed in their trust." The attempt
on Chester succeeded, but General Lambert falling upon the
Royalist levies at Winnington Bridge on August the 19th completely routed them. Sir Thomas Powell was taken prisoner,
and Sir Thomas Myddelton besieged in his Castle of Chirk and
compelled to surrender. But events were now moving fast. By
the end of the year General Monk at the head of the army in
Scotland had himself declared for a free Parliament. Marching
south he soon after (Feb. 3, 16$\frac{59}{60}$) entered London in triumph.
The " Rump " of the long Parliament dissolved itself, and issued
writs for the summoning of the new Parliament demanded. The
elections for this new Parliament (which from being irregularly
summoned came to be called " The Convention Parliament ")
were held forthwith. For the county of Denbigh, Sir Thomas
Myddelton, of Chirk, was elected.[3] Elsewhere scarce any

---

30. The following notes of disbursements made by Sir Thomas at Wrexham at this
election may be interesting (for copies of which I am indebted to Mr. W. M. Myddelton) :—

" Mr. Perry, of Wrexham, his bill of charge at the eleccon there, x*li.* xiii*s.* vi*d.*
Paid Captaine Baker, his noate at the said eleccon xi*li.* xiiii*s* and his noate of x*li.*
　　xiii*s.* ix*d.* for quarteringe in the time of Cheshire riseinge, in all paid him
　　xxii. vii*s.* ix*d.*
Pd. at the eleccon at Wrexham at the severall houses and otherwise as followeth:—
To the ringers v*s* ; seven ordinaries at the Sheriffes quarters iiii*s.* viii*d.*, and
　　for beere there ii-. iiii*d.* ; 13 ordinaries at Mrs. Harvies, house viii*s.* viii*d.*,
　　and for beere and tobacco v*s.* x*d.*, in all xiii*s.* vi*d.*
To the troopers then there xl*s.*, and to the foote company xx*s.*
At Mr. Joseph Tyler's house for beere and tobacco, v*s.* vi*d.*
At Rees Davies his house for bread and cheese, beere and tobacco, xvi*s.*
At Mr. Bell's house for 52 ordinaries, xxxiiii*s.* viii*d.*, for beere and Tobacco, xxvii*s.*,
　　and for hay for the horses there iiii*s.*, in all iiii*li.* v*s.* viii*d.*
For 27 ordinaries at Mr. Henry Jones, xxvii*s.* at 12*d.* a peece, for 33 more at viii*d.*
　　xxii*s.*, and for beere and Tobacco xviii*s.* viii*d.*, in all iiii*li.* vii*s.* viii*d.*
To the music at Captaine Bakers v*s.*, and at Mrs. Peirce xxx*d.*
Edward Rees, of Wrexham, for beere ix*s.*'

but Royalists (mostly Presbyterians) were returned. Almost immediately after Parliament was assembled, a motion was brought forward for the restoration of the monarchy. Charles, in view of his recall, had meanwhile composed his famous *Declaration of Breda*, and this was now read in the House. Herein, he promised, among other things liberty of conscience[31] and a general indemnity. The cautious Sir Matthew Hale was for appointing a Committee to settle the conditions of the king's return. But the loyalty of the Presbyterians was so irrational in its exuberance that they were nearly all for restoring the king without conditions, and holding his kingly declaration as sufficient. Charles was accordingly unanimously recalled. He was proclaimed on the 8th of May, 1660, and entered London on the 29th.

74. One of the first acts of the Parliament, after the restoration of the monarchy, was to enact that all incumbents who had been ejected, for whatever cause, from their benefices during the interregnum should forthwith re-enter upon the same. In accordance with this enactment Mr. Ambrose Mostyn, the Presbyterian Vicar of Wrexham, had to make way for Mr. Rowland Owen, who had been ejected at the beginning of the Parliamentary epoch. In April, 1661, Philip Henry records of Mr. Mostyn that God "hath at present provided" for him "a little sanctuary at Lord Saye[32] in Oxfordshire;" and on December 16th, 1663, hearing of his death in London during the previous week, writes, "that he is now at rest in ye Lord, being taken away from ye evil to come. From Calamy we learn that Mr Mostyn remained with Lord Saye, as his chaplain until his lordship's death, 'and afterwards removed to London and liv'd with Mr. Johnson, a Nonconformist minister in the city, where he dy'd.'" A very good account is given by Calamy of Mr. Mostyn's character, as a preacher and as a man, and this account is quoted in Dr. Thos. Rees' *History of Protestant Nonconformity in Wales*, where it may be consulted.

75. On the 29th of December of this same year (1660) the Convention Parliament was dissolved. To the new Parliament only 56 Presbyterians were returned. This was due in part to the Anti-Puritan reaction which had now definitely set in, and in part to the manipulation by the Government of the elective bodies. The success of the High Church and Absolutist parties at the election of 1661 relieved them from the necessity of resting on the Presbyterians for support, and gave them the opportunity of attempting to pay off old scores, and crush out Puritanism altogether. The *Declaration of Breda*[31] in which toleration had been promised should have prevented this attempt. The *Declara-*

31. "We do declare a liberty to tender consciences, and that no man shall be disquieted or called in question for differences of opinion in matters of religion which do not disturb the peace of the kingdom."—From *Declaration of Breda*.

32. William Fiennes, Viscount Saye and Sele, of Broughton Castle, Oxon., died April 11, 1662.

tion of Breda had been followed moreover by the *Declaration of Worcester House*, wherein the conditions were indicated under which the liberty promised was to be granted. These conditions most of the Presbyterians or Royalist Puritans were now willing to accept. To an episcopacy they had no rooted objection; for peace sake they were prepared to accept a liturgy, provided a certain liberty were conceded to them, so that they should not be required to say things which they did not believe, or do things which they could not reconcile with their consciences; and it was this very liberty which was promised them in the *Declaration of Worcester House,* which promised a revision also of the old Church Service, to be effected by a free Conference, composed of an equal number of Episcopalian and Presbyterian divines. But by the time this Conference ("the Conference of the Savoy") met, the elections had taken place, and the bishops, neglecting the terms of their commission, which directed that "what was needful should be done to satisfy tender consciences," felt themselves able to treat the Presbyterians, not as coadjutors, but as lawless objectors to what was already settled. So the Prayer Book came to be revised without reference to Puritan susceptibilities. It must be admitted that the behaviour of the Presbyterians in the day of their power had not a little to do with the unjust and ungenerous treatment which they afterwards received. But however intolerant they had been they were now willing to do everything except "damn their souls" (as one of them said) to secure comprehension. And, inasmuch, as it was due to them that monarchy and episcopacy were now restored, they certainly deserved better treatment. It certainly seems also a grievous pity that so grand an opportunity of securing a comprehensive and truly national church should have been thrown away.

76. The old persecuting statutes of Queen Elizabeth were still unrepealed, and these began now to be freely used against Puritans. Strong feeling was thus excited. Incautious words which may have been used by some were twisted into indications of a general plot against the Government. Spies were employed, and information was solicited which would show such evidence of the disloyalty of the Presbyterians and Independents as might justify the coercive measures against them that were contemplated. No such evidence was found, but among the reports, supposed to contain it, collected at this time is a letter from Captain Thomas Baker (see Note 9) of Wrexham, of which Dr. Stoughton, who saw it at the State Paper office, has given[38] the following account :—

"The same day (Sept. 2, 1661), Thomas Baker, of Wrexham, writes to Henry Bishop a letter, which finds its way, with many others, into the Secretary's (Sir Edward Nicholas) cabinet. He rejoices that those 'at the

38. *Church and State Two Hundred Years ago,* page 232.

stern' of the good old ship are beginning in earnest to look about them, for
their enemies assuredly are not idle. People now talk very high—dangerous
people, who have served three apprenticeships in rebellion. It is plain they
plot another rising. 'Wrexham is the most factious town in England. Jones,
Ludlow, and Harrison, all belong to it' (Note 34). Oh, that the king had a
standing army! He, Baker, valiant man, 'can raise a hundred old royalists,
who never rebelled, and never would!' Baker trusts the king will trust
Cavaliers, and no others; of course he is a Cavalier, and, moreover, has been
imprisoned. He has the promise of a company in case of an army being
raised; in short, this informant will be glad of anything he can get."

77. However baseless were the accusations against the Presbyterians and Independents that now began to be circulated, they
served their purpose in rendering easier the passage through
Parliament of the *Act of Uniformity,* which made the Church a
sect and laid the foundations of the older dissent. This Act
received the royal assent on the 19th of May, 1662. Thereby
every minister of the Church of England, if not already episco-
pally ordained, was required to undergo ordination; to declare
that it was "not lawful on any pretence whatever to take arms
against the king . . . or [against] those commissioned by
him; to repudiate the *Solemn League and Covenant;* and, finally,
not merely to *accept* the Book of Common Prayer, but publicly
to declare his "unfeigned assent and consent to all things in the
said book contained." And this Act was to come into force on
the Feast-day of St. Bartholomew next following. If any one
disabled from preaching by the Act "should nevertheless preach
or lecture, any two justices of the peace or the chief magistrate
of any town corporate were authorised to commit him for three
months to the common jail without bail or mainprice." Every
schoolmaster also, or tutor in a private family, was only permitted to teach after licence obtained from the bishop of the
diocese, and, before such licence could be obtained, was required
to declare his belief in the unlawfulness, under any circumstances
whatever, of bearing arms against the king. Under the provisions of this Act about 2,000 ministers, who preferred poverty
to dishonour, were ejected, and prevented at the same time from
following the only other calling—that of a schoolmaster or tutor—
which most of them were fitted to take up.

78. Among those in the neighbourhood of Wrexham who
who were thus ejected may be named the Revs. Robert Fogg,
M.A., of Bangor-is-y-coed, Richard Taylor, of Holt, Matthew
Jenkins, of Gresford, and the famous Philip Henry, of Worthenbury. The ejected included some of the most pious and learned
ministers of the Church, and their former parishioners still, in
many cases resorted to them in private houses, and, at times

34. It has already been explained (see sec. 10) how Colonel John Jones was connected
with Wrexham. That General Harrison and Colonel Ludlow did not "belong to" the
town is quite certain. Captain Baker, however, knew Wrexham very well, and it is probable therefore that these officers were *connected with* the town in some way.

when no service was going on at the parish church.   To prevent
these gatherings, the *Conventicle Act* was passed (July 1, 1664).
This Act decreed " that only five persons above sixteen years of
age, besides the family, were to meet for any worship, domestic
or social.   For the first offence on the part of him who officiated,
the punishment was three months' imprisonment, or a fine of
five pounds ; for the second, six months' imprisonment, or a fine
of ten pounds; for the third, transportation for life, or a fine of
one hundred pounds.   Those who permitted conventicles to be
held in their barns, houses, or outhouses, were liable to the same
forfeitures ; and married women. taken at such meetings, were
to be imprisoned for twelve months, unless their husbands paid
forty shillings for their redemption.   The power of enforcing the
Act was lodged in the hands of a single Justice of the Peace,
who might proceed without the verdict of a jury, on the bare
oath of an informer."   The *Conventicle Act*, which was to be in
force for three years, was renewed in 1669.   " In its new shape
it inflicted a fine of five shillings on every hearer for the first.
and ten shillings for the second ; twenty pounds each on the
preacher and owner of the house where the meeting was held,
and one hundred pounds on any magistrate who might have
neglected to inflict the penalties at the request of the informer.
Of these fines, one-third was to go to the informer, one-third to
the king, and one-third to the poor."

79. If Parliament decided against Comprehension, it should
have allowed Toleration. but not merely did it refuse this, but
pursued the ejected ministers with an almost fiendish malignity,
and in 1665 passed the *Oxford* or *Five Mile Act*, which required
that no ejected minister, unless he had subscribed the declaration
contained in the *Act of Uniformity*, or taken a prescribed oath of
non-resistance, should either live in, or come within five miles of
the place wherein he had aforetime preached, under a penalty
of forty pounds, or six months' imprisonment.

CHAPTER II

Nonconformity in Wrexham from the Restoration to the Formation in the town of two Distinct Congregations—Presbyterian and Independent.

1. Of the Parliamentary Acts affecting the Nonconformists enough was said at the close of the first chapter to enable us to understand the incidents connected with local Nonconformity which have now to be detailed.

2. As to the Presbyterians, most of them wished earnestly to conform, and would have done so if the provisions of the *Act of Uniformity* had been less exacting than they were. Some, torn asunder by conflicting motives, shut their eyes and conformed for good and all. Others conformed provisionally, and as little as they could, and patiently waited for a better time. There were several Presbyterians among the churchwardens of the Pre-Toleration epoch. Philip Henry, writing on March 11, 1663, speaks of " the Presbyterian interest "—" the middle between two extremes "—as being " of late eclipst and clouded " at Wrexham, an enfeeblement due, in his opinion, to the want " of a faithful minister to goe before them."[1] Nevertheless, many of the Presbyterians held together, meeting in secret for worship and communion, and daring all. Philip Henry, writing on June 12, 1664, says that Mr. Taylor[2] and many more about Wrexham were bound over to appear at Quarter Sessions for a private meeting at which yei were deprehended." He makes also the following entries as to the persecution of Non-conformists at Wrexham, but gives no hint as to whether the sufferers were Presbyterians or Independents :—

" June 13, 1663, John Jones and others excommunicated for Nonconformity."
"August 14, 1664, Mr. George Bostock, of Holt, Justice of Peace [probably of Plas Bostock] dyed. His death occasioned by a surfet of drink which hee took at ye time of ye quarter sessions at Llanrwst whither he had bound over certain of ye inhabitants in and about Wrexham, who were deprehended

1. Mr. Ambrose Lewis (see chapter 1. sec. 71) to whom it was natural to look for the fulfilment of this function, had felt himself constrained to conform, and would have had his licence as schoolmaster refused if he had not done so.
2. Although Captain Taylor [see chapter 1, sec. 7(6)] was an Independent in 1651, he appears in the later part of his life to have inclined to the Presbyterian way.

at ye meeting to their no small trouble. And now just before the Assize ye
Lord took him away by a remarkable stroke, for verily Hee is a God yt
judgeth in the earth ; O that man might hear and fear ; and Lord goe on
to plead ye cause of thy poor suffering people in all the three nations for
Jesus's sake."

"Feb. 25, 1665. A meeting at Wrexham surprised, Sabb day was sennight,
some payd 5lb, some went to prison for three months, accord. to the Act.
Lord let ye libertyes of thy people be precious in Thy sight."

3. These meetings were not confined to the town, and at the
Quarter Sessions held July 14th, 1668, Alexander Powell, yeoman,
of Dutton-y-brain, was fined £4 10s. (his kinsman, Sir Thomas
Powell, being then upon the bench), for being present at a conventicle held at the house of Urian Weaver, yeoman, of the same
township.[3] These names are interesting. Alexander Powell
was the son of the John Powell who was mentioned in chap I.
sec. 14 (8), and the father of the John Powell who will be mentioned hereafter. He was buried at Holt, June 29th, 1685.
Urian Weaver's farmstead was the predecessor of that which is
now called "Park Farm." Following the custom of nearly all
the Presbyterians of his time, Urian Weaver had his children
baptised at his parish church (Holt), but was himself buried,
when he died, not in the parish graveyard, but in an enclosed
corner of a field, still called "The Burying Ground Croft," adjoining his own house, and here his tombstone may still be seen
together with the tombstone of his widow, and of one William
Taylor, Taylor being the name of an old family of yeomen long
settled in the manor of Isycoed, to which family Captain Edward
Taylor belonged.[4] Urian Weaver's estate was afterwards sold to
Dr. Daniel Williams, in the hands of whose trustees it still
remains. He had a son of the same name who was buried at
Holt, January 9th, 1757.

4. The *Independents* of Wrexham, among whom the Baptists
must be included, caring nothing for "comprehension," and only
asking to be let alone, held, doubtless, their usual meetings, the
persecuting laws notwithstanding, as often as they could. But
they worshipped, of course, in secret, and we hear little of them at
this time. But we know that they were not extinguished, and
that in February, 166⅔ Mr. John Evans, being invited to assume
the pastoral oversight of them, settled in Wrexham as their
minister.

3. At the same sessions Ellen Roberts, the wife of Edward Roberts, tailor, of Wrexham, was presented for being present at a conventicle on the 30th of June, and was saved
by her husband from imprisonment by payment of the statutory fine of forty shillings.

4. Although the present tenant is most tender and reverential in his treatment of
these gravestones, the last tenant destroyed one of the four formerly there. It seems
desirable therefore to put on record the inscriptions on the three gravestones that remain.
They are as follow:—(1) "Here lyeth the body of Urian Evanson, alias Weaver, who departed
this life August the 24th, Anno Do. 1686 ;" (2) "Here lyeth the body of Margaret, the wife of
Urian Evanson, alias Weaver, who deceased December the 22nd, 1687 ;" (3) "William
Taylor was interred the 5th day of November, 1690 " The fourth gravestone, I have
been told, commemorated another member of the Taylor family.

5. As Mr. Evans remained in Wrexham until the end of his life, and was a notable figure among the Welsh Nonconformists of his time, it is necessary to give here some particulars relating to his life. The best account of him that I can find is that contained in Mr. Samuel Palmer's Continuation of Calamy's *Nonconformists' Memorial*. This account, therefore, I shall now quote, making such additions as I am able, or, as it may seem desirable to give. :—Mr. John Evans "was born at Great Sutton, near Ludlow. His father (Rev. Matthew Evans) and grandfather were successively rectors of Penegoes, near Machynlleth. He was educated at Balliol College, Oxford. He left the University sooner than he intended, because he was unwilling to submit to the Parliamentary visitors. Returning to his father in Wales he was ordained presbyter at Brecon by Dr. Mainwaring, Bishop of St. David's, November 28, 1648, but soon after saw reason to alter his thoughts about Conformity, upon which some papers passed between him and his father, who was very zealous for the hierarchy. He was admitted one of the itinerant peachers of Wales, and was successively master of the free schools of Dolgelley and Oswestry." He was appointed master of Oswestry school in 1657 on the recommendation of no less a personage than the Protector, Oliver Cromwell himself,[5] and was ejected at the Restoration. "When he was ejected, he and his family were reduced to low circumstances, and his necessities were once so great, that he was forced to sell a considerable part of a large library for present maintenance. . . . He was a man of good learning, great gravity and seriousness, of a most unblameable conversation, and a laborious and judicious preacher." In the interval between his ejectment from Oswestry school, and his settlement at Wrexham, Mr. Evans is described as ministering to congregations at Oswestry, Llanfechan, and Llanfyllin. Captain Edward Lloyd, of Llwyn-y-maen (near Oswestry), writing soon after the Restoration, describes Mr. Evans as an "Anabaptist," but the captain does not appear to have been a very veracious person, and as the word "Anabaptist" carried a reproach with it, probably applied it without much enquiry as to its accuracy to those of whom he wished to speak evil. Mr. Joshua Thomas, however, says that an old member of the Baptist congregation at Wrexham told him in 1756 that Mr. Evans " baptized no one by sprinkling towards the end of his ministry." Spite of this, there is no real evidence that he was what is called a "Baptist;" he is described in two contemporary documents as an "Independent," and with this description we shall have to be content.

5. The Protector's letter of recommendation is printed in the Appendix to Carlyle's *Oliver Cromwell's Letters and Speeches.*

6. Mr. Evans was twice married. By his first wife he had a daughter, Mary, the wife of the Rev. Timothy Thomas, who was ejected after the Restoration from Morton Chapel, near Oswestry, and who became afterwards chaplain to Mrs. Baker, of Sweeney Hall. Mr. Thomas died in 1676. His widow[6] gave birth, seven months after her husband's death, to a son, Timothy, who was brought up in his grandfather's house at Wrexham, and became, at 20, minister of a church at Pershore, where he was succeeded at his death (Jan. 10, 171⅔) by his son of the same name. Mr. Evans' second wife was a daughter of Colonel Gerrard, Governor of Chester Castle, and widow of the famous Vavasour Powell. By her he had a son, John, afterwards Dr. John Evans, who will be mentioned again.

7. Soon after he came to Wrexham Mr. Evans assumed the pastoral oversight, not merely of the Independents, but also, in a provisional way, of such Presbyterians as still held together in the town. Of his later history an account will be given farther on.

8. The sufferings of the Quakers at this troublous time will be best detailed in the chapter devoted to the History of the Friends in this town and neighbourhood—Chapter VI.

9. It was in this time of deepest darkness for local Puritanism that a young Wrexhamite consecrated himself to the work of the ministry, who afterwards played an important part in the development of the Noncomformity of this town, and became somewhat famous outside it—Daniel Williams. He must have been born about 1643 or 1644, though there is no record of his baptism in the parish registers of either of those years. Was he not rather born *near* than *in* Wrexham? Who his parents were is not known. Edmund Calamy says of him :—" As well as I knew him, I can yet say nothing of his parentage and extraction, or even his education with regard to learning." He had a sister Elizabeth, married to Mr. Hugh Roberts, of Wrexham, the names of both of whom will often again be mentioned. He was connected somehow with the family of the Merediths of Allington,[7] who were of the same stock as the Merediths of Pentrebychan and Leeds Abbey, Kent. He speaks also of his cousin, Richard Edwards, who was dead in 1711, but whose widow (Dorothy) and father (Hugh Edwards) still survived. He mentions his cousin, the Rev. Stephen Davies, of Banbury (see ch. iii., sec. 2). And he mentions at the same time his " cousin, Kath. Taylor, of Wrex-

---

6. Her tomb in the Dissenters' Burial Ground is thus inscribed:—"Here lyeth the body of Mary Thomas, daughter of John Evans and widow of Mr. Timothy Thomas, who died July 7, 1693." Her daughter, Elizabeth, is also buried in the same place. She carried on a grocer's business at the corner of Church Street and Town Hill.

7. In his will (signed June 26, 1711) he left his "largest silver tankard" to his "cousin Richard Meredith, Esq." and all the money due by him to the testator. He left also £100 to that son of the said Richard Meredith, who bore the testator's name, and £100 to Elizabeth West, sister of the same Richard. It was of the Merediths also that Dr. Daniel Williams bought the estate in Allington (Trefalun Farm) which his trustees still hold.

ham," who appears to have been connected with the Mr. John Taylor, who will be mentioned in a later chapter (ch. iii., sec. 22). Other probable local connections will be indicated as we proceed (see ch. iii., secs. 2, 17 and 18). Dr. Daniel Williams has himself told us that from the time he was five years old he did nothing but read and learn, and that he began to preach when he was only nineteen years of age. It could not have been very long after this that Lady Wilbraham, of Weston (Salop), introduced him to the Countess of Meath, who took him with her as her domestic chaplain to Ireland. Where he lived and how long a period elapsed between the time that he began to preach and the time that he went out of this country is not clear. Soon after he got to Ireland he was elected minister of the Wood Street congregation, Dublin, and there remained for many years. While in Dublin he made himself so notorious by his opposition to Roman Catholicism (I am afraid a strain of truculence streaked his better qualities) that he believed his very life to be in peril and thought it best to leave Ireland altogether. This, accordingly, in the year 1687, he did, and, in the year following, accepted the pastorate of the important Presbyterian congregation, meeting in Hand Alley, Bishopsgate Street, London—a position he continued to fill to the end of his life. He was twice married, and both his wives brought him wealth. His second wife was one of two daughters of M. Georges Guill,[8] and the widow of Mr. Francis Barkstead (the son of Colonel John Barkstead, one of the regicides). In London we will leave him awhile until we have carried on the history of Nonconformity in Wrexham beyond the time of the *Act of Toleration.*

10. Under the stress of the penal laws so many of the wealthier Puritans of Wrexham ostensibly conformed, that in an official report, made in 1669, to the Archbishop of Canterbury, it was stated that, " in this parish [Wrexham] are schismatics many, but all or most of them are of ordinary condition."

11. But the pressure of persecution was now to be relieved for a while. On the 15th March, 1672, Charles II. issued his *Declaration of Indulgence* by which on his own responsibility, he suspended the exercise of the persecuting statutes, and promised to grant licences to preach to all Presbyterian, Independent, and Baptist ministers who should make application, the houses in which they proposed to preach being also required to be licensed.

12. Mr. John Evans took advantage straightway of the *Indulgence* to obtain a licence for Congregational worship in Wrexham at the house of Edward Kenrick, and for Presbyterian worship at the house of John Hughes.

13. Edward Kenrick, often called " Edward John Kenrick " (that is " John Kenrick's Edward " from which we conclude that

8. M. Guill was a Huguenot refugee; his other daughter married the well-known Dr, Joseph Stennett, the elder,

his father's name was "John"), was an inhabitant of Gwersyllt. He had two houses in Wrexham, both situate in Hope Street, one of them being that which was afterwards, and is still, called "The Talbot." In the barn belonging to this house, after the accession of William III., and until the year 1762, the Independent congregation regularly met, and it was probably these premises that were in 1672 licensed for the meetings of the Independents. Of Edward Kenrick's son, Samuel, the ancestor of the Kenricks, of Wynne Hall, I shall afterwards have something to say. Another son, John, was a walker in Bersham, with a shop on Town Hill, while a third, Daniel, was probably the ancestor of the Kendricks, of Gwersyllt. Besides these three sons, he had two daughters—Martha, who died unmarried in 1705, and Elizabeth, who married Thomas Robinson, joiner, of Wrexham, who had a son of the same name and calling, about whom something will hereafter be said. Edward Kenrick's widow died June, 1698, and was buried in the Dissenters' Graveyard, where her tombstone may still be seen. She left £3 to Mr. John Evans, the Nonconformist pastor, and 10s. to his son of the same name, afterwards Dr. John Evans.

14. Besides the house of Edward Kenrick, in Wrexham, two other houses in the neighbourhood of the town (both in the township of Cristionydd and parish of Ruabon) were at the same time licensed for Congregational worship. One of these was a house belonging to Roger Kynaston, Esq., (the son of the John Kynaston, Esq., already mentioned, ch. i. sec. 11.) probably Cefn-y-Carneddau or Plas Kynaston, the house in which Mr. Kynaston himself lived. The preacher licensed to officiate in this house was Philip Rogers.[9] The other place licensed for Congregational worship was a house belonging to Captain William Wynne, not Wynne Hall, which is in the hamlet of Bodylltyn, but a house on the same estate in the adjoining township of Cristionydd. The licensed preacher here was Richard Price, who had also the pastoral oversight of the churches at Ruthin, Glyn, and Sweeny Hall.

15. The Presbyterians met in 1672 under the protection of the *Declaration of Indulgence* at the house of John Hughes, of Wrexham. Who John Hughes was, and where he lived, I have not been able with certainty to ascertain, but I believe that he was a bookseller[10] and lived in Hope Street, his house standing on the site of the houses now numbered 3 and 4.

---

9. I suspect this was the same Philip Rogers, who was in 1675 (see sec. 19) one of the elders of the Independent Church at Wrexham. He is described in 1660 as a "yeoman, of Esclusham" and in 1666 as "a barker [that is, tanner] of Esclusham," and was in the last-named year, together with Margaret, his wife, "presented" by the churchwardens for not going to church.

10. John Hughes issued a token thus described by Mr. Jas. W. Lloyd, of Kington:—"[ob.] JOHN HUGHES. 1666—I. K. H., and an object resembling a pair of eyeglasses, [Re] OF WREXHAM—HIS HALFPENY."

16. The following entries from Philip Henry's diary relate to the assemblies held at John Hughes' house:—

"July 3, 1672. I preacht at Wrexha at Mr. Hugh's house, having first show'd both his licence and mine to the Justices who endors'd their names on the backside."

"July 31, 1672. I preacht the second lecture at Wrexham at John Hugh's house. [Text] Luk 17, 26, &c., security and sensuality like to bee raigning sins in Gosp. times—Lord, awaken people to see it, lest the day come upon them at unawares. Mr. Goodwin, of Bolton,[11] had preached before in ye morn. and repeated again in the evening."

"Aug., 1672. I said to Mrs. Figes, in my own house, speaking of the meeting place in Wrexham being a barn, that wheat in a barn is better than chaff in a church."

17. The last entry is curious, and unless we conclude that Mr. Henry was speaking of the Independent meeting place, his remark implies that the Presbyterian services on John Hughes' premises were also conducted in a barn.

18. The king's *Declaration of Indulgence* raised a great storm in Parliament. It was thought unconstitutional (as it undoubtedly was) that the king should set aside, of his own pleasure, laws that had been duly passed, and it was feared also that in thus favouring the Protestant Nonconformists, the king was only making a first move towards the toleration of the Roman Catholics, a toleration which but few even of the Independents were as yet prepared to accept. The Presbyterian members themselves joined in the clamour against *The Indulgence*, and on March 8, 167¾ the king felt constrained to cancel it, after it had been in force scarcely a year.

19. The Nonconformists of Wrexham were now again exposed to the persecuting laws, but they seem never to have lost the start which the year of toleration had given them, and from this time began to increase in numbers and influence. Mr. Henry Maurice, minister of the Nonconformist churches in Brecknockshire, writing in 1675, describes the Independent church at Wrexham as fully organized, having " Mr. John Evans, a person of great sobriety and godliness," as pastor, Mr. John Browne, Captain William Wynne, Philip Rogers, and other elders ; Evan Roberts, and other deacons. Mr. John Browne and Captain Wynne have already been mentioned (see ch. 1, sec. 7 (10) and sec. 61). Philip Rogers had been licensed in 1672 (see sec. 14) to preach at Captain Wynne's house in Ruabon. Rees and Thomas in their *Hanes Eglwysi Annibynol Cymru* speak of Deacon Evan Roberts as the brother-in-law of Dr. Daniel Williams, but in this I think they must be mistaken ; he lived in Bieston, occupying the farm which now belongs to the poor of Wrexham ; he and his wife, Margaret, were presented at the Quarter Sessions,

11. Rev. Richard Goodwin ejected from the vicarage of Bolton (Lancashire) under the *Act of Uniformity*, and the founder of Nonconformity in that town, where he died December 12, 1685.

E

held at Wrexham, October, 1663, for not going to church. Mr.
Maurice adds that the members of this church "were Independents from the beginning; yet are they very moderate, so that
some few Baptists are of their society."

20. After a time the Presbyterians joined with the Independents
to form a single congregation under Mr. Evans' ministry. Mr.
Joshua Thomas (*Hanes y Bedyddwyr*) says that this united congregation met in part of a large house afterwards called "The
Red Lion" ("The Lion" in High Street.) The congregation met
also sometimes, it appears, at Bryn-y-ffynnon, a part of which
house Mr. Evans, the minister, during the latter part of his life,
himself occupied.

21. It was almost impossible for the Presbyterians, with their
widely scattered congregations, to carry out, in the presence of
the penal laws, their ecclesiastical system, or for them to exist
at all save, as separate and disconnected churches. They were
thus driven by force of circumstances to adopt the Independent
system of church government. As to doctrine, they were Evangelical Calvinists like the Independents, with this difference, that
while the latter interpreted their system of doctrine with great
strictness, the Presbyterians interpreted it more freely, and
began already to develope a tendency towards Arminianism, which
became more marked as time went on, and had, afterwards, as
we shall see, important consequences. But for the present, this
difference of attitude towards Christian doctrine did not hinder
the two congregations from worshipping together.

22. Some light is thrown on the history of Nonconformists
in Wrexham during the time of The Second Persecution (1673-
1689) by certain additional particulars which Mr. Samuel
Palmer gives (in his edition of Calamy's *Nonconformists'
Memorial*), of Mr. John Evans' life. Mr. Evans kept at Wrexham "private assemblies in his house or neighbourhood through
most of the hottest times. Some gentlemen of considerable rank
(knowing his abilities in school-learning), sent their sons to
board with him for several years, which was some relief to him
under violent persecutions. About the year 1681 he was earnestly
pressed to conform by the bishop of the diocese, Dr. William
Lloyd, who at first expressed a particular regard to him, and
offered him a very good living; but, upon his positive refusal,
prosecuted him with great severity, and upon his personal
soliciting against the Bishop in open court, the magistrates
imposed heavy fines from time to time, and he was sued to an
outlawry.[12] But it was remarkable that though these measures
obliged him to keep the doors constantly locked for some years,
he escaped better than many who were not so eagerly pursued;

---

12. There is printed in Appendix XIV. of Sir J. B. Williams' *Life of Philip Henry*, an
undated letter from Mr. John Evans to his flock, at a time when he was himself compelled
by the force of persecution to absent himself from the town.

the most officious informers not being able to gather one of the
fines laid upon him. Nor was his person ever seized but once
upon the road (notwithstanding frequent warrants), and then he
was soon released by the mediation of a person of honour who
often generously took his part. There is reason to think that
his hardships, and the frequent journeys he was forced to take
by night, impaired his health and brought on that weakness [loss
of memory] under which he laboured."

23. One of the persons of honour who, we may be sure, pro-
tected Mr. Evans was Mary, Lady Eyton, the second wife and
relict of Sir Kenrick Eyton, Knt., of Eyton Isaf.[13] She was not
merely herself a Nonconformist (though Sir Kenrick had fought
on the king's side in the Civil War), but she actually occupied
in 1699, and probably before, a part of the house (Bryn-y-
ffynnon), ancther part of which was occupied by Mr. Evans.
She was thus very favourably placed for befriending him. She
lies buried in the Dissenters' Grave Yard, Rhosddu Road, where
her tomb bears an inscription which may still be read, "Here
lyeth the body of Dame Mary Eyton, widow, relict of Sir Kenrick Eyton, of Eyton, Kt. [She] departed this life the 13th day
of February, 1701 And in the — 2nd year of her age."

24. I learn from the books of Matthew Henry's chapel at
Chester that in May, 1687, the Rev. Wm. Tong (afterwards
author of *The Life of Matthew Henry*) went to Wrexham, and
there remained several months. He, doubtless, acted as assistant to Mr. Evans.

25. Towards the end of 1688 King James the Second fled from
his throne, and the Prince of Orange, under the title of William
the Third, ascended it. This event necessarily brought into
power the party ("the Country Party," as it was called), which
was most favourable to the Dissenters ; and early in the following
Spring, *The Toleration Act*, which conceded liberty of worship
to such Protestant Dissenters as were Trinitarian, was pushed
through the two houses of Parliament, and received the royal
assent on the 24th of May, 1689. The scope of this measure
might well have been enlarged, for it left the *Test* and *Corporation Acts* still unrepealed, and excluded Unitarians and
Roman Catholics from its operation ; but it was too eagerly
welcomed by the Nonconformists to be in any way criticized.

26. In Wrexham the Dissenters actually anticipated the passing of the Act by arranging for the ordination there of Mr. Jenkin
Thomas. Mr. Evans was now becoming feeble, and his memory
began to fail, and Mr. Thomas was probably intended to be his
assistant. He had been educated at the well-known academy of

13. Lady Eyton was a daughter of Sir Francis Bickley, Bart. ; her first husband was
Sir William Hoo, of the Hoo, Herts ; she had, by Sir Kenrick, one son and two daughters,
of whom the elder, Mary, married Sir Henry Bunbury, Bart., of Stanney, Cheshire, who
occupied in 1669 another part of Bryn-y-ffynnon, and the younger, Amy, married Jasper
Peek, Esq., of Cornish, grandson of the John Peek, Esq., mentioned in ch. i. sec. 11 (2).

the Rev. Samuel Jones, Brynllywarch, Glamorganshire, which may be regarded as now represented by the Presbyterian College, Carmarthen.

27. The Nonconformists of Wrexham were now able to worship without concealment, and it was at this time probably that they resumed the occupation of the barn belonging to the house afterwards called "The Talbot," which had been licensed in 1672. It stood where the Talbot stables now are, and was entered from Stryt-y-Syfwr (Queen Street.) Three pounds a year rent were paid for it; there was a loft in the upper part which was sometimes sub-let. The whole premises belonged to Samuel Kenrick, himself a Dissenter, son of the Edward Kenrick who owned them in 1672. This Samuel Kenrick lived at the Fawnog Farm, Bersham. He had five sons and two daughters. His sons were:—Edward, afterwards Rev. Edward Kenrick, of Bron-y clydwr (see sec. 33); Samuel, afterwards a dyer of Wrexham and Esclusham; John, afterwards the Rev. John Kenrick, of Wrexham; Joseph, of whom I can learn nothing; and Daniel, of Hope Street, Wrexham, where the shops numbered 3 and 4 now are, and who was a chandler. Of Samuel Kenrick's two daughters, Deborah was the wife of Daniel Edwards (otherwise called "Bedward" or "Ab Edward"), who was perhaps the same Daniel Edwards who was then tenant of Plascoch, Stansty, and Mary was the wife of a certain Mr. John Jones, of Wrexham. Samuel Kenrick died in the year 1716; the list of the expenses of his funeral is so curious that I have copied it entire and given it in a foot-note.[14]

28. Now that *The Toleration Act* had passed, and Presbyterians, Independents, and Baptists were joined together in a single congregation, which, moreover, was a large and wealthy one, the Dissenters of Wrexham might be excused for believing that their troubles were nearly over. They were, however, on the eve of a convulsion which was to rend them asunder, breaking them into separate congregations that were not again to be united.

---

14. "Funerall Expences" [of Mr. Samuel Kenrick, in handwriting of his son; Rev. John Kenrick, Presbyterian minister, of Wrexham.]

	£	s.	d.
Paid Mr. Powell for Biscake	01	15	00
Paid sister for Beef and sowte (suet)			
Pd. Sam. Price the grave cutter	00	02	00
To Mary Rogers for Cakes, allowing 6s. wch she owed my father		09	00
To Thomas Jones of ye Raven for Ebulon (?)		08	00
To Alex. Robinson for Beer	1	00	00
To Hugh Jones for Ale		11	00
To Coz. Robinson for coffin, crape, etc.	2	10	0
To Benj. Parry for Gloves	2	11	06
To Coz. R. Benjamin for Tobacco and Sugar		07	09
Pd. to Mr. Jno. Broadfoot for hat bands		11	00
Item to Jeffrey Thomas for Heriott		07	06
Item to John Clubb for a graveston		19	00
Dec. 21. Mr. Moulding for Probate of my fa. will	1	12	00
In all...	10	03	09
Will proved at St. Asaph, Dec. 20, 1716			
Sum should be	13	3	9

29. We shall best follow the steps which led to this division by carrying on to a later stage the history of Dr. Daniel Williams from the point at which we dropped it in sec. 9.

30. Mr. Daniel Williams' wealth, character, and abilities fitted him to take a prominent position among the London ministers, and he was called, when the well-known Richard Baxter died in 1691, to take the latter's place as Tuesday lecturer at Pinners' Hall. Here he presently became entangled in what was called " the Crisp controversy," and strongly attacked the ultra-Calvinism which the Presbyterians had generally given up, but which the Independents for the most part still held. Mr. Williams was, on his part, accused of Socinianism. Much feeling was thus excited, and the result was that the co-operation which had been established in London between the two denominations was brought to an end.

31. The Crisp controversy excited great interest in Wrexham, where Mr. Daniel Williams was well known. As the matter came to be discussed much bitterness was introduced, and sides were freely taken. One of the members of the church who opposed most violently Mr. Daniel Williams' opinions was Thomas Edwards, Esq., of Rhual, near Mold, a man of learning and position,[15] who ultimately (in 1669) contributed to the controversy an able but most intemperate work, called " Baxterianism Barefaced."[16] Mr. John Evans, the minister, took the same side, but bore himself in a way which retained him the respect of those who felt constrained to take an opposite course. Among those who took

15 This Mr. Edwards was the last in the male line of the Edwardses of Rhual, and the son of Evan Edwards, Baron of the Exchequer in Chester, who built Rhual and was descended from Edwin ap Goronwy, Prince of Tegeingl. He was sheriff of Flintshire in 1684, and had as such to dance attendance on Sir George Jeffreys, the Chief Justice (see ch. 1, sec. 71), and he exposed to his gibes, which m ist have made his office particularly distasteful to him as a Dissenter. He married, in 1672, Jane, daughter of Robert Davies Esq., of Gwasaney, by whom he had an only daughter, Mary, who married Walter Griffith, gentn., of Llanfyllin, who founded the family of Griffith of Rhual. Mr. Edwards appears to have often supplied the pulpit at Wrexham when there was no regular minister, or when he was absent. He was a Baptist, and Mr. Joshua Thomas (*Hanes y Bedydwyr*) says that " he kept a meeting at his house [at Rhual] and there commonly baptized," making a place for this special purpose near it. He seems to have died before 1702. The Griffiths of Llan-fyllin, into which family Mary Edwards married, were themselves strong Dissenters. In 1708 land for a chapel at Llanfyllin was given by Mr. Nehemiah Griffith, who is described as brother of Mr. Thomas Griffith, of Rhual, and who I take to be the same Nehemiah Griffith who erected the well-known column of Maes Garmon, near Mold. At some time between 1708 and 1722, Mrs. Ann Parry, of Rhual, bequeathed (see App. III, *Receipts*) a small sum to the poor of the Old Meeting, Wrexham. The burial-places of several of the Rhual family are shown in the Dissenters' Grave Yard in this town, but the inscriptions on their tombs cannot now be read. I have been unable to trace with certainty the descent of the Griffiths of Rhual, but from various references to them, I conjecture that Walter Griffith had two sons, Thomas and Nathaniel, and that the former was succeeded at Rhual by his son of the same name. Before the middle of last century the Griffiths had ceased to be Dissenters.

16. The offensiveness of tone indulged in this book towards those who swerved in any degree from the strait paths of orthodox Calvinism is very marked. Richard Baxter and Daniel Williams are especially singled out as the objects of the author's spleen. Yet the book, although now absolutely unreadable, is an able one, and well-written, and it is certain that Mr. Edwards was an honest, well-meaning, and conscientious man. To show the author besides of two pamphlets :—*A plain and impartial enquiry into Gospel Truth*, and *A Short Review, with some Remarks upon the Union in the late Agreement in Doctrine among the Dissenting Ministers in London*,

this opposite course and eagerly championed Mr. Daniel Williams' opinion were, not merely the Presbyterians, but many who had hitherto been reckoned Independents; the Kenricks, for example, and the Wynnes, of Ruabon. The end of the matter was that before the year (1691) was over, the Presbyterians and those who sympathised with them drew off and formed a new congregation, leaving the meeting-house in the occupation of the Independents and Baptists. The Rev. Matthew Henry, of Chester, and the Rev. James Owen, of Oswestry,[17] sympathised with the seceders, and helped them until they should be able to get a regular minister. The latter of these writing, November 26th, 1691, to Mr. Philip Henry bespoke a sermon from him for the new congregation in Wrexham, and told him that the Presbyterians there were united while Mr. Evans' people were divided, and that the meetings of the former were actually better attended than when Independents and Presbyterians worshipped together. The explanation of this probably was that many Presbyterians were now joined with the new meeting who had hitherto attended the parish church. We know, at any rate, that the venerable Ambrose Lewis, who had formerly conformed, was now not merely a worshipper with the Presbyterians, but resumed sometimes his earlier function of preaching.[18] If the Presbyterians of Wrexham had any settled minister before 1702 I have not been able to discover his name (but see note 1, ch. iii.). Where, moreover, they at this time met is not certain. The chapel in Chester Street was not built before 1697, perhaps not before 1699 or 1700. I find, however, in the rate-books for 1699 and 1700 (but not afterwards), Samuel Kenrick charged for " shop and *meeting-house* " on the north side of College Street, and it must have been here, I think, in one of two shops occupied by Samuel Kenrick, that the Presbyterians met until their chapel was built. This Samuel Kenrick was either the Samuel Kenrick who owned the other meeting-house or his son, the dyer, of the same name.

32. Having thus sketched the initiation of what now came to be called " The *New* Meeting " or Presbyterian congregation in Wrexham, let us follow for a few years the fortunes of " The *Old* Meeting " or Independent congregation. Mr. John Evans was still minister, but was old and feeble, and had *probably* an assistant—Mr. Jenkin Thomas. His grandson, Mr. Timothy Thomas, who was being trained for the ministry, did not attain the age of 20 until 1697, and then went to Pershore, while his son, John

---

17. Mr. Owen seems in fact to have exercised, at first from Oswestry, and after 1700 from Shrewsbury, a general supervision over the congregation; so much so that Mr. Samuel Hignett in his will speaks of him as having been its pastor; but this, strict y speaking, does not appear to have been the case. That Mr. Owen came over often, however, to lecture and administer the sacrament is certain.

18. He was buried in Wrexham church or churchyard January 2, 1698-9. His son, also named Ambrose Lewis, was a churchman. The present Mr. Bamford-Hesketh, of Gwrych Castle, Abergele, is descended from him. For a fuller account of the descendants of Mr. Ambrose Lewis see my *History of the Parish Church of Wrexham.*

Evans, junior, at that date only 17 years old, was away from home undergoing that long period of study and accumulation[19] which was afterwards to bear such good fruit. Mr. Jenkin Thomas was, however, afterwards sent at the charge of the Independent Board, to the University of Utrecht, and was there during the years 1699 and 1700. Mr. John Evans, junr., meanwhile, returned to Wrexham to assist his father a little before the latter's death. This event happened in 1700. A little while before Mr. Evans died, when it was said to him that he was going to his Father's house, he cheerfully answered : "It will not be well with me till I am there." He was buried in the Dissenters' graveyard, where his gravestone bears the following inscription : "Here lyeth the body of the Revd. Mr. John Evans, late of Bryn-y-ffynnon, and minister of God's word in Wrexham, who deceased in the 72nd year of his age, July 16, And was interred July 19th, 1700." His funeral sermon was preached by the Rev. David Jones, pastor of the Independent church at Shrewsbury. I find from the rate books that his widow, Mrs. Evans, was still living in Bryn-y-ffynnon in the year 1705.

33. Mr. John Evans was invited at his father's death to succeed the latter as minister of the Old Meeting, but he made it a condition of the acceptance of this offer that the two congregations should be again united. This was found not to be practicable, and it soon become evident that he sympathized very much more with the opinions of the Presbyterians than with those of the Independents. Thereupon he appears to have been invited by the Presbyterians to become minister over *them*, and to have accepted the offer. At any rate, we soon afterwards find Mr. Jenkin Thomas again settled in Wrexham, and when Mr. Evans was ordained at Wrexham (Aug. 18, 1702) with the exception of this same Mr. Thomas, all the ministers present were Presbyterians—Rev. Matthew Henry, of Chester, Rev. Charles Owen, of Warrington, Rev. James Owen, of Shrewsbury, Rev. Francis Tallents, M.A., of Shrewsbury, and the Rev. Samuel Benion, M.D., afterwards also of Shrewsbury. At the same time Mr. Edward Kenrick was also ordained. This Mr. Kenrick was the eldest son of the Mr. Samuel Kenrick mentioned in sec. 27, and had married one of the three daughters of the well-known Mr. Hugh Owen, of Bron-y-clydwr,

---

19. Mr. John Evans "was educated for the ministry, first, by the Rev. Thomas Rowe, who kept an academy at Newington Green, London, a gentleman of extensive learning and great urbanity (son of the Rev. John Rowe, M A., of New Hall, Oxford, preacher at Westminster Abbey); and afterwards, by the Rev. Richard Frankland, of Rathmall, Yorkshire, whose academy is considered to be in some sense the ancestor of Manchester New College. Having completed his academical course, Mr. Evans settled in Shropshire as chaplain in the family of Mrs. Rowland Hunt [of Boreatton], sister to Lord Paget. . . . . In this quiet retreat the young chaplain employed his time most diligently. He read all the Christian writers of the first three centuries, besides studying a vast amount of criticism." —Jeremy's *Presbyterian Fund and Dr Williams' Trust.*

in the parish of Llanegryn, Merionethshire,[20] and after the death
of his father-in-law (March 15, 1699), and of his brother-in-law,
Mr. John Owen (June 27, 1700), went to live at Bron-y-clydwr,
which fell to him as his wife's portion, and undertook the
pastoral oversight of the dissenting congregations at Bala, Dolgelley, and elsewhere which his father-in-law had gathered. He
died in 1741, and was buried at Llanegryn on the 6th of May in
that year. His son, John Kenrick, Esq., of Bron-y-clydwr,
appears ultimately to have conformed. The family of Kenrick,
of Bron-y-clydwr came to an end in the person of Hugh Owen
Kenrick, who died Aug. 16, 1821, aged 36.

34. The two congregations—the Old Meeting and the New—
were now definitely constituted, so that they not merely never
came together again, but followed henceforth different lines of
developement. It will therefore be necessary henceforth to sketch
the history of each congregation separately. I shall accordingly
in the two chapters following deal first with the history of the
New Meeting, and secondly with the history of the Old Meeting,
an order which is adopted merely for reasons of practical convenience.

20. Hugh Owen, of Bron-y-clydwr. A long and interesting account of this self-denying
and apostolic man will be found in Rees' *History of Protestant Nonconformity in Wales*, pp.
281-285. He was descended from the Lewis Owen, Baron of the Exchequer of North Wales,
who was murdered by banditti at Dinas Mawddwy. Abigail, another daughter of Mr. Hugh
Owen, was the second wife of Thomas Owen, gentleman, of Llunllo, Merionethshire (see
App. note 2), and a third daughter was the wife of Mr. Wm. Farmer, of Whitley, co.
Salop, and mother of the well-known Rev. Hugh Farmer, of Walthamstow.

CHAPTER III

History of the New Meeting (at first Presby= terian, afterwards Independent), from the time of the first building of the chapel in Chester Street to our own days.

1. For some time after the Presbyterians had drawn off from the Old Meeting they appear, as already has been explained (see ch. ii. sec. 31) to have used as a meeting-house a shop in Camfa'r Cwn (College Street) which was fitted up for that purpose. But the Rev. Daniel Williams, of London (he did not receive his diploma of D.D. until 1709), who had himself furnished the occasion for their secession, having offered a piece of land if the Presbyterians of Wrexham would build a chapel upon it, this offer was accepted. The land selected was the site of two houses (formerly belonging to John Lewis, gentleman) in Chester Street, next the great pool, which occupied the space in front of the present municipal buildings, the whole situate in what was called "The Lampint," which was then the name of a district including the land lying about the lower part of Chester Street and on each side of the present Lambpit and Holt Streets. On March 23, 169⅞, Mr. Daniel Williams leased this site for 99 years, from the feast of the Annunciation then next ensuing, to twelve trustees who covenanted to erect thereupon such buildings as had been agreed upon, and to render for the same a rent of four peppercorns yearly on the feast of the Annunciation of the Blessed Virgin, if the same should be lawfully demanded. The following are the names of the twelve trustees (the other parties to the indentures of lease executed) :—John Hunt, Esq., of the city of Chester ; Thomas Hunt, Esq., of the Middle Temple, London ; Andrew Kenrick, Esq., and Matthew Henry, gentlemen, both of the city of Chester ; James Owen, gentleman, of Oswestry ; John Mollineux, merchant, of Liverpool ; Hugh Roberts, Hugh Davies, senr., Edward Mainwaring, Stephen Davies, Thomas Bowker, and John Wynne, gentlemen, all of Wrexham.

2. It seems desirable to give brief notices of some of the twelve trustees named in the lease of 1698. Of the Revs. MATTHEW HENRY and JAMES OWEN enough has been elsewhere

said. Messrs. JOHN HUNT and THOMAS HUNT were sons of Col.
Thomas Hunt, of Boreatton, Shropshire, member for Shrewsbury in the Long Parliament, and brothers of Rowland Hunt,
Esq., of Boreatton. Mr. ANDREW KENRICK was of the family
of K nrick. of Woore, Salop, and I believe son of Richard
Kenrick, Esq., of Woore, by his wife, Rebecca, daughter of
Maurice Gethin, Esq., of Plas Cerniogau, in the parish of Cerrig-
y-Drudion. Mr. HUGH ROBERTS was the husband of Elizabeth,
sister of Dr. Daniel Williams. By trade he was a currier and
corvisor, and his house was where the two houses now stand
that are on each side of Cutler's Entry, in Charles Street. He
had also lands in the Fields of Wrexham, and it was, I suppose,
in virtue of these that he is described as " gentleman " in the
trust-deed. For further particulars relating to him see note 6.
Mr. HUGH DAVIES was a member of an important local family, one
branch of which is now represented by Chas. Salusbury Mainwaring, of Galltfaenen, Esq. He was a son of Hugh Davies,
gentleman, of Wrexham, (son of David ap John Robert), by his
wife Eleanor Puleston. At one time an ironmonger in High
Street, he afterwards retired from business and built a large
house at the top of Pen-y-bryn, Wrexham, afterwards called
" Prospect House." The tablet that once stood in the front of
this house has since been inserted in the front of the cottages

that occupy its site, and bears the inscription :— $\boxed{\begin{array}{c} \text{D} \\ \text{H} \quad \text{R} \\ \text{1676.} \end{array}}$, that is,

Hugh and Ruth Davies. Mr. Hugh Davies owned a portion of
the tithes of Wrexham. He was churchwarden in 1671-2, and
was buried March 6. 170$\frac{3}{2}$ in Wrexham churchyard. JOHN
MOLLINEUX, merchant, of Liverpool, married Eleanor, only
daughter of Edward Davies, gentleman, of Wrexham, eldest
brother of the Hugh Davies just named, by whom he had a
son, John Mollineux, of Liverpool, the younger. Mr. STEPHEN
DAVIES was a son of the Mr. Hugh Davies already named. He
afterwards became a Presbyterian minister, and as such settled
before 1711 in Banbury, where he was still living in 1717. Dr.
Daniel Williams speaks of him as his " cousin," and made him
the residuary legatee of his will. Of Mr. THOMAS BOWKER I know
nothing. Mr. EDWARD MAINWARING was a friend of Philip
Henry, who once (in 1673) stayed at his house, and appears to
have kept " a solemn fast there." He was a draper in Hope
Street, but is quite as often styled " gentleman " as " draper "
in the parish registers. In the latter part of his life he occupied
a large house on the south side of Lampint Street close to the
end of Chester Street. He was twice married, and had several
children, all of whom were baptized at the Parish Church, and
he himself, like other Presbyterians, served once the office of
churchwarden. His daughter, Sara, married (December 19, 1699)

Mr. John Travers, of Wrexham, afterwards of Trefalun House, who ultimately came into possession of all Mr. Mainwaring's Wrexham property. Mr. Edward Mainwaring died February, 170⅞, and was buried on the 11th of that month in the parish churchyard. Mr. JOHN WYNNE, the last of the twelve trustees, lived at this time in a largehouse opposite Bryn-y-ffynnon in the upper part of Hope Street, but afterwards at The Court, Wrexham, and at Wynne Hall, Ruabon. He was a barrister, and was often called "Councillor Wynne." He was of the family of Wynne, of Efenechtyd, and apparently brother of Captain William Wynne, of Wynne Hall, Ruabon [see ch. i. sec. 7. 10)] He is said to have married Elizabeth, daughter and heiress of Thomas Juxon, Esq., of East Sheen, in the parish of Mortlake, and widow of — Douglas, Esq. Mr. John Wynne died March 171⅝, and was buried at Ruabon. His widow, whose will was proved January 28, 1722, is said to have been buried in the Dissenters' graveyard, Wrexham, but her tomb cannot now be found.

3. Although the site of the chapel was conveyed in 1698, the chapel itself does not appear to have been ready for occupation before the year 1700. The meeting-house in Camfa'r Cwn, at any rate, was still charged for as such in the year last named, and it was not until 1701 that what had been used as a meeting-house there was charged as a shop. Nor was it apparently until August 17, 1702, when Mr. JOHN EVANS, junr. (see ch. ii, sec. 33) was ordained, that the Presbyterians had any regular minister at all.[1] Even then, Mr. Evans did not remain long as minister of the congregation. Perhaps his former relations with the members of the Old Meeting rendered his present relations with them intolerable. Anyhow, he soon made up his mind to leave Wrexham, and in the year 1704 resigned his charge. Thereupon, Mr. Daniel Williams invited him to become his own assistant at Hand Alley Chapel, an offer which he gladly accepted, and here, first as Mr. Williams' assistant, and afterwards as his successor, he remained until the end of his life. Here, he not merely took a leading place among the London Nonconformists, but also acquired a certain literary distinction. His excellent "Discourses on the Christian Temper" (published in 1723), are still read, and are still worth reading. "He collected materials for a *History of Nonconformity* from the time of Henry VIII. to that of the Civil Wars in the time of Charles I., and for that purpose perused an

1. It is true that Matthew Henry in his Diary speaks of being present on June 18th, 1700, at an ordination service at Macclesfield, at which Mr. Stephen Hughes, of Wrexham, was one of the candidates. But as I have never met with the name of this Mr. Hughes in any of the local records, I have not ventured to insert his name in the text. As to Mr. Evans even, it is not *absolutely*, but only *nearly* certain, that he was, between 1702 and 1704 the regular and settled minister of the congregation. Recurring to this Mr. Stephen Hughes, I cannot resist the impression that he was the same person as the Mr. Stephen *Davies*, who was one of the trustees of 1697-8, and who became afterwards the Presbyterian minister at Banbury. Being the son of Mr. *Hugh* Davies, he would be called, *according to the Welsh custom*, Stephen *Hughes* rather than Stephen Davies.

incredible number of books. A part of his MS. collections on
this subject, marked A, B, (containing references to the remaining parts C, D, and E), is still in Dr. Williams' Library; what
became of these remaining parts is not known. It was the
author's intention to publish his work in two folio volumes, and
he had fairly transcribed and finished a part of it when death
overtook him in the prime of life. The other MS. left by Dr.
Evans is a quarto volume containing statistics obtained in 1717
or 1718 (corrected and altered by interlineations and corrections
down to 1729) of Presbyterian, Independent (and Baptist) congregations throughout England and Wales. Dr. Evans received the degree of D.D. from the Universities of Edinburgh and
Glasgow in 1729. He died May 23, 1730, in his 51st year, and
was buried in Dr. Williams' tomb in Bunhill Fields. He left a
library of 10 000 volumes. There is a fine portrait of him at the
Library (Grafton Street.) He was soberly orthodox, and
moderate, not running into any extremes, and disposed to think
well of and honour those who differed from him," when they
" appeared upright and deserving. In the controversy of 1719
he was found among the non-subscribers."—Walter D. Jeremy's
Presbyterian Fund and Dr. Daniel Williams' Trust. Dr. Daniel
Williams left Mr. Evans £50, his " repeating watch," and the
lease of a house in Plum Tree Lane.

4. Mr. John Evans was succeeded as minister by Mr. NATHANIEL
LONG, son of the Rev. George Long, M.D., Presbyterian minister
of Newcastle-under-Lyme. Mr. Long lived in the house (mentioned in sec. 2), which Mr. John Wynne had before occupied
The course of his ministry here was a short one ; he died July,
1706, and was buried in the churchyard on the 17th of that
month, where his daughter, Eleanor, soon after (November 20)
followed him. Mr. Matthew Henry was present at his funeral,
and has left us the following account, of him :—" He had been
about three months declining of a consumption ; he walked out
but the day before he died ; he was about thirty years of age, a
serious, good young man, and likely to have been very useful
there."

5. On Mr. Long's death, Mr. JOHN KENRICK, a member of the
congregation, the third son of the before-named Mr. Samuel
Kenrick (see ch. ii, sec. 27), was chosen pastor. He was
ordained, with three other candidates, at Nantwich, October 21,
1707, on which occasion the Revs. Matthew Henry, Dr. Holland,
and eighteen other ministers were present.

6. Soon after Mr. Kenrick became minister, Mr. John Powell,
of Holt[2] died (September, 1707), and his will (proved at Chester,
March 15, 170⅞) came into operation. This will contains the
following clause :—" Item, I give, devise, and bequeath to Master

2. He was the son of the before-mentioned Alexander Powell, of Is-y-coed (see ch. I.
sec. 3.)

Long, now a Nonconformist minister of the lately new built chappell in Wrexham, all those two parcells of land, which formerly were in three parcells, that I lately purchased of the said Mr. Eddows [previously described as ' Mr. Eddows, iron-monger, of Whitchurch, in the county of Salop,'] and the rents, issues and profitts thereof during the term of his naturall life, and after his decease to the surviveing Minister that shall be elected and chosen to preach and officiate in the said chappell for ever." These lands, which still belong to the minister of the Chester Street (Presbyterian) Chapel, are situated near the present Vicarage at Holt. Their rent in Mr. Kenrick's time was £4, and is now about £11 a-year. In the latter part of his life (July 29, 1742), so as to assure the enjoyment of them to his successors, Mr. Kenrick conveyed these lands to trustees, namely, to John Travers, Esq., of Trefalun,[8] William Travers, gentle-man, of Lincoln's Inn,[9] John Wright, tanner, of Wrexham, (see *Hist. of Par. Ch. of Wrexnam*, page 98, note 145), and Thomas Collins, glover, of Wrexham,[3] who covenanted to pay the rents and profits of the said parcels of land to whomsoever should be elected after the death of Mr. Kenrick to succeed him as minister, "provided that in case the said congregation of Protestant Dissenters should be dissolved, or should be by law restrained from having such minister, teacher, or preacher as they shall elect, or should for the space of twelve months, in case of the death or removal of any minister officiating there, neglect or omit to elect or appoint some other person to officiate as pastor, minister, or teacher of the said congregation, or in case such person, so elected or appointed, should after such election, for the space of six months, neglect or refuse to officiate as pastor . . . then, and in any of the said cases, the said deed and every clause, matter and thing therein contained should cease, determine, and be utterly void."

7. The death of Mr. John Powell was soon followed by that of Mr. Samuel Hignett, of Ridley Wood, near Holt, another bene-factor to the New Meeting. Mr. Tong tells us in his *Life of Matthew Henry* that the latter, while minister of Chester, often used to contrive to meet his father, Mr. Philip Henry, at some place between Chester and Broadoak, where they would preach and pray together. Ridley he mentions as one of the places at which these meetings took place, and by Ridley I have little doubt he means Ridley Wood, Mr. Hignett's house.[4] By his will, dated April 1, 1706, Mr. Hignett left " to the Society of Christ's members and people belonging to the meeting place in Wrexham called ye New

---

3. Thomas Collins lived at this time on the west side of Church Street, but after-wards for many years, and until his death, in a large house in High Street, where are now the shops of Mr. Rowland, druggist, and Mr. Heywood, watchmaker.

4. If not Ridley *Wood* it must have been Ridley *Farm* not far distant, which was meant. The latter had been the farm of Richard Presland, Captain Edward Taylor's father-in-law (see ch. I, Note 8.)

Chappell, whereof James Owen was formerly pastor [see chapter 2, note 17], one hundred and fifty pounds of current mony of England to be payd to the minister and chiefe members of yt Societye to be distributed amongst Christ's poore needy members and people according to their necessity and ye discretion of ye minister and chiefe members of yt congregation." Mr. Hignett bequeathed also a similar sum to the poor of the Old Meeting, Wrexham, £100 to the poor of Matthew Henry's congregation at Chester, and a further bequest to the poor of the parish of Holt. The only one of his relatives mentioned in his will was his cousin, Cornelius Hignett, gentleman, of Frodsham, who lies buried in St. John's Church, Chester. He left his house, lands, books, furniture, etc., to his servant, Hannah Randles, whose descendants have ever since enjoyed them. He was buried March 3, 170⅞, in the orchard adjoining his house, and around his grave was built a red brick square enclosure with an arched entrance in one of its walls, all which enclosure still stands, and mantled with ivy, looks pleasing and venerable. Within is Mr. Hignett's gravestone, having the following inscription upon it :—
"Here lyeth the body of Mr. Samuel Hignett, mariner, who died the first day of March, 1707, and was buried in this place on the third day of the same month according to his own will and appointment."

8. During the later years (1710-1714) of Queen Anne, the Tories were in power, and the Dissenters were in daily peril of losing the liberties which they had acquired. When Queen Anne died (August 1, 1714), however, the Whigs were clever enough to secure the quiet succession of the Elector of Hanover (George I.) to the throne. But the Tories bitterly resented this setting aside of the Stuart family, and broke out at various places in the following year into riots, the first rumblings of the rebellion which flamed out in the north later in the same year. These riots were mainly directed against the Dissenters, who were among the staunchest friends of the Hanoverian succession. The meeting houses at Llanfyllin, Shrewsbury, and Manchester were destroyed. The New Meeting-house, Wrexham, was also destroyed, and the Old Meeting-house (see ch. iv. sec. 5) much damaged. The best account of the Wrexham riots is contained in the following extracts[5] from the note-book of Mr. Kenrick himself, the minister of the New Meeting :—

5. These entries, together with various private memoranda and notes of baptism performed by Mr. Kenrick, are contained in a set of blank leaves attached to one of the almanacks, for 1715, of John Jones (" Philomath "), ofthe Caeau, Wrexham. This almanack and note book I myself once saw at Somerset House, but had then no time to do more than extract a few memoranda which were not included in the set of extracts from it which I already possessed. The entries above given are copied from a transcript made by Mr. Samuel Kenrick, banker, of Wrexham, great grandson of the writer. On the title page of the Almanack are the words, " Rhodd yr Awdwr "—*Gift of the Author.* The author or compiler of the Almanack—the Mr. John Jones above-named—was a member of Mr. Kenrick's congregation, and the latter has recorded in the note-book his baptism of three of Mr. Jones's children—Margaret, John and Hugh. I find John Jones assessed in the rate books

July 15, 1715. There was a riot of the Tradesmen, and some of the principal inhabitants of the town.

16. The rioters broke into our Meeting-house at Wrexham, pulled down the pulpit and pews, and threw them into the pool ; broke down the Door and Battered the windows. The Old Meeting House was uncovered, the slates and laths and walls destroyed the same night.

17. Being Lord's Day the Children and young people did a great deal of harm to the New Meeting House.

Being Lord's Day, Mr. Williams and I preached at Mr. Hugh Roberts'[8] House to a numerous and mournful assembly. From that day till the Old Meeting House was repaired Mr. Williams continued to preach the Word and administer the Sacrament at Mr. Roberts,' as I at Mrs. Nicholls.[7]

18. The Colliers came to town to assist and protect the rioters. We applied to Mr. Watkin Williams [afterwards the first Sir Watkin Williams-Wynn] who was at an Audit same day in Wrexham. He came with his hat in his hand, and desired them to forbear. He took away one of them along with him, and told them not to do anything while they stay'd in town. Afterwards the colliers were prevailed upon, and prevented from mischief until evening, and for fear. At night the town people did a great deal of Harm, uncovering the roof, breaking the timbers, demolishing the entire walls, breaking the door frames and window frames.

19. In the evening they came to their work again.

20. The rioters are at it.

21. A great deal of Harm done.

28. At it in a most violent manner, staid till morning, then went about town in a most violent manner.

30. Last night these workers of iniquity were again employed.

Aug. 1. Being the King's Ascension to the Throne was not at all observed at Wrexham except by the Dissenters, who had a sermon preached that day and their shops shut. But there was no Bell-Ringing, no Bonfire, nor Illu-

for the Caeau from 1704 until after 1732. He appears to have died in 1738, and to have been buried in the Dissenters' Graveyard. He was probably the son of Mr. Hugh Jones of the Caeau, whose tombstone is still visible in the Dissenters' Burial Ground. Another noted "almanaciwr," or Welsh almanack maker, of that time, was Thomas Jones, of Shrewsbury who charged John Jones, of Wrexham, with stealing materials out of the almanacks which he former had produced.

6. Mr. Hugh Roberts (see sec. 2) died October 1st, 1715, before the riots, which he witnessed, had burnt themselves out, and was buried in the churchyard. Mr. Kenrick makes in his note-book the following entry concerning him :—"Our good friend, Mr. Hugh Roberts, died, a Faithful, useful, and Judicious Christian, who laid himself [out] unweariedly to do good. He obtained a good report of all men, and of the truth itself, of whom I can safely say to his honour, that he, having served his generation according to the Will of God, fell asleep. I have none like-minded, who naturally care for the things of Christ. A great loss to all North Wales. Help, Lord, for the godly man faileth. We shall daily feel the loss of him, especially in our present circumstances, our meeting house being destroyed, and our troubles increased. There is none left here that will so cheerfully and earnestly undertake that work."

7. This Mrs. Nicholls lived at a large house in High Street, where the premises of Mr. C. K. Benson now are. She appears to have been the widow of John Nicholls (or Nicolas), linen-draper, who had lived in the same house. Mary Nicholls, who was probably her daughter, married (February 4th, 1700-1) Richard Benjamin, grocer, and the High Street house, which thus came to the latter, continued in the possession of the Benjamins, until all the property of the latter was sold at the end of the last or the beginning of the present century. The Benjamins owned also the estate of Hafod, the house and shop in Town Hill which Mr. Phillips now occupies, the large house in the churchyard at the back of the house last-named, a large house and shop in Hope Street, where the shop of Messrs. Hughes and Sons now is, and various lands in the Town Fields. They had also an estate called "Rhosnessney" in that portion of the township of Erlas nearest the hamlet called by that name, and here nearly all the later members of the family lived. Richard Benjamin, grocer, above-named, died October 9th, 1749, and was buried in the Dissenters' Graveyard. He was descended from Richard Benjamin, butcher, who was in 1620 living in the house on Town Hill, describe.1 above, having obtained it by his marriage with Ermin, daughter of Thomas Goldsmith, gentleman, of Wrexham.

mination—the Ordinary Marks of public rejoicing.   But the Windows were broken in a certain inn where some loyal persons were drinking the King's Health etc.

Sept. 15, 1715. Informations were given in at the Great Sessions at Ruthin against 31 of the rioters.

Oct. 20. The King's Coronation Day. The Bells rung, but at night great Riots and Disorders committed.   The Dissenters' Bonfires put out, their windows broken, the Meeting Houses threatened, and the Mob beat at the door.   Treasonable songs were sung about the Town, and great disorders allowed.

" They went about the streets and made noises like Dogs—Behold Fire out of their Mouths, Swords were in their lips."

" Lord be not merciful to any wicked transgressors."

Nov. 14. No ringing of Bells, no Illumination, no bonfire except at a Dissenter's House, tho' there was Abundant demonstration of joy on account of the Successes of the Rebels at Preston.

Nov. 22. The great news of the victory over the Rebels in Scotland, but no public demonstration of joy at Wrexham.

There were great threatenings by the wild and bygotted Rabble respecting the Rebels from the North, who came as far as Preston in Lancashire with a design of coming up towards London, but were happily prevented by the King's Forces under Major-General Wills, who came down with special orders to attack them wherever he met them.   He was to have had Ten Regiments under his command, but he attacked the Rebels before his Troops all came up, and forced them, after a bloody engagement, to surrender prisoners at discretion.   There were signs and appearances of a kind Providence that the Rebels were so entirely swallowed up at once.   Suffered to come down so far so that the disaffected might discover themselves, yet no further that the Loyal people might be put out of fear.   This Blow to the Rebels quieted the Mad and disaffected in this Town, who were so violent and daring, so outrageous and cruel.

One person who had been the great encourager of the Mob in pulling down the Meeting Houses was actually at Preston, and taken with the Rebels there, he had gone with a desire to acquaint them about the forwardness they were in to receive them here, and to direct and encourage them in their rebellious progress.   He was discharged and returned to Wrexham.   The bells were rung for his Escape and safe return.

May 28, 1716.   Being King George's Birthday, but little ringing
        29   A very great riot and ringing all day.
June 7   Thanksgiving Day. They did not begin till far in the
                day. No sermon.
        10   They began to ring about 8 o'clock, and continued ringing only when chiming for service time till late at night. They wore feathers in their hats and oak boughs and openly blessed the Pretender.

Mch 28, 1717. The rioters being removed by certiorari to the Crown Office their trial came on at Salop.   Edward Pul   and David B The witnesses were H[ugh] Burton, Richard ab Edward, Mary H and H D   .

July 27, 1717   Received from the Government, per Mr. William Travers, the Ten Pounds which I lent towards the expense of rebuilding our Meeting house.

9. The task of rebuilding the New Meeting was taken in hand as soon as the riots had completely subsided, and there was promise of a quiet time. The Government made a large grant of money for this purpose. The new chapel lay east and west, with its east front towards Chester Street. The form and arrangements will be best understood from the plan hereto appended, it being

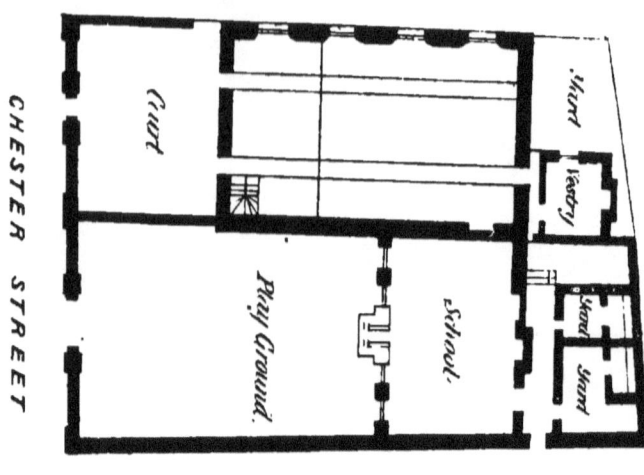

PLAN OF THE PRESBYTERIAN CHAPEL, CHESTER STREET,
WREXHAM,

*Of the School, and of other buildings there pertaining to it, all pulled down
in the year 1840.*

remembered, however, that the school-room shown on the plan was not built for about fifty years later. The two doors in the east front gave entrance to two aisles which ran the whole length of the chapel. There was a gallery at the east end, and the pulpit was opposite. This latter was in three tiers. In the lowermost desk was "the clerk" (as he was always called), who started the tunes, and in other ways assisted the minister. The minister conducted the first part of the service in the middle desk, and went into the uppermost to preach the sermon. The carved oak of the pulpit and gallery was heavy but handsome. The big clock in the gallery front is the same that has been until lately in the Market Hall. The date 1716 was on the outside of the east front.

10. When a return was made in 1715 to Mr. John Evans (see sec. 3) of the strength of the Dissenting congregations throughout the country, the average attendance at the Presbyterian Chapel, Wrexham, was given as 230, and the congregation was declared to have included 20 tradesmen, 29 voters for the county, and three for the boroughs.

11. Dr. Daniel Williams, of London, one of the fastest friends of the Presbyterian cause in Wrexham, died January 26th, 171⅚, soon after the incidents just described. He made many personal bequests (some of which have been already mentioned), and a host of bequests for the furtherance of various religious, charitable, and philanthropic projects in which he was interested. Of these last, only such will here be dealt with as are connected in one way or another with the subject of this book.

12. Dr. Williams left his estate in the township of Burton (parish of Gresford) to his sister, Mrs. Elizabeth Roberts and her husband, Mr. Hugh Roberts (see sec. 2), for the term of their several lives, subject to a yearly charge of £6 "to Mr. Kenrick, or other the Presbyterian dissenting minister in Wrexham," and of £10 to a schoolmaster, to be nominated by her sister and her husband, "to teach 20 children to read and write and instruct them in the principles of religion." After the death of Mr. and Mrs. Roberts, the £6 and £10 just mentioned were to become £10 and £15 respectively, the £10 to be paid annually "to Mr. Kenrick whiles he continues pastor of that congregation where he now preacheth, and the same sum to his successors in the said congregation whiles it remains in its present constitution Presbyterian," and the £15 to the schoolmaster at Wrexham who should thenceforth instruct 25 boys there instead of 20.

13. Dr. Williams also bequeathed for public purposes his collection of books, which he had recently enriched by the purchase of Dr. Bates' library of 6,000 volumes, and to which were subsequently added the 10,000 volumes which Dr. John Evans (see sec. 3) had collected. These were arranged in a house in Red Cross Street, which was opened in 1727, and which

F

henceforth became known as " Dr. Daniel Williams' Library."
Here the deputies of the three denominations (Presbyterian,
Independent, and Baptist), the trustees of the Presbyterian
fund, and the members of Dr. Daniel Williams' trust were accustomed to meet. Here was kept a register of births, baptisms,
marriages and deaths in Nonconformist families, and the building
became the headquarters of the Older Dissent. The Library
which, by continued additions, has since become a very fine
collection of religious, mystical, philosophical, and historical works,
has recently found a new home in Grafton Street, Gower Street,
London.

14. Dr. Daniel Williams' will, which was signed, sealed, and
attested, was dated June 26, 1711, but the doctor subsequently
(August 22, 1712) made various interlineations in it, and added
a codicil relating to the disposition of certain estates which he
had acquired since the date of the will. These interlineations
and this codicil were, however, not duly witnessed, so that his
sister, Mrs. Elizabeth Roberts, as his heir-at-law, became entitled
to all such property as he had not legally devised. Mrs. Roberts
thereupon declared her opinion that her brother had "not expressed in the distribution of his charity such regard for North
Wales and Denbighshire, the place of his nativity, as the great
number of poor and ignorant inhabitants there might have hoped
from his extensive charity," and expressed her intention, while
willing to promote the general intentions of her said brother, to
rectify his omissions in the respect named. By an indenture,
therefore, dated March 25, 1720, she conveyed to Dr. Daniel
Williams' trustees the estates inherited from her brother on the
condition that they should pay to trustees, whom she should
appoint, £60 a-year out of the issues of the said estates, to be
disposed of as she, by her hand in writing, duly attested,
should direct, and that the residue should be applied according to
the purposes declared in the codicil of her brother's will.

15. Among the trustees appointed by Mrs. Roberts were Andrew
Kenrick, Esq., of the city of Chester (see sec. 2) ; John Kenrick,
minister of the Gospel, of Wrexham ; John Travers, draper, of
Wrexham,[8] and William Travers, gentleman, of Clement's Inn,
London.[9]

---

8. Mr. John Travers was one of the wealthiest members of the Presbyterian congregation, Wrexham. His first wife was Sarah Mainwaring, daughter of Edward Mainwaring,
draper, of Wrexham (see sec 2), to whom he was there married, December 19, 1699; by her
he had several children, of whom only one son, Edward, appears to have survived. Mrs.
Sarah Travers died July, 1707, and was buried at Wrexham. Mr. Travers came into possession of his father-in-law's property at Wrexham, as well as of his business there, which
he carried on for many years, although he appears to have been in reality trained for the
legal profession. He married, secondly, at Wrexham (June 11, 1717), Anne, widow of
Gerard Eyton, Esq., of The Office, Wrexham (see *History of Parish Church of Wrexham*,
page 141, note 39), and eldest daughter of Simon Thelwall, Esq., of Llanbedr, by whom he
had a daughter, Anna Maria (baptised at Wrexham, July 18, 1718, buried at Gresford, March
28, 1746-7), and a son, William (baptised at Wrexham, April 18, 1721). His other son, Robert,
was also probably a child of his second marriage. Mr. John Travers ultimately relinquished
his business at Wrexham, and (about 1720) became agent for the Trefalun Hall Estate,

NONCONFORMITY OF WREXHAM. 67

16. By deed poll, dated February 23rd, 1724, Mrs. Roberts directed her trustees to pay £20 yearly (afterwards, as we shall see, altered to £10), to Mr. John Kenrick, Presbyterian minister, of Wrexham, and his successors, and various sums of money, amounting in all to £37 10s., yearly to seven Presbyterian ministers in North Wales and to their successors, and " fifty shillings, the residue of the said £60, to [John] Williams, of Wrexham, minister of the Gospel, whilst he should continue to officiate as such, at the Old Meeting Place at Wrexham afore-said, where he had of late years usually officiated as such, and after his death or removal, to pay the said Fifty shillings yearly to such other minister or ministers of the Gospel as should officiate as such in the Old Meeting Place, and if there should be no such, then to any other minister or ministers of the Gospel of the Presbyterian persuasion officiating within any of the counties of North Wales."

17. Afterwards, by another deed poll, dated November 11, 1725, Mrs. Roberts altered the application of the £20 she had formerly allotted to Mr. Kenrick, and she now devised £10 (instead of £20) to " John Kenrick whilst he should continue to officiate as minister of the Gospel at the said new erected Meeting Place at Wrexham aforesaid, where he then usually officiated," and directed that "after his death or removal the same Ten pounds per annum should be paid to such Minister or Ministers of the Gospel, of the Presbyterian persuasion, usually officiating at the said Meeting Place for ever." The other half of the £20 previously devised to Mr. Kenrick was now directed to be thus applied : —£6 per annum were to be paid to Joshua Eddowes, of Wrexham, ironmonger,[19] during his life, and after his decease to such person or persons as she, the said Elizabeth Roberts, should hereafter appoint ; £2, another portion of the said £10, were to

and steward of the manor of Marford and Hoseley. Henceforth he lived at Trefalun Hall, where he died December 26, 1748, aged 74. His wife died the following year. William Travers, one of his sons, succeeded him as agent to the aforesaid estate, and as steward of the manor of Marford. He was the first of the Traverses who lived at Trefalun *House*, formerly the estate of the Langfords, now of the Townshends, and which the Traverses must have purchased. He was a captain in the Denbighshire militia, and Justice of the Peace for the county. He died without issue, October, 1765, and was buried at Gresford. Edward Travers, the eldest son of Mr. John Travers, was a member of the Honourable Society of Lincoln's Inn, and ultimately succeeded his brother William at Trefalun House, where he died August 21, 1777, and was buried at Gresford. His widow, Ursula, married George Johnson, Esq., of Chester. She left a life interest in the Trefalun property to Mr. Richard Twiss, who in 1807 is described as of Stour Street, Chelsea, and whose son the Rev. Robert Twiss, D.D., set up to the Traverses the monument in Gresford Church which may still be seen there. The eldest son of Dr. Twiss is the present Sir Travers Twiss. There was a third son of Mr. John Travers—Robert,—who was a merchant in London, and who died February 23, 1781.

9. This Mr. William Travers could not have been Mr. John Travers' son, but was, perhaps, his brother.

10. Mr. Joshua Eddowes was a member of the Presbyterian congregation ; his shop and house were on Town Hill, where Messrs. Phillips' shop now is ; he was a grocer, as well as an ironmonger, and, probably, in some way, related to Mrs. Roberts ; buried in Wrexham churchyard, May 7, 1733.

be paid yearly to " Eleanor Hughes, spinster,[11] for life, and after her decease to such person and persons who, for the time being, should officiate as clerk (see sec. 72) of the said new erected meeting for ever ; " and £2, the residue of the said £10, to " Samuel Jones, of Wrexham, glover, during his life, and afterwards to be distributed by the minister among the [poor] members of the Presbyterian congregation, usually resorting to the said new erected meeting place, for ever."

18. Finally, by a codicil, dated November 21st, 1727, Mrs. Roberts directed that the £6 a year devised by her for life to Joshua Eddowes should after his death be paid " to Thomas Radcliffe, of Wrexham Abbot, and Catherine, his wife, and to their heirs for ever, to be disposed of by them in charitable uses according to their discretion." Thomas Radcliffe (or Ratcliffe) was a glover and skinner in Pen-y-bryn, having the premises which now form Mr. Sisson's brewery, and he was buried in the churchyard, February 21, 1760. I do not know whether he was a Nonconformist, but I think it probable that his wife was a kinswoman of Mrs. Roberts.[12] His daughter, Esther, married (December 24, 1725) Mr. Edward Evans, skinner, of the Brook-side,[13] the founder of an influential family of local Presbyterians, one of the present representatives of which, Mr. Thomas Evans, of Birmingham, now enjoys the £6 a year left by Mrs Roberts to Thomas and Catherine Radcliffe. Catherine, a second daughter of these last, married (July 17, 1722) Mr. John Williams, tanner,[14] of " Ireland " (that is, Island Green), Wrexham, and had a daughter, Esther, who married her cousin, Thomas Evans, son of

---

11. Eleanor Hughes was also probably a connection of Mrs. Roberts. She was doubtless, the same Eleanor Hughes who left to the poor of the New Meeting the house in Hope Street (No. 19), which, since 1884, when it was rebuilt, has been the shop of Messrs. Phillips and Co., tea merchants (see sec. 44).

2. Her name before marriage was Hughes; she was, perhaps, a sister of the Eleanor Hughes mentioned in the last note. I believe she belonged to the Hughes of Heol Pwll y Kiln, a family of small gentry in the township of Acton. There is a tradition among Thomas Radcliffe's descendants that he was, somehow, connected with the Dr. Radcliffe who founded the Radcliffe Library, Oxford, and that the doctor was accustomed, regularly, to visit his kinsfolk at Wrexham. I am afraid this tradition cannot be trusted.

13. This Edward Evans had several children :—(1) Esther, afterwards the wife of Hugh Burton, grocer (see note 20), died November 8, 1800, aged 82; (2) Thomas, born November 17, 1734 (see note 24), afterwards a skinner in the Brookside, but not on the same premises as his father; (3) John, born 1737, afterwards a linen draper (see sec. 48), who married (Octobter 25, 1764) Elizabeth Buttall; (4) Jane, born 1738, afterwards the wife of John Pearce, skinner, of the parish of Holt; and (5) Katherine, born 1741, who died unmarried at the age of 20. Mr. Edward Evans died August 2, 1746, aged 46, and was buried in the churchyard, near the tower, where also his second wife (died February 29, 1740-1 aged 30) was buried.

14. The above-named John Williams had, by his wife Catherine, besides his daughter Esther, a son, John Williams the younger, who established a tannery on the premises a part of which his grandfather Radcliffe also occupied. His sister Mary married (June 5, 1751) Mr. Timothy Beardsworth, of Liverpool, whose son, John Beardsworth (who also, owned the estate of Bron Wylfa, in Esclusham Above) succeeded his uncle in the tannery which many still remember as " Beardsworth's." The Williamses and Beardsworths were, like most of their kinsfolk, Presbyterians. John Williams the elder died June 1, 1753 aged 40; John Williams, the younger, August 14. 1788, aged 48; and John Beardsworth March 16, 1812, aged 52; all being buried in the Dissenters' graveyard. The son of Mr. John Beardsworth, also named John, succeeded his father in the Penybryn Tannery, but failed in business, and died in Welshpool workhouse.

the before-named Edward Evans. Now there appears to be an opinion among the Evanses that they are in some way connected by blood with Dr. Daniel Williams. If this notion is well grounded, they are connected with him. it is probable, rather as descendants of this afore-named Katherine Ratcliffe than of the afore-named John Williams.

19. Mrs. Roberts gave to the Presbyterian congregation, Wrexham, the older of the two communion-cups which it possesses. This is a large two-handled silver drinking-cup made, as I learn from Mr. Wilfrid Cripps, in London in the year 171⁷/₈ by Joseph Crane. It is 5½ inches high, and has a diameter at the mouth of 5¼ inches. It bears the following inscription :—*The gift of Eliz. Roberts*. The other cup is somewhat smaller in diameter, but is also two-handled, and has the same general outline as the first. The hall-marks upon it are not very clear, but Mr. Wilfrid Cripps thinks it was made in London in the year 175⁰/₁ by John White. Each cup has its corresponding plate or paten.

20. Mrs. Elizabeth Roberts died January 172³/₄, and was buried in Wrexham churchyard.

21. In the year 1736 [or 1738] I find mention made of Mr. George Hampton, of Wrexham, as " a student lately returned from Glasgow," and " a studious and promising young man." He had been baptized as a child at the Presbyterian Chapel, Wrexham, his baptism being recorded (Dec. 7, 1716) in Mr. Kenricks' note book, wherein he is described as a " son of Mr. Hampton." The only Mr. Hampton mentioned in the rate books at that time was Mr. William Hampton, tanner, of Bridgefoot (see *Hist. Par. Ch. of Wrexham*, p. 96, note 124). What afterwards became of Mr. Hampton I have been unable to learn.

22. I have already given a sufficiently full account of the parents, brothers, and sisters of the minister of the New Meeting —the Rev. John Kenrick, and it is now time to say something of his personal history. He married (Feb. 14th, 172²/₃), at Ruabon Parish Church, Mrs. Sarah Taylor, widow, of Wynne Hall, Ruabon, and thus acquired Wynne Hall, and founded the family of the Kenricks, of that place. Mrs. Taylor, now become Mrs. Kenrick, was the granddaughter of the Captain William Wynne who has already been two or three times mentioned. Sarah, daughter of this Captain Wynne, married (March 24th, 1694) the Rev. Archibald Hamilton, parish minister of Corstorphin, near Edinburgh, by whom she had one child only, Sarah Hamilton born September 9th, 1695. After Mr. Hamilton's death (April, 30th, 1709), the widow[15] and daughter came to England, ultimately settling in Wrexham, and living in the Beastmarket (Nov. 15th).

15. The widow died August 14, 1724, and was buried in the Rhosddu Road graveyard, where her tombstone may still be seen. There are portraits of her and of her husband at Wynne Hall.

Mr. John Wynne (see sec. 2), brother of Captain Wynne, was now the owner of Wynne Hall. In a codicil to his will dated February 22nd, 171⅚, he bequeathed his house, cottage, lands, together with his house in Trefechan and "the standing goods" he bought of his father, to his "niece [that is, his *grand* niece], Sarah Hamilton, provided she take my wife's advice in the disposal of herself in marriage, according to instructions left with my wife for that purpose." In accordance with these arrangements, Sarah Hamilton, the younger, married, October, 1715, at Wrexham Church, "John Taylor, gentᵐ;," who had a small estate in Esclusham Below. I have been unable to identify this Mr. Taylor, but he was evidently a Nonconformist, and I should not be surprised if he was a son of the Mr. Edward Taylor, junr., of Pickhill, who has been mentioned in note 7, chapter I., or at any rate, a member of the same family as he. Mr. Taylor died suddenly at Wynne Hall, January 14th, 172⁰, having been "well the Day befor," and was buried in Ruabon church-yard four days after, leaving, it would seem, no children behind him. His widow, as we have seen, married subsequently the Rev. John Kenrick.

23. The Rev. John Kenrick had, by his wife Sarah, six sons and three daughters. The youngest son, Daniel, died an infant, and a daughter, Sarah, died unmarried, May 23, 1757, in the 23rd year of her age. Of the eldest son, afterwards the second John Kenrick, of Wynne Hall, born August 31, 1725, I shall hereafter speak. Archibald, the second son, born June 23, 1727, was afterwards an apothecary in Wrexham, living in a large house on the North side of Town Hill, which was formerly called "The Greyhound.[16] "He died in a fever taken in his attendance upon a patient," May 12, 1762, leaving behind a widow (born Margaret Wilkinson, see Append. Note 9) and a child Sarah (see Append. I, 133.) To the third son, Samuel, born June 17, 1728, the whole of the next paragraph will be devoted. William, the fourth son, born March 10, 17²⁹₃₀, was a brazier in Wrexham (see Append. I, 72), living in the large house in Hope Street, which his uncle Daniel had previously occupied (see ch. II, sec. 27); he was buried in the Dissenters' Graveyard, May 22, 1793. Edward, the youngest of the sons, born September 20, 1731, founded in 1765, in conjunction with his brother, Samuel, the well-known Bewdley Bank, which is still in existence; he died in 1799.

16. The mother makes in her note-book the following remarks as to her son Archibald :—"It was a great trial for me, for he was a Tender Dutyfull son. Blessed be God who snported me; he lived be oved and died Lamented and Revered. Mr. Boult preached his funeral sermon fr. Samuel 3, 18, *It is the Lord, let him doe what seemeth him good;* he said he was dutyfull son, a tender, loving Husband, and a kind, indulgent Father, and however he was hurried in the Day he wod not neglect family Duty at night: he was but three days sick."

24. Mr. Samuel Kenrick (the Rev. John Kenrick's third son) was an excellent classical scholar and modern linguist. He translated, it is said with great fidelity and spirit, " one of our celebrated tragedies" into Italian. He was tutor to Mr. Alexander Millikin, a rich young Scotchman, and twice made with him the tour of Europe. He had a fine collection of rare books, many of which he picked up in his Continental travels. The record of his visits to the courts of Sardinia and the Palatinate and to Rousseau and Voltaire is very interesting. Rousseau he found " a poor depressed melancholy misanthrope," but Voltaire " full of spirit, vivacity, and intelligence." At Ferney, while one of Voltaire's plays was being acted he was much amused "to see the old man [the author] jump upon the stage and with the most grotesque gesticulations drive the poor frightened actors about the stage." In 1776, he founded with his brother Edward, the Old Bank at Bewdley, there being then no banking business in the whole county of Worcester. He seems to have been a man in whom a wide culture was united with a rare grace of manner, a simple and unaffected piety, and such downright honesty, kindness, and goodness as won him the love of all who knew him. The following account, written by one of his family, of his later days, seems worthy of being quoted :—

" Mr. K [enrick] always read without glasses, and it has often surprised strangers to see him reading the Greek Testament when past 80 years of age without any assistance of this kind. A favourite Greek Testament lett him by a very dear friend was his constant companion; indeed, the sacred volumes (comparing them in different languages such as Latin, Greek, Italian and French), were his solace and delight, and were his constant companions while able to sit up, and, when confined to his bed, his piety and resignation to the Divine will never forsook him for a moment, nor his affectionate attachment to those who stood weeping around his bed ; all his fear was least he should injure their health by their close attendance upon him. But the worth of his valuable character will be best appreciated by the love and affection of all ranks to his memory; from the poor man upwards, all were attached to him, for it was his delight to do them good. Mr. Kenrick was a decided Unitarian, totally free from prejudice or bigotry, and was incapable of saying a harsh word, or of doing a rude or uncivil action ; he was patient and uncomplaining under the most trying sufferings, and thankful for the smallest attention."

25. The Rev. John Kenrick was minister of the Presbyterian Chapel, Wrexham, for nearly forty years, and died in harness at the last. The following account of his death was written by his widow five or six years afterwards :—" My dear Husband, Mr. Kenrick, died January 28, 174⅚, aged 61; he preached the day befor; God wonderfully preserved me, for I was near a week without food. God in a gracious manner made good His promis to the Widow and Fatherless, for my children were disposed of into comfortable places. Blessed be God! Lord grant they may be kept fr. the polution of the world thro' Lust, and may live to the praise and glory of God who has been so good to us."

26. There is another account, which, because it is more detailed, and contains besides an estimate of Mr. Kenrick as a man and minister, it may be worth while here to give. It is contained in a private letter written soon after the minister's death, evidently by a lady, who signed herself " E T "—initials which probably stand for the name of Miss Elizabeth Thomas, a member of the congregation[17] :—

ACCOUNT OF GOOD DEAR MR. KENRICK, OF WREXHAM, HIS DEATH.

" He died on a Monday morning, February 7th, 1744. He preached twice on Lord's Day, went three miles home, got up in the morning, went to prayer, then eat his breakfast as cheerful and well as ever, got up as brisk to go to his study, in the middle of his hall dropt down dead without a groan, or the least motion of life after. As good Enoch, he walked with God and did not see death ; for God took him. Oh eternally happy dear soul ! He has been a great many years prepared to meet his God. If there is anything good, if there is anything praiseworthy, think of these things ; he has them all to the greatest degree I ever knew any. His good will and kindness extended to all the world. In his earnest prayer for them, and ever doing all the service and good he could to all within his reach. But what he was to his friends is not to be exprest, so humble, so tender and sympathizing ; quite a disinterested friend. But he has his reward on high.

' There he doth see and hear and know
All he desired or wish'd below,
And every power finds sweet employ
In that eternal world of joy.'

" I could write and weep his loss all day, but I am so affected I shall scratch what I believe you can't read, so will only tell you that whole sheets would not contain half his real goodness, nor the great loss he is ; for there are few ministers in these days will do much for nothing. He would go twenty or forty miles to heal a breach in any congregation, or do any good to the cause of religion, though all was at his own charge. But I will say no more ; dear Mrs. Kenrick is a lovely example of submission and trust in God.
                                                                E.T."

27. I have seen notes of two sermons preached by Mr. Ke·rick in the early part of his ministry ; they appear to have been plain, practical, and Scriptural—good average specimens of the Puritan preaching of the time.

28. Mr. Kenrick is said to have exhibited, in the latter part of his life, tendencies towards Arianism ; when we remember that this tendency was very marked in the case of his successor, and that some of his own children went a long way in the direction of Unitarianism, we are quite prepared to give credit to this statement, though we are reminded, when we read the entries in his wife's note book, of the warm but narrow piety of another phase of theological thought.

29. Mrs. Sarah Kenrick survived her husband more than thirty years ; in the latter part of her life she lived in the large house of Messrs. W. and J. Prichard, and was buried Oct. 27, 1775,

17 She was a daughter of the Rev. Timothy Thomas (see ch. ii, sec. 6), and herself died not long after (Jany. 1, 1747-8), and was buried in the Dissenters' Grave Yard.

aged 79, in the Rhosddu Road Burying Ground, where, however, neither her own tomb, nor that of her husband, can now be found, being doubtless among those that have been wantonly robbed of their brasses. The books which she especially mentions in her will, and to which, therefore, she was probably particularly attached, are Matthew Henry's *Commentaries;* the works of Richard Baxter; Dr. John Evans' *Sermons;* Dr. Manton's *Sermons;* the *Life of Philip Henry;* the *Life of Matthew Henry;* the *Life of Col. Gardiner;* Bennett's *Christian Oratory;* White's *Power of Godliness;* Fleming's *Fulfilling of the Scriptures;* and the works of Dr. Howe.

30. I have spoken of the supposed Arian tendencies of the Rev. John Kenrick, and of the more pronounced Arianism of Mr. Boult, his successor. Now Arianism, or something like it, was, so to say, in the air throughout nearly the whole of last century, and it is necessary here to say something of it as a tendency of the time, so that we may thereby the better understand its local manifestations. The general intellectual movement, called " Rationalism," which was characteristic of the 18th century, took among religious people the form of a tendency towards the simplification of dogma, or a *re*-presentation of it under an aspect consistent with " human reason " and the prevailing philosophy. Early in the century, the movement called " Latitudinarianism," a movement represented in various ways by Dr. Samuel Clarke, by Whiston, and by Dr. Hoadley, Bishop of Bangor, made great headway in the Established Church. This movement at first scarcely affected the Nonconforming churches, and when it began to affect them, it was, speaking broadly, the Presbyterians only that were influenced by it. There were many reasons why this was so. The Presbyterians had by this time relinquished all hope of being included in the Established Church, and had accepted the position forced on them by law of Protestant Dissenters. But they still showed their feeling for unity by laying less stress on narrow doctrinal distinctions than on essential principles of agreement.[18] They had thus no fierce doctrinal instincts to oppose to the new tendencies. The Presbyterian congregations were also drawn on the whole from a wealthier and more leisured class than the Independent and Baptist congregations, and included a larger number of people than these last, who were themselves liable to be affected by the new drift of thought. So that when a Presbyterian minister *Arianized,* it was generally easier for him than for an Independent to carry his congregation with him. Moreover, the trust deeds on which the Presbyterian chapels were settled, were nearly all " open trusts," and contained no specification of doctrine.

18 What they held as essential were, first, the reality of the divine life in the soul and of direct and personal communion with God, and, next, the absolute and exclusive authority of Scripture.

31. Now when the Rationalistic movement had once really set in, the doctrine of the Trinity would, we may be sure, not long be allowed to remain unchallenged. But the movement having reached the Presbyterians, these, in accordance with the Puritan doctrine of the supremacy of Scripture, approached the discussion almost wholly from the Scriptural standpoint, and it was urged on the one hand, and denied on the other, that the Arian conception of Christ was more consistent with the general drift of Scripture, and with its particular texts, than the Athanasian. The Arian ministers still appealed to Scripture, and it is curious to notice how slightly their phraseology was altered by the change which their doctrine had undergone.

32. Many of the Presbyterian congregations that had become more or less Arian went on gradually from Arianism to Socinianism, and from Socinianism to Unitarianism, still calling themselves "Presbyterian," for Unitarian worship was not yet tolerated by law. Other of the Arianized congregations, frightened by this development, or influenced by the evangelical revival due to Methodism, swung back to orthodoxy, and these and the congregations that had never Arianized at all now discarded the name "Presbyterian" altogether, and called themselves henceforth "Independents." Thus, most of the old Presbyterian churches are now Independent, while those that retain the name "Presbyterian" are Unitarian in doctrine. But among all the old Dissenting congregations of North Wales it was only in the Presbyterian congregation at Wrexham that Unitarianism obtained any footing at all, and even here it came to nothing in the end. Nevertheless, there was for a long time among the Presbyterians of Wrexham a decided tendency towards Unitarianism, and it has therefore been necessary for us to take account of this tendency, and put it in its true light as a local manifestation of a more general movement.

33. The Rev. John Kenrick was succeeded as minister of the Presbyterian Chapel, Wrexham, by the REV. FRANCIS BOULT. Mr. Boult had been trained at the Carmarthen Academy, and became then minister of the Presbyterian congregation, Newmarket, Flintshire—his native town : here he remained for ten years, and then (in 1743) went to Shrewsbury, to become assistant to the well-known Job Orton, minister of the High Street Chapel there. From Shrewsbury, after rather more than a year's residence, he came in 1745 to Wrexham, where he remained for the rest of his life.

34. The grandfather of the Rev. Francis Boult was also named Francis Boult. He was a nailor, and lived in Pen-y-bryn, Wrexham, and was buried December 13, 1707, in Wrexham churchyard. He had several children, but I shall only speak here of two of his sons—William and John. William Boult, born about 1675, married Mary, the widow of Joseph Buttall, of

Wrexham, who will again be mentioned. John Boult, the other son (baptized in Wrexham Church, January 2, 167ᵢ), settled at Newmarket, Flintshire, and became a member of the Dissenting congregation there. I find him described as " John Boult, gentleman." He had by his wife, Lowry, three sons,—John, Francis, and William. John was the father of the Rev. John Boult, for some time Presbyterian minister at Congleton, and of William Boult, who was ancestor of the Boults of Liverpool. Francis, the second son, was afterwards the Presbyterian minister of Wrexham. William, the third son, married a Miss Ellen Braddock, and lived at Chester, but died by drowning before the birth of his only child, Ellen. Besides the three sons, there was also a daughter, Ellen, who appears afterwards (in 1784) to have gone to live with her brother, Francis, at Wrexham. Much of this information I owe to Mr. Joseph Boult, of Liverpool.

85. According to the tradition of the congregation and of his own family, Mr. Boult was an Arian in doctrine, though I think it was only in the latter part of his ministry that he was decidedly so. But he appears to have been unaggressive and disposed to lay less stress on doctrine than on practice, and there is no evidence of his having had any disagreement with the members of his congregation, most of whom still adhered to the doctrines of Evangelicalism.

36. Mr. Boult never married, but soon after his settlement in Wrexham, or but a little while before, he made an offer of marriage to Miss Mary Quarrell, daughter of Mr. Timothy Quarrell, tanner, of Llanfyllin. Almost at the same time, John Kenrick, Esq., of Wynne Hall, a member of his congregation, and the eldest son of his predecessor, offered his hand to the same lady. Mr. Quarrell applied to the Rev. Job Orton, of Shrewsbury for advice under these perplexing circumstances. The old minister in his reply expressed his own high opinion of both the suitors, and suggested that the young lady should herself decide between them. Miss Quarrell was soon after married to Mr. Kenrick.

37. The Mr. Kenrick just named—the second John Kenrick, of Wynne Hall, lived for many years at Plas Gwern, Wrexham, which has within the last few months been destroyed. He had seven children, all but one baptised by Mr. Boult, his wife's former suitor :—

(1) Mary, baptized November 19, 1751 [See App. I, 102.]

(2) John, baptized October 10, 1753, afterwards the third John Kenrick, of Wynne Hall, of whom more will hereafter be said (see sec. 64.)

(3) James, baptized May 13, 1757, afterwards a grocer and chandler, in Hope Street, Wrexham, and living where the shop of Messrs. Hughes and Sons, booksellers, now is. Here he also started a bank, to which he subsequently devoted all his time,

and which he transferred to new buildings next his old shop, where the National Provincial Bank now is. He was an odd man, and all sorts of queer stories are told of him. He died of a fall from his gig at Parkgate, September 26, 1824. He left no legitimate issue, but devised his banking business to his nephew Samuel, son of his brother Timothy.

(4) Timothy, baptized February 6th, 1759. He was (1779-1784) a tutor in the Dissenting Academy at Daventry, and subsequently for twenty years Presbyterian minister at Exeter. In the later years of his life he became a decided Unitarian. He was the author of an *Exposition of the Historical Writings of the New Testament*, in three volumes. He married (as his second wife) Elizabeth, sister of the Rev. Thomas Belsham, of Hackney College. One of his sons, the late Rev. John Kenrick, M.A., of York had a wide reputation as a classical scholar and Biblical critic: he was also a ripe antiquarian, and had a fine literary taste. Another son, the Rev. George Kenrick, a Unitarian minister, was also very well-known. Samuel Kenrick. a third son, succeeded his uncle James in Kenrick's Bank, Wrexham, and married his cousin Mary Anne, a daughter of his uncle Mr. Archibald Kenrick, of Bewdley. The Rev. Timothy Kenrick died suddenly while on a visit to this neighbourhood, and was buried in the Dissenters' Graveyard, Wrexham, August 26, 1804, where his tomb may still be seen.

(5) Archibald, baptized November 12, 1760, afterwards a hollow-ware manufacturer at Bewdley, ancestor of the Kenricks of West Bromwich and Birmingham.

(6) Martha, baptized June 18, 1762, who married the Rev. James Parry (see App. Note 45) ; she died at Chester August 3, 1853.

Besides the above-named, Mr. John Kenrick had a daughter, Sarah (the date of whose birth is not known to me), who married Ralph Eddowes, tobacconist, of Chester (son of John Eddowes, of Chester, of the family of Eddowes, of Whitchurch, Salop), by whom she had at least thirteen children, one of whom, Sarah, was the mother of Mr. Peter Swinton Boult, of Liverpool. Mr. Ralph Eddowes was a determined champion of political liberty and famous in the annals of Chester for having taken legal proceedings against the Corporation of Chester in a well-known case. Disappointed and disgusted, he afterwards emigrated to Philadelphia, U.S.A., where he died March 29, 1883, aged 82.

38. The second Mr. John Kenrick, whose children have just been enumerated, died July 15, 1803, and was buried in the Dissenters' Graveyard, Wrexham, where also was buried his widow, who died at the age of 83, October 10, 1801.

39. We must now return to Mr. Boult. He was a man very methodical and exact in his habits, and as soon as he was installed minister made out a " *List of the members of the Church of Christ*

assembling at the Chapel in Chester Street, Wrexham," to which list he subsequently added various valuable annotations. This list, with its continuation down to the year 1817, I have printed in Appendix I. He also began to keep a register of baptisms and burials at which he officiated, and this register is very full, precise, and interesting. The only earlier register, which the congregation possessed, is, properly speaking, not a register at all, but only the private note-book (see note 5) of the Rev. John Kenrick for the years 1715-1718. These and the later registers are now in the charge of the Registrar-General at Somerset House.

40. On March 2, 1748, a new set of trustees for the £60 a year devised by Mrs. Elizabeth Roberts was appointed. The following are the names of these trustees :—" John Travers, late of Wrexham, now of Trevalyn, gentleman (see note 8) ; William Travers, late of Symonds Inn, Chancery Lane, now of Lincoln's Inn, gentleman (see note 9) ; ffrancis Boult, of Wrexham, gentleman ; John Kenrick, of Ruabon, gentleman ; Richard Benjamin[19], of Rhosnessney, gentleman ; John Wright, the younger, of Wrexham, tanner [see Appendix I (62)] ; Job Orton, of Shrewsbury, gentleman [Rev. Job Orton] ; John Kenrick, of Bron y-clydwr, in the county of Merioneth, gentleman (see ch. ii, sec. 33) ; Randle Keay, of Newmarket, in the county of Flint, gentleman ;[20] Ebenezer Keay, of Whitchurch, in the county of Salop, gentleman ;[20] Timothy Quarrell, of Llanfyllin, gentleman (see sec. 86); and Richard Jennings, of Newtown, in the county of Montgomery, mercer."

41. The congregation had at this time in their possession various sums of money which had at different times been bequeathed for the use of the minister or for the benefit of the poor. Mr. Hignett's was one of these bequests. What was the source of the other legacies we have now no means of ascertaining, all the earlier books of account belonging to the chapel having perished. But we know that in 1752 the sums in hand amounted all told to £175. It was resolved to invest these funds in actual property, and a favourable opportunity of doing this now presented itself. A little lower down the street, south of the chapel was a large house (now " The Long Pull "), which had long been in the possession of the Rosindale family. Between this house

19 This Mr. Benjamin was son of the Richard Benjamin, *grocer*, who is mentioned in Note 7. He was buried in the Dissenters' Burial Ground, Feb. 20, 1750. His son was the Richard Benjamin, gent., of Rhosnessney, who married Elizth. Dannald, and was buried in the Dissenters' Grave Yard, March 16, 1763.

20. The Keays belonged to an old Nonconformist family in this district. Philip Henry often mentions his friend, Mr. Randle Keay of Willington (and Croxton, in the parish of Hanmer), as well as his son and successor of the same name and place. Randle Keay, *of Newmarket*, was the son of the second of these two : he married his kinswoman, Margaret, daughter of Ebenezer Keay, gentn., of Newmarket, and there lived for many years : towards the end of his life he was quite blind, and died (Dec. 1782, aged 85,) at the house of his kinsman, Mr. Joseph Lee, of Redbrook. His wife had one brother, the above-named Rev. Ebenezer Keay, his fellow-trustee, who was minister of the Dissenting Chapel, Whitchurch, from 1739 to 1779. I owe many of these particulars to the Rev. Canon M. H. Lee, of Hanmer.

and the chapel were four cottages, a bakehouse, and a piece of land behind, which Dr. Michael Rosindale had leased and erected a cock-pit thereon. These premises,[21] which belonged to a certain Richard Owens, were heavily mortgaged, and were in November, 1752, purchased of Richard Owens and of the mortgagee with the £175 of trust funds which have just been mentioned. They were conveyed to the after-named persons as trustees :—The Rev. Job Orton, of Shrewsbury ; the Rev Ebenezer Keay, of Whitchurch ;[20] the Rev. Francis Boult, of Wrexham ; Randle Keay, gentleman, of Newmarket ;[20] John Kenrick, gentleman, of Ruabon (sec. 37) ; Archibald Kenrick, apothecary, of Wrexham (sec. 23) ; Thomas Collins, glover, of Wrexham ;[3] John Roberts, maltster, of Wrexham ;[21] and John Wright, the younger, tanner, of Wrexham, [see Appendix 1, (62.)]

42. By a separate instrument, dated April 25, 1753, the above-named trustees undertook to apply the rents of the four cottages " for the support, relief, and maintenance of the minister for the time being of the said congregation," who is more fully again described as " minister of a congregation of Protestant Dissenters usually assembling in Wrexham aforesaid, to perform Divine worship at a place there commonly called The New Meeting," and the rents of the residue of the said premises for the use and benefit of the poor, indigent, and distressed members, and other poor hearers of the said congregation.

43. The cock pit purchased with the other property in 1752 continued to be used as such until far on into the present century, being let by the trustees to the successive tenants of the Red Lion in High Street. At the last it was used as a cooper's shop. It was only pulled down when, in 1884, the new schools were built.[23]

21 These premises are described in 1628 as " one p'cell of waste land|sometyme covered with water adjoyneing to the garden or p'cell of land called Place y Kyll in Lampynt, and one messuage, one cottage, one bakehouse, one barne, and other buildings lately built upon the said p'cell of waste, p'cell of the said Manor of Wrexham with their app'tenance, and now in the tenure or occupation of the said Hugh ap David or his assigns of the yearely [chief] rent of eight pence."
Ten years later the premises are described as consisting of " a certaine messuage or tenement in Wrexham, scitnat and lying in a certayne place called Lampitt in Chester Lane . . . . and also one shope, one Barne, a garden with a yard or backside to the same messuage or tent belonging."
In 1677 they are described as situate in a certain street called " The Lampant."
In 1712 " The Cockpitt " or " conveniency for flighting of cocks " is for the first time mentioned.

22. John Roberts, maltster. His was the large malt-house in Lampint Street ; died February 24, 1766, aged 48, and was buried in the Dissenters' Graveyard.

23. It may be well here to bring the history of the property next the chapel down to date. Between 1752 and the present time the cottages appear to have been rebuilt and the rents re-apportioned. In 1884, in order to provide a site for the new schools, it became necessary to take down one of the cottages and half another. The trustees of the new schools, therefore, determined to buy of the trustees of the old property the whole of the latter, getting thus for themselves a free hand. The rents of the whole of the property then amounted to £52 15s., whereof the minister received £17 and the poor £35 15s. But the premises were in a condition which would shortly demand the expenditure upon them of a large sum of money, and by an independent valuation made by an agent of the Charity Commissioners, their value was estimated at £1,050. This sum was accordingly paid to John James, Esq., of Plas Acton, and Thomas Painter, Esq. of Wrexham, the sur-

THE COCK-PIT.

(As standing in 1883. From a photograph by A. Seymour-Jones, Esq.)

44. In the year 1773 Eleanor Hughes, spinster, of Wrexham (see sec. 17), died, and was buried, April 6, in the Dissenters' Graveyard. She appears to have left her house in Hope Street (now No. 19) to the poor of the New Meeting, subject to two rent charges of five shillings each, payable respectively to the ministers of the Old and the New Meetings, and intended, it is said, to buy them each a goose. The house was a very small one, and in the rate books for 1808-1828 was only assessed at £1 a year. In 1884 it was rebuilt, and let to Messrs. Phillips and Co., tea merchants.

45. In the following year, on the death of Miss Deborah Buttall, April 12, 1774, at the age of 45, the endowments of the Presbyterian Chapel were still further increased, but this time for the exclusive benefit of the minister. Miss Buttall, by her last will and testament, dated February 15, 1772, bequeathed to James Buttall, ironmonger, of London (see sections 46 and 47), to John Kenrick, gent[n]., near Ruabon, and to Thomas Evans, skinner, of Wrexham,[24] the sum of £100, "upon trust that they place it out at interest, or otherwise, in the best manner they can, for the benefit of the minister at Wrexham who for the time being doth, or may be called to officiate statedly at the meeting-

viving Trustees of the old Poor's Trust, who invested the sum in the names of the official Trustees of Charities in 3 per cent. annuities of the value of £1,051 6s. 3d., yielding per annum £31 10s. 8d. This sum is received by the trustees of the new Poors Trust, created May 17th, 1886, who are under obligation to apportion it so that the minister shall receive £10 17s. 3d. yearly, and the poor £21 3s. 5d. The trustees of the new schools purchased for £400 at the same time a shop in Henblas Street, making thus the shape of their own land symmetrical and giving them the control of the entrance to it.

24. This Mr. Thomas Evans was the eldest son of Mr. Edward Evans, skinner of The Brookside (see Note 13) ; his skinyard was that which had been formerly the tanyard of Mr. John Wright [see Appendix I (2), and (62)], and forms now the site of the old Pentrefelin Brewery. He married January 25th, 1760, his cousin Esther Williams (see Note 14), and had by her eleven children of whom the eight after-named reached adult age :—
    (1). Thomas, baptised May 2, 1763, afterwards a tanner at Island Green ; married Miss Margaret Benjamin (see App. note 26), and subsequently entered a bank in Birmingham, in which city his own son Thomas still lives.
    (2). Sarah, baptised Nov. 18, 1765, afterwards the wife of the Rev. Wm. Browne (see sec. 59).
    (3). Esther, baptised April 4, 1767, afterwards the wife of Mr. Jas. McCulla, of Liverpool.
    (4). John, baptised Feb. 27, 1770, afterwards a currier of Chester, and is buried in the graveyard of Matthew Henry's Chapel there.
    (5). Catherine, baptised April 29, 1771, afterwards the wife, first of Captain [Richard?] Meller, and next of Thos. Barton, gentleman, of Liverpool.
    (6). Edward, baptised April 20, 1772, afterwards a tanner, in business on the premises which his father had before occupied. One of his sons, Mr. Edward Evans, velvet manufacturer, of Manchester, is still living, and has communicated to me many reminiscences of the old Presbyterian families of Wrexham.
    (7). Benjamin, baptised July 1, 1774, afterwards a tanner in The Walks; finally emigrated to the United States, and died in New York.
    (8). Joshua, baptised Aug. 7, 1778, afterwards, first a muslin manufacturer at Bolton, Lancashire, then a manufacturer of charcoal and pyroligneous acid at Liverpool. His son, William, became one of the foremost leaders of the Anti-Corn Law League, and was the father of Mr. F. W. Evans, now member of Parliament for Southampton.
Mr. Thomas Evans, the elder, was one of the most prominent among the Presbyterians of Wrexham; he died Dec. 14, 1793, aged 59, and was buried in the Dissenters' Graveyard, Wrexham, where, on his tombstone, he is described as "a tender husband, an affectionate father, and a faithful friend ; in all his public transactions, a man of trust and integrity." His widow long survived him, living in her later years at The Talwrn, Esclusham Above : she died May 25, 1827, aged 92, and was buried with her husband.

house of which the said ffrancis Boult is pastor at present, so that he and all succeeding ministers may receive all the interest and produce accruing from the said one hundred pounds for ever." Afterwards, the above-named Mr. James Buttall, now definitely settled in Wrexham, having added to the sum bequeathed by Miss Buttall a further sum of £18, the trustees purchased therewith 3 per cent. Bank Annuities of the nominal value of £133 6s. 8d., and on February 3, 1776, transferred the stock to the trustees of Dr. Daniel Williams in trust to carry out the provisions of Deborah Buttall's will, with the further proviso that "in case the worship in the said meeting-house shall wholly cease for the space of seven years, the said sum of £133 6s. 8d., Bank Annuities, shall be transferred to the Fund (for the relief of Protestant Dissenting Ministers in the country), commonly called The Presbyterian Fund."

46. The Miss Deborah Buttall just-named, in the entry relating to her burial in the New Meeting Register, is said to have been "the daughter of Mr. Jonathan Buttall, of London." She evidently lived with Mr. James Buttall, of The Groves, Wrexham, and was buried in the same tomb as Mrs. Elizabeth Buttall— Mr. Buttall's wife. Now on this tomb (in Rhosddu Road Graveyard) Deborah Buttall is called the sister of Mrs. Elizabeth Buttall, but as Mrs. Buttall is described in the register of the New Meeting as the daughter of Mrs. Sarah Pain (widow of the Rev. Edward Pain, of Winchester), what is *possibly* meant is that Deborah Buttall was the sister of Mrs. Elizabeth Buttall's husband. We should then conclude that Mr. James Buttall, of The Groves, was the son of Jonathan Buttall, of London.[25] If, on the other hand, Deborah Buttall was the actual sister of Mrs. Elizabeth Buttall, then Mr. Jonathan Buttall must have been the first husband of Mrs. Pain, and we should be at liberty to identify Mr. James Buttall, of The Groves, who we know was born in 1719, with the James, son of George Buttall, who was baptized in the Presbyterian Chapel, Wrexham, on the 14th of January in the year named ; and I myself think this alternative the more probable.

47. Whether Mr. James Buttall was the son of George or of Jonathan Buttall, the main points of his history are perfectly clear. He was a wealthy ironmonger of the Strand, in the parish of St. Martin, London. About the year 1765 he began to prepare for his retirement from business and settlement in Wrexham "his native place," by purchasing various crofts and pieces of land lying between the Chester and Rhosddu Roads. Among these were, as we shall hereafter see (see ch. iv. sec 19), a croft and other property belonging to the trustees of the Baptist Chapel. Nearly all these purchased lands, which amounted

25. We find from the register that a certain " Jonathan Buttall, from London," was buried in the Dissenters' Graveyard, Wrexham, April 27, 1754.

in all to over 20 acres, lay within the Old Common Fields of Wrexham, and still in part consisted of quillets, or separate strips of land lying in fields partly owned by others. And various exchanges had to be made with other quillet holders before he could get a sufficiently continuous tract of land to warrant him in beginning to build his house. This house, afterwards called "The Groves," was built in the middle of "Pant-y-crydd," one of the old Town Fields, wherein in 1765 Mr. Thomas Meredith, of Pentrebychan, had a quillet which cut the field into two.[26]

48. Mrs. Elizabeth Buttall—Mr. Buttall's wife—died (March 13, 1767) while these arrangements were still in progress, and soon after he settled at "The Groves," his wife's mother—Mrs. Sarah Pain—also died (January 25, 1773 in the 80th year of her age), and was in little more than a year followed by Miss Deborah Buttall, all of whom (see sec. 45) were buried in the Dissenters' Graveyard, Rhosddu Road. Thus Mr. Buttall was left in his large house alone. The only one of his kindred left in the town was Mrs. Elizabeth Evans (perhaps his daughter or daughter-in-law), wife of Mr. John Evans, clothier (see Appendix, note 13), and who afterwards, her husband having retired from business, came to live near him at The Yspytty.

49. Mr. Buttall was a Presbyterian, and gave during his life a beautiful chandelier to the Chester Street Chapel, and at his death made a bequest to its minister, which is now of the annual value of £6. He died November 15, 1793, aged 74, and was buried in the Dissenters' Graveyard, where upon his tomb it is stated that—"by [a] regular course of sobriety, industry, and integrity he acquired [a] fortune in London, and ended his life in this his native place, much respected by all who knew him."

50. In 1789 the old property of the Buttalls in Pen-y-bryn and Lampint Street, Wrexham,[27] which had before been described in the rate books as belonging to James Buttall, Esq., is returned as belonging to Jonathan Buttall, Esq. Now as there is no evidence that Mr. James Buttall had any son who survived him, it is exceedingly likely that the Jonathan Buttall just-named was no other than Gainsborough's Blue Boy. In view of this probability I have for several years been collecting every scrap of information available as to the Buttall family, without, however, being able by any means to lay my hands on all the facts that are essential to a satisfactory treatment of the point raised. The considerations that will be presented in the next paragraph may

26. The next field northward, "Pant-y-glover," which Mr. Buttall also purchased, contained two quillets belonging to this same Mr. Meredith, one of which Mr. Buttall acquired by exchange. Other quillets, however, lying in the midst of his property, could not be obtained, and remained down to our own times. A full account of this curious system of tenure, and of its origin, will be found in my History of Ancient Tenures of Land in the Marches of North Wales.

27. The Buttall property in Pen-y-bryn consisted originally of three messuages next below what is now "The Red Cow," and the property in Lampint Street was composed of a house, orchard, and croft on the north side of the way,

G

be nevertheless put in evidence, and such of my readers as are in possession of further information will then be able to judge as to how far these considerations point.

51. Gainsborough's "Blue Boy"—Jonathan Buttall—is known to have been the son of Mr. Jonathan Buttall, a wealthy Londoner, who, for many years, carried on the business of an ironmonger in Greek Street, Soho, at the corner of King Street, and who died in 1768. This business is said to have been established under the name Buttall as early as 1728. Now, although Buttall is by no means a common name, in Wrexham the Buttalls were very numerous, and they appear to have been all related one to another. They were, moreover, all, so far as I can make out, either smiths or ironmongers, and were, almost without exception, Nonconformists. One of these Buttalls, James, afterwards of The Groves, went, we know, to London, and settled there. So, I believe, did another member of the family—Joseph Buttall, smith, whom I find described as uncle of this same James. His widow, at any rate, was married *in London* to her second husband. Now this Joseph Buttall (who, I believe, was a son of Joshua and Deborah Buttall,[28] of Pen-y-bryn), married at Wrexham (Dec. 4. 1703), Mary Shone, and was by her the father of Jonathan Buttall, who was baptised Nov. 22, 1717 at the New Meeting House. Wrexham ; and this Jonathan Buttall, I cannot help thinking, was the father of the Jonathan who was the father of *The Blue Boy*. "The Blue Boy" seems, at any rate, to have inherited the property that Joseph Buttall's father owned in Wrexham. In what has been said, the manner of " The Blue Boy's " connection with this town may not have been quite exactly stated, but of the fact of that connection there can, I think, be no doubt.

52. A little before Mr. James Buttall's death, the question of building a school-house on the waste ground adjoining the chapel began to be discussed. The Rev. Thomas Davies had already been established in Wrexham before 1767,[29] as a Dissenting Schoolmaster, receiving, in consideration of his instructing 25 boys to read and write, the £15 a year left by Dr Daniel Williams for that purpose, and taking besides such private pupils as he could get. The building in which he at first kept his school was the Old Friends' Meeting House in Holt Street, which, for many years before, the Society had ceased to occupy. This meeting

---

28. Joseph Buttall died March 10, 1724, and was buried in the Dissenters' Graveyard, Wrexham. His widow was married (September 30, 1727) to William Boult (see sec. 34), whom she survived and was also buried in the same Graveyard, May 15, 1766. The Joshua Buttall who died March 3, 1719, aged 35, a leading member of The Old Meeting, was apparently a brother of Joseph, and so also was George (or Jonathan) the father of James.

29. Mr. Davies married (May 11, 1767), at the Parish Church, Wrexham, Miss Lucy Griffiths, who died seven months afterwards, and was buried (December 15, 1767) in the Dissenters' Graveyard. Mr. Davies himself died February 10th, 1783, and was also buried in the same graveyard. After his death, the Rev. Wm. Browne, the minister of the chapel, carried on the school.

house was, however, probably far from being in good repair (it was not many years after taken down altogether), and the Presbyterians determined to erect a properly furnished and seemly building, which should be used as a day-school for the children of Nonconformist parents. I judge, from various indications, that this building was erected about the year 1781, but cannot speak on this point with absolute confidence. The arrangement of the desks in the school was, it is said, particularly good. Proper offices and a good playground were attached (see plan opposite page 65).

53. Twenty-two years were yet to run of the lease of the chapel premises, but since a large sum of money was now to be expended in erecting the school-house, it was thought fitting to take out a new lease of the whole for 39 years from the time of the expiry of the lease then in existence—from 1797, that is, to 1836. The rent under the new lease was still a pepper-corn one. The following are the names of the new trustees :—Rev. Francis Boult ; James Buttall, gent[a]·, of Wrexham ; John Kenrick, gent[a]·, of Ruabon ; William Kenrick, brazier, of Wrexham (see sec. 23) ; Thomas Evans, skinner, of Wrexham ;[24] Thomas Gittins, gent[a]·, of Erbistock [Hall] ; John Evans, clothier, of Wrexham ;[13] John Kenrick, the younger, gent[a]·, of Ruabon (see sec. 64) ; and Hugh Burton, grocer, of Wrexham.[30]

54. In 1781, Mr. Richard Harris, of Shrewsbury, made a bequest of "the annual interest of £100 towards the support of the minister for the time being who shall stately preach to a Protestant Dissenting congregation in Wrexham, in the county of Denbigh, where the Rev. Mr. Boult now preacheth." This interest—£3 10s. a year—is paid by the trustees of the High Street Chapel, Shrewsbury. In what way Mr. Rd. Harris was connected with the New Meeting, Wrexham, I do not know, but I find that a sister of Mr. John Wynne, one of the first set of trustees of the chapel, married a Mr. Harris, and it was thus, perhaps, that the connection came about.

55. Towards the end of 1783 Mr. Boult, who by this time was an old man, found it impossible any longer to perform unaided the full work of the ministry. A certain Mr. William Browne, eventually his successor, then only 21 years of age, was therefore chosen to assist him. Mr. Boult died April 16, 1787, aged 77, at the house of his sister-in-law, Mrs. Ellen Boult (see sec. 34), at

---

30. The Burtons were an old family of tenant farmers and small freeholders in the township of Stansty. They were nearly all Puritans, and John Burton, the first of them that I can find mentioned, died fighting on the side of the Parliament [see chap. I. sec. 14 (1).] The Hugh Burton mentioned above was the fourth of the name. His shop was in High Street, where Mr. J. F. Edisbury's shop now is. His wife, Esther, was a daughter of Edward Evans, skinner (see note 13). Amongst his children may be mentioned John, afterwards of The Yspytty (see note 31) ; William, who ultimately succeeded him in business (see Appendix, note 44) ; Edward, who settled in Chester ; and Catherine, afterwards the wife of Mr. John Painter. Mr. Hugh Burton died September 22 1780 aged 59 and was buried in the Dissenters Graveyard, Wrexham.

Chester, and was buried in the Dissenters' Graveyard, Wrexham. Both his own sister, and the sister-in-law just named, died soon after, and were buried in the same place. For many years before his death Mr. Boult lived at a house in Chester Street, which is still standing, and which is now numbered 36. He left an annuity of £2 to the minister, who should succeed him at the New Meeting, and also a small sum of money for the repair of the houses next the chapel that belonged to the poor.

56. The annuity just mentioned was the last of many endowments bequeathed at different times to the congregation of the New Meeting, Wrexham.[55b] None of these endowments is hampered by any conditions as to doctrine. I have given in Appendix II. a list of them all in due order.

57. Mr. Boult being dead, his assistant, the REV. WILLIAM BROWNE, became the regular and settled pastor of the church, and so continued until the end of his life.

58. Although Mr. Browne was not an Arian, he was like his predecessor in this respect that he hated polemics, and preferred as a preacher to deal with those central truths as to which all honest men and good Christians are agreed, rather than with those points of doctrine as to which the Presbyterians of the time were divided. He was thus well adapted to be the minister of a congregation the members of which ranged in their theological opinions from definite Evangelicalism to definite Unitarianism, but who were willing nevertheless to join in a common worship and have religious fellowship one with another. But if Mr. Browne was broad, liberal, and tolerant, there is no reason to doubt the sincerity of his Evangelicalism, and it seems quite certain that in his time the tendency towards Unitarianism which had manifested itself in the Presbyterian congregation was, except in the case of certain families, definitely arrested. Spite of this, Unitarians continued to be admitted as members up to the very end of Mr. Browne's life. This would hardly have happened if the Evangelicals, who all along appear to have been in a large majority, had not been either consciously tolerant or superlatively complacent and easy going. It is clear, in any case, that they possessed little of that enthusiasm of which the Methodists of the time had so plentiful a store. The local Presbyterians of the last quarter of the 18th century were for the most part decorous, reputable, conscientious, devout, lovers of liberty, fairly intelligent, often scholarly, but wanted warmth

30b. It should be noted how large a proportion of these endowments was given to the congregation during the period, when *as to doctrine* its conditions of membership were very broad, and when, *as to church-government*, it was already practically Independent. When the right of the present congregation to its endowments is denied on the ground that those endowments were given *to Presbyterians*, the answer is, that we have to consider what was meant in England and Wales by the name "Presbyterian" during the latter half of last century, not what was then meant by that name in Scotland, nor what is now meant by it in Wales.

and colour, and had little or none of that fiery force which sought out the unwilling and the lost, and compelled them to be saved.

59. Mr. Browne was a man of rather a fine presence, and in the later years of his life possessed an appearance so venerable as always to draw towards him the eyes of strangers. He married (April 27, 1787), directly after his election as sole minister, Sarah, eldest daughter of Mr. Thomas Evans, skinner, of the Brookside. He lived, first of all, at the Priory, then at Pentre-felin House, next in a house on the east side of Regent Street, and finally in Pen-y-bryn, where the Eagle Brewery now is.

60. Mr. Browne carried on, in the school-house next the chapel, the school which had aforetime been kept by the Rev. Thomas Davies (see sec. 52), taking at the same time several private pupils, some of whom boarded at his house. When he gave up the school he appears to have been succeeded as master, about the year 1800, by the Rev. James Parry (see Appendix I., 192).

61. Mr. Browne had four children, one son and three daughters. His son William, born August 4, 1789, was afterwards a skinner and tanner, having, in Pentrefelin, the premises formerly occu-pied by Edward Jackson (see Appendix I., 180), and afterwards a tannery next the Bridge House, at the bottom of what is now Willow Lane. He died July 1, 1819, when only 30 years of age, his wife, Mary, having died four years before.

62. The Rev. William Browne's three daughters were singu-larly beautiful. They were called " the Meeting-house bells [belles]." One of them, whom an uncle or some other relative took to an exhibition of pictures in London, was almost as much looked at as the pictures were. The eldest daughter, Sarah, born February 12, 1788, was married (May 22, 1810), to Mr. John Jones, mercer, of High Street (see Appendix I ., 208), by whom she had several children, one of whom (Miss Sarah Jones, of Bowdon) is still living ; she died March 12, 1820, aged 32, and was buried in the Dissenters' Burial Ground. Abigail, Mr. Browne's second daughter, born June 27, 1791, married (Novem-ber 21, 1814), Mr. George Snelson, bookseller, of Nantwich, by whom she had at least two children, and died December 19, 1818, aged 27. The third daughter, Caroline Evans Browne, born November 9, 1791, married (March, 1822) William Bowker, tallow chandler, of Bolton, Lancashire, who had been a boarding pupil with her father, and who, after a short residence in Wrex-ham, emigrated to Canada or to the United States.

63. On January 19, 1797, the after-named new trustees for Mrs. Elizabeth Roberts' legacies were appointed :—John Kenrick, cheese factor, late of Whitchurch, in the county of Salop (see sec. 64) ; James Kenrick, grocer, of Wrexham [see sec. 37 (3)] ; Rev. William Browne ; William Wilkinson, Esq., of The Court, in the parish of Wrexham (see Appendix note 9) ; John Burton, mercer,

of Wrexham ;[31] Thomas Evans, tanner, of Wrexham (see note 24); John Beardsworth, tanner, of Wrexham (see note 14); William Burton, grocer, of Wrexham (see Appendix, note 44); Benjamin Evans, tanner, of Wrexham [see note 24 (7)] ; and John Hayton, the younger, wire manufacturer, of Gwersyllt.[82] In January, 1799, new trustees were also appointed for the property next the chapel belonging to the poor and minister. The following are the names of them :—Rev. William Browne ; James Kenrick, grocer, of Wrexham ; John Beardsworth, tanner, of Wrexham ; Thomas Evans, tanner, of Wrexham [see note 24 (1)] ; John Painter, stationer, of Wrexham ;[83] Benjamin Evans, tanner, of Wrexham [see note 24 (7)] ; John Kenrick, gentleman, of Little Coton, in the county of Salop; John Hayton, the younger, wire-drawer, of Gwersyllt (see note 32) ; John Evans, currier, of Chester [see note 24 (4)] ; Edward Evans, tanner, of Wrexham [see note 24 (6)] ; and Joshua Evans, muslin manufacturer, of Bolton, in the county of Lancaster [see note 24 (8).]

64. Of the Mr. John Kenrick, described in the trust of 1797 as " late of Whitchurch," and in that of 1799 as " of Little Coton," afterwards the *third* John Kenrick, of Wynne Hall, a somewhat fuller account must be given than would go in a foot-note. Having grown to manhood, he went, after a short residence at Chester, to live at Whitchurch, where he was in business as a cheesefactor. Here he was living as early as 1782, and remained until about 1797. In 1799 he is described, as we have seen, as of Little Coton, near Bridgenorth, where he appears to have lived until, by the death of his father in 1803, he came into possession of Wynne Hall. He was a decided and avowed Unitarian. He married (September 13, 1781) Sarah, eldest daughter of Samuel and Sarah Savage, of Clay Hill, in the parish of Enfield, Middlesex, Mr. Savage being a great grandson of the well-known Philip Henry.[84] Mr. Kenrick had, by his wife, Sarah (Savage) twelve children :—

81. Mr. John Burton occupied the shop in High Street (now Mr. Scotcher's) in which Mr. John Evans, mercer (see Appendix, note 17) had formerly carried on business. He was twice married, his first wife being Elizabeth, a daughter of Mr. James Jones, tanner, of Pont Tuttle. He had (besides three children that died young), one son and three daughters :— (1) Elizabeth, born August 17, 1796 ; (2) John, born March 24, 1798, died February 18, 1818, aged 20; 3) Mary Anne, born December 2, 1801, married Rev. John Pearce, Mr. Brown's successor at Chester Street Chapel; and (4) Margaret (by his second wife, born October 24, 1813) who married September 6, 1831, Mr. Edward Jay, a son of the famous Rev. William Jay, of Bath. About the beginning of the century Mr. Burton retired from business and went to live at the Yspytty, where he continued to the end of his life. He died October 20 1813, aged 51, and was buried in the Dissenters' Graveyard. He was a very rich man.

82. John Hayton, the younger, son of John Hayton, the elder (see Appendix, note 11) died January 8, 1813, in the 55th year of his age, and was buried in the Dissenters' Graveyard Wrexham.

83. Mr. John Painter, whose shop was where that of Mr. Potter now is, married (October 3, 1798), Catherine, a daughter of Mr. Hugh Burton (see note 30), by whom he had three children—(1) John, killed October 15, 1833, by a fall from his horse (2) Mary Anne, who became (June 29, 1816), the first wife of the late Mr. John James; and (3) Thomas, who has died (Jan. 16, 1889, aged 82) while this work is going through the press.

84. There is at Wynne Hall an original diary of Philip Henry, which doubtless came into the family through Sarah Savage.

(1) John, born June 29, 1782; died in London, aged 21.

(2) Sarah, born July 28, 1783; died unmarried September 21, 1852, and was buried in the Dissenters' Graveyard, Wrexham.

(3) Mary, born October 18, 1786; died unmarried July 7, 1844, and was buried in the Dissenters' Graveyard, Wrexham.

(4) Martha, ; married (1817) George Lewis, surgeon, of Wrexham (see ch. V., sec. 12), and had eleven children, of whom five are buried in the Rhosddu Road Graveyard, and another, William Kenrick Lewis, was afterwards a surgeon in Wrexham, and died in 1856.

(5) Elizabeth, born March 15, 1788: married Jean Paul Eppelin, a Swiss gentleman.

(6) Lydia, born August 25, 1789.

(7) Samuel Savage, born October 25, 1790; married, in 1830, Hannah Edwards, by whom he had one daughter: in 1657 was living at Mouton Prêtre, Saint Heliers; died soon afterwards.

(8) Dorothy Quarrell, died young.

(9) Richard, born March 11, 1794; died in London, May 7, 1816.

(10) William, born July 24, 1798, and, by the death of all his elder brothers, came ultimately into possession of the Wynne Hall estate. He married Sarah, daughter of Mr. James Edmondson, of Lancaster, by whom he had six children, all of whom are still living. He died January 9, 1865, and was buried in the Dissenters' Graveyard.

(11) Ann, died young.

(12) Edward, born February 10, 1801; married Phœbe Hopkins, by whom he has issue; emigrated to the United States, where he still lives.

Mr. John Kenrick, the father of the above-named twelve children, died April 21, 1823, aged 70: his widow died August 8, 1839, aged 80. Husband and wife were buried in the Dissenters' Graveyard, Wrexham.

65. I have decided to print the after-given extracts from an account, written by one of his daughters, of Mr. John Kenrick's last sayings, not merely because they illustrate the character of an important member of the congregation, but also, first of all, because they exhibit the devotional side of the Unitarianism which, after 1820, was proscribed in the Chester Street Church; and next, because they show that, after that proscription, the project was once entertained of starting a distinctly Unitarian congregation in Wrexham :—

My trust is in the mercy and goodness of God as declared by our Saviour Jesus Christ, and it is my hope that those principles which, tho' with many frailties, I have endeavoured to govern my life, may so guide and direct my children that we may *all* meet in Heaven. The Bible has been my comfort and support; you cannot have a better guide. There is an Exposition of it[meaning my Uncle Timothy's Exposition of the New Testament] which has enabled me to understand some parts of it much better. Some say we [Unitarians] take away the Mediator, but I believe in Him, and trust in Him and in His divine mission as sent by God for the salvation of man. You may not be thought so well of by the world for professing these sentiments, but if your conduct be upright and consistent, you will be respected at last. The time will come when the Bible will be more read and the Gospel will be better understood; the progress tho' slow is sure and certain. If a few pious people are inclined to meet together, I know there are many in this neighbourhood, tho' it may be in a humble way at first. I hope my children will assist and do their part. Mr. Greenhow [Mr. *Robert* Greenhow, see note 43] told me *he* would, and some others, referring to Mr. G., said:—" He is a worthy man." . . . . Soon after he repeated, with much fervour, the Lord's prayer in the following manner:—" *Our Father which art in Heaven, hallowed be thy name!*" "May it be sanctified! may it be kept holy!" *Thy kingdom come.* "It will come." *Thy will be done.* "It *shall* be done; and it shall be done" *on earth as it is in Heaven. Give us our daily bread. Forgive us our trespasses as we forgive them that trespass against us,* "only as we forgive them." "*Lead us not into temptation, but deliver us from evil, for ever and ever, Amen.*" . . . . . . Exhausted with fatigue he said:—"You will now read something. I much admire our Lord's Sermon on the Mount." Repeating some parts of it, Eliz^{th.} then read the 103rd Psalm, after which each one repeated some suitable hymns, with which he appeared pleased, and some time after said:—"My God is my strength: my God is my hope. He will support and bless me. I know in whom I have believed, and that he is able to keep what I have committed to Him. May God support me in my last hour."

66. There was one important member of the congregation during the later years of Mr. Boult's ministry and the earlier years of Mr. Browne's, who because he was not connected with any of the trusts just recited, nor belonged to the inner circle of church membership, has not hitherto been mentioned. This was Mr. Richard Kirk, of Bryn Mali, afterwards of Gwersyllt Hill. who was concerned, more, perhaps, than any man of his time, in the developement of the mineral resources of this district. All his children were baptised in the Presbyterian chapel, and thirteen members of his family including his wife (Mrs. Ellen Kirk died April 8, 1827, aged 82) lie buried in the Rhosddu Road Graveyard. He settled in the neighbourhood a little before 1775, coming from Chapel-en-le-Frith, in Derbyshire, having recently married Miss Ellen Venables.[35] Mr Richard Kirk was the father of Messrs. James, George, and Richard Kyrke, deceased (note the changed spelling of the name in the second generation!) the grandfather of the present Mr. Richard Venables Kyrke, J.P., of Pen-y-wern, and the great grandfather of Mr. Richard H. Venables Kyrke, of Nant-y-ffrith. Towards the end of his life he left the Presbyterian chapel and joined the communion of the Church of England. He died April 13, 1839, aged 92.

67. About the year 1820 a Sunday School in connection with the chapel was started, which has been carried on ever since.

68. The Rev. William Browne died May 5, 1820, aged 58, having been for 37 years minister of the congregation, and was buried in the Dissenters' Graveyard, where his wife, who survived him nearly nine years (died January 9, 1829), also lies.

69. The death of Mr. Browne, and the necessity of electing a successor to him, brought the doctrinal differences that existed within the congregation to a head. The Trinitarians, affected by the evangelical revival then in progress, were less disposed than formerly to tolerate the doctrine of the Trinity being treated in any way as an open question. Meanwhile many of the Arians

---

35. Mr. [James] Venables was charged in the rate books for Cae Hick in the township of Broughton-in-Bromfield as early as 1770. He died October, 1786, aged 84, and both he and George Lowe Venables, of Broughton [his son ?], who died October 10, 1776, aged 43, are buried in the Dissenters' Graveyard.

of the congregation had become Unitarians. This was the case with two of the most important Presbyterian families—the Kenricks, of Wynne Hall, and the Evanses, of Wrexham. The Burtons, on the other hand, the richest family in the congregation, were decided evangelicals, and so were still most of the members of the church and congregation. Mr. John Pearce, a student from Wymondley,[86] who had been supplying during Mr. Browne's illness, was an evangelical of the militant type, one who put in the forefront and made essential the distinctive doctrines of Evangelicalism, and the orthodox portion of the congregation proposed that he should now be invited to accept the pastorate. This proposition was carried, the Unitarians for the most part voting against it, and the congregation became henceforth of the ordinary Independent type, and ceased, except on official occasions, to call itself "Presbyterian." Several of the Unitarians soon after left the town ; Mr. John Kenrick and Mr. Robert Greenhow died, and those who took their place did not call themselves Unitarians, so that in a very short time the heterodox element completely died out.

70. The Rev. JOHN PEARCE married, April 24, 1821, at the parish church, Mary Ann, second daughter of the late Mr. John Burton (see note 31) of The Yspytty, and it was at the Yspytty that he thenceforth lived. His wife brought him several thousand pounds as her marriage portion. He appears to have had by her fourteen or fifteen children (once two, and again three at a birth), of whom nine grew to maturity. His two sons—Edward Burton, and Robert—are both living ; the first in Australia, the second at the Cape of Good Hope, but are unmarried. One of his daughters, Mary Ann, now deceased, became the wife of Mr. Milne, of the Ecclesiastical Commissioners' Office ; and another, Ellen, also deceased, the wife of the late Rev. Cadwaladr Evan, a well-known Congregational minister in Australia.

71. In 1824, the first organ was set up in the chapel ; it was a small instrument, purchased for £70, which had formerly been in the parish church of Holywell, and was replaced, in 1836, by an organ which had previously stood in Saint Mark's, Liverpool, and which was presented by the late Mr. John James—then the voluntary organist. The present instrument, which is a very fine one, was built in 1879, at a cost of about £200, by Messrs. C. and J. Whiteley, of Chester, a large portion of the older organ being incorporated with it.

72. The setting-up of the organ in 1824 brought to an end the succession of " the clerks of the Meeting," who had followed one another without interruption since the chapel was first built, and

---

86. Mr. Pearce was born at Whitechurch (Hants) in 1795, was educated at Wymondley College, and before he came to Wrexham preached for a time on trial at Lymington, Hants. Mr. Pearce's eldest brother—the Rev. James B. Pearce—was minister first at Clavering, Essex, and afterwards at Maidenhead.

whose main function was to occupy the lowermost tier of the
"three decker," to give out the hymns, and start the tunes. The
following is as complete a list of these curious old functionaries
as it is now possible to compile :—

——1752. JOHN JAMES, [buried in Rhosddu Road Grave-
             yard, June 8, 1752.]

——1768. JOSEPH LARGE, [buried in Rhosddu Road Grave-
             yard, October 4, 1768.]

——1813. FRANCIS EDWARDS, [see App. I. (98) : buried in
             Rhosddu Road Graveyard, Oct.
             4, 1813.]

1813-1824. RICHARD WILLIAMS, [see App., note 86.]

73. The clerk's endowment was henceforth paid to the organist
who has been accustomed to use it as wages for the organ blower.

74. On January 8, 1834, a further lease of the meeting-
house was obtained from Dr. Daniel Williams' trustees. The
following are the names of the trustees to whom the lease was
granted :—Rev. John Pearce ; John James, solicitor (the late
John James, Esq., of Plas Acton); Isaac Senior, wire-drawer
(see App., note 50); William Jebb, gent^n.;[37] Charles Tomkinson,
grocer ;[38] Thomas Painter, bookseller (the late Thomas Painter,
Esq.) ; Edward Jones, architect ;[39] Edward Jones, ironfounder ;[40]
Barnabas Gregory, perfumer ;[41] and John Randles, shoemaker[42] —
all of Wrexham ; William Kenrick, gent^n., of Wynne Hall [see
sec. 64 (10)] ; and Richard Greenhow, gent^n., of Gardden
Lodge[43]—both in the parish of Ruabon ; and William Dobie,

37. Mr. Jebb, who came from the neighbourhood of Wem, was really a music-master
in the town and the organist at the chapel. He married (January 2, 1832), as his second
wife, Anna Jones, widow, of Wrexham, and died here.

38. Charles Tomkinson, of Mount Street, his shop and house being next The Nag's
Head, on the site of Tuttle Street, which then entered York Street at a different point. He
lived afterwards in King Street. His son, Samuel, is still, or has been, a prominent member of the South Australian Parliament, and his daughter, Mary, became the wife of the
late Mr. Frank Roberts, bank manager, of Oswestry.

39. Edward Jones, architect, a son of Mr. John Jones, of The Linen Hall, and brother
of Mr. John Jones of High Street (see Appendix, note 46) : he died at his house in Queen
Street, next the Linen Hall, April 1, 1833, aged 39, and was buried in the Dissenters' Graveyard.

40. Edward Jones, ironmonger and ironfounder, a son of Mr. Thomas Jones, gunsmith, of Town Hill, and a brother of Thomas Cambria Jones, the poet : his foundry was in
Tuttle Street, and his shop in High Street, where that of Mrs. Scott, milliner, now is. He
afterwards went to live at Chester.

41. Barnabas Gregory, who came from Wem, had a hairdresser's and "fancy" shop,
where the insurance offices in High Street now are.

42. John Randles, of York Street, afterwards of High Street, where his grandson's
widow still lives; "for 35 years a deacon of Chester Street Congregational Church, and a
preacher of the Gospel"; died March 23, 1874, in 77th year of his age, and was buried in
the Rhosddu Road graveyard.

43. Richard Greenhow, afterwards of King Street, Wrexham, nephew of the Mr.
Robert Greenhow, aforetime of Kendal, who died August 29, 1829, aged 72, and was buried
in the Dissenters' Graveyard, Wrexham. Mr. Richard Greenhow married Elizabeth,
daughter of William and Elizabeth Woollatt, of London, Mrs. Woollatt (born Elizabeth
Savage), being a sister of Mrs. John Kenrick (see sec. 64) of Wynne Hall, and a descendant
of Matthew Henry. Mr. Greenhow afterwards became manager of the Southsea Colliery,
and ultimately went to Liverpool, where he died. He had six children.

surgeon, of Hoseley, in the parish of Gresford." The indenture conveys, at a peppercorn rent, the premises to the above-named trustees for 21 years from the expiration of the last lease (1835 to 1856) "if the congregation from time to time assembling in the said chapel shall so long continue Presbyterian, according to the will of the said Daniel Williams as aforesaid, except and always reserved to the said lessors, their heirs or assigns, the free use of the schoolroom, part of the premises hereby demised, at their will and pleasure during all the term hereby granted, so and in such manner that the same may be occupied by the schoolmaster for the time being of their own appointment, and that the management of the school may be under their inspection and direction, as heretofore used and accustomed."

75. Mr. Pearce was the schoolmaster under Dr. Daniel Williams' will, but always appointed a deputy. The new schoolroom beneath the chapel, however, was found so dark and unpleasant and the instruction given at the British School had now attained so high a reputation, that about the year 1848 the scholars taught under Dr. Daniel Williams' will were transferred to the care of the master of the British School, who, *ultimately*, received the whole of the endowment, which, under the scheme of the Endowed School Commissioners, was increased, in 1875, to £55 a year, payable for the education of about 35 children.

76. The lease of 1834 had not long been signed before Mr. Pearce began to agitate for the building of a new chapel. The old chapel he looked upon as untasteful and antiquated, and he was anxious to have his pastorate connected with the erection of a larger and more imposing structure. A larger chapel was, indeed, thought to be called for by the considerable increase which the congregation had undergone since Mr. Pearce had become the minister. As, moreover, the old meeting-house had been in existence for 125 years, it was supposed to be in "a state of decay." Under the circumstances the church and congregation were persuaded to pass sentence on the old building. How far, however, this building was from being "in a state of decay," was discovered when it came to be taken down. And if its exterior was plain, it was neither unseemly nor displeasing, while its interior was far handsomer than the interior of the building which took its place. In 1840, however, the old chapel was destroyed, and all its furniture became the property of the contractor. The old clock long found a refuge in the Market Hall, where it, until lately, remained; but what became of the beautiful old chandelier, I have not been able to learn.

44. Mr. Dobie was the father of the present well-known Dr. William Murray Dobie of Chester.

77. As the ground was held under a lease which had now only 16 years to run, it was necessary, first of all, to surrender it and take out one for a longer period. On May 1, 1840, accordingly, a lease for 99 years (from Dec. 25, 1839, until Dec. 25, 1938), was granted. This lease, for which £200 were paid, contains a reservation as to the boys' school similar to that contained in the lease of 1834. The names of the trustees in 1840 are identical with those of 1834, except that for Messrs. Jebb, Tomkinson, Edward Jones, architect, and Edward Jones, ironfounder, are substituted the names following:—Edward Jackson, gentleman, of Bersham;[45] Charles Griffiths, gentleman, of The Court, Wrexham;[46] William Simmons, glazier, of Wrexham;[47] and Hugh McGill, bookseller, of Wrexham.

78. The new chapel was built symmetrically on the site of the old meeting-house and schoolroom and of their respective courts, so as to leave an equal space on each side, and was set back a little from the street. The new schoolroom beneath the chapel was larger than the old, and contained provision for girls as well as boys, but, being partly underground, was dark, dismal, and unhealthy. The architect was Mr. Edward Welch, of Liverpool, and the builder Mr. Michael Gummow (father of the late Mr. Jas. Reynolds Gummow; see also ch. v., note 14.), of Wrexham. The total cost was £2,611 18s. 10d. The chapel was opened April 21, 1841, when the Rev. William Jay, of Bath, preached morning and evening. At subsequent services Dr. Raffles, of Liverpool, and Revs. Messrs. Fletcher, of Manchester, and Luke, of Chester, preached. The list of subscribers included the following names:—Rev. John Pearce and Miss Burton, £300; John James, Esq., £110; Mr. Wm. Simmons (see note 47), £70 5s. 10d. (amount of his bill for glazing); Sir Robert Henry Cunliffe, Bart., £20; Richard Kirk Esq. (see sec 66), £20; John Lockie, Esq.,[48] £20; Rt. Hon. Lord Mostyn (the first lord), of Mostyn, £20; Sir Watkin Williams-Wynn, Bart. (the last Sir Watkin), £20; Charles Griffiths, Esq. (see note 46), £20; Thomas James, Esq. (father of Mr John James), £14 10s.; William Kenrick, Esq., of Wynne Hall, £10; Mr. Thomas Painter, £10; Col. Myddelton-Biddulph, of Chirk Castle, £10; John Burton, Esq., of Minera, £10; Samuel Cotton, Esq. (secretary of Dr. Daniel Williams' trustees), £10; Thomas Griffith, Esq., surgeon, of Queen Street,

45. Edward Jackson, son of the Edward Jackson, dyer, mentioned in note 43 of Appendix.

46. Charles Griffiths, a son of Mr. Edward Griffiths, of Cae Glas, Esclusham Above; he married (January 3, 1838), Eliza, second daughter of Mr. Francis Morris, of The Court, Wrexham, and afterwards lived for many years at the King's Mills, owning at the same time several other mills in the neighbourhood, so as to have almost a monopoly of the trade; died at Brooklands, Salop Road, Sept. 14, 1885, aged 85.

47. William Simmons, Pentrefelin, Wrexham; died July 23, 1859, aged 67, and was buried in the Dissenters' Graveyard.

48. Mr. John Lockie lived in King Street, and was a member of the congregation he was a retired secretary of the Phœnix Fire Office.

£5; John Griffith, Esq., of Hereford (a son of the last named), £1; Mrs. Griffith, of Hereford, £6; Miss [Theresa] Griffith (a daughter of John Griffith, Esq., and a member of the Chester Street Church), £12; Thomas Taylor Griffith, Esq. (the well-known surgeon, another son of Thos. Griffith, Esq.), £5 5s.; Mrs. Roberts, £5; Wm. Williamson, Esq., of Greenfield, Holywell, £5; F. R. Price, Esq., of Bryn-y-pys, £5; Thos. Fitzhugh, Esq., of Plas Power, £5; Mrs. Lee (of Talwrn, in the parish of Bangor, a daughter of Mr. Richard Jones; see *History of Parish Church of Wrexham*, p. 219, note 37), £5; Mrs. Jones, of Talwrn (mother of last named), £3 10s.; Dr. Phillips Jones, of Chester (son of last named), £3; John Townshend, Esq., of Trefalun House, £5; Mr. Henry Jackson (excise officer), £5; Mr. Robert Ankers (spirit merchant, of High Street), £5; William Dobie, Esq. (see note 44), £5; and Mr. Wm. Phillips, £5.

79. By the year 1842 Mr. Thomas Evans, then of Birmingham [see Note 24(1)] was the only surviving trustee of the property next to the chapel that belonged to the minister and to the poor. On November 23, 1842, therefore, Mr. Evans conveyed it to new trustees, all of whose names are now familiar to us :—Rev. John Pearce; John James, solicitor; Isaac Senior, wire-drawer; Richard Greenhow, gentleman; Thomas Painter, bookseller; Edward Jones, ironmonger; Hugh McGill, bookseller—all of the town of Wrexham; William Kenrick, gentleman, of Wynne Hall; Edward Jackson, gentleman, of Bersham; and Charles Griffiths, miller, of King's Mills.

80. I have now to speak of the painful circumstances under which Mr. Pearce's ministerial career in Wrexham was brought to an end. Liberal in his expenditure, and with a large family growing up about him, Mr. Pearce became anxious to increase his income, and thought that in coal-mining he had found a ready means of doing so. In conjunction, therefore, with Mr. Richard Gough, tobacconist, of Chester, he began about 1835 to purchase the Broughton Hall estate, known to be rich in coal. The whole of this estate, which was owned in various undivided third and sixth parts, passed ultimately into the possession of Messrs. Pearce and Gough, who then started "The Southsea Colliery," and sank what is now called "The Broughton Old Pit." Of this colliery the Mr. Richard Greenhow already mentioned (see Note 43), after the manager at first appointed had left, became manager. This colliery in Mr. Pearce's hands never really paid, absorbed all his capital, and demanded more. Borrowing only postponed and made more calamitous the inevitable day of reckoning. It would serve no useful purpose to revive the incidents of this painful portion of Mr. Pearce's history. It must suffice to say that in 1853 he became hopelessly insolvent, and the colliery and all that belonged to him were sold by the

sheriff.[49]   When his effects were seized, the old books of account and minutes of meetings were at his house : these must have been seized with the rest, treated as waste paper, and destroyed.

81. There was nothing for Mr. Pearce after this but to resign. This he accordingly did, and went to live in the Isle of Guernsey. Going hence in 1857 to visit some relations of his at Great Marlow, Essex, he there suddenly died, July 3rd, aged 61 years. Mrs. Pearce is still living.

82. And now with the following brief account of Mr. Pearce's successors we will bring this chapter to an end :—

(1). Rev. Francis Birkinshaw Brown ; born June 10, 1819, at Mansfield, Nottinghamshire ; son of Mr. Thomas Brown, of that town, by his wife Martha (Birkinshaw) ; trained (1842-7) at Highbury College ; minister (1847-1855) of the Quay Meeting, Woodbridge, Suffolk ; accompanying his friend, the Rev. John Rogers (see ch. v., note 11) on a visit to Wrexham, and, preaching in the Chester Street Independent Chapel, received (1855) an invitation from the church there to be its minister—an invitation which he accepted ; resigned August, 1877, after ten months' ill health ; retired to Birmingham, where he remained about ten years, and now resides at Coed Efa, near Wrexham.

(2). Rev. Henry J. Haffer ; born November 1, 1850, at Dublin ; trained at the Western College, Plymouth ; his first charge at Kingston, near Dublin, which he resigned at the end of twelve months on account of the breakdown of his health ; after a rest of five months, accepted the pastorate of the Chester Street Congregational Church, Wrexham, beginning his ministry there on the first Sunday in June, 1878, and being ordained on the 16th of July following. After ten years of faithful service, Mr. Haffer has recently (July, 1888), brought his connection with the Chester Street Congregational Church to an end, and is now minister of the Congregational Church, Dulwich Grove, London. He claims kinship with the poet Oliver Goldsmith, through his mother, who was a daughter of Mr. Thomas Bradley, of Rich View, county Kilkenny.

49. Mr. Pearce's partner died soon after (Feb. 26, 1856, aged 52), and was buried in the Dissenters' Graveyard.

CHAPTER IV

Ibistory of the Old Meeting (at first Inde= pendent afterwards Baptist), from the year 1700 to our own time.

1. When Mr. John Evans, junior, declined the offer made to him that he should succeed his father in the pastorate of The Old Meeting, it was Mr. Jenkin Thomas (see ch. ii, sec. 33), formerly the old minister's assistant, who now became his successor. As such, he was already settled here in August, 1702, when, as we learn from Mr. Matthew Henry's diary, he was present at the ordination of the above-named Mr. Evans. During his residence in Wrexham he was married at the parish church to Martha Griffiths, of Wrexham Regis, of whom I have been able to learn nothing. His marriage is thus recorded in the parish register :— "[Oct., 1707] 28. Mr. Jenkine Thomas techer of the barne & Martha Griffiths of w.r. were Maryed." Mr. Thomas was still minister of the Meeting between June and Christmas, 1708, but appears to have left before the end of that year. Of his subsequent history nothing can be ascertained, though Dr. Jenkins, writing in 1750, says that he was buried in the Rhosddu Road Graveyard.

2. A little before Mr. Jenkin Thomas' removal (or death) the members of The Old Meeting came into possession of the £150 left them by Mr. Samuel Hignett (see ch. iii, 7), for the use of the poor. The following is the clause in Mr. Hignett's will in which this money is bequeathed :—" I give and bequeath to the Society of Christ's members and people belonging to the meeteing house in Wrexham, called The Barn, whereof Jenkin Thomas is overseer, one hundred and fifty pounds of Currant money of England to be payd to ye minister, Elders, and undertakers of that Society to be distributed among Christ's poore, needy mem- bers according to their nessissity & ye discretion of ye heads of ye congregation." How the greater part of this money was dealt with is shown in Appendix III ; the residue of it was employed in purchasing the premises on a portion of the site whereof the Baptist Chapel now stands.

3. And now for several years no regular minister was appointed. The Rev. Timothy Thomas,[1] the grandson of Mr. John Evans, the elder (see chap. ii., sec. 6), came over, however, regularly once in three months from Pershore, and the Revs. Thomas Baddy,[2] of Denbigh, David Jones,[3] of Shrewsbury, and William Jervice,[4] of Llanfyllin, and others, rendered occasional help. These ministers, who came to Wrexham on horseback, were paid five shillings for each visit (a visit which must have taken three or four days) and a small allowance, varying from a shilling to half-a-crown, was also sometimes made for oats and hay for their horses. At last the REV. JOHN WILLIAMS was chosen minister. He is mentioned for the first time in the church accounts in the year 1714, and I do not think he can have settled here much, if at all, before this date. Mr. Joshua Thomas says that he had been preaching for some time before at Y Fenni, Monmouthshire. He was the son of Captain John Williams, of Llangollen, of whom I copy from Rees' *History of Protestant Nonconformity in Wales* the following account :—" Mr. John Williams, commonly called ' Captain Williams,' having been for some time a captain in the army, was a very popular itinerant preacher. It appears that he had also been a member of Parliament for one of the Welsh counties. He joined Mr. V [avasour] Powell in the protest against Cromwell's policy. It seems that he exercised his ministry chiefly in the counties of Montgomery, Radnor, and Denbigh. Llangollen, in Denbighshire, was the place of his residence during the latter part of his life. He was a great sufferer after the Restoration. The time of his death is unknown. His death was attended with very brutal circumstances. The corpse was carried to the churchyard and buried there ; but it was soon after dug up by his savage enemies, so that his friends had afterwards to perform the painful office of re-interring it, which was done privately in his own garden."

4. Mr. Williams is charged from 1716 to 1724 in the parish rate books for a small house in what is now Queen Street, apparently part of the Talbot ; yet I find him in July, 1715, and

---

1. I find from the Parish Registers that a Mr. Timothy Thomas—I suppose the one above-named—was married (January 1, 1695-6) in Wrexham Church to "Mrs. Anne Edisbury, of W.R." [Wrexham Regis].

2. Thomas Baddy (Badi, a familiar form of Madoc) minister of the Dissenting congregation at Denbigh, from about the year 1693 to his death in June, 1729. He had been educated at the academy of Mr. Richard Frankland, of Rathmel (Yorks.), where he and Mr. John Owen (see ch. ii., sec. 33) of Bron-y-clydwr, entered on the same day, November 25, 1689. His wife was Anne, daughter of Robert Salusbury, Esq., of Galltfaenan. He had a brother, Mr. Owen Baddy, a schoolmaster of Wrexham, who lived in a house in College Street, where the Commercial Inn now is, and who was buried in Wrexham Churchyard, October 29, 1734.

3. David Jones, successor of Rev. Titus Thomas (brother of the Rev. Timothy Thomas, Mr John Evans' son-in-law) in the pastorate of the Independent Church, Shrewsbury ; the son of a freeholder in the parish of Llangollen ; a pupil of Rev. Samuel Jones, of Bryn Llywarch (ch. ii., sec. 26), whose eldest daughter he married ; died at Shrewsbury, 1718.

4. William Jervice, minister of the Dissenting congregation at Llanfyllin from 1703 until the time of his death (1743); buried in Llanfyllin Churchyard.

at other times, described as "of Rhual," and it was at Rhual that he died. He was probably connected with the Edwardses or Griffiths of that place, and spent much of his time there.

5. Soon after Mr. Williams became minister of the Old Meeting, on July 12th, 1715, the Tory riots broke out in Wrexham which have been already particularly described in chapter iii. These riots continued, so that on the Saturday following, having pulled down the pulpit and pews and smashed the windows of the Presbyterian Chapel, the mob came into Queen Street, and wrecked the Independent meeting-house also. "The old meeting-house was uncovered, the slates and laths and walls destroyed the same night" (Rev. John Kenrick's diary). The next day being Sunday, the two congregations met together at the house of Mr. Hugh Roberts (see chapter iii., note 6), where both Mr. Kenrick and Mr. Williams preached, and where the latter continued regularly to conduct services until his meeting-house was put into proper repair. Mr. Samuel Kenrick, the owner of the meeting-house, appears to have obtained compensation from the Government for the damage done to his property.

6. In the year 1715, the congregation of the Old Meeting, though it included some Baptists, was composed mainly of Independents, and Mr. Williams had declared himself to be an Independent, that is, a Pædo-Baptist, when he was elected a minister of it. But he had not been here long before he became much troubled as to what was the proper form and who were the proper objects of the ordinance of baptism. He gave much attention to the subject, and finally came to the conclusion that they were right who advocated the method of immersion and were opposed to the baptism of children, and he himself, thereupon, submitted to be re-baptized. Mr. Williams' change of opinion on the point of baptism greatly strengthened, of course, the Baptist element in the church, and led, in the end, to the congregation becoming wholly Baptist. All the settled ministers who followed Mr. Williams were Baptists, as all those who came before him had been Independents. This process of transformation was much hastened by the secession to the Presbyterians of many members who continued to believe in the baptism of children. The congregation of the Old Meeting never recovered from the effects of this secession.[5]

7. In the very year in which the dispute as to baptism took place, a return was compiled (see chapter iii., sec. 3) at the instance of Dr. John Evans, of the Dissenting congregations throughout the country. From this return it appears that the average attendance at the Old Meeting, Wrexham, amounted to 150, and

5. Even the Robinsons, a notable local Dissenting family (see App. notes 56 and 57) who continued for some time longer connected with the Old Meeting, ultimately joined the New. On the other hand, several of those who had at first connected themselves with the New Meeting afterwards rejoined the Old, when the question of baptism came to be discussed : among these were Arthur Lewis (Note 13) and Peter Chaloner (Append. note 65).

H

included 20 tradesmen, 23 persons having votes for the county, and three having votes for the borough. This return should be compared with that made at the same time as to the size and composition of the Presbyterian congregation.

8. I cannot find that Mr. Williams was ever paid any salary;[9] but the congregation lent him a sum of money (see App. iii., sec. i.), for which he had to pay five and six per cent. interest. Few, indeed, of the early Nonconformist ministers received anything more than the most miserable pittance. They were expected to work hard, submit to ignominy, contempt, and persecution, forego the fair incomes which their talents and education (for most of them were learned men) would have fitted them in other situations to acquire, and to provide for their own material wants as well. Those of them that did not enjoy private incomes tried often to earn a little money by teaching, or accepted allowances from wealthy Dissenters. We may think these men mistaken in many of their opinions, but we cannot refuse them the homage which duty, unflinchingly done, merits.

9. Mr. Joshua Thomas (*Hanes y Bedyddwyr*), writing from the report of many who well remembered him, says, that "Mr. John Williams was a mild, humble, affectionate man, with a very beautiful evangelical gift. His peculiar power lay in edifying the saints, in comforting them and establishing them in the truth. He was a holy and loving man, and an example of godliness to all."

10. Mr. Williams died in 1725, at Rhual (I suppose at the house of Mr. Griffith), and was buried in the Dissenters' Graveyard, Wrexham, where his tombstone bears the following inscription: — " M. S. R [everendi] V [iri] Johannis Williams, V [erbi] D [ivini] M [inistri]. Nec minus fuit officiorum hominis Christiani exemplar quam didasculus. Christo obdormit D [ie] M [artis] Octob. 5, 1725, A [nno] Ætatis 63 apud Rhual com. Flint." His widow survived him.

11. After Mr. Williams' death there was no settled minister for many years, but the Rev. Wm. Jervice, of Llanfyllin (see note 4) and William Williams, of Newmarket,[7] came with fair regularity, and among those who occasionally supplied were Mr. Oulton,[8] Mr. Parr (here at the beginning of 1727), a Mr. Lewis, whom I cannot identify (here July, August, and September, 1728),

---

6. In the last year of his life, Mrs. Elizabeth Roberts left (see ch. iii., sec. 16), fifty shillings a year to Mr. Williams and his successors, but he himself never received any benefit from the bequest. He had, however, it is probable, like many of his successors, a small grant from the Independent Fund.

7. William Williams, minister of the Dissenting congregation, Newmarket, Flintshire, from about 1721 to 1728; ultimately for many years minister at Tredustan, Brecknockshire. "He was an excellent scholar, and a laborious and successful preacher."

8. Described as "from near Nantwich"; here in July and November, 1725. I suppose he was the same Mr. John Oulton who succeeded (in 1748) Mr. John Johnson (see Append. note 68) in the pastorate of the Byrom Street Baptist Chapel, Liverpool.

and Mr. Stennett (here December, 1728, and January, 173⅜),
doubtless Dr. Joseph Stennett, son of the Rev. Joseph Stennett,
the elder.
12. At the end of 1728, Mr. John Phillips, of Rhyd Wilym,
(Carmarthenshire) came on trial, and remained nearly a year but
did not permanently settle.[9]   After a long interval, either in 1733
or 1735, or perhaps both in 1733 and 1735, Mr. Edmund Jones
was here as a temporary supply. This was the Edmund Jones,
afterwards Independent minister of Pontypool, who ultimately
became so well known for his apostolical zeal and holiness, as
well as for his writings. His mystical writings are very curious,
and his *History of Apparitions* is still sought after. The fact of
Edmund Jones' residence in Wrexham is, I believe, absolutely
forgotten in the town. That fact explains, however, his minute
acquaintance with certain phases of our local history, as evidenced
for example, in his *Life of Evan Williams.* Here, perhaps, also
it was that he became especially interested in Morgan Lloyd,
whose mystical writings appear to have so much influenced him.
At the beginning of 1735, Mr. David Williams came on trial, but
did not stay. Later in the year, Mr. Morgan Harry was here for
a while, having recently been ordained at Y Blaenau (Monmouthshire), of which congregation his father—Mr. John Harry—was
minister.. But he was speedily summoned home to assist his
father, and on the death of the latter (December 20, 1737), succeeded him at Blaenau, where he died February 174⅞, aged 42.
He was one of the ablest of the Welsh Baptist ministers of his
time, and though his stay at Wrexham was so short, was long
remembered here, and subsequently two or three times visited
the town. Mr. Joshua Thomas says that Mr. Rees Williams,
aforetime minister of Trosgoed, Brecknockshire, also ministered
at Wrexham for a time about this date, but I can find no mention
of him in the church books.[10]   Finally, in the year 1737, according to Mr. Thomas, Mr. EVAN JENKINS came on trial, but soon
after left, having received a call from Exeter, which he accepted.
At Exeter he stayed about a year and a half, being ordained at
Pen-y-garn, near Pontypool, Monmouthshire, of which congregation he had been a member. But in 1740, being definitely invited
to settle in Wrexham as pastor of the Old Meeting, he decided
to do so, and here remained until his death. I learn from Mr.
Joshua Thomas' *Hanes y Bedyddwyr,* that he was the son of Mr.
John Jenkins, a very noted man in his time, who was for a very
long time pastor of the Rhyd Wilym congregation, and who died
July 3, 1733, aged 77 years. Evan, his son, afterwards became

9. He went from Wrexham to London 'but stayed nowhere long, and died in 1761,
near Castell Gwent.

10. Mr. Rees Williams had been compelled to resign the pastorate of Trosgoed for
what were held to be heretical opinions concerning the person of Christ, and ultimately
left the ministry altogether.

a member of the congregation at Pen-y-garn, and there was called
to the ministry. The year after his settlement at Wrexham he
married. His wife appears to have belonged to a local family.
He had several children. One son, William, died at sea while still
young. His eldest son, afterwards Dr. Joseph Jenkins, born
August, 1742, was himself also ultimately minister of the Old
Meeting. Two daughters—Mary (died December 2, 1798, aged
54), and Anna (died July 11, 1815, aged 68)—kept for many years
a draper's shop at the corner of Church Street and High Street.

13. Soon after Mr. Jenkins came hither (in November, 1747),
the land in Chester Street on which the present Baptist Chapel
stands, with much property adjoining, was purchased. This property, which had formerly belonged to Lady Jeffreys, of Acton
Hall, but which had since been acquired by Messrs. Griffith Speed
and Edward Whetnall (*see Hist. of Par. Ch. of Wrexham*, page
203, note 2j, and page 103, note 215), is described as consisting of
two dwelling-houses in Chester Street, of five cottages near the
north end of the said dwelling-houses, and of a quillet or croft at
the north end of these last. This croft extended for about 240
feet along Chester Road, which latter took then at this point a
somewhat irregular course, and did not run as now between
nearly straight and parallel lines. The following are the names
of the trustees to whom Messrs. Speed and Whetnall conveyed
the premises:—Evan Jenkins, minister of the Old Meeting;
Daniel Kenrick, of Wrexham (see ch. ii. sec. 27) ; Evan Roberts,
smith, of Wrexham ; Richard ffennah, yeoman, of Brymbo;[11]
Benjamin Jones, stonecutter, of Wrexham;[12] John Jones, mason,
of Wrexham (lived in Queen Street) ; and Arthur Lewis, yeoman,
of Brymbo.[13] The property was purchased with £40, the residue
of Samuel Hignett's and other bequests formerly made to the
poor of the Old Meeting (see Appendix iii., sec. 1.) Seventeen
pounds, borrowed of the Rev. Francis Boult of the New Meeting,
were expended in putting the houses into proper repair, and it
was intended, when this loan had been repaid, to devote the
rents to the relief of poor and indigent members of the congregation. In December, 1758, three of the above-named grantees
(Evan Jenkins, Daniel Kenrick, and Evan Roberts) being dead,
and the loan of £17 paid off (Mrs. Gwen Price's legacy of £9
being used for that purpose)[14] the premises were conveyed to a

11. Richard ffennah held one of the farms called "Glascoed "; he was probably the
son of Peter ffennah (see App. note 62).

12. Mr. Benjamin Jones lived where now is No. 85, Chester Street: he married,
August 24, 1750, as his second wife, Hannah Clubb, apparently daughter of John Clubb (see
Append. note 60), and so acquired the house in Abbot Street, which had formerly belonged
to the latter. He was one of the staunchest supporters of the Baptist cause in Wrexham,
and a man much beloved. He died January 21, 1780, aged 76, and was buried in the Dissenters' Graveyard, Wrexham.

13. Arthur Lewis, of the Fron Farm, Brymbo, great grandfather of the present Mr.
John Lewis, solicitor; died July 6, 1762, aged 82, and was buried in Rhosddu Graveyard.

14. "Gwen Price, late of Denbigh, buried June 9, 1755 "—Presbyterian Register.

new body of trustees, which included, besides the surviving members of the original trust, three new trustees, namely Thomas Jones, tailor, of Wrexham,[15] Joseph Jones, of Wrexham, mason, and Samuel Jones, of Erddig, yeoman, who, out of the rents of the property, after discharging all rates and taxes levied, and executing all repairs necessary, were to pay the yearly interest of £9 to " the minister of the congregation of Protestant Dissenters usually assembled for Divine worship in the chapel or Meeting-house called or known by the name of " The Old Meeting House," and to apply the residue of the said rents for the relief of the poor and indigent members of the said congregation.

14. During Mr. Jenkins' ministry communion was established between the church of the Old Meeting, Wrexham, and the Baptists meeting at Cefn, near Newbridge, in the parish of Ruabon, who had hitherto been Arminian in their opinions. The Baptists at Cefn met in a building partly used as a dwelling-house, in which they continued to assemble until the erection of the present chapel there, but which was originally designed for a Friends' Meeting House (see ch. VI., sec. 10). They were, in 1786, incorporated into a distinct church, under the pastoral care of Mr. Jenkin Davies.

15. Mr. Jenkins was a pious man, a diligent pastor, and a fluent speaker both in the English and Welsh tongues. In an account of him, written in Mr. Joshua Thomas' own handwriting, Mr. Jenkins is described as " very personable, of a good and venerable appearance, of a middle stature, full made [and] rather fat." During the latter part of his life he suffered much from ill health and appears to have had an assistant. The name of this assistant was Henry Phillips. He had been a member of the church at Pen-y-garn, from which church, it will be remembered, Mr. Jenkins himself came. He must have been here as early as 1751, for I find his name, " Mr. Henry Phillips, of Wrexham," in the list of subscribers to Richards' Welsh Dictionary, a work which was published in the year just named. After Mr. Jenkins' death he went to Nantwich.

16. Mr. Joshua Thomas strikingly says of Mr. Evan Jenkins that in 1751 he preached at the Cymmanfa (Annual Assembly), at Hengoed, but that before the new Cymmanfa came round, he had joined the Cymmanfa above. He was buried in the Dissenters' Graveyard, Wrexham, where " Mr. Morgan, of Salop (see Appendix, note 69), spoke over his grave," and where his tombstone, bearing the following inscription could formerly be seen :— "Underneath are deposited the remains of the Rev. Mr. Evan Jenkins, late minister of the Baptist congregation in Wrexham, who, after a life holy and exemplary, studiously laid out and

15. Thomas Jones, died June 13, 1786, and was buried in the Dissenters' Graveyard.

laboriously spent in the service of God and for the welfare of immortal souls, finished his course with joy in the 40th year of his age, March 23, 1752."

17. And now, after a long interval, during which the congregation had no settled minister, MR. DAVID JONES was, in 1755, chosen as such. He came from Pembrokeshire, and was baptised at Moleston, in that county, having been a Methodist at first. During his residence in Wrexham he lived in the more northern of the two larger houses in Chester Street belonging to the poor, and for this he paid 19s. 6d. a year.

18. Mr. Jones was very acceptable as a Welsh preacher. At Cefn Bychan, where he regularly preached, some came to hear him from the top of Glyn Ceiriog, and invited him to visit them there. This he several times did, so that a congregation was presently gathered in the Glyn and many were baptized. In 1762 the members there built a chapel for themselves, and two years after were incorporated into a distinct church, which, in 1768, was received into the Cymmanfa. In 1770 a call was given by the church at the Glyn to Mr. John Hughes, a member among them, who now for four years continued minister there (see App., note 92). The Baptists at Cefn continued until 1786 to be members at Wrexham. Communion was also established about (or somewhat before) this time between the Baptists of Wrexham and those of Brassey Green, near Bunbury, Cheshire.[16]

19. But the most important incident that occurred during Mr. Jones' ministry was the abandonment of the old barn which had for so long been used as a meeting-house. This had for many years been falling into ruin, so that the rent had now been reduced from sixty to fifty shillings a-year. Mr. Jones was for a long time very busy in collecting money, and ultimately succeeded in gathering an amount which warranted him in beginning to build both in Wrexham and the Glyn. Both chapels were opened in 1762. The Wrexham chapel was set up at the south end of the croft in Chester Street belonging to the poor of the Old Meeting. It was very small, 40 feet long by 20 feet broad. Soon after the chapel was built Mr. James Buttall, of London (see ch. iii. sec. 47) being about to retire from business and settle in Wrexham (whence his family had come), purchased various fields and quillets of land between Chester Street and Rhosddu Lane, and commenced to build there a large house for himself, which he called "The Groves." He purchased also for £70 a 500 years' lease of all the property in Chester Street belonging to the poor of the Old Meeting, all except the actual site of the

---

16. The meeting house at Brassey Green, " about 36 feet by 40, with a small house adjoining for the minister, was erected about the year 1715, by Mr. Thos. Walley, of Rhode Street, and was bequeathed by him for the use of the Particular Baptists," (Urwick's *History of Nonconformity in Cheshire.*) The names of several of the Walleys of Cheshire occur in the lists of members of the Baptist Chapel, Wrexham, and upon tombstones in the Rhosddu Road Burying Ground.

THE OLD BAPTIST CHAPEL.

Pulled down 1875. (From a photograph by Mr. Thos. Griffiths.)

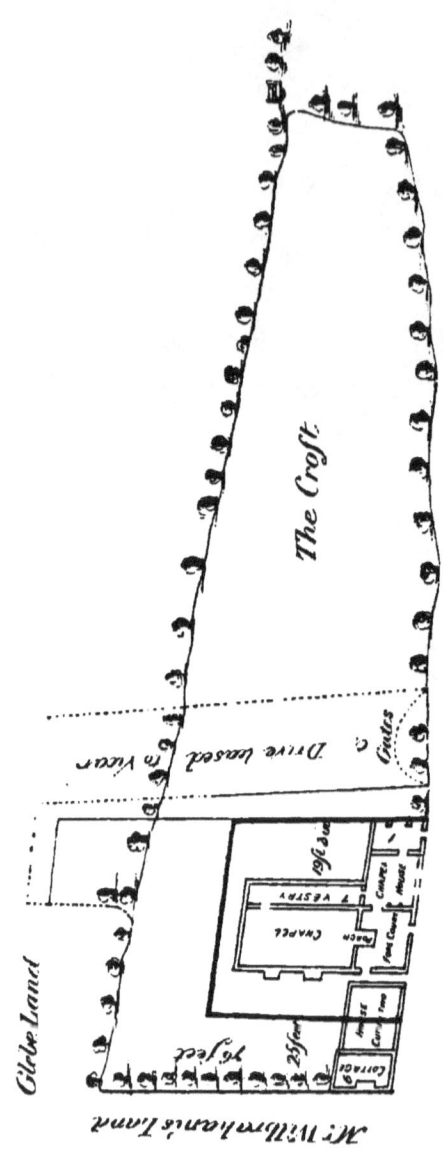

PLAN OF THE BAPTIST CHAPEL, CHESTER STREET, WREXHAM,

AND OF THE PROPERTY BELONGING TO IT, IN THE YEAR 1778.

N.B.—All outside the thick black line was sold to Mr. Jas. Buttall.

chapel there, and the area within which it stood ; buying, that is to say, the croft, the strip of land behind the chapel, the five old cottages, and the land on the south side of the chapel which included one of the two larger houses there and part of the other (see the plan.) Mr. Buttall intended at first his carriage drive to go round by the back of the chapel, and along its south side into Chester Street over the site of the houses—a plan not carried out. Although not a Baptist, he was a Nonconformist and friendly purchaser, and declared that in giving for a part of the premises nearly twice what had been given for the whole, he desired to provide the trustees with funds to build a minister's house. The trustees, therefore (June, 1776), covenanted with him that they would, with the £70 paid them, build a substantial dwelling-house on the north side of the chapel "for the use of the minister for the time being to be by such minister occupied or enjoyed, or otherwise to apply the rents and profits thereof for the use and benefit of the poor members of the said congregation."

20. Mr. Buttall (or his executors) subsequently sold the houses on the south side of the chapel to Mrs. Mary Puleston (widow of Philip Puleston, Esq., of Hafod-y-wern) who then lived at the present Vicarage, from whom they passed to her son-in-law, Colonel Bryan Cooke, of Gwasaney.

21. The sale of these houses and of the land all round the chapel left the trustees no room for expansion,[17] and in 1826 they were obliged to purchase back from Philip Davies Cooke, Esq., of Gwasaney (son of the Col. Cooke mentioned in the last paragraph, and father of the present Mr. Philip Bryan Davies Cooke), the houses and land on the south side of the chapel, for which they gave £80; they purchased back also from Mr. Ephraim Parkin, of the Groves, for £73 17s. 6d., a part of the land behind and on the north side of the chapel, which they had before sold to Mr. Buttall.

22. Although Mr. David Jones had been in many ways so successful, his relations with some of his flock do not appear to have been wholly satisfactory. The truth is his command of the English tongue is said to have never been perfect, and at last, in 1770, he terminated a series of unpleasant incidents by resigning his charge. He then went to live at Adwy'r Clawdd, where, four years after, he died. He was buried in the Dissenters' Graveyard, Wrexham, where his tomb, with an inscription, of which the following is a part, may be seen :—" Mr. Dafydd Jones o Adwy'r Clawdd, yr hwn a ymadawodd bywyd hwn ddydd Sadwrn y 5ᵈ· o fis Mawrth, 1774, yn y 51 flwyddyn o'i oed." His daughter, Rachel (buried June 10, 1766), lies somewhere in the same

---

17. In this arrangement also the claims of the poor of the congregation, for whose benefit the property had been acquired, were forgotten. To satisfy those claims, the rent of one of the old houses belonging to the property was ultimately set aside, and when, on the building of the new chapel, this house was pulled down, the church passed a resolution, declaring its liability to a yearly charge of £10 for the relief of its poor.

graveyard.   I always fancy him to be the " Dafydd Jones " who
wrote a Welsh book, printed in Wrexham by Richard Marsh,
entitled " Histori Nicodemus."

23. After Mr. Jones' resignation a long interval occurred,
during which the Rev. John Hughes, of the Glyn, and many other
ministers, whose names will be found in Appendix III, took turns
in supplying the pulpit.   At last MR. JOSEPH JENKINS, M.A.
(afterwards Dr. Jenkins), son of the Rev. Evan Jenkins, a former
pastor of The Old Meeting, accepted an invitation to fill his
father's place, and was, in 1773, ordained.

24.   Mr. Jenkins was born in Wrexham, and after his father's
death (which occurred when he was nine years old) continued,
it is probable, to live here with his mother.   In 1759 he went to
London, where " he learned Greek and Hebrew, under the care
of Dr. Walker ; " and thence, in 1761, as one of Dr. Ward's
exhibitioners, to King's College, Aberdeen, where he remained
until 1765, in which year he took his degree, and returned to
Wrexham. He had begun to preach in Scotland, but his doctrinal
opinions were as yet unfixed, and he had not been baptised.
Subsequently, he became tutor in a family whose mistress was a
sister of Dr. Stennet.   So he came under the Doctor's influence,
and subsequently underwent a moral and intellectual change,
which left him in no doubt as to the course he ought now to take.
In 1766 he was baptised by Dr. Stennet, and became a
member of the latter's church. In 1769 he returned to Wrexham,
from which place he exercised, for a time, a sort of pastoral oversight of the Independents who had seceded from the Old Nonconformists' Chapel in Crook's Lane (now Trinity Street),
Chester, and were then meeting in Common Hall Lane, in that
city.   Finally, as we have seen, in 1773, he definitely accepted
the pastorate of the Old Meeting, Wrexham.[18]

25. Soon after Mr. Jenkins' appointment to the pastorate, the
Chapel-house (the house provided for the minister), was enlarged
by the addition of another story, and a loft, intended for Mr.
Jenkins' study, was at the same time built above the vestry,
which ran along the north side of the chapel. This loft was
ultimately made to open into the chapel, forming a kind of
gallery, and presenting a very curious appearance.

26. This enlargement of the chapel-house was made in consequence of Mr. Jenkins' marriage which took place not long after
his settlement here.   By his wife, Mary (her surname being probably " Fossey,"[19]) he had several children, of whom I find

---

18. Nearly all the facts above detailed, as to the early history of Dr. Jenkins, have
been gleaned from Mr. Joshua Thomas' *Hanes y Bedyddwyr*.

19. I have seen by the kindness of Mrs. Jenkins, of Huddersfield (the widow of Mr.
Evan Jenkins, one of Dr. Jenkins' grandsons), a letter addressed from Watford, June 15,
1786, to Mr. Joseph Jenkins, junr., of Wrexham (Dr. Jenkins' eldest son), by " his very
affectionate aunt, Rebecca Fossey." Miss Charlotte Fossey appears to have been living
with Dr. Jenkins in 1779.

the following mentioned :—Joseph, born in 1778, died March 7, 1789 ; Mary Fossey, born in 1781, died February 25, 1845, aged 64 ; Fossey, died an infant ; William Fossey, afterwards a draper in Wrexham, and Anna, born December 5, 1786. Mrs. Jenkins died July 6, 1791, aged 35, and was buried in the Dissenters' Graveyard. Mr. Jenkins soon after married again, and had by his second wife at least one child, Sarah Load Jenkins, born June 15, 1793.

27. To the clear and orderly mind of Mr. Jenkins, the precision, interdependence and completeness of the doctrines of Calvinism were very attractive. He was a rigid doctrinarian, clad in impenetrable mail from head to foot. As a disciplinarian also, he was strict, impartial, and inflexible. With all this, he was a thoroughly honest, good, and pious man, as all who knew him could not but acknowledge.

28. Mr. Jenkins published two volumes of sermons, entitled *Discourses on Select Passages of Scripture History*, printed at Shrewsbury, 1779, by Joshua Eddowes. He was the author also of the after-named pamphlets, of which the first two at least were published at Wrexham :—

A Week well Spent ; or Serious Reflections for every day in the Week. 1791. Price 1d.

A Calm Reply to Mr. DeCourcy's Rejoinder on the Subject of Baptism. 1798. Price 9d.

Reflections on the Apology of the Rev. Theophilus Lindsey, being a Defence of the Doctrine of the Trinity against the Objections of that Author. Price 1s.

The Orthodox Dissenting Minister's Reasons against subscribing the Articles of the Church of England. Price 2d.

The Christian's Strength, A Sermon. Price 6d.

A Defence of the Baptists. London, 1795.

A sermon preached by Mr. Jenkins, at Chester, on the occasion of a terrible explosion of gunpowder there, was translated into Welsh by the Rev. Benjamin Evans, of Llanuwchllyn, and printed (1772) by Richard Marsh, of Wrexham, under the following title :—*Pregeth ar y achlysur chwythiad arswydus Powder-gwn yn Ngharlleon Gawr.*

29. Mr. Jenkins' love of order was shown by the business-like footing on which all affairs pertaining to the congregation were placed during his pastorate, and by the care with which its records were henceforth kept.

30. He began immediately to keep a "church-book" preceded by a solemn covenant (see Appendix IV. sec. 1) which all the members of the church were required to sign, and which contains minutes of the church meetings thereafter held. From this church-book I have printed in Appendix IV. a selection of extracts which will give a better notion of the doctrine, discipline, and administration of the church during Mr. Jenkins' pastorate, and of the character of Mr. Jenkins himself, than anything will give that I can myself say.

31. I think Mr. Jenkins must also then have begun to keep a register of the burials conducted by him in the Dissenters' Burial Ground, Rhosddu Road.   If so, however, this register of burials has since been lost, the earliest register belonging to the Baptist congregation that has been preserved not beginning until 1785.[20] The entries in this earliest existing register are remarkably full and precise, and are all, except a few late and discontinuous ones, in Mr. Jenkins' large, clear, and characteristic writing.

32. Mr. Jenkins, during his ministry at the Baptist Chapel, introduced a public ceremony, by which the newly-born children of members of the church and congregation, were not, of course, baptized, but named and dedicated to God.   There are many entries in the register relating to such dedications.   Of these entries, the following may be quoted as a specimen :—" Anna, daughter of Joseph Jenkins, of Wrexham, in the county of Denbigh, and Mary, his wife, was born on Tuesday, the fifth day of December, 1786, at half-an-hour after 12 o'clock at noon, and was dedicated the twenty-fifth day of the same month by the said Joseph Jenkins, Baptist minister in Wrexham."

33. By March, 1778, only three of the trustees of 1758 were still alive :—Messrs. Benjamin Jones, Joseph Jones, and Thomas Jones; and of these, the second-named wished to be relieved of his trust.   By indentures of lease and release, accordingly, dated 3rd and 4th of March of the year named, the residuary trustees conveyed the chapel and chapel-house to John Matthews, weaver,[21] of Wrexham, and William Lloyd, cordwainer,[22] of Wrexham, to be, by them, reconveyed to the aforesaid Benjamin Jones and Thomas Jones, as well as to the Rev. Joseph Jenkins, M.A.; to Joseph Jones, linen-draper, aforetime of Wrexham, but then of the Old Jewry, city of London ; to Daniel Roberts, edge-tool maker,[23] of Wrexham ; to John Mellor, hosier,[24] of Chester ; and to John Hughes, farmer, of Pont Newydd, in the parish of Ruabon. The conditions of trust recited in the indentures of March, 1778, include a stipulation that the trustees and members of the church, society, or congregation of Protestant Dissenters of Wrexham, of which Joseph Jenkins was then minister (or the major part of those members), should " from time to time elect, nominate, and appoint the minister or ministers that should

20. This at any rate was the earliest register shown me at Somerset House; but there is strong evidence of there having been an earlier one belonging to the chapel.

21. John Matthews, of Pen-y-bryn, occupying the premises there belonging to the Buttall family (see ch. iii, note 27). Abraham and Isaac Matthews were his sons. He died February 2nd, 1800, aged 80, and was buried in the Dissenters' Graveyard.

22. William Lloyd, cobbler, custodian of the Burying Ground, died February 22nd 1786, aged 66, and was buried in the Dissenters' Graveyard.

23. Daniel Roberts [see App. iv, 3 (1) (7) and (15)] died August 11, 1792, aged 46, and was buried in the Dissenters' Graveyard.

24. Mr. John Mellor was a plumber as well as a hosier, and was a member of the Church at Wrexham, because there was at that time no Baptist congregation in Chester. He was afterwards, with others, " dismissed " to form a church there [see App. iv., 3 (13)].

statedly officiate and administer the ordinances of religion in the said chapel or Meeting House, *such minister or ministers to be of the Antipædobaptist persuasion.*" Something must be said as to the last clause of this stipulation. Hitherto there had been in none of the trust-deeds pertaining to the congregation even the vaguest definition of any specific doctrine, or set of doctrines, to the teaching of which the church was committed; and though, except in the matter of baptism, the congregation had never varied from the doctrinal standards to which, when it first came into existence, it had adhered, its trust-deeds had been even more " open " than those of the Presbyterian congregation. And here, in the trust-deed of 1778, we find for the first time expressed a reference to doctrine.

34. Mr. Jenkins had not been in Wrexham very long before he became involved in a dispute with the Presbyterians as to the rights which the latter claimed in the Rhosddu Road Burying Ground. The freehold of this ground, there can be no doubt, belonged to the congregation of The Old Meeting. Nevertheless, members of the New Meeting, had for *at least* 40 years been permitted to bury their dead there without the payment of any fees. And in 1746 the Presbyterian minister had begun to keep a regular register of the burials conducted by him in what he called "The Meeting Yard." It is probable, however, that the congregation of the Old Meeting found the fees they received for church folk who were there buried with their relations or ancestors, and from the money yielded by the sale of the grass, after-grass, and trees that grew in it, inadequate to meet the charges of its maintenance. At any rate, they determined in 1774 to demand a fee for every Dissenter, not belonging to the Old Meeting, that was buried in the Rhosddu Road Graveyard, of not less than 2s. or more than 3s. This fee the Presbyterians refused to pay. At the March Assizes of 1779, accordingly, William Lloyd (see note 22) the custodian of the graveyard, acting on behalf of the Old Meeting, levied a fine upon the burying ground, and, no uses being declared of the said fine, conveyed the ground by indentures, bearing date the 3rd and 4th of August, 1779, to the Rev. Joseph Jenkins, John Meller (see note 24), Joseph Jones [mason], and John Hughes [farmer, of Newbridge] as trustees. These trustees were under obligation to allow the minister and male members of the Old Meeting to fix the rates for burial in the Graveyard, and determine who should be buried therein, paying all the emoluments of the said graveyard to the minister of the Old Meeting and his successors.

35. In the trust-deed of 1778 the church of the Old Meeting is *incidentally* described as not merely " Antipædobaptist,' but as " professing the doctrine of co-equal Trinity in Unity, justification by the imputed righteousness of Christ, personal and unconditional election to eternal life, and the final perseverance of the

saints." This was the first attempt made to commit for ever the Old Meeting to a definite scheme of doctrine, all the earlier trust-deeds, except the deed of 1778, being absolutely free and open. For this reason the congregation whose history is now being related, will be called henceforth " the Baptist Congregation," and no more the " Congregation of the Old Meeting."

36. In dealing with the provisions of the trust-deed of the Burying Ground, we have wandered from the dispute as to the right claimed by the Presbyterians to bury therein. The Presbyterians acknowledged that the Baptists of Wrexham owned the Dissenters' Graveyard, but claimed an immemorial right to use it as a burial ground for the members of their congregation, and they still continued to use it. The Baptists locked the Graveyard, but the Presbyterians forced their way into it. Mr. Jenkins, acting on behalf of the trustees under the deed of 1779, finally brought an action for trespass against William Kenrick (see ch. iii., sec. 23.) James Kenrick (see ch. iii., sec. 37 (3), Francis Edwards (see App. I, 99), Richard Humphreys, and John Reese, which came on for trial at the Great Sessions, holden at Wrexham, on Tuesday, the 18th of March, 1788. The pleadings seem to have been lengthy, but ultimately an arrangement was reached by which the claims of the Presbyterians were in effect conceded. Of this arrangement the following is the official record :—"Saturday morning. The jury being empanelled and sworn to try the issue, it is ordered, by and with the consent of the parties, their respective counsel and attorneys, that a juror be withdrawn, and that the present and future members of the Presbyterian Meeting now existing in the town of Wrexham, and the friends, being Presbyterians, of such present and future members, and the relations of such present and future members, whether Presbyterians or not, who at the time of their death shall be part of the families of such present and future members, shall have a right of being buried as heretofore in the Burying Ground in the Pleadings to this cause mentioned, paying to the gravemaker to be from time to time appointed by the members of the [Baptist] Old Meeting, of which the plaintiff is now pastor, 2/- for every man, 1/6 for every woman, and 1/- for every child under the age of ten years, together with the power of setting up tomb-stones. And that the members of such Presbyterian Meeting shall have one key to the said Burying Ground, and shall and may keep a register of their own births and burials as they have hitherto done. That the Old Meeting may appoint a gravedigger from time to time, and that the present and future members of the Old Meeting, or such person as shall be by them appointed, shall be entitled to the pasture, trees, and herbage of the said Burying Ground, with liberty to occupy and enjoy the same as they shall think proper. And that they shall plant such trees as

they shall think fit in the present hedgerows of the said Burying Ground. That the ministers may speak over the graves of their respective friends. That the present and future members of the Old Meeting shall have a general right of burying all persons in the said Burying Ground as heretofore, and that each party shall pay his own respective costs of this suit. That this Agreement shall be made a rule of this Court, and a regular deed or instrument drawn up between the trustees of each meeting at their equal expense and executed by them, and one part of such deed delivered to the members of each Meeting ; such deed or instrument to be approved and settled by Mr. Leycester and Mr. Richards, the Counsel, on behalf of all parties ; and, in case they shall disagree, then by such third person as they shall appoint as an umpire."

37. The fees mentioned in the above-given record as payable by the Presbyterians were really no more than those due to the gravedigger, and included no payment for the graves themselves. It seems to me, however, that the Baptists were justly entitled, by reason of their undoubted ownership of the graveyard, to levy a fee for Presbyterian burials therein, though in view of the long use of the burial ground by the Presbyterians, such fee should have been very small. But the Baptists were, on the other hand, in my opinion, quite wrong in refusing, as, in 1785, they did [see App. IV. sec 3 (16)] any right of burial whatever in the graveyard, to the members of the congregation of Independents newly formed at Pen-y-bryn. The congregation of The Old Meeting was itself originally composed of Independents, who allowed Baptists to have communion with them. While still composed mainly of Independents this congregation acquired the Rhosddu Road Burying Ground, and received the money wherewith the premises in Chester Street were purchased. But, ultimately, the congregation became, in due course of development, wholly Antipœdobaptist, so that when, in 1776, two Independents sought admission to its membership, they were required to sign a declaration [see App. IV. sec. 3 (8)] that they would in no case, and at no time, seek, on a vacancy of the pastorate, to prevent the election of an Antipœdobaptist minister. The Baptists were, by true succession, under an open trust (or rather in the absence of any trust), the legal owners of all the property of the Old Meeting, but the Independents of Pen-y-bryn were *in doctrine* (that is in respect of the point of baptism), more truly the representatives of the founders of that meeting than the Baptists were, and had *in equity*, as good a right as they to be buried there. Ultimately, the right of burial in the Rhosddu Road Graveyard was conceded to all Dissenters and their friends on payment of a burial fee of 5s., in addition to the fees of the gravedigger.

38. In 1780 the Baptist Chapel was enlarged and repaired, and a bapistry formed. To meet the charges involved in these operations, Mr. Jenkins collected the sum of £68 12s.

39. About the year 1790 Mr. Jenkins received from one of the Scotch Universities the degree of D.D.

40. The last entry in the Chapel Register in the hand-writing of Dr. Jenkins occurs under date June 13, 1794. It was therefore about this time that he must have left Wrexham. He went to London where he became, first of all, pastor of a church in Blandford Street. Here, however, he did not stay long, and after a short while accepted the charge of the Baptist congregation at Walworth, where he remained until his death. He died of an attack of apoplexy, February 21, 1819, and was buried in Bunhill Fields. Some of his descendants live now at Huddersfield (see note 29.) There is a portrait of him attached to the two volumes of Dr. Jenkins' *Sermons* published in 1779.

41. When Dr. Jenkins left Wrexham, Mr. ROBERT ROBERTS, a deacon of the church, acted as minister. Mr. Roberts was a weaver, and lived in one of three or four cottages which formerly stood where Leaside, Rhosddu, now is. He became a Sandemanian, and by making " Ramoth Jones " (Rev. J. R. Jones, of Ramoth, Merionethshire) acquainted with the doctrines of Sandemanianism, was the means of introducing those doctrines into North Wales. Under Mr. Roberts' ministry the congregation declined, until at last services ceased to be regularly held. He was still minister in 1799, and received as such at that time a small payment—the balance of the rent of the houses in Chester Street.

42. Somewhere about this time the roof of the cottage on the south side of the chapel fell in; the upper floor was re-built and roofed anew by the Misses Mary and Anna Jenkins (the sisters of Dr. Jenkins), to whom the cottage was thereupon mortgaged. It was found necessary also to spend £50 upon the repair of the Chapel House, and this money was borrowed from Dr. Jenkins.

43. The Baptist cause in Wrexham was now temporarily extinct, and its property charged with debt, but it was presently to be revived, and to become stronger than ever.

44. The occasion of this revival was the settlement within the town of three Baptists from elsewhere. Mr. John Ratcliffe[25]and his wife, from Manchester, and Mr. Richard Price, who afterwards became the minister, from Newtown, Montgomeryshire. Mr. Ratcliffe put himself in communication with the Rev. John Palmer, the Baptist minister of Shrewsbury. who came over to Wrexham several times, and ultimately (Sept. 25, 1805), definitely reconstituted the church, as described in App. IV.

25. I think this must be the Mr. Ratcliffe who was then, according to the rate-books, living next the Town Mill in Pentrefelin; if so, he must have died or left the town by the year 1815.

sec. 4. MR. RICHARD PRICE was shortly afterwards called to the pastorate of the church, and regularly ordained. It was agreed to give him an annual salary of £50, which was afterwards increased to £60. As Mr. Price lodged with Miss Jenkins at the chapel-house, he was probably an unmarried man.

45. Mr. Price resigned the pastorate towards the end of 1809, and was succeeded by a certain MR. THOMAS BARRACLOUGH, who was ordained at the beginning of 1810. There are several references to him in the chapel accounts, given in Appendix IV. One of the houses in Chester Street was fitted up to accommodate him. He lived scarcely eighteen months after coming to Wrexham, dying June 28, 1811, aged 71 years. He was buried in the Rhosddu Road Graveyard, where he is described on his gravestone as " a sincere minister of Jesus Christ."

46. And now, after a long interval, the REV. GEORGE SAYCE became minister of the chapel. He was certainly settled here as such in 1819, and probably in the year before, if not as early as 1817. Mr. Sayce was born at Bishop's Castle, in the county of Salop, September 8, 1793. He was a tall, stout, well-proportioned man. He had been a tallow chandler at Shrewsbury, and worked somewhat at his business after he came to Wrexham, eking out thus an income which was at first very small. Spite of the necessity thus put upon him—a necessity which, while it lasted, he nobly and frankly met—he managed to find time for ministerial labours which, looking now at their mere amount, were nothing less than amazing. And he was a successful as well as a laborious minister. The congregation, hitherto very small, increased until the chapel was filled : the Sunday School became a flourishing institution, and the debts that had hitherto been so heavy a burden upon the trustees were nearly all paid off   But the duties connected with his own congregation, large as was Mr. Sayce's conception of those duties, were not enough to satisfy his hunger for work. He sought out and availed himself of every opportunity which presented itself for rooting his denomination in the villages around, preaching in cottages, barns, and in the open-air, the common people everywhere hearing him gladly. And it was to his labours mainly that the Baptist churches at Holt, Wheatsheaf, and Bowling Bank owe their origin.

47. Soon after Mr. Sayce became minister a portion of the Chapel-house (formerly Dr. Jenkins' study) was taken into the chapel, so as to form a schoolroom, the upper floor being already used as a gallery, and these two floors still exist, having been preserved when, in 1875, the chapel was rebuilt.

48. In 1820, all but one of the original trustess being dead, a new trust was incorporated. The following are the names of the trustees of 1820 :—Joseph Jones, formerly of Wrexham. linendraper, but then of Cleaver Street, [London ?], gentleman ; Isaac

I

Matthews [linen] weaver;[25a] Joseph Griffiths, grocer;[26] George Sayce, tallow chandler [the minister]; Richard Sudlow, grocer;[27] Evan Morris, skinner;[28] John Price, glazier; and William Fossey Jenkins, draper,[29] all of Wrexham; John Walley, farmer, of Carwarden, Cheshire (see note 16); Benjamin Jones Griffiths, draper, of Oswestry;[30] and Thomas Sudlow, hatter, of Liverpool.[31]

49. Mr. Sayce married in 1836, at the parish church, Oswestry, Anna, daughter of Mr. Richard Griffiths, of that town, and sister of two of the trustees above-named. He had one son, Benjamin Jones Sayce, now of Liverpool, whose name is associated with the first practical application, in 1864, of the "collodio-bromide of silver process" on which modern photography is founded.

50. Although Mr. Sayce was naturally a strong man, he died comparatively young, and suffered much from ill-health (palpitation of the heart and acute dyspepsia) during the latter part of his life. This was due in part to the excessive labours he had undergone, and in part to the unfavourable conditions under which those labours were often executed. Towards the end of the year 1845, feeling himself no longer equal to the full work of the ministry, he was compelled, to the great grief of his congregation, to resign his charge, and, leaving the Chapel-house, where he had hitherto lived, went to reside in King Street. Here, February 20th, 1847, he died, aged 52, and was buried in the Rhosddu Road Graveyard. His widow did not long survive him, dying December 19th, 1849, aged 50, and was buried with her husband.

51. After Mr. Sayce's resignation, Mr. Joseph Pike, son of the author of "*Persuasives to Early Piety*" (a book formerly to be

25a. Isaac Matthews, son of John Matthews (see note 21), and at that time living in the same place; afterwards custodian of the Rhosddu Road Graveyard, where he was buried, January, 1848.

26. Joseph Jones Griffiths, of Hope Street, where he occupied the house and shop that Mr. Charles Davies, tailor, now has; afterwards of King Street: a son of Mr. Richard Griffiths, shoemaker, of Oswestry; for many years a deacon of the Baptist Church, Wrexham; was thrice married; died November 5, 1869, in his 83rd year, and was buried in the Dissenters' Graveyard.

27. Richard Sudlow, assistant to his brother, Mr. J. B. Sudlow, grocer, of Town Hill died July 7, 1866, aged 75; buried in Rhosddu Road Graveyard.

28. Evan Morris, predecessor of Messrs. Jones and Rocke (now J. Meredith-Jones, and Sons), and uncle of Evan Morris, Esq., the present Mayor of Wrexham.

29. Wm. Fossey Jenkins, a son of the Rev. Dr. Jenkins, at this time a draper at corner of Church and High Streets, afterwards a wool merchant of Chester Street: his son Evan (born February 2, 1806), afterwards settled in Huddersfield: one of his daughters was the first wife of Mr. Wm. Bayley, bookseller, of Wrexham. Mr. W. F. Jenkins was buried in the Rhosddu Road Graveyard.

30. Benjamin Jones Griffiths, brother of the Mr. Joseph Jones Griffiths, mentioned in note 26, and of Mrs. Sayce; "for many years an honoured deacon in the Bootle and Wrexham Churches": died at Wrexham November 24, 1871, aged 85, and was buried in the Rhosddu Road Graveyard.

31. Thomas Sudlow, son of Mr. Joseph Sudlow, of Underhill, near Oswestry, brother of the Messrs. Rd. and J. B. Sudlow, mentioned in note 27, and of Mr. William Sudlow, confectioner, of Hope Street, Wrexham, who was the father of the present Mr. John Sudlow, draper, also of Hope Street.

found in almost every Evangelical library), supplied for several months, but, ultimately, the Rev. Joseph Clare was elected minister.

52. Of Mr. Sayce's successors I will content myself with giving an annotated list :—

1846-1853. JOSEPH CLARE.[31a]
1854. THOMAS BROOKS [Removed to Wallingford].
1856-1857. ENOCH GRIFFITHS.[32]
1858. ABRAHAM ASHWORTH [Removed to Bramley, Yorks., where he died, Aug. 27th, 1854, aged 54].
1861-1865. JOHN LYON.[33]
1865. Supply by ISAAC THOMAS WILLIAMS [from South Wales.]
1866. FREDERICK PERKINS [from Farringdon, removed to Keysoe, Beds].
1870. JOHN B. BRASTED [removed to London].
1874. SAMUEL DAVID THOMAS [from Monmouth, removed to King's Lynn].
1879-1886. DAVID RHYS JENKINS.[34]

53. The existing chapel and schoolrooms were built in 1875, at a cost of £2,200, being set symmetrically upon the site obtained by pulling down the old chapel and the two houses south of it.

31a. Joseph Clare, removed to Perth; died June 13, 1860, aged 43, at Durdham Down, near Bristol, and was buried in the Arno's Vale Cemetery, Clifton. He had a son, the Rev. Wm. Clare, of New South Wales, who was also a Baptist minister.

32. Mr. Enoch Griffiths was a man of singular mental force: he died December 7, 1757, aged 45, and was buried in the Dissenters' Graveyard. "He was a faithful labourer and earnest servant, and was suddenly called to his rest."

33. Mr. Lyon married while in Wrexham Miss Sibree, a daughter of a Congregational minister in Birmingham: after leaving Wrexham he qualified as a surgeon, and devoted himself to the service of the Liverpool Medical Mission: he died at Birkenhead in the year 1881.

34. Mr. Jenkins came from Salford, and on leaving Wrexham became minister of East Street Baptist Church, Southampton. While in this town he published a volume entitled "The Eternal Life, and other Sermons."

CHAPTER V

History of the Pen-y-bryn Congregation (Independent).

1. Although, strictly speaking, the Pen-y-bryn congregation does not belong to "The Older Nonconformity of Wrexham," there is a sense in which it may be regarded as an offshoot from the latter. The congregation of the Old Meeting, though it remained Calvinistic and orthodox, and retained in other respects the old Puritan temper, had become exclusively Antipædobaptist. The congregation of the New Meeting, on the other hand, though it recognised the baptism of children and had adopted the Independent form of church government, had become Arminian and Latitudinarian. The want of an Independent congregation of the ordinary type was, therefore, felt by many. Accordingly, in 1783, or a little before, several persons agreed to found such a congregation. Some of these had belonged to one or other of the two older meetings, and others had been, it is not improbable, "awakened" under the preaching of the Methodists. They are said to have met in an old pin factory close to the site of the present chapel. A confession of faith and a church covenant were drawn up. The former, strictly orthodox and Calvinistic, is most minute in its definitions; the latter is touching in respect of the high obligations to which it bound those who set their hands to it. On the 1st of March, 1783, twenty-one persons signed the covenant, and signified their adherence to the aforesaid confession of faith by lifting up their hands, and were thereupon duly recognized as a church by the Rev. Edward Williams, D.D., of Oswestry, and the Rev. William Armitage (see Appendix, note 83), of Chester. The following are the names of the 21 signators:—William Ellis;[1] Frederick Jessamin [see Appendix I. 121]; John Jones, flaxdresser;[2] Michael Williams; James Jones; John Jones; Abraham Matthews [son of John Matthews, weaver, see ch. IV., note 21]; John Griffiths; Robert Jones [Mount Street, died March 9, 1834]; Thomas Wilcoxon; Thomas Jones; Joseph Harvey; William Jones [of Pen-y-bryn: died at Flint, January 5,

---

1. William Ellis, watchmaker, lived on south side of Church Street, in the corner house next the churchyard; he was afterwards deacon of the church; died April 8, 1827, aged 80, and was buried in the Dissenters' Graveyard.

2. John Jones, flaxdresser, of Town Hill, occupying the house and shop now numbered 3; in 1799 or a little before he removed to Wilderness Row, Goswell Road, London, where he carried on business as a broker. He will be mentioned again (see sec. 17.)

1823]; Mary Bellis; Ann Williams; Hannah Jones; Mary Owens; Esther Wilcoxon [afterwards Mrs. Jessamin]; Hannah Matthews [daughter of John Matthews, weaver, see ch. IV., note 21]; Richard Bickerton [see Appendix I., 127]; and Hannah Wilcoxon. Three of these 21 afterwards experienced the rigour of the discipline exercised in the new church, and were expelled from its communion.

2. Before the church was formally incorporated an invitation was addressed to Mr. Jenkin Lewis, assistant tutor at the Independent Academy, Oswestry, to become the pastor of it. Mr. Lewis came a year on trial, and was then duly elected and ordained. I learn from the *Hanes Eglwysi Annibynol* that he was born August 12, 1760, at Brithdir Uchaf, in the parish of Gelligaer, Glamorganshire, and was the eldest son of Malachi and Cecilia Lewis, who were members at the old chapel, Cefn-coed-y-cymmer, Merthyr. A broad and liberal education given to him as a boy was supplemented by five years' study at the Independent Academy, Abergavenny. When Dr. Benjamin Davies, the tutor, resigned, the Academy was removed to Oswestry, so as to be under the charge of Dr. Edward Williams. Hither Mr. Lewis, who now became assistant tutor, followed it in June, 1782, and hence, in December of the next year, he removed to become minister of the new Independent congregation at Wrexham. Mr. Lewis is said to have been a man in whom much dignity and sweetness of manner were united with a clear and strict piety and genuine learning.

3. The grant of £5 a year from the Independent Fund was transferred to the Pen-y-bryn congregation, soon after its formation, from the Baptist congregation which for fifty years before had enjoyed it. It is exceedingly likely, the congregation being small and poor, that Mr. Lewis's salary, as minister, was for a long time merely nominal.

4. In 1788 a site for a chapel was secured. On November 3 of that year Mr. William Edwards, tanner, of The Palis,[3] and his eldest son Mr. Thomas Edwards, tanner, of the same, conveyed to Mr. John Jones, flaxdresser (see note 2) for a nominal sum (10 shillings), but under a perpetual yearly rent of £3, payable to them, their heirs and assigns, two pieces of land, a part of the Palis property, of which the first piece had a frontage to Stryt Draw, and the second piece adjoined the first. These pieces of land are thus described in the indentures of feoffment :—

---

3. The Palis property extended from the top of Stryt Draw (now Chapel Street), round into Bridge Street, almost to the bottom of the hill and backwards to the brook. The house upon it is represented by that now occupied by Dr. R. J. Evans. In later times it came to be called, by a mis-spelling of its name, "The Palace," and thus the before-mentioned Mr. Thomas Edwards, who was a wealthy man, got to be commonly called "The King," as his brother John was called "The Duke." "Palis," however, is an adopted Welsh word, and means simply a place enclosed with *pales.*

" All that plott, piece, and parcel of ground (part of a field, close, or parcel of land of them the said William Edwards and Thomas Edwards) situate, lying, and being in Pen-y-bryn in the township of Wrexham Abbot. . . . . . containing by admeasurment 21 yards in length to the front of a street or lane called Street Draw, and in depth, from the said street or lane backwards, 16 yards, and which said plott, piece, or parcel of ground adjoins a dwelling-house in the holding of John Taylor. And also all that other plott, piece, or parcel of ground adjoining to the last mentioned, extending from the lower side of a hovel in a yard or backside in the holding of Evan Lloyd to the said last mentioned plott of ground in a direct line, and containing in breadth 20 feet or thereabouts, and in length 7 yards for thereabouts."

5. On the ground thus secured the existing chapel was built, together with a vestry and a house ("The Chapel-house") for the minister's use. I have been quite unable to gather any particulars as to the cost of these operations, or as to the way in which that cost was met.

6. Among the 46 members subsequently admitted by Mr. Lewis were John Barton (admitted October 3, 1784, died April 9, 1820), of Madeira Hill, who, though a poor man, exercised by virtue of his piety considerable influence in the congregation ; Gwen Matthews (admitted March 6, 1786), wife of Mr. John Mattews, weaver (see ch. IV., note 21) ; Richard Browne (admitted November 5, 1790);[4] Samuel Garner (admitted November 1, 1795);[5] Hannah Garner (wife of last-named, admitted same time); Jane Browne (wife of Mr. Richard Browne, admitted March 4, 1796) ;[4] Alexander Wylde Thornley (admitted October 5, 1798) ;[6] and Ann Thornley (first wife of last-named.)

7. In 1791, Dr. Edward Williams resigned the tutorship of the Independent Academy, and Mr. Jenkin Lewis was appointed his successor. The Academy was, therefore, removed from Oswestry to Wrexham, where it remained for 21 years. The students had private lodgings in the town, and received instruction, I suppose,

4. Mr. Richard Browne was a solicitor who lived for more than 20 years in the house in Pen-y-bryn, which Mr. Caldicott, smith, now occupies, but about the year 1808 built Pen-y-bryn House in Stryt Draw, where he resided until the time of his death, becoming possessed ultimately of considerable property. He married, first (May 9, 1793) Miss Jane Jones, of the parish of Wrexham, by whom he had many children of whom several died young, but three reached maturity—Richard, who died in 1823, at the age of 26 ; John, who married and had issue ; and Jane, who became the wife of the late Mr. Charles Bowen Teece, solicitor, of Shrewsbury. He married, secondly (November 19, 1822) Miss Ann Edgworth, only daughter of John Edgworth, Esq., of Bryn-y-grog,|in the parish of Marchwiel, and aunt of Thomas Edgworth, Esq., the first Mayor of Wrexham. He died March 8, 1826, aged 71, and was buried in the Dissenters' Graveyard.

5. Samuel Garner, farmer, of Felin Broughton, and Coed Efa: belonged at first to the Baptist congregation, and was in 1812-3 one of the churchwardens of the parish. Garner's Hill takes its name from him. He died May 8, 1827, aged 77.

6. Mr. A. W. Thornley was a well-to-do hatter, who occupied three quaint old gabled shops next the Town Hall on the site of Nos. 1 and 2, Hope Street. His first wife died in 1826, and he subsequently (May 17, 1833) married Miss Mary Ann Levingstone, sister of Mr. Moses Levingstone (see note 10.) When the old Brookside Tannery, formerly the property of Mr. Edward Evans (see Appendix, note 47) was offered for sale, Mr. Thornley bought it, and so gave his name to what is now called "Thornley Square," while "Mary Ann Square" commemorates the name of his wife. A large portion of the land belonging to the tannery was presented by Mr. Thornley as a site for the British Schools, erected in 1844, to the building fund of which his wife contributed £100. He died, March 17, 1854, aged nearly 84, and was buried in the Dissenters' Graveyard. He was succeeded in his business by his son, Mr. Robert Thornley, who ultimately sold it to the late Mr. Edward Jones and now lives in Birkenhead.

in the chapel. Of these the following may be mentioned :—
William Williams, afterwards of the Wern, eloquent and beloved;
John Roberts, for many years of Llanbrynmair ; Thomas Powell,
author of various religious and doctrinal works, and the translator
of Calvin on the Psalms; Robert Everett, afterwards so well
known in the United States as " Dr. Everett " ; and Michael
Jones, late Principal of one of the Independent Colleges of Bala.
Some of the students of the Academy started the Welsh churches
at the Wern and Harwood (now Brymbo) within the old parish
of Wrexham, as well as other churches, now large and flourishing,
beyond the parish bounds.

8. Mr. Jenkin Lewis married, firstly, April 24, 1787, Miss
Jane Jones, daughter of John Jones, gentleman, of Coed-
y-glyn, Wrexham, who died March 15, 1802, aged 56, and was
buried in the Dissenters' Graveyard. He married, secondly, the
widow of the Rev. Wm. Armitage (see App., note 83) of Chester.
He had no children.

9. Mr. Lewis was the author of a pamphlet, of which the
following is the title :—"*Natural Evil from God : being the
Substance of a Discourse delivered at Pen-y-bryn Meeting House in
Wrexham, on the General Fast day, April 19, 1793, by Jenkin Lewis.
Wrexham : Printed by J. Marsh, 1793.*"

10. Although Mr. Lewis was a singularly able man and much
beloved by his people, he was not a popular preacher, and the
congregation never under his ministry became a large one. This
want of success, or apparent want of success, at last troubled him
very much, so that when, towards the end of 1811, the presidency
of an academy intended to be established in Manchester was
offered to him, he eagerly caught at it. This academy turned out
a failure, and Mr. Lewis then became the minister of Hope Chapel,
Casnewydd, Monmouthshire, where he remained until the end of
his life. He died August 11, 1831, aged 71, and was buried in the
graveyard of the old Heol-y-felin Chapel. About six months
before his death, he received the degree of D.D. from one of the
American Universities, but never used it. (*Hanes Eglwysi
Annibynol*).

11. When Mr. Jenkin Lewis left Wrexham, the Independent
Board offered the tutorship of the Academy to the REV. GEORGE
LEWIS, D.D., of Llanuwchllyn, the members of the Pen-y-bryn
church inviting him at the same time to become their minister.
Both offers were accepted. Of the history of a man so well
known as Dr. Lewis, little need be said here. The apprehensions which his avowed Republicanism excited had long since
been quieted by his manifest attainments as a theologian. And
his reputation was now considerable. Already, his *Drych
Athrawiaethol* (" Doctrinal Mirror "), a work on systematic
theology, had appeared, and he was now engaged on his

Esboniad ar y Testament Newydd ("Exposition of the New Testament") which ultimately appeared in seven volumes.

12. Mr. George Lewis, a son of Dr. Lewis, who for many years was a surgeon in Wrexham, married Miss Martha Kenrick, of Wynne Hall [see ch. III., sec. 64 (4)]. He lived in a large house in Hope Street, which formerly stood between the Rainbow and the National Provincial Bank.

13. Dr. Lewis only remained three years (1812-1815) in Wrexham, during which time he admitted only twelve members, a fact which seems to show that he was scarcely more successful than his predecessor in giving to the Pen-y-bryn congregation that enlargement which was desired.

14. In 1815, Dr. Lewis accepted a call from the Congregational Church at Llanfyllin, and was permitted by the Independent Board to remove the Academy thither.[7] While the Academy was at Llanfyllin, a young man—Edward Davies – from the little church of Harwood (now Brymbo) in the parish of Wrexham, joined it as a student, who, when the Academy was again removed to Newtown, became theological tutor in it, and afterwards married Dr. Lewis's daughter. When the Academy underwent its final removal and became the Brecon Independent College, Mr. Davies was appointed classical tutor in it, and so continued until 1854. His father—also named Edward Davies —was a native of Minera, and lies buried in the Dissenters' Graveyard, Wrexham, where his tomb may still be seen.

15. Dr. Lewis was succeeded at Pen-y-bryn Chapel by the Rev. GEORGE WEIDEMANN, who only remained from March 1, 1816, to July 3, 1818. He admitted seven members, one of whom was John Clarke, a young man who afterwards became an evangelist in the employment of the Home Missionary Society. The congregation must at this time have increased at a greater rate than the Church, for it was in Mr. Weidemann's time that the gallery, taken down in 1881, was erected.

16. The fourth pastor was Mr. SAMUEL BELL, who came as a candidate, April, 1818, was called in July following, and was ordained in November, 1819. He found 46 members, and admitted 32. Among these was John Harrison, son of John Harrison, glazier (see *Hist. Par. Ch. of Wrexham*, page 109, note 280 f) and afterwards of Plas Coch. In June, 1823, Mr. Bell resigned the pastorate and went to Lancaster, and an interval of four years then followed, during which there was no regular minister.

17. Hitherto no trustees had been appointed, and the chapel, its site, and all the property pertaining to it, still stood in the name of Mr. John Jones, who for more than a quarter of a century had lived in London. On the 11th of February, 1826,

7. Dr. Lewis died at Newtown, June 5, 1822.

however, Mr. Jones conveyed the whole property to trustees, and a formal trust deed was executed. The trustees were Alexander Wylde Thornley, hatter ;[6] Richard Browne, gentleman ;[4] John Wilcock, gentleman ;[8] William Simmons, plumber and glazier (see ch. III., note 47); William Woods, cabinet maker ; John Harrison, yeoman (see sec. 16); Hugh Davies, grocer; and John Smith, watchmaker ;[9] all of Wrexham ; and Peter Jarvis, nailor, of Felin Buleston. The trustees engaged that they would " from time to time and at all times thereafter permit and suffer the said chapel or meeting-house to be solely used for religious worship by Protestant Dissenters of the Independent persuasion," and that they should " permit and suffer such minister or ministers to officiate and administer the ordinances of religion in the said chapel or meeting house as should be of the Independent per-suasion respecting church government," and as "should hold, pro-fess, preach, and embrace the truths contained in the Westminster Confession of Faith, and in the larger and lesser catechism con-tained therein," and also the doctrinal articles of the Church of England in the plain, literal, and grammatical sense thereof," such ministers being "duly elected by the majority of the church or society holding the doctrines aforesaid, such majority of the church, consistent with the Independent form of church govern-ment, always to have the power to remove the minister and to appoint another in his room and stead." The next body of trustees was not appointed until 1873. and the above-quoted stipulations as to the Westminster Confession, the larger and lesser catechism, and the doctrinal articles of the Church of England were, I believe, not then repeated.

18. After Mr. Bell left in 1823 there was no regular pastor, but at last Mr. WILLIAM WATERFIELD, who came on trial in January, 1827, was invited to remain, and was ordained on May 7th of the same year. He found 42 members, and admitted 68. Among the 68 were Moses Levingstone,[10] admitted June 5, 1829; Mary Ann Levingstone (sister of last named, admitted same time, after-wards second wife of Mr. Alex. W. Thornley); Mary Garner (daughter of Mr. Samuel Garner, of Broughton, afterwards wife of Mr. Robert Jones, of Glan-yr-afon) ; John Rogers[11] (ad-

8. Mr. Wilcock lived in his own house on the east side of York Street, next below " The Hop Pole " (now " The Black Horse "). He had been a flaxdresser, and was brother to Mr. Thomas Wilcock, of Plas Noble, in the parish of Marchwiel. He married his second wife (who afterwards married the Rev. Aaron Francis) when he was more than 80 years of age. Died October 26, 1850, aged 88, and was buried in the churchyard.

9. John Smith lived at this time, as his father before him, in a house next the Wynn-stay Arms, now incorporated with it: afterwards retired from business and lived in Salusbury Park : he was a deacon here : died February 23, 1868.

10. Mr. Moses Levingstone was Adjutant of the East Denbighshire Militia, and was engaged in the suppression of the Irish Rebellion : he died November 30, 1787, and was buried in the old cemetery, " having served his king and country for the space of 46 years."

11. This John Rogers was afterwards the well-known Congregational minister of that name, who, after many years' successful labours at Lowestoft and Rendham (Suffolk), in

mitted September 3, 1830); John Smith (see note 9, admitted
December 31, 1831); Mary Smith 'wife of last named, admitted
same time) ; John Houghland (joiner, of Plas Gwern) ; Thomas
Matthews[12] (admitted May 3, 1833) ; Ann Matthews (admitted
and removed same time as last) ; and Martha Lewis (admitted
December 2, 1831, wife of Mr. George Lewis, see sec. 12).

19. Mr. Waterfield resigned in August, 1837, leaving 61 mem-
bers. He was followed by MR. RICHARD BROWN, who came as
candidate May 20, 1838, and was ordained December 26, in the
same year. In his time were added 60 members to the church.
Among these were :—Robert and Sarah Thornley, of Fairfield
House (see note 6) ; John Davies, Street-yr-hwch ; Thomas and
Eliza Davies, Old Sontley ; Eliza and Hannah Rawson,
Pickhill Hall[13] (admitted February 1, 1839) ; Samuel Jones,
Glan-yr-afon (admitted May 31, 1839 ; died January 30, 1845) ;
Michael and Sarah Gummow, Wrexham Fechan[14] (admitted
August 30, 1839), and Sarah Hilditch.

In accordance with the plan to which I have always, as far as
possible adhered, of dealing but lightly with the events of the
last fifty years, it must now suffice to give the following
annotated list of the ministers who succeeded Mr. Richard
Brown :—

    1843-1846. JAMES ADAMS.[15]
    1846-1852. AARON FRANCIS.[16]
    1853-1855. JOHN CLARKE.[17]
    1855-1860. JOHN G. SHORT.[18]
    1860-1864. J. HARVEY PICKERSGILL [came hither from
       Marsden, Yorks.].

London, and at Bridport, died at the last named place, June 24, 1871, in his 56th year. As
his " Memoirs " have been written by Dr. A. Moreton Brown, it is unnecessary for me to
give here any particulars of his life. Dr. Brown, however, has omitted to give the names
of his parents. John Rogers was, I find, the son of William and Hannah Rogers : his
father was a smith and lived in Pentrefelin, and the child was baptized November 15, 1815
at the Parish Church of Wrexham.

    12. Thomas Matthews, of Hope Street, afterwards a deacon, dismissed April 1
1846, to Newington Church, Liverpool.

    13. These ladies were, I believe, daughters of Geo. Rawson, Esq., a retired Yorkshire
manufacturer, who for some time lived at Pickhill Hall, and who was himself a member at
the Baptist Chapel, and now and again preached there. They had formerly been members
at Salem Chapel, Leeds, and afterwards removed to Leamington.

    14. Mr. Michael Gummow was a builder, the grandfather of the present Messrs. W.
H. and M. J. Gummow, of Wrexham : died May 21, 1876, aged 74, and was buried in the
Dissenters' Graveyard.

    15. Mr. Adams, on leaving Wrexham, became a member of the Free Church of
Scotland.

    16. Mr. Aaron Francis came from Ruthin, where he had been minister of the Welsh
Congregational Chapel : married the widow of Mr. John Wilcock, of Wrexham (see
note 8), and became afterwards the minister of the English Congregational Church at Rhyl,
where he died Dec. 12, 1882, aged 70.

    17. During Mr. Clarke's time the salary was £100 a year and the chapel house free.

    18. Mr. Short came hither from Plunkett Street, Dublin, and was here very successful ;
the chapel during the latter part of his ministry was always crowded, and he was exceedingly popular among the working men. He removed, in 1860, to Spring Head, near Manchester. He died at Omagh July 27, 1866, in the 42nd year of his age. "Mr. Short was a
man of a clear head and a warm heart."

1864-1865. WILLIAM EDWARDS [afterwards of Kilsby].
Interval.
1868-1873. THOS. FRANCIS NATHAN.
1876-1885. WILLIAM TILLER [previously minister of English
Congregational Church, Ruabon].
1886.　　 WILLIAM OLIVER, M.A.[19]

In the year 1881, Mr. Tiller being then minister, the chapel was repaired throughout, the gallery removed, the old seats replaced by new, a porch added, an apse formed in which a rostrum, taking the place of the old two-decker, was set, and a large school built at the back, on the site of a cottage which was purchased and pulled down, and of the old schoolroom, which was very small. Nearly £700 were expended in making these alterations.

19. Mr. Oliver was educated at New College, London, and at the University of Glasgow; was, from 1872, for ten years Classical Professor at the Congregational College, Brecon, and from November, 1863, to April, 1886, kept a private Grammar School at Holywell.

CHAPTER VI

History of The Friends' Meetings at Wrexham and Rhuddallt.

1. The circumstances under which the principles of the Society of Friends first obtained a footing within the district of which Wrexham is the centre have been duly set forth by George Fox himself, the founder of the Society. In his published Journal, under date 1654, we find the following entry :—

"While Friends abode in the Northern parts a priest of Wrexham, in Wales, whose name was Morgan Floyd [Lloyd], having heard reports of us, sent two of his congregation into the North to inquire concerning us, to try us, and bring him an account of us. But when these triers came down amongst us, the power of the Lord overcame them, and they were both of them convinced of the truth. So they stayed some time with us, and then returned into Wales, where afterwards one of them departed from his convincement, but the other, whose name was John ap John, abode in the truth, and received a part in the ministry in which he continued faithful."

2. In the history of the Welsh " Friends," the John ap John mentioned by George Fox takes an important place, and it becomes therefore necessary to ask who he was and where he lived. To these questions, however, the records of the Society supply no clear answer. Richard Davies, of Cloddiau Cochion, near Welshpool, his fellow-labourer, mentions John ap John several times, but merely speaks of him as living " near Wrexham, in Denbighshire," and says nothing as to his rank or calling. George Fox also, who mentions him again and again, never tells us where he lived, though he describes him as having been at first a member of Morgan Lloyd's congregation at Wrexham. The difficulty of identifying him is much increased by the fact that the name he bore was at that time a very common one. Nevertheless, it may now be regarded as absolutely established that this John ap John lived in the township of Trevor, in the parish of Llangollen, and within a short distance of Ruabon.[1] And with this conclusion certainly agrees the fact that Ruabon rather than Wrexham was at first the head-quarters of the Society of Friends in this district.

3. George Fox tells us in his journal that in 1657 he came from Bristol into Wales, visiting first " The Slone," then Cardiff, Swansea, and finally Brecon, where were Thomas Holmes and

---

1. Can he have been the John ap John ap William, a freeholder of Trevor, who married Catherine, one of the daughters of John Trevor Esq., of Trevor Hall and Valle Crucis Abbey?

John ap John. The latter spake in the streets. Afterwards in the same year, George Fox and John ap John passed again into Wales through Montgomeryshire and Radnorshire to Leominster, thence travelling to Tenby, Pembroke, Haverfordwest, Pembroke, Dolgelly, Carnarvon, and Beaumaris, the last-named being "a town wherein John ap John had formerly been preacher." After crossing the Menai Straits, they set forward on horseback "and about five in the morning," says George Fox, "got to a place within six miles of Wrexham [probably the house of John ap John] where that day we met with many friends, and had a glorious meeting, and the Lord's everlasting power and truth was over all, and a meeting is continued there to this day. Next day we passed thence into Flintshire, sounding the day of the Lord through the towns, and came into Wrexham at night. Here many of Floyd's people came to us, but very rude, wild, and airy they were, and little sense of truth they had ; yet some were convinced in that town. Next morning one called a lady sent for me, who kept a preacher in her house. I went, but found both her and her preacher very light and airy, too light to receive the weighty things of God. In her lightness she came and asked me if she should cut my hair ; but I was moved to reprove her, and bid her cut down the corruptions in herself with the sword of the Spirit of God. So, after I had admonished her to be more grave and sober, we passed away ; and afterwards in her frothy mind she made her boast that she came behind me and cut off the curl of my hair. But she spoke falsely." From Wrexham George Fox went on to Chester.

4. We have seen that, according to George Fox, some were " convinced " in Wrexham on the occasion of his visit in 1657 to that town, and soon after this date we begin to meet with the names of various "Friends" resident in Wrexham. Richard Davies, of Cloddiau Cochion, speaks of a letter dated " Wrexham, 9th of 1st month, 1662," left with him by James Parkes, who had recently come out of the North, entitled "A Lamentation and Warning unto all the Professors in North Wales, especially those about Wrexham, in Denbighshire, and Welshpool, in Montgomeryshire whom formerly I have walked with in a Fellowship and Worship, till the Lord awakened me out of sleep," etc.

4b. At the Quarter Sessions, held at Wrexham in October, 1663, it was intimated that several Quakers were already in prison, and the Grand Jury presented the names of other inhabitants of Wrexham as " Quakers," and " for not coming to church." The following are the names presented :—Brian Sixsmith, William Lewis, and John ap Edward. Of these, John ap Edward was a butcher, and this is all I know of him. Brian Sixsmith was a draper in High Street, next the Golden Lion, whose Quakerism had already got him into trouble. In the Quarter Sessions, held at Ruthin in the January before, the oath of allegiance being in open court tendered to him, he had then refused to take the same, but had begged for time to consider the matter, which request was granted. His name soon after disappears from the rate books. William Lewis was a corvisor, whose house and shop were at the foot of Town Hill, where No. 12, Mr. Williams' shop, now is. He issued a token, which has been thus described by Mr. Jas. W. Lloyd:—*Ob.* William Lewis, 1666. The Cordwainers' Arms, W.A.L. *Re.* In Wrixham. His Half-Peny,½. "W.A.L." stands for William and Ann Lewis, Ann being the name of his wife, who was also presented by the churchwardens for not going to church.

4c. One of the staunchest members of the Society of Friends in the town of Wrexham at a later date was John James (see sec 18), and I suppose it was this same John James, together with John Meredith, both of Wrexham, who, at the General Sessions, held at Ruthin, July 14, 1668, were fined for being present at "several conventicles," the first £2, and the second £5, or in defanlt, to be sent for three months to "the Comin Goale."

5. Besides these, the after-named, living in the neighbourhood of Ruabon, were also presented by the Grand Jury in October, 1663, as "Quakers":—John ap John, of Trevor; Catherine Edwards, of Trevor; Roger ap Shone, of Pen-y clawdd; and Thomas ap Hugh, of Chirk. John ap John is now very well known to us. Of the two last-named nothing can or need be said, but of Catherine Edwards, otherwise called Catherine ferch Edward, I must not omit to give here some account. She was one of the four daughters and co-heiresses of Edward ap Randal, gentleman, of Rhuddallt Isaf, the latter being a small estate of about 85 acres in the parish of Ruabon.[2] Her father came of a noble line, being descended from Llewelyn Eurdorchog, Lord of Iâl (Yale). She was the wife of David ap Edward, of Trevor, and having purchased the rights of her sisters in her father's estate, was able to bestow it upon her only son, Richard, who, from his father's Christian name, assumed the surname of Davies. Catherine ferch Edward was probably one of the first converts of John ap John, and her son, Richard Davies, gentleman, of Rhuddallt Isaf, one of the most influential of the early supporters of Quakerism in this district. A meeting began to be held at Rhuddallt which was continued in the lifetime of his son and successor, and was still in existence in 1724. Mr. Richard Davies married Anne, daughter of John Barnes, of Warrington, and was living, as we shall hereafter see, in the year 1708. He

2. Nearly the whole of the hamlet of Rhuddallt, which contained, besides Rhuddallt Isaf, several small freehold estates, has long been included within Wynnstay Park. Most of its ancient names and landmarks have thus been obliterated, and I have therefore found it quite impossible to ascertain where the house of Mr. Davies stood. James' Farm within the Park and Plas Newydd outside it, both belong to the now almost forgotten hamlet of Rhuddallt.

had two sons, Edward Davies, his successor, who was living in 1723, and John Davies, of whom I can learn nothing.

6. In the year 1670, John Robinson, Esq., of Upper Gwersyllt, laid an information against various persons present "at a seditious conventicle" (that is, a meeting for worship) held on the 12th of June of that year at the house of John ap John, of Trevor. These persons were fined in all £20 15s., a very large sum in those days, two-thirds of which sum were paid to Mr. Robinson as informer, the remaining third going to the king. That a Justice of the Peace and man of honour should not merely have harried these harmless folk, but have taken in doing so the reward of an informer, may well awaken our surprise.

7. The year before John ap John and his fellow-worshippers were thus plundered, the former made, together with Richard Davies, of Cloddiau Cochion, an evangelistic tour in South Wales. Of this tour Richard Davies, in his *Autobiography* has left us an account, a part of which account may suitably be here quoted: —" About the year 1669, my ancient, well-beloved, and dear companion, John ap John, and I took our journey for South Wales to visit our friends and brethren in those parts. . . . . We declared the Word of the Lord both in Welsh and English. My friend, John ap John, was very sound and intelligible in the Welsh language. He deserved the right hand of fellowship, for he was my elder and the first Friend that I heard declare in the English tongue ; and though he was not perfect in that language, yet he had the tongue of the learned to such as were spiritual. . . . . At Cardiff John ap John suffered great persecution, and in other parts of that country, before I was convinced. I suppose he might be prisoner there in 1653 or 1654."

8. In 1675, Richard Davies " went to John ap John's, near Wrexham, in Denbighshire, and visited Friends there," and on the 28th of the 7th month in the year 1681 met him at the half-yearly meeting at Swansea. After this last-named year I do not find John ap John once mentioned.

9. Mr. Edward Davies, who succeeded his father in his estate was also a Quaker, and the Friends continued to meet at Rhuddallt. The Rhuddallt meeting was still in existence in 1724 when it is described as belonging to the Nantwich monthly meeting. But I think that not very long afterwards Mr. Davies must have died, or the estate have passed into other hands. It is certain, at any rate, that somewhere about this time the Friends' meeting was removed from Rhuddallt to Cefn Bychan in the adjoining township of Coed Cristionydd.

10. The house at Cefn, in which the Friends met after Rhuddallt Isaf was closed to them, and which, it is said, they themselves built as a meeting-house, can readily be identified, inasmuch as it was subsequently let to the Baptists (see ch. IV., sec. 14), and continued to be used by them until the existing

Baptist Chapel at Cefn Bychan was built. It is a rather large
building with unusually thick walls, and is now used as a dwelling
house and butcher's shop. It stands by the roadside, between
New Bridge and Cefn Bychan Railway Station, and adjoins the
present Baptist Chapel. The upper storey probably formed the
meeting room, while the ground floor was fitted up as a dwelling
house. Some land belonged to it.

11. Mr. Joshua Thomas (*Hanes y Bedyddwyr*), writing in 1778,
says that the Friends built their meeting-house at Cefn as early as
1700, if not before that date. If this was so (which seems hardly
likely), this meeting-house, although situate at Cefn, must have
retained the name of the house at which the Quakers had at first
met, for the Rhuddallt Friends' meeting is mentioned, as we have
seen, in 1724. We see also from the statement just recorded
that Mr. Thomas was mistaken in supposing that the Friends'
meeting had ceased to exist, and that their meeting-house had
passed into the occupation of the Baptists by about the year
1715. It is certain, nevertheless, that the Baptists had enjoyed
the use of the building at Cefn Bychan for many years before
1743, but when precisely the Friends' meeting there came to an
end, I have not been able to ascertain.

12. Towards the end of the seventeenth century the want of a
Friends' Burying Ground in this district came to be very much
felt. In 1682 accordingly, a piece of land was purchased at
Holt, a place convenient not merely for Bromfield and the adjoining parts of Cheshire, but also for the northern portion of the
hundred of Maelor, where Quakers were then rather numerous.
The land purchased was a corner strip, containing about 240 yards
square, nearly opposite the entrance to the churchyard, bounded
on the east by the main road leading to Holt Bridge, and on the
north by Holt Green. It was bought (Feb. 23, 168$\frac{1}{2}$) for the sum
of £4, of Thomas Taylor, yeoman, of Worthenbury, by Arthur
Paynter, yeoman, of Church Shocklach, and John Newton,
yeoman, of Caldicot. It is thus described in the deed of sale :
"All that small piece or parcell of land situate or being w^{th}in
the Towne of Lyons al^s Holt, adjoyning there to a greene called
Crosse Greene, incompassed wth a brick wall, contayning in
breadth seventeene yards and in length fourteene yards, formerly
the land of John Yardley, of Holt." There was never a meeting
house erected upon this piece of land, and I do not think that
many burials ever took place within it. It continued in the possession of the Friends until about forty or fifty years ago, when it
was sold by them. It is now a strawberry patch, but is still
called "The Quakers' Yard." It will be mentioned again in a
later paragraph.

13. It is now time to turn to the history of the Society of
Friends in Wrexham itself.

K

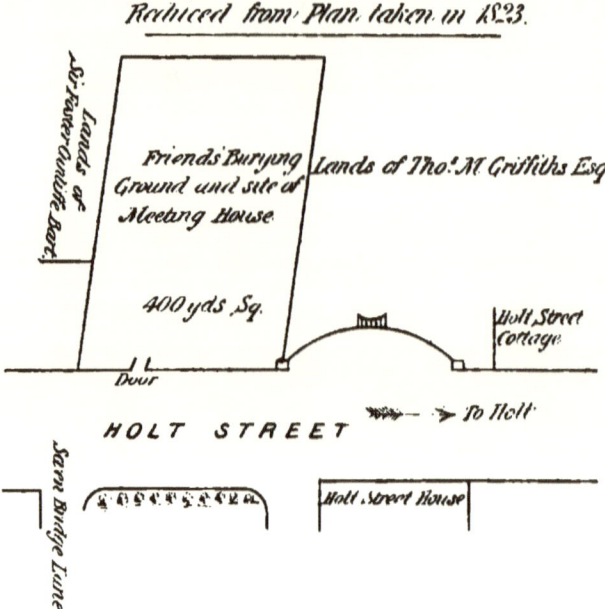

PLAN OF FRIENDS' BURYING GROUND, AND SITE OF MEETING
HOUSE, WREXHAM.

14. About the beginning of the last century the Friends resident in Wrexham determined to have a meeting-house of their own. On April 7, 1708, accordingly, John James, dyer (see sec. 18), and Hannah Newton, flaxdresser (see sec. 19), both of Wrexham, and Richard Davies, gentleman, of Rhuddallt (see sec. 5), purchased for £32 15s., of Thomas Kynaston, gentleman, of l'enley, two recently erected cottages, together with the gardens belonging to the same, situate in the Lampint (see ch. III., sec. 1), in the street which is now known as Holt Street. The site of these premises is accurately represented in the plan hereto appended which was made in 1823. The premises are thus described in the deed of purchase :—" All those messuages and houses lately erected by him the said Thomas Kinaston, and all that parcell of land whereon the said messuages now stand, lately purchased [on Nov. 20, 1668] by the said Thomas Kinaston," of Roger Williams, Catherine his wife, and Alice Jones, " in a streete there called y Lampint, alˢ Street y Lampint, alˢ the Lampitt Street, situate between the lands late of Sir Robert Hanson, Knight, deceased, now in the tenure or possession of Sʳ John Wynn, Knight and Baronet, his undertenants or assigns, on the north and west partes, and the lands late in the tenure or possession of Sir John Conway, Baronet, on the east parte, and the Queen's highway there on the south parte, contayning in length along the said highway side eighteen yards or thereabouts, and contayning in breadth from the said highway unto the Lands [late] of the said Sir Robert Hanson on the northe part ffive and twenty yards or thereabouts."

15. It seems probable that part of the two cottages purchased was fitted up as a meeting-house and the other part let out at rent, or used, at any rate, as a dwelling, and it is certain that a portion of the land was set apart as a burial ground. Towards the cost of fitting up the meeting-house the Friends of the Frandley, Morley, and Nantwich monthly meetings largely contributed. Frandley forwarded £14 10s., Morley £9 16s., and Nantwich £4 3s., in all £28 9s. 4d.

16. I have seen the original licence obtained at this time for the house in Holt Street, as a place of worship. It was granted at the General Sessions for the county of Denbigh, held in July, 1708, at Wrexham, there being then upon the bench : Sir John Wynn, knight and baronet, of Wynnstay ; Kenric Eyton, Esq., of Lower Eyton ; the Rev. Robert Wynne, S.T.P., Chancellor of St. Asaph ; Ellis Lloyd, Esq., of Pen y lan ; Peter Ellice, Esq., of Croes Newydd ; and Ellis Meredith, Esq., of Pentrebychan. The licence is thus worded :—" Att the request of the people called Quakers, residing in and about Wrexham, the house of John James, dyer, is by the court allowed for a place of meeting for the said Quakers to worship God in their own way.— John Evans, Cler. Pac."

17. Of John James and Hannah Newton, two of the three Friends concerned in the purchase of the premises above described, something must now be said.

18. John James, who has already been mentioned (see sec. 4c) was a dyer, whose dyehouse was in or near the Brookside, and who lived nearly all his life at the house in Town Hill, which Mr. E. R. Palmer, shoemaker, now occupies. He was a very staunch Quaker until his death. In 1733 he proposed to the Nantwich monthly meeting a place suitable for a meeting-house at Denbigh, and offered £5 towards fitting it up. The offer was accepted, and the place was completed for £10. He died about the year 1740, and left £5 to the Nantwich monthly meeting.

19. Hannah Newton was a flaxdresser, whose shop in Town Hill was where that of Mr. J. E. Powell now is. She appears to have ultimately married Robert Owen, also a flaxdresser, who had for a long time a shop in Town Hill on the site of the shop now occupied by Mr. C. E. Evans, draper. This Robert Owen was apparently, after Mr. John James, the chief support of Quakerism in this town. Neither of them ever paid church-rates. In the church-rate parochial assessment for 1724, there is written against the name of John James the words : " Says on his conscience he can't pay," and against the name of Robert Owen the words : " *Will not* pay." Robert Owen died about the year 1727.

20. In 1723 so as to secure the meeting-house and burial-ground at Wrexham, and the burial-ground at Holt, for ever to the use of the Society of Friends, Robert Owen and Hannah, his wife, at the Great Sessions for the county of Denbigh, held at Wrexham, April 5th, 1723, levied a fine upon the said premises to Edward Davies, gentleman, of Rhuddallt (see sec. 5); Thomas Andrews, yeoman, of Worthenbury ; and Joseph Urian[3] yeoman, of Eyton, in the county of Denbigh; and four days later (April 9th) a formal deed of trust was entered into between the parties to the aforesaid fine. Of this deed the following extract contains all the essential points :—" That as for, touching or concerning the Building in the said parish of Wrexham . . that it shall and may be a place for the worship of Almighty God by such well-disposed people (commonly called Quakers) as shall think fitt there to do for ever, and that the same shall not att any time thereafter be any otherwise employed by any person or persons whatsoever, likewise that the said parcells of land in the said severall parishes of Wrexham and Holt aforesaid, are hereby intended forever to continue, remaine, and be for a Buriall place of all such person or persons as shall have a will or desire

---

3. There was a *Ruth* Urian, a Quakeress, who lived in Wrexham. She was a flax dresser, and in 1704 succeeded Hannah Newton (see sec. 19), in the shop in Town Hill, which the latter had till then occupied. In 1717 she is described in the rate books as having " gone."

to be buried in the same, and the families of all such persons whomsoever as are or shall att any time hereafter be buried in the said parcells of land in the said parishes of Wrexham and Holt, shall, by the consent of the said Edward Davies, Thomas Andrews, and Joseph Urian, and their heirs, have free Ingress, Egress, and Regress into and upon the said premises for the making of graves and Buriall places for the Buriall of Bodys of such persons aforesaid."[4]

21. The burial-register and minutes of the Wrexham Meeting can now nowhere be found, so that of the history of that meeting it is impossible to present henceforth those details concerning which we naturally enquire. We learn, however, from the minutes of the Nantwich Meeting that, in 1724, the Wrexham Friends subscribed £4 16s. towards the erection of the Nantwich Meeting House, and that in the early part of 1740, "the friends of Wrexham Meeting having been visited, a good account is given of the service thereof."

22. Spite of the favourable report just quoted, I do not think the meeting long survived the death of John James, which appears to have taken place in that same year. When precisely it came to an end, I cannot say. But in 1744 the meeting house (or that part of it which was used as a dwelling) was occupied by a tenant who, for the first time, paid church rates in respect of it. This rather looks as though the meeting was already extinct, and it is certain that after this date I can find no indication of there being more than two Quakers in the parish one of which two—Mr. Benjamin Harvey—subsequently joined the Established Church, and on July 10, 1753, being then 23 years of age, was baptised at the Parish Church.

23. From about 1767 to about 1781 the meeting-house was let, as already has been explained, to the Rev. Thomas Davies (see ch. III. sec. 52) for a Presbyterian day school. Before the end of the century it appears to have fallen or been taken down, so that the property henceforth consisted of no more than a piece of land—the burial-ground and the site of the old meeting-house. This piece of land was let in September, 1801, for £2 a-year, to Thomas Griffith, Esq., who lived at Holt Street House on the other side of the street, and who owned also and used as a garden the land on the east side of the burial-ground immediately opposite his house. The burial-ground was separated from Mr. Griffith's garden by a brick wall, and this wall in 1805 was taken down by Mr. Griffith, he covenanting with the trustees to rebuild it whenever required to do so, making it nine inches thick and five feet six inches high. And the said burial-ground or plot of land was

---

4. The only notice as to actual burials in the Meeting Yard at Wrexham that I have met with occurs in a memorandum furnished by Mr. Francis Smith. This memorandum records that on 12th day, 1st month, 1728, "Benjamin Bangs gave 30s. for two burials at Wrexham." Benjamin Bangs was a rather noted minister belonging to the Cheshire meeting who devoted much of his time to visiting the meetings in North Wales. He died in 1741.

declared at the same time to be 79 feet seven inches long (from north to south) and 47 feet nine inches broad (from east to west). The burial-ground still forms a part of the garden or croft adjoining, and is still let to the occupier of Holt Street House.

24. Since the first part of this chapter was in type I have learned from Simpson's *Account of Llangollen*, now out of print, that an old house called "Plas Eva" or "Plas Evan," near the Sun Inn, Trevor, close to the road leading from Llangollen to Ruabon. had formerly attached to it a field, containing some gravestones, which was called "Mynwent y Quacer" or "Quaker's Graveyard." "In cutting the canal, the earth from the excavation was thrown upon the old graves and the inscribed stones that lay upon the surface." It is very probable, therefore, that it was at Plas Evan that John ap John lived, and this the more, as there appears to be a distinct tradition at Trevor that Friends' meetings were at one time held at Plas Evan.

Chapter VII.

The Roman Catholics of Bromfield.

1. It may be worth while to say something of the Roman Catholics who were living in the district during the latter part of the 17th and beginning of the 18th century.[1]
2. The chief of these were the Trevors of Upper Esclus and Cae Glas, in the township of Esclusham Above. In 1663 Thomas Trevor, gentleman, was presented by the grand jury as "a recusant" and as "constantly absent" from church. Nevertheless, all his children had been baptized at the parish church: his sons, Matthew and Robert, married into Protestant families, and one of the children of the Mr. Robert Trevor just named, was also baptized (July, 1682) at the parish church. I can find, however, no record in any of the parish registers of the baptism of any of the other children of this Mr. Trevor, and there can be little doubt as to all these Trevors being really Roman Catholics. In Cosin's list of " Names of the Roman Catholics, Non-jurors, and others who refused to take the oaths," in 1715, after the accession of George I., appears the name of John Trevor, gent⁰·, of Esclusham, son of the fore-named Robert Trevor. The family of Trevor, of Upper Esclus, died out with Mr. Richard Trevor (brother and heir of the last-named John Trevor) who deceased April, 1790, having previously sold part of his estate, and left the rest heavily mortgaged.
3. Among the other "papists" in this neighbourhood presented by the Grand Jury in 1663 were the brothers Eustace, Edward and Sylvanus Crue; Thomas Bostock, innkeeper; John Prince, barber; and James Owens, mason, all of Wrexham; and Edward Williams and his son of the same name, of Llai. Eustace Crue was an apothecary, having his house and shop where the Conservative Club in High Street now is : he was settled in Wrexham at least as early as 1649, and he died in 1705. I have printed in my *Hist. of Par. Ch. of Wrexham* (see page 217) the Latin inscription on the tomb of this Mr. Crue. Edward, his brother, had also a shop in High Street. Sylvanus Crue, goldsmith, was the well-known engraver of that name (see *His of Par. Ch. of*

1. The period which I have selected for treatment prevents me from dealing with the case of Mr. Richard Gwyn, otherwise White, who as a Roman Catholic, was cruelly martyred October 15, 1584, at Wrexham. Moreover, the very full account of this pitiful incident given in the third volume of *The History of Powys Fadog* is so touching, that I could not in any case have ventured to abbreviate it, or put it in my own words. The account, however, should be read by those who think that religious persecution in this country was practised by one church and one party only.

Wrexham, page 211, note 12). Mr. Thomas Bostock kept the inn in High Street, known successively as " The George," "The Spread Eagles," and " The Wynnstay Arms :" he was buried in the parish churchyard, March 22, 1670. The George and Bryn-y-ffynnon were then the two largest houses in the town.

4. A little later, the name of another Roman Catholic occurs— Mr. James Goodwyn, apothecary. He lived at first in High Street, but afterwards in Beastmarket Street in the house which is now numbered 22. He is mentioned in the rate books for the first time in 1668, and for the last in 1701. Edward Lhwyd, the antiquary, speaks of him in one of his letters.

I.

List of members belonging to the Presbyterian Chapel, Chester Street, Wrexham (1748–1818), begun by Rev. Francis Boult, and continued by the Rev. Wm. Brown, with annotations by one or other of them.

[When a date is appended to a name, this represents the time when the person named was admitted as member. My own additions are always put within brackets. A.N.P.]

1. Mr. [John] Travers	Ob^t Dec. 22nd, 1748 [see ch. iii., note 8.]
2. Mr. [John] Wright, senr.	Died 17th Dec., 1752 [see Hist. Par. Ch. of Wrexham, page 98, note 145.]
3. Mrs. Wright	Dead.
4. Mr. [Thos.] Collins	Died 14th Nov., 1753 [see ch. iii, note 3.]
5. Mrs. Collins	Dead.
6. Edward Evans	Departed this life 2nd Aug., 1746 [see ch. iii, note 13.]
7. Henry Roberts [of Llai]	Buried 20th Feb., 1776.
8. [Mary] Roberts, his wife	Died 19th April, 1761.
9. Kenrick Cross	[Shoemaker, of Beastmarket St.; died March 10, 1794, aged 85.]
10. Peter Fenner¹	Buried 23rd May, 1759.
11. Mr. John Hampton	Removed to London.
12. John Pierce	Died 21st Nov., 1746.
13. Mrs. Kenrick, widow	Buried 27th Oct., 1775 [widow of Rev. John Kenrick.]
14. Miss Owens, now Mrs. Hatchett²	Dead.

1. Peter Fenner, described in the Register as " of Plas Teg " [parish of Hope]: doubtless the farming tenant of the Plas Teg land. Before the passing of the *Act of Toleration*, the Rev. James Owen (see page 54) was once preaching at " one Mr Fenner's in Hope parish " when the persecuting zealots broke in, and carried off the whole company to Mold. Mr. Owen and Mr. Fenner were committed to Caerwys jail. and the rest of the congregation bound over to appear at the Assizes. The notes of Mr. Owen's sermon, which were in Latin, gave much trouble to the justice before whom he was taken.

2. Martha Owen, daughter of Thomas Owen, Esq., of Llynllo, Montgomeryshire (descended from Idnerth Benfras), by his second wife, Abigail, one of the daughters and co-heirs of the Rev. Hugh Owen, of Bron-y-clydwr (see ch. II., note 20). She was the sister and heir of Dr. Hugh Owen, of Shrewsbury, and married (December 11th, 1748), at Gresford, Richard Bulkeley Hatchett, Esq., of Lee, Salop, becoming by him the ancestress of the Bulkeley-Owens, of Tedsmore, Salop.

15. Mrs. Dannald[3]	Dead.
16. Mrs. Brereton[4]	Died 25th Feb., 1753.
17. Mrs. [Elizabeth] Thomas	Died 1st Jany., 174$\frac{7}{8}$ [see ch. iii, note 17.]
18. Mrs. Jones, clothier	
19. Mrs. [Catherine] Williams, midwife	[Buried June 25, 1782, aged 82.]
20. Elizabeth Kenrick, widow[5]	Dead.
21. Mrs. Rotheram	Removed to London.
22. Widow Eliz. Jones [of Pen-y-bryn]	Departed this life 30th Sept.,1752
23. Mrs. Sarah Buttall	Buried 13th March, 1760.
24. Widow Mary Jones	Departed this life 4th Aug., 1752 [sister of Rev. John Kenrick, see ch. ii, sec. 27.]
25. Rebecca Jones, her daughter	[Died unmarried; buried in Dissenters' Graveyard, April 27, 1762.]
26. Mary Samuel[6]	Dead.
27. Sarah Randles	Dead.
28. Mary Jones, midwife	Buried 4th Jany., 1749 [Described in register as "Sister of Simon Jones."]
29. Deborah Edwards	Died 3rd May, 1749 [Sister to Rev. John Kenrick, see ch. ii, sec. 27.]
30. Rebecca Edwards	Settled in London. [Probably daughter of (29)].
31. Mary ap Edward	Died 4th July, 1755.
32. Maudlin Nicholas	[Buried in Dissenters' Graveyard, June 25th, 1770.]
33. Catherine Fletcher	[Otherwise "Williams"; buried in Dissenters' Graveyard, Oct. 11, 1758.]
34. Betty Jones	
35. William Matthews[7]	Buried 2nd March, 1758. [Described as of "Parish of March-wiel."]
36. [Gwen] Matthews, his wife	Buried 30th Dec., 1760.
37. Mary Morton	Died 29th July, 1753 [widow of Alexander Morton.]
38. Deborah Bithel, the elder	[Widow; buried July 20, 1774.]
39. Lucy McCaig	Removed.

3. The widow of John Dannald, surgeon, of Wrexham ; her daughter, Elizabeth, married Richard Benjamin, gentleman, of Rhosnessney (see note 15) : she was buried in Wrexham Churchyard, April 20th, 1769.

4. Margaret, wife of John Brereton, tallow chandler, of Hope Street, and daughter of Richard Benjamin, grocer, of High Street (see ch. III., note 7) ; buried in Dissenters' Graveyard, Wrexham, February 28th, 1753, aged 51.

5. Elizabeth Kenrick, widow of Samuel Kenrick, dyer, of Brookside, who appears to have been brother to the Rev. John Kenrick; buried in Dissenters' Graveyard, May 25th, 1758.

6. Mary Samuel, widow of Robert Samuel, farmer, of Plas Coch, Stansty; buried in the Dissenters' Graveyard, July 18th, 1755.

7. It is nearly certain that the above-named William and Gwen Matthews were the parents of Joanna Matthews, the maternal grandmother of the Right Hon. Anthony J. Mundella, and it is quite certain that Samuel Matthews, also mentioned above (No. 43), was her uncle. Her parents being dead, she accompanied her uncle to Leicester. She subsequently married Mr. Thomas Alsopp, of Tamworth, and died at Leicester about the year 1834, aged 80, being buried in the graveyard of the Great Meeting (Unitarian) there. Mr. Mundella says that she was "remarkably well educated as compared with the women of her day," .. "very proud of her Welsh descent, and of the Welsh people, whose love of learning was a constant theme of pride and satisfaction with her."

40. Ellen Davies	Died 17th July, 1749. [Described in register as " Wife of Thos. Davies."]
41. Mrs. [Tabitha] Taylor	Died April 26, 1748. [Lived on north side of Camfa'r Cwn.]
42. Martha Jeffreys	Removed to London.
43. Samuel Matthews (see note 7)	Settled in Leicester.
44. Elizabeth Mackaig	[Wife of Hugh McKey; buried Dec. 8, 1775]
45. John Mackaig	Sept. 6, 1747 ; died 14th Feb., 1753 [of Beastmarket Street.]
46. Ruth Buttall	Died 2nd March, 1755. [Described in register as " of Abbot Street, widow."]
47. Hannah Matthews	7th Feb., 174⅞ ; removed to Stourbridge.
48. Mary Reynolds	Aug. 7, 1748.
49. Ann Shefton	Sept. 4, 1748 [widow, buried May 4, 1763.]
50. Elizabeth Woolridge[8]	5th Feb., 1748 ; buried at the old churchyard.
51. John Whittaker [farmer] of Issacoed	Sept. 4, 1748.
52. David Humphreys, Miner, Minera	2nd July, 1749. [Buried in Dissenters' Graveyard, Dec. 24. 1765.]
53. Hannah Parry	Recommended by a minister from Ireland [widow; buried from poor house, Nov. 18, 1763.]
54. Mrs. Davies, of the Beastmarket.	
55. Deborah Ithel, the younger	
56. Mrs. Kenrick, junr., Ruabon	[Formerly Miss Mary Quarrell, of Llanfyllin, see ch. iii, sec. 36]
57. Daniel Reynolds, senr.	[Shoemaker, of Town Hill.]
58 & 59. Mr. Isaac Wilkinson and his wife	Removed to Bristol.[9]
60. Mrs. [Mary] Fullelove	Buried 7th Aug., 1756. [Wife of Mr. Thos. Fullelove, of the Forge or Wiremill.]
61. Mr. James Craig[10]	
62. Mr. John Wright [junr.]	[Tanner, of the Brook Side ; buried in Dissenters' Graveyard, Feb. 25, 176⅘.]
63. Mrs. Moulton	

8. "Mrs. Woolrich, Gunsmith, W.R." Buried October 8th, 1763.—*Par. Reg.*

9. Mr. Isaac Wilkinson, who came hither from North Lancashire, was living at this time at Plas Grono, and carrying on at Bersham the blast furnaces, cannon foundry, and iron works, which afterwards became so well known. They were not in his hands successful, and he ultimately (soon after 1761) went to Bristol, where he was also unsuccessful in business, and became wholly dependent on his two sons, who remained behind. These, and especially John, afterwards of Brymbo Hall, the elder of them, speedily made the Bersham Works a great success. William, the other son, was a member of the Presbyterian congregation ; he lived first at The Court, Wrexham, and finally at Plas Grono, and was buried in the Dissenters' Graveyard, March 5th, 1808. He married, I believe, a Miss Elizabeth Stockdale: two infant daughters of his were baptized at the Presbyterian Chapel. John and William Wilkinson at first worked together, but afterwards quarrelled, and were never reconciled. A third son of Mr. Isaac Wilkinson—Henry—died (June 26th, 1756) while the former was still living at Plas Grono, and his gravestone may still be seen in the Rhosddu Road Burying Ground. Mr. Isaac Wilkinson had also a daughter, Mary, who was married (June 13th, 1762) to the famous Dr. Joseph Priestley, afterwards of Birmingham, but then a tutor in the Dissenting Academy, Warrington.

10. Mr. Craig, a Scotchman, lived at this time in High Street, where the Conservative Club now is, afterwards in Church Street, on the site of Mr. Collens' shop.

64. John Hayton, of the Furnace.[11]
65. Joshua Matthews, son of Thomas Matthews; removed.
66. Mrs. Jones, wife of Samuel Jones [Butler] at Erthig.
67. Mrs. [Martha] Quarrell [widow][12] of Llanfylling. [Buried in Dissenters' Graveyard, Aug. 18, 1767, aged 80.]

68. Mrs. Doro. Quarrell[12]	[Buried in Dissenters' Graveyard, July 28, 1767, aged 80.]
69. Mr. John Kenrick, Ruabon	April 1, 1759. [The *second* of the name, son of the Rev. John Kenrick.]
70. Mr. Thomas Evans	May 6, 1759. [See ch. iii, note 24.]
71. Sarah Senior	June 1, 1760.
72. Mr. Wm. Kenrick, Brazier	Aug. 3, 1760. [Fourth son of Rev. John Kenrick; see ch. iii., sec. 23.]
73. Barbara Samuel	Aug. 3, 1760.
74. Mrs. Elizabeth Buttall[13]	Jan. 3, 1762.
75. Mrs. Evans, Mr. Evans skinner's wife[14]	March 6, 1763.
76. Mrs. Benjamin, junr.[15]	May 1, 1768.
77. Glass Edwards, widow	Jan. 1, 1764. [Widow of Henry Edwards.]
78. Elizabeth, wife of Mr. Walter Robinson[16].	Jan. 6, 1765.
79. Ellen, the wife of Charles Edwards	Removed to Ireland.

80. Mrs. Cross, widow, aunt of Mr. T. Evans, skinner; removed.
81 & 82. John Evans, clothier, and his wife.[17]
83 & 84. John Pierce, skinner, and his wife.[18]

85. Mr. John Kenrick, Plas Gwern	[Second John Kenrick, of Wynne Hall (see ch. iii., sec. 37); already once mentioned in the list.]
86 & 87. Mr. Jas. Buttall, of London, and his wife	[see ch. iii., sec. 47.]
88. Miss [Deborah] Buttall	[See ch. iii., sec. 45.]

89. Mrs. Anne Williams, midwife.

11. John Hayton was at this time a workman at Bersham Furnace, and lived at the Little Fawnog. He afterwards started the Gwersyllt Wire Works, which his son John subsequently carried on. He died 22nd August, 1803, aged 76 (or 78), and was buried in the Dissenters' Graveyard.

12. Both these ladies were now living at Wynne Hall, and had formerly lived at Llanfyllin. One of them was the widow of Mr. Timothy Quarrell, of Llanfyllin, and the mother of Mrs. Kenrick, of Wynne Hall.

13. This lady must be, I think, the "Mrs. Elizabeth Buttall," of "The Groves," who married Mr. John Evans, but, if so, is mentioned again as (82).

14. Mrs. Esther Evans, daughter of Mr. John Williams, tanner (see ch. III., note 14); as a widow lived at the Talwrn, Esclusham Above; died May 28, 1827, aged 92, and was buried in the Dissenters' Graveyard.

15. Mrs. Elizabeth Benjamin, daughter of Mr. John Dannald, surgeon, of Wrexham, (see note 3) wife of Richard Benjamin, gentleman, who was son and successor of the Richard Benjamin, gentleman, mentioned in note 19, ch. III. Her son, Richard Benjamin, gentleman, of Rhosnessney, married Sophia Bruen, daughter of Mr. John Meller, of Wrexham (see *History of the Parish Church of Wrexham*, page 109, note 280a).

16. Mr. Walter Robinson was a linen draper from Scotland, whose shop in High Street, was where that of Mr. R. O. Jones now is.

17. Mr. John Evans, clothier, was brother of Mr. Thomas Evans, skinner, (see ch. III, note 24): his shop was in High Street, where that of Mr. Scotcher and another shop adjoining now are : he married Elizabeth Buttall (see ch. III, sec. 48), and lived during the latter part of his life at the Yspytty ; died February 24th, 1796, aged 59, and was buried in the Dissenters' Graveyard.

18. John Pearse, skinner, of the parish of Holt, buried in Dissenters' Graveyard, October 13th, 1768, aged 38 : his wife Jane, who was a sister of Messrs. Thomas and John Evans (see note 17), was also buried there, August 11th, 1774, aged 38. Their daughter, Esther, was afterwards the wife of Edward Jackson, dyer, (see note 43.)

90. Edward Boddwa, weaver [Beddoes ?]   Dead.
91. Mary James, Ruabon[19]
92. Sarah Howell, of Adwyrclawdd, wife of Samuel Howell [wheelwright and pumpmaker.]
93. Charles Edwards, cobbler   Dead.
94. Mrs. Hannah Robinson   Dead. [Buried in Dissenters' Graveyard, July 15, 1774.]
95. Ann Williams, servant to Mr. Evans, the skinner, Nov. 3, 1771 ; removed.
96. Deborah Jones   12th May.
97. Jonathan Large   7th June, 1772.   [Maltster ; buried March 31, 1778.]
98 & 99. Francis Edwards, weaver, and his wife Anne, Sept. 6, 1772. [Francis Edwards, clerk, see ch. iii., sec. 72.]
100. Mary Francis, the wife of Wm. Francis, shoemaker, Pentrefelin, Nov. 1, 1772.
101. Elizabeth Edwards, Mr. Buttall's servant, Dec. 6, 1772.
102. Miss Mary Kenrick,[20] Mr. Kenrick, of Plas Gwern's daughter, and
103. Dear Rebekah Robinson, both admitted 7th Feb., 1773 ; removed to London. [Probably a daughter of Mr. John Robinson, see note 67.]
104. Tabitha Hughes, sister of John James [the clerk, see ch. iii., sec. 72] ; admitted Sept. 5, 1773.
105. John Kenrick, son of Mr. Kenrick, of Plas Gwern ; removed to Chester.[21]
106 & 107. Samuel Bickerton, of Erbistock, and Mary his wife. She goes [so!] 1793.[22]
108 & 109. Mr. Thos. Gittins and his wife, of Erbistock [Hall.]
110. Miss Molly Kenrick, of Ruabon.[23]
111. Miss Sally Kenrick, of Ruabon ;[23]   Removed to Chester.
112. John Kenrick, junr., Ruabon   [Already mentioned under (105).]
113. Rev. Mr. Davies   [See ch. iii., sec. 52.]
114. Debby Cross   ⎫
115. Debby Collins   ⎪
116. Mrs. [Elizabeth] Adderley, wife of John Adderley ⎪   Should have been
117. Mrs. Edwards, sister of Deborah Ithel   ⎬   mentioned before.
118. Mrs. Ann Jones[24]   ⎪
119. Mrs. [Esther] Burton[25]   ⎭
120. Miss Benjamin, daughter of the late Mr. Berjamin, of Rhosnessney.[26]
121. Frederick Jessamine.[27]

19. Mary James, a daughter of John James, the late clerk, (see ch. III, sec. 72) : not having been baptised in infancy, she now, at the age of 21, underwent that ordinance.

20. Mary Kenrick, eldest daughter of the second John Kenrick, Esq., of Wynne Hall (see ch. III, sec. 87).

21. This Mr. Kenrick was afterwards the *third* John Kenrick, Esq., of Wynne Hall (see ch. III, sec. 64.

22. Samuel Bickerton, farmer, afterwards of Stryt-yr-hwch, Sontley ; buried in Dissenters' Burial Ground, Nov. 11, 1793, aged 75.

23. The Misses Molly and Sally Kenrick were daughters of the *second* Mr. John Kenrick, of Wynne Hall (see ch. III, sec. 87). The former has been already mentioned as (102). When members left the town, and afterwards returned, their names were re-inserted in the list of members.

24. Mrs. Anne Jones, second wife of Mr. John Jones, carpenter, of the Linen Hall.

25. Esther, wife of Mr. Hugh Burton, grocer, of High Street, and a daughter of Mr. Edward Evans, Skinner (see ch. III, note 13): died Nov. 8, 1809, and was buried in Dissenters' Graveyard.

26. Margaret Benjamin, daughter of Richard Benjamin, gentleman, of Rhosnessney, by his wife Elizabeth (Dannald); afterwards married (May 12, 1776) to Mr. Thomas Evans, tanner, of Island Green, son of Mr. Thomas Evans, skinner.

27. Frederick Jessamine, glover and earthenware dealer; lived in the middle of the east side of Church Street : he was afterwards one of the 21, who in 1788, started the Independent Church in Pen-y-bryn ; died July 6, 1804.

122. John Bickerton, son of Mr. Bickerton, of Street yr Uch [Stryt yr hwch, see note 29.]

123. William Johnson, of Pentrefelin   Admitted Sept. 1, 1776 ; removed to the North.

124. Thomas Jones, Tailor   April 6 1777 [Died June 13, 1786, aged 53, buried at Rhosddu Road.]

125. Elizabeth Lloyd, of the Hope Street, widow. Oct. 5, 1777.[28]

126 & 127. Richard Bickerton, son of Samuel Bickerton [see 106], and Sarah his daughter.[29]

128. Thomas Whetnall, sawyer   1778 [Buried in Dissenters'Graveyard, Feb. 19, 1800, aged 84.]

129. Thomas Large, Newmarket   Dead 1793 [Buried in Dissenters' Graveyard July 15, 1793.]

130. Elizabeth Rogers, Daughter of Thos. Rogers, Shoemaker [of Pen y bryn]; removed to London.

131. George Gibbs, Mr. Buttall's Servant Gardener, 1778 ; removed.

132. Mrs. Sarah Hayton, Wire Mill   1778.[30]

133. Miss Sarah Kenrick, the late Apothecary's daughter.[31]

134. Debby Jones, Mrs. Deb. Jones's niece, both admitted 1 July, 1781.

136. Elizabeth Robinson, Daughter of Mr. Walter Robinson (see note 16), Jany. 6, 1782.

137. Mary Chaddock, of Wern y Sergeant   Admitted Sept. 1, 1782.

138. Ellen Boult, my sister [see ch. III, sec. 34] admitted Member 3 Oct., 1784.

139. Mr. James Phœnix   Admitted a member 1784.[32]

140. Miss Ann Price   Admitted a member 1785, removed to Chester, 1789.

141. Mrs. Elizabeth Brown   Admitted a member at the same time. Dead.

142. Miss Martha Kenrick[33]   Admitted a member 1785.

143. Mr. Mulcaster[34]   Admitted 1786.

144. Miss Sarah Price   Admitted a member Jany. 1, 1786 ; removed to Chester 1789. Dead.

145. Mr. Joseph Senior   1787 [of the Wire Mill ; buried in Dissenters' Graveyard, June 24, 1811, aged 63.]

146. Mr. [John] Lloyd, Grocer, Town Hill   Admitted a member 1787, Dead. [Lived where Mr. Stant's shop now is.]

147. Mrs. Brown (my wife)   Admitted a member 1788 [see chap. III, sec. 59.]

148. Mr. Kenrick Cross   Admitted 1788. Dead

---

28. Widow of Thomas Lloyd, breeches maker : she was one of the Kenrick family

29. Mr. Richard Bickerton was afterwards one of the 21 who in 1783 formed the Independent Church in Pen-y-bryn.

30. Wife of Mr. John Hayton, the elder, of Gwersyllt [see (64)]; buried in Dissenters Graveyard, February 20, 1799, aged 74.

31. Daughter of Mr. Archibald Kenrick, apothecary, of Wrexham (see ch. III., sec. 23) by Margaret his wife.

32. James Phœnix was a farmer and lived at the house which is now The Travellers' Inn, Hightown.

33. Martha Kenrick, daughter of the second John Kenrick, Esq., of Wynne Hall, by Sarah (Quarrell) his wife, afterwards wife of the Rev. Jas. Parry, [see ch. III., sec. 37 (6)] of Chester ; died at Chester, August 2, 1853, aged 91.

34. George Mulcaster, cordwainer, of Charles Street, next Eagles Inn ; buried in Dissenters' Graveyard, April 17, 1812, aged 85.

149. Mrs. Cross, wife to Kenrick Cross   Admitted a member 1789.
150. Mr. John Burton [see ch. III, note 31] Admitted a member 1789.
151 & 152. Mr. William Senior and his wife [Margaret], admitted Jany. 3, 1790, Mr. Senior dead.[35]
153. Mr. William Burton (see note 44)   Admitted 7 Nov., 1790. Dead.
154. Mrs. Jane Evans, widow   Admitted Feb., 1791.
155. Mr. [Rd.] Williams, Hatter[33]
156. Mrs. [Hannah] Williams, wife of Mr. Richard Williams, Hatter, Admitted June, 1791 [Died 27 Augt., 1831, aged 72]
157. Mrs. Dauncey (?) from Holt   Admitted June, 1791. Dead.
158 & 159. Mr. [Richd.] and Mrs. [Cath.] Grant, from Holt, admitted August, 1791 [gone to] Drayton.
160. Mrs. Price, Glover   Admitted 1792, now gone to Liverpool.
161. Esther Pierce, Niece to Mr. John Evans, and living with him, admitted 1792.[37]
162. Miss Catherine Evans[38]   Admitted 1793.
163. Mrs. Wilcox   Admitted Nov., 1793.
164. Eleanor Rowland   Admitted Jany. 5, 1794.
165. Mrs. Ann Kenrick, wife of Francis Kenrick, Shoemaker, admitted Feb. 3, 1794. Dead. [Buried Jany. 31, 1810.]
166. Mrs. Lloyd, Daughter of Elizth. Lloyd, Hope Street, who is also a member [see note 28] admitted Feb. 3, 1794.
167. Mrs. Margaret Hughes, widow to Mr. John Hughes, admitted Sept., 1794. Dead.[39]
168. Mrs. Ann Ellis   Admitted 4 Jan., 1795.
169. Mrs. Mary Chipwell   Admitted 4 Jan., 1795.
170. Mrs. Mary Adderley   Admitted Jan. 4, 1795. [Widow of Joshua Adderley, died 9 June, 1818.]
171. Mrs. Mary Collins   Admitted Feb. 1, 1795. [Wife of Wm. Collins, glover.]
172. Mrs. Jane Thomas   Admitted Feb. 1, 1795.
173. Mr. Daniel Ellis   Admitted Nov. 1, 1795. Removed to Chester.
174. Mrs. Mary Lloyd, Beast-market   Admitted 1795. Dead.
175. Mr. [Wm.] Matthews [shoemaker]   Admitted Aug., 1796. [Lived where Mr. Southern's shop now is in Charles street.]
176. Mr. [Wm.] Baugh [farmer] (formerly in communion with the Baptist Society). Admitted Aug., 1796.
177. Miss Esther Evans[40]   Admitted Sept. 1796.

---

35. William Senior, of Gwersyllt; buried in Dissenters' Graveyard, September 8, 1812, aged 67; his wife (also buried there, April 2, 1849) was one of the Haytons of Gwersyllt.

36. Richard Williams, afterwards "clerk of the meeting" and of the Machine, Hope Street (next to "Nelson's Arms"); died July 5, 1823, aged 63, and was buried in the Dissenters' Graveyard.

37. Esther Pearse, daughter of John and Jane Pearse (see note 18), afterwards wife of Edward Jackson, skinner (see note 43); died January 25, 1818, aged 59, and was buried in the Dissenters' Graveyard.

38. Catherine, daughter of Mr. Thomas Evans, skinner, baptized April 29, 1771, afterwards wife of (1) Capt. Richard Mellor and (2) of Thos. Barton, gentleman, of Liverpool.

39. Widow of John Hughes, shoemaker, of west side of York Street, next below Black Horse; died August 28, 1801, aged 47.

40. Esther, daughter of Mr. Thomas Evans, skinner, baptised April 24th, 1767, afterwards wife of Mr. James McCulla, of Liverpool.

178. Miss Catherine Burton[41]   Admitted Oct., 1796.
179. Mrs. J. Burton[42]   Admitted June, 1797.
180. Mr. [Edward] Jackson, dyer[43]   Admitted 1797.
181. Mr. Birch   Admitted 1798.
182. Mr. William Burton[44]   Admitted 3 Feb., 1799.
183. Mrs. Mary Jones, Castle yard   Admitted 1799.
184. Mrs. Robins, near the Vicarage   Admitted 1799.
185. Mrs. Mary Francis, Abbot Street   Admitted 1799.
186. Mrs. [Ann] Hayton, Wire Mill   Admitted 1800.   [Wife of John
                                              Hayton,the younger,Gwersyllt,
                                              see ch. III., note 32.]
187. Mrs. Mary Hughes.
188. Mrs. Matthews, Charles Street   Admitted Dec. 7, 1800. [Wife of
                                              (175).]
189 & 190. Mr. and Mrs. Kenrick, Wynn Hall. [Mr. Kenrick already
       mentioned, see 105.]
191. Jane Roberts
192. Rev. Mr. Parry, schoolmaster.[45]
193. Ann Williams, Charles Street.
194. John Jones, Castle yard   Admitted 1805.   Removed.
195 & 196. Mr. Jones, hatter, and wife   1805.
197. Ann Minor, widow [of Henry Minor, smith].
198. Francis Kenrick   1807.   [Buried Dec. 16, 1810.]
199. Mrs. Elizabeth James.
200. Mrs. Elizabeth James' niece.
201. Mrs. [Esther] Stubbs [widow of Thos. Stubbs, schoolmaster of Lady
       Jeffreys' School].
202. Mr. Samuel Redrop   [Died July 5, 1821, aged 79.]
203. Mr. William Brown, my son [see ch. III., sec. 61]. Dec. 3, 1809.
204. Miss S. Brown, my daughter [see ch. III., sec. 62]. Dec. 3.
205. Mr. Joseph Yates.
206. Mrs. Yates.
207. Mr. Redrope   4 March, 1813.
208. Mr. [John] Jones, clothier.[46]
209. Mrs. [Margaret] Burton, Queen Street. Second wife of Mr. John
       Burton (see ch. III., note 31), of the Yspytty.
210. Mr. E. Evans[47]   March, 1813.

41. Catherine, daughter of Mr. Hugh Burton, grocer (see ch. III, note 30), baptized November 11th, 1768, married, October 10th, 1798, Mr. John Painter, by whom she became the mother of the late Mr. Thomas Painter ; died June 18th, 1824, and was buried in the Dissenters' Graveyard.

42. Elizabeth, first wife of Mr. John Burton, of the Yspytty (see ch. III, note 31); died July 23rd, 1810, aged 43, and was buried in the Dissenters' Graveyard.

43. Edward Jackson, dyer, of Pentrefelin ; married (January 1st, 1797,) Esther Pearse, (see note 37) died April 4th, 1811, in the 72nd year of his age, and was buried in the Dissenters' Graveyard.

44. William Burton (already once mentioned), grocer, of High Street, brother of Mr. John Burton (see ch. III, note 31), lived where Mr. Edisbury's shop now is ; died February — 1811, aged 44, and was buried in Dissenters' Graveyard, leaving a widow, and one daughter, Elizabeth, afterwards the wife of Enoch Gerrard, accountant, of Chester.

45. Rev. James Parry, schoolmaster, of Dr. Daniel William's school, Wrexham, afterwards of Chester ; married Miss Martha Kenrick, of Wynne Hall [see ch. III, sec 37, (6)] ; died at Chester, April 20th, 1848, aged 72.

46. John Jones, clothier, of High Street, where Mr. Scotcher's shop now is, elder son of Mr. John Jones, of The Linen Hall, husband of Sarah, eldest daughter (see ch. III, sec. 62) of the Rev. Wm. Brown ; died Nov. 4, 1826, aged 89, and was buried in the Dissenters' Graveyard.

47. Edward Evans, third son of Mr. Thomas Evans, skinner, and brother of Mr. Thomas Evans, tanner : he was himself also a tanner, and had the Tannery where is now the old Pentrefelin Brewery ; died in 1839 ; father of the present Mr. Edward Evans, of Manchester.

211. Mr. E. Evans [probably a mistake for *Mrs.* E. Evans, indicating Jane (Kempster) Mr. Edward Evans' *second* wife.]
212. Mrs. E. Andrew — May, 1813
213. Mrs. [Eliz.] Beardsworth — 1813. [widow of Mr. John Beardsworth, see ch. III. Note 14.]
214. Mrs. Jackson [see (161)] returned after being with the Methodists, 1813.
215. Miss Mary Ann Hayton — 1813. [Daughter of Mr. John Hayton, jun., of the Wire Mill, Gwersyllt, see ch. III. note 32.]
216. My daughter Abigail [Browne] — 1814. [See ch. III. sec. 62]
217. Mrs. [Mary] Samuel, Plasgoch⁴⁸ — 1814.
218. Miss [Mary Anne] Burton⁴⁹ — 1814.
219 and 220. Mr. and Mrs. Edwards — 1815.
221. Mr. Rogers — 1815.
222. Mrs. Abigail Jones — 1816.
223. Mr. Howell — 1817.
224. — Salisbury — 1817.
225. Eliz. Edwards — 1817, [Died June 6, 1821.]
226. Mr. Isaac Senior⁵⁰ — 1817.
227. Mr. Joseph Senior [of the Moss] — 1817.
228. My daughter Caroline [Browne, see ch. III. see 62]
229. Mr. Hugh Morris — Sept. 1817.[Shoemaker, of York-street, east side]
230. Miss [Sarah] Kenrick, Wynne Hall — 1817.
231. Miss E [lizabeth] Kenrick, Wynne Hall — 1817.
232. Miss M [ary] Kenrick, Wynne Hall — 1817. } 51.
233. Miss L [ydia] Kenrick, Wynne Hall — 1817.
234 and 235. Mr. and Mrs. Stokes — Dec. 1817.
236. Mrs. Davies, Rhosddu⁵² — March 1, 1818.

II.

List of Endowments belonging to the New Meeting, Wrexham.

I. Endowments for Minister :—

			£	s.	d.
1. Land at Holt	.. ..	(see ch. III., sec. 6) about	10	0	0
2. Dr. Daniel Williams' annuity	{ ,, ,, 12)		10	0	0
3. Mrs. Elizabeth Roberts' ,,	{ ,, ,, 17)		10	0	0
4. From Trustees of Poor ..	{ ,, note 23)		10	17	3
5. Miss Deborah Buttall's annuity	{ ,, sec. 45)		4	0	0

48. Widow of Mr. Watkin Samuel, of Plas Coch; died January 31, 1823, and was buried n the Dissenters' Graveyard.

49. Mary Ann, second daughter of Mr. John Burton, of The Yspytty; born Dec. 2, 1801, afterwards wife of the Rev. John Pearce: is still living.

50. Isaac Senior, wire-worker, of High Street: his house and shop occupied part of site of the entrance to the present Market Hall: he was a deacon of the church; died July 6, 1848, aged 56.

51. These four ladies were daughters of the third Mr. John Kenrick, of Wynne Hall (see ch. III sec. 64): they kept a school at Bryn-y-ffynnon.

52. Maria, wife of Thomas Davies, of Rhosddu Farm (now Walnut Tree Tavern.)

L

			£	s.	d.
6. From the Presbyterian Fund, Mr. James Buttall's bequest .. .. .. (see ch. III., sec. 49)			6	0	0
7. Mr. Rd. Harris' annuity .. („ „ 51)			3	5	0
8. Rev. Francis Boult's annuity („ „ 55)			2	0	0
9. Miss Eleanor Hughes' „ („ „ 44)			0	5	0
			£56	7	3

II. Endowments for Poor :—

1. From 3 per cent. Annuities (see ch. III., sec. 41-43)	21	3	5
2. Miss Eleanor Hughes' charity („ „ 44)	49	10	0
	£70	13	5

III.

Selected Extracts from Old Account Book belonging to the Old Meeting.

The first entry in this book is dated June, 1708. The book opens with an account of "how Mr. Hignett's 150 pounds were disbursed" (see chap. IV. sec. 2). A portion of this legacy being kept in hand, the remainder was lent, generally at 6 per cent. interest, to various persons in the town and neighbourhood. Thus Mr. Hugh Burton (see chap. III. note 80), of Stansty, had for years on loan £40 (afterwards reduced to £20) of this money, and as soon as the Rev. John Williams was established as minister of the meeting, first £20 and afterwards £40 of it were lent him, on which sums he regularly paid interest to the day of his death. The moneys in hand, together with the interest received from the loans, were applied in payment of the current expenses of the church and congregation, and in doles to the poor members of the same. The congregational expenses (the chief item of them being the £3 paid yearly as rent of the Meeting-house) were singularly small, and the greater part of the money disbursed was expended in gifts to the poor, in small loans bearing no interest, and in other forms of poor relief.[53] And as the sums annually expended were always in excess of the interest received from the monies lent, these latter were gradually called in and applied as income until at last only about £40 of the principal remained. Various other small legacies and donations, bequeathed and given to the congregation, did no more than delay this process. We

---

53. Between March 26, 1709, and December 31 of the same year, £13 1s. 0d. were distributed in charities, and £3 lent without interest.

are now prepared better to understand the extracts that have been selected for insertion. These extracts, for clearness sake will be grouped under the two heads of I, Disbursements, and II, Receipts.

I. Disbursements :—

			£	s.	d.
June the 24th, 1708, to crismas, 1708 . . . gave Mr. Jenkin Thomas (see ch. IV., sec. 1 and 2) arrears due to him from the congregation			5	0	0
November 2, 1709.	Gave Elizabeth Bronbodell[54]			3	0
December 4, ,,	payd for cutting a grave for a poor woman, a minister's daughter and the coffine			5	6
4, ,,	Gave Joshua Buttalls (see ch. III. note 28) for to buy a coate for Thos. Ellis			3	0
4, ,,	Gave Joshua Buttalls to give the poor at seuerall times		3	0	0
February 8, 1710.	Gave Mr. Samuel Jones, a minister of South Wales[55]			5	0
August 26, 1711.	gave a coffine for Sam: Fenna			6	0
Sept. 29, ,,	Gave Mr. Baddy (see ch. IV., note 2)			5	0
October 10, ,,	payd for the grass of his horse..			1	0
Nov. 19, ,,	gave Jane Ethell [Ithel] to pay her rent ..			10	0

[Between July 15 and October 26, 1711, £10 were given away to the poor, one poor man (John Randles) getting as much as £2 10s.]

			£	s.	d.
July 12, 1712.	Payd me Uncle Samuell Kenrick[56] the sum of eight pounds for arrears of rent for the meeting (see ch. II. sec. 27) instead of the Collection that the rent use to be payd out		8	0	0
22, ,,	gave for berring [burying] Elizabeth Owens, coffin and crape			9	0
22, ,,	gave a Coffin and Shute of Crape for Elizabeth Reeves			9	0
May 26, 1713.	gave Mr. Pugh, minister, for a horse to Sallop and his charges red lion			5	6
26, ,,	payd Joshua Buttalls (see before) for his [i.e., Mr. Pugh's] diet and his brother's diet ..			5	0
March 10, 171¾.	Payd for a Coffine for ould Ann, 4s. 0d. Shute of crape, 2s. 6d.		0	6	6
March 10, 171¾.	Payd for coales wⁿ shee was sick, and candles and other		0	5	11½
Dec. 31, 1715.	made a Coffin and Shute of Crape for Katherine Edwards		0	10	0
	payd for drink for the berring [burying] ..			2	6

54. Elizabeth Hughes, of Bron Boodle. Bron Boodle was a cottage and enclosure within what is now Erddig Park, near "The Court." It had originally belonged to John Boodle, of Wrexham.

55. The Rev. Samuel Jones (or John), minister of Cilfowyr, Pembrokeshire : died there June 21, 1746, aged 80.

56. This was written by Mr. Thomas Robinson, joiner, whose mother was the sister of Mr. Samuel Kenrick, of the Fawnog (see ch. II., sec. 27), so that the Rev. John Kenrick of the New Meeting and Mr. Thos. Robinson were cousins. Mr. Th. Robinson lived in Stryt y Syfwr (now Queen Street), in a house represented by that now occupied by Mr. Ashton Bradley.

£ s. d.

Sept. 3, 1716.	Payd Cozin John Kenrick[57] for to make up the rent for the meeting	
July 23, 1717.	gave Mr. Morgan Thomas[58]	5 0
Nov. 24, 1723.	Gave Joseph Edwards[59] and Joshua Buttalls (see before) to give ye poor	10 0
August 30, 1725.	payd Samuell Edwards for a fortnight's diet for Hannah Powell, and for there looking after her 3s. a week for 2 weekes	6 0
November 1,1725.	gave Mr. Baddy (see chap. IV. note 2) which came from [i.e., the fees derived from] ye berring place for 1725 fro: Jo[n]. Clubb[60] ..	10 0
Feb. 16, 1725-6.	Gave John Clubb the 30s. from Ruall (see ch. II. note 15) his accounts show how he disbursed it	1 10 0
July 18, 1726.	gave Ruth for sweaping the Meeting	1 0
March 12, 172⁶⁄₇.	gave to make up a ginny for Mr. Parr ..	2 6
	payd for Mr. Whilliams (see ch. IV. note 7) horse, hay, and gauve him	5 0
	payd for 2 nights' hay for Mr. Jeruie's horse and bateing	1 0
May 22, 1727.	gave Katherine Whilliams, widow, by Ruthin . . . . . . in the world—an ould member of this congregation	5 0
May 22, 1727.	payd John Clubb for hedgeing the berring place	9
	gave Sarrah Powell, at Travor, a poor member	2 6
June 6, ,,	payd for bottles of Claret for ye use of congregation..	5 9
August 19, ,,	Payd Daniel Abedward [ab Edward] one pound which they layd out upon Hannah Powell account when out of order	1 0 0
Sept. 29, ,,	for a coffin for Mary Burton	6 0
Nov. 6, .,	Gave Mr. John Davies, minister at swansy,[61] when sick in town	5 0
Jany. 20, 172⁷⁄₈.	Hugh Burton's wife when Lieing in and for rent to Samuell Edwards	18 9
April 3, 1728.	Gave Mr. Whilliams, of Newmarket (see ch. IV., note 7)	5 0
	for a month's diet when sick at our houses ..	10 0
	payd Roger Whitticar to bring Mr. Whilliams to Newmarket, 4 dayes	4 0
April 6, ,,	gave Petter Fennah[62] his jurney and horse to Llanvollin, with a Letter from ye Congregation to Mr. Jervyes and ye Congregation ..	7 0

57. This was written by Mr. John Robinson (see note 67).

58. The Rev. Morgan Thomas was in 1718 minister of Goltre, in Monmouthshire: he afterwards sometimes supplied the pulpit of the Baptist congregation at Hengoed, Glamorganshire.

59. Joseph Edwards was an elder of the Old Meeting.

60. John Clubb, mason, lived at the honse in Abbot Street, now occupied by Mr. Fred. Jones; married August 5, 1711, Hannah Buttall, who was a daughter of James Buttall, of the Lampint: from her he appears to have derived the house on the east side of Abbot Street, next the old Vicarage, which belonged to him; died about the year 1746.

61. The Rev. John Davies, assistant to the Rev. Morgan Jones, minister of the Baptist congregation at Swansea; died 1743, aged 73.

62. Peter Phennah was a farmer living at one of the farms in Brymbo, called Glascoed, and one of the chief members of the Old Meeting.

May	29,	,,	payd for a nighls grass for Mr. Whilliams, his [horse]		6
July	2,	,,	payd for 2 bottles of wine for ye congregation	6	0
Dec.	12,	,,	Payd Mr. Stennett (see ch. IV., sec. 11) to goe to his Junny	10	0
			Payd to make up his horse hire..	5	0
			,, Mr. Stennett for his Jurny	10	0
			,, Mr. [John] Phillips (see ch. IV., sec 12), for his Jurny	15	0
Dec.	31,	,,	,, for oates for Mr. Phillips hors		9
Jany.	11, 172⅜.		Gave Mr. John Whilliams, tanner (see chap. III, note 14) to give the poor..	7	6
Feb.	10,	,,	payd for another pound candles		6
Apl.	2, 1729.		pd. for a Load [? a pannierful] of coales ..		6½
	9,	,,	payd towards Mr. Phillips diet	2 0	0
			,, for 2 bottles of wine		6 0
	21,	,,	pd. for bread and washing cloth		1 0
			,, ,, 4 nights' hay for Mr. Gerues' (see ch. IV, note 4) horse		2 0
June	8,	,,	gave Ruth for sweaping the meeting		1 0
July	28,	,,	payd sweaping the top meeting [? the loft] ..		6
Aug.	19,	,,	for Mr. [Rev. John] Phillips (see ch. IV, sec. 12)..		2 0
Sept.	11,	,,	mad a coffin for Lowry [Williams]		6 0
,,	16,	,,	Simon [Jones ?] for Hedgeing and for ditching the new churchyard for putting rails ..		1 0
			payd for Mr. Phillips horse grass		6
Jany.	10,17⅔⁰.		Paid Roger Burton[63] for the Edgrew[64] for Mr. Phillips, his horse	16	0
June	3, 1734.		Paid Peter Fenner (see note 62) for Mr. [Edmund] Jones horse		6 0
Jany.	25, 173⅘.		Paid Mr. Williams (ch. IV., note 7) the sum of 3 pounds fro. the Colect [collection ?] mony yt. was in hand: either to pay him or to pay Peter Chalinor[65] for his diet : of this £3 pd. there was 2 pd fro. the Col . . . [collection] and one pd. from Hugh Burton Interest woh was to pay Mr. Ken[rick] one year's Rent		
March,	21	,,	Paid Peter Chalinor too pounds which I had fro. Ruall, being one years interest for the year 1733 for Mr. Edmon. Jones (see ch. IV. sec. 12) Diet	2 0	0
	12,	,,	Paid Mr. David Williams (see ch. IV., sec. 12) from the Colections at Dore	1 10	0
April	25, 1735.		Paid Mr. David Williams	2 0	0
May	4,	,,	,, for a letter from Bristo		5

63. Roger Burton, mercer : his shop was at the corner of High Street and Church Street; buried in the Churchyard, November 23, 1731.

64. "Edgrew," generally corruptly called "headgrow," is the local English name for "aftermath" or "after-grass." It is the only word remaining (unless "eddish" be another) which contains the old English prefix ed -now everywhere else replaced by the Latin prefix "re"—which has not nearly so sweet a sound. Surely "ednew" (edniwian) is a better word than "renew," and "edkindling" (edcenning) than "regeneration."

65. Peter Chaloner (often called "Chandler,") shoemaker (?) of Hope Street, where the shop of Mr. A. Rhys Jones now is; was one of the chief members of the Old Meeting, though either he, or his father, had been at first a member of the Presbyterian congregation.

			£ s. d.
June	26, 1735.	Paid Wm. Davies[66] fro. South Wales	5 0
	28, „	„ for Mr. [Morgan] Harrys (see ch. IV. sec. 12) and Mr. David's [Mr. Davies] horses ..	1 2
		„ for Mr. Watts Psalms	1 6
July	13, 1735.	Paid Simon Parry for grass for Mr. Morgan Harry's horse	2 7
		„ Mr. Morgan Harry (see before)	1 1 0
August	11, „	Gave Mr. Wms. for Wate's Hims [Watts' Hymns]	1 6
		Pd to Mr. Garvis fro ye poors mony Colect ..	2 6
		Ditto to John Samll for Glassing	3 5
Jan.	12, 173⅚.	Gave Mr. Stennet (see ch. IV., sec. 11) ..	10 0
	20, „	Pd Mr. Stennet for a letter from Mr. Harry's father (see before)	5
	. 1736.	Pd Mr. Stennet for a London letter	5
		Paid for a pound of Candels	5
		Pd to Debro Robson for Mary Ellis Srowd ..	3 6
		„ for Drink for Mary Ellis Burriall	2 0
		„ for Mary Ellis Cofins—to Jno. Robinson[67]	7 6
Feb.	12, 173⅞.	Sarrah Powell had a Brown Lofe from Thos. Sweetnam	4
Mch.	15, ' „	Payd Simon Jones, Sawer, for the new churchyeard (see note 87) work 10 0	
		He had more fro the Cooper .. 5 0	
		„ „ „ „ the Turner .. 7 0	
		„ „ „ in outsides Slabes .. 2 6	
		[he] Rec. for kides 1 0	
		Recd. fro Jno. Robison[67] 8 0	
		————	1 13 6
May	10, 1737.	Paid Peter Chalinor for a pair of Shoes for Whitegar gerle [Whittaker's girl]	1 10
October	3, 1737.	Gave for a load of lime	10
January	1, 1738.	Paid Jno. Edwards a day's work	1 4
October	25, „	Jno. Clubb (see note 60) paid to Mr. Morgan Harry (see ch. IV. sec. 12) from the 8s. 11d. in my hand	5 0
Feb.	8, 174½.	Paid for a pd. of Candels to Daniel Ken[rick, see ch. II. sec. 27]	6½
		Paid Jno. Samuell for Repairing ye Glass Windows of ye ould Meeting	2 1
Sept.	3, 1741.	Gave for a quart of wine..	1 6
October	11 „	Paid John Huse for a paire of Shose	2 4
Jan.	1, 174¾.	Paid Simon Jones for making between us and the loft	1 6
Feb.	21 „	Paid for a load of Coles [? a pannier-ful] ..	6
August	29 „	Gave Mr. [Evan] Jenkins for wt he gave Mr. Jonson[68]	5 0

66. The Rev. Wm. Davies had previously been assistant to the Rev. Griffith Jones, pastor of Pen-y-fai, Glamorganshire: in 1737 he emigrated to Pennsylvania, and there died in the year 1768.

67. John Robinson, joiner, of Stryt y Sytwr, son of the Thos. Robinson already mentioned (see note 56), and succeeded the latter in his house and business; married, January 25, 1733-4, at Gresford, Deborah Edwards, who was probably his cousin (daughter of Daniel and Deborah Edwards, see ch. II., sec. 27). He appears to have afterwards left Wrexham, and I suppose he was the same "John Robinson, joyner, from Chester," who was buried in the Rhosddu Road Burial Ground, May 12, 1773.

68. Doubtless the Rev. John Johnson, minister of the Byrom Street Chapel, Liverpool. So zealous a Whig and Hanoverian was he that when in the following year, during the rebellion of 1745, Prince Charles Edward, the young Pretender, invaded Lancashire,

October	9, 1743.	Gave Mr. Harry (see ch. IV. sec. 12)	5	0	
May	7, 1744.	Gave Mr. Jenkins	10	0	
Feb.	3, 174⁴⁄₅.	Gave Mr. Brown	5	0	
July	4, 1745.	Paid Mr. John Kenrick [a year's] rent for the Meeting House	3 0	0	
October 7,	,,	Gave Mr. Jenkins	1 0	0	
Dec. 29	,,	,, Mr. Bostock [here again in Sept., 1749]	5	0	
June	29, 1746	,, Mr. Oulton [see ch. IV. note 8; here again in January following]	5	0	
July	6, 1746.	Paid Mr. [Daniel] Kenrick Towards horse Hair [hire?]	1	6	
Jan.	3, 174⁶⁄₇.	Paid Mary Evans towards her rent	6	0	
April	11, 1747.	Paid Rich^d. Davis for fencing in Chester Street [around property recently acquired there (see ch. IV., sec. 13)	3	0	
July	1, ,,	Paid for Sweeping ye Chimy		2	
Sept.	21, ,,	Paid Rent [of the Meeting House]	2 17	6	
Jany.	28, 174⁸⁄₉.	Gave towards Sam^ll. Edw^ds. Coffin	5	0	
,,	8, ,,	Gave Mr. Morgans.⁶⁹ [This entry often recurs]	5	0	
Sept.	16, 1749.	Paid Rent [of the Meeting House]	2 10	0	
May	10, 1751.	Paid for Camging Cups [Communion Cups]		6	
Dec.	25, ,,	Paid for Building and Repairing at Chester Street	1 8	2	
August	20, 1752.	Gave Mr. Miles Harry⁷⁰	10	0	
July	7, 1753.	Pd for cutting Mr. Morgan grave (see note 69)	2	0	
Dec.	28, ,,	Pd William Hughs for paveing before ye Houses in Chester Street	5	11½	
March	9, 1754.	Pd for Tining⁷¹ ye Buring Yard	2	3	
		Pd. for seting of quicksets in the Burying ground		10	
		pd for Thach and Thach-Pricks, and to Thatcher and his man in Chester Street ..	10	0	
Jany.	31, 1756.	pd on account of Work and Materialls for ye fitting up of them Housis in Chester Street for Mr. [David] Jones [the minister] ..	1 4	2	
		For a load of Coles		7	
March	27, 1756.	Pd for Thatching of Mr. Jones House [Rev. D. Jones] and thach and thach-pricks ..	6	1½	

In "bread and wine" between 2/- and 1/8 a month were at this time expended.

he enlisted in the Regiment of Volunteers formed at Liverpool, to assist the king's forces Afterwards, on account of the dissatisfaction caused in his congregation by preaching what was called "Sabellianism," he drew off and built a new chapel in Stanley Street, where he continued until his death in the year 1791, at the age of 90. His followers were called "Johnsonian Baptists." He was succeeded at Byrom Street by the Rev. John Oulton. Mr. Johnson's name is mentioned again in the chapel accounts in August, 1744, and in March, 1752.

69. Rev. Wm. Morgan became minister of the Baptist congregation at Shrewsbury in 1748 and subsequently came very frequently to Wrexham, especially after the death of Mr. Evan Jenkins. In 1753 he set out with the intention of attending the Assembly at Halifax, but became sick on the way, returned from Liverpool to Chester, and there died. Thence his body was brought to Wrexham, and buried in the Dissenters' Graveyard (see App. III., July 17, 1753.)

70. Rev. Miles Harry was one of the most eminent Baptist ministers in Wales at that time: he was for many years pastor of Pen-y-garn, Monmouthshire, where he died in the year 1776, aged 76.

71. To "tine" is to hedge, or to trim or repair a hedge.

		1758.	pd for advice on account of our being refused a licence to Edward Edwards' House in the Glinn (see ch. IV., sec. 18)	6	0
Nov.	12, ,,		To Hugh of ye New Bridge	1	0
Feb.	4, 1759.		pd for ye Stamps and drawing ye writeings for ye houses in Chester Street	11	0
July	22, ,,		pd Edward Jones for mending the Little door to the Burying yard	2	6
Jany.	27, 1760.		paid for Mr. Rees Hire five nights[72]	2	6
			gave him out of the box	5	0
Feb.	15, 1761.		Old Marey at ye Glinn	1	0

[The following entries belong to 1761, but the exact dates are not given :]

		paid for Mr. Rees hors 1/, for his shurts 1/5 ..	2	5
		Hed out of the Box to finish for his sherts ..		6
		A Briddil for Mr. [Rd.] Jones's Hors[76].. ..	2	0
		Gave to Mr. Smith and Mr. Rees	5	0
		paid for 2 loads of cols 1/2, for 2 Beesoms 1d.	1	3
		,,　,, 2 pound of candel	1	0
		,, to Elizabeth Rogers's funeral	8	0
		,,　,, Edward Moris of ye Glinn	5	0
		,,　,, a Table Cloth to the meeting	4	0
May	6, 1762.	to Mr. Jacob Rees 2s. 6d., for his hors 8d. ..	3	2
		Paid for clanin Mr. Rees' watch	1	0
July	8, ,,	,, to Marey Evans her half-year pay for cleaning the meeting-house in order to pay the Landlord his rent	6	6
		for a Hors to Ruthin 2s. 6d., for Expencis 2s. 6d.	5	0
		for the atorney oharge 5/-, Clark of the peace 6d...	5	6
		paid for a horse to Elsmar	1	6
September, 1762.		Mr. Rees' paid for		6
		Given him at his going [twice]..	5	0
Jany.	13, 1763.	paid to Mr. Kendrick one pound seaventeen shillings and sixpence, being 3 quarters of a year's [rent] Due the 4th of August, 62 ..	1 17	6

[The above is the last entry of payment for rent of meeting-house.]

		22. ,,	paid for hay for Mr. Thos[73] hors	2	0
			,, ,, the Stabil and Looking after the Hors	1	6
March	26, ,,		for velvet for the coshin	14	0
		,,	Mr. Jones [the minister] for 2 Leters from Mr. Thos. of Lemster (see note 73)		2
			gave to Mr. Thomas of Lemster [Here again, May 19, 1765 and June 17, 1768]	2	6

71. The Rev. Jacob Rees, formerly (1738-1745) at Olchon, Herefordshire ; buried at Pen-y-fai, Glamorganshire, where he had at first been member and assistant minister, April 17, 1772, aged 90.

73. This was the Rev. Joshua Thomas, Baptist minister at Leominster, the well-known author of *Hanes y Bedyddwyr ymhlith y Cymry*. He died at Leominster, August 25 1797, aged 78.

[The following entries belong also to 1763 :—]

		paid to Mr. Garside[74] for pleding the ac[tt] for a Licence for the Glinn (see ch. IV. sec. 18)	6 6
		„ for an underside of ye cushing, 1/4 for an inside cloth 1/-	2 4
		„ for sand to clane the puter	½
		„ for tining the croft and Buring ground and for quicksetts	9 9
Jan.	3, 1764.	paid towards the briefs[75] the[y] being not read	2 0
April	„	„ for Mr. Smith's hors	1 6
June 3,	„	„ for saddle Bars to ye Little Window ..	3
		Paid to Mr. Garset [Gartside (see note 74)] towards ye Licence for ye Glinn	5 0
Aug. 5,	„	Pd for Mr. Rices Horse [Mr. Rees here again in May and August, 1765]	8 0
Aug.	26, 1764.	And for mending the Clock	1 4
Nov.	18, „	Gave Mr. Blakeshaw	5 0
July	14, 1765.	„ Mr. Evans[77]	3 11
Dec.	1, „	„ Mr. Poulson	5 0
Jan.	5, 1766.	pd John Ingram for Latches to the window shutters	1 0
Feb.	16, „	pd Richard Price for ash plants for the Burying yard	2 0
Mch.	2, „	Gave to Mr. Phillips [see Mch. 26, 1771] ..	2 6
Apl.	21, „	„ „ Mr. Hall[78] .. .. .. ' ..	5 0
Oct.	19, „	„ „ Mr. Jenkins [afterwards minister of the congregation]	9 0
	23, „	Gave to Mr. Daniel Garnon[79]	2 0
Sept.	13, 1767.	„ „ Mr. Rice, of Carmarthen[80]	2 6
Jan.	13, 1769.	pd to Benjn. Jones for Copeing of the garden wall sout[h]end and carriage..	1 0 0
Mch.	5, „	Gave Lydia of the New Bridge [Lydia Price, see note 95]	5 0
May	16, „	„ to Mr. David Evans[81]	4 6
Aug.	25, „	pd to Mr. Morgan Evans (see note 77) ..	4 0
Feb.	25, 1770.	„ for a Lock to the Door of the burying yard	1 0
Oct.	21, „	„ Wm. Lloyd, for the minister's Horses, 10 nights	5 0
		Mr. Evan's Hors paid for 2 nights at the Talbot	1 7
		Pd for Mr. Wood of Chester Horse	1 0
		„ for a letter to Dr. Stennett	3

74. Danvers Gartside, attorney, of Hope Street (see *Hist. Par. Ch.*, note 26, p. 216).

75. Briefs were letters-patent issued under the great seal authorising the making of collections in places of worship for an object specified in the briefs. They were abolished in 1828.

76. The Rev. Richard Jones, minister of Y Dolau, Radnorshire, from 1750 to 1768 when he was expelled. He preached at Wrexham once a quarter.

77. Probably the Rev. Morgan Evans, of Y Trallwm [see Aug. 20, 1769.]

78. The Rev. Samuel Hall, minister of Byrom Street Baptist Chapel, Liverpool, and successor of Mr. Oulton, 1765-1772.

79. A Mr. "D. Garnen," was assistant minister about this time at Ebenezer Chapel, Pembrokeshire: he preached at Wrexham afterwards once a year until 1774.

80. The Rev. Owen Rees, assistant to the Rev. Stephen Davies, of Carmarthen; was in Wrexham again May, 1768; March and September, 1769; and May and August, 1770.

81. The Rev. David Evans, minister of Y Dolau, where he succeeded Mr. Richard Jones (see note 76). He came from the church of Cilfowyr.

Mch.	10, 1771.	paid for whitewashing the house let to Miss Griffiths[82]		2	0
May	26, „	„ „ Mr. Phillips of Angleseys Horse to the Egls [now Wynnstay Arms]		2	0
		„ „ Mr. Matthews Chester horse.. ..		1	6
		„ „ 2 cart loads of Coals		14	4
Dec.	22,	Collected for & paid to James Williams of Ochton [? Olchon], Herefordshire		13	0
May	3, „	to Mr. Jenkins [afterwards minister of the congregation]		5	0
July	19, „	to Rev. Mr. Phillips [see May 26]		2	6
Mch.	14, 1773.	Pd for making Room for ye Bier		1	9½
May	5. „	for whitewashing the meeting to John Catridge & 1 pound of glue		5	6
July	3, 1774.	Mr. Armitage's horse[83]		1	0
Dec.	4, „	paid for 25 pitches of coal[84] at 8½		17	8½
Mch.	5, 1778.	Pd for Mr. Ashworth's Horse		2	0
June	6, „	pd to the Rev. Mr. Jones		2	6
May	12, 1779.	„ for whitewashing and painting ye meeting		10	0
Sept.	29, 1780.	Mr. Hurst's Horse..		1	3
July	22, „	Filling the Baptistry twice			6
Oct.	20, 1782.	Mr. Crabtree's Horse			10
		Do. Mr. Ecking[85] in July..		3	6
Jany.	3, 1783.	Lock for the door under the pulpit		1	8
Oct.	9, 1784.	payd for three pounds of Candles		1	8½
Dec.	10, „	3 Save-alls			3
March	14, 1786.	Locks for the Burying Ground and repairing the Hedge of ditto		8	6
July	13 „	three briefs (see note 75)			6
March	2, 1790.	Sweeping meeting 6 weeks		1	6

The last regular entry relating to the chapel and congregation occurs in January, 1792, about which time Dr. Jenkins resigned. Then follows a number of charges for repairs to the meeting and large house [chapel-house, which was let at £11 11s. a year, free of taxes]. Of these charges the following may be given :—

Sept.	29, 1794.	Hinges for door under Stairs in Vestry ..			7
		Pumpmakers Bill	3	3	0
		painting, glazing, etc.			
		Beer for workmen at different times		2	0
April	11, 1795.	Half-years' taxes		18	4½
July		Shutters to Stop ye Window on the Garratt Stairs		2	0
February,	1796.	Owing to the greatness of water standing on the walk at the end of meeting was oblidge to get wooden troughs to meet those on the large house.			

82. This was the house on the South side of the chapel, formerly occupied by the Rev. Dd. Jones.

83. Rev. Wm. Armitage was the first regular minister of the Independent Chapel, in Common Hall Street, Chester, now represented by that in Queen Street. Mr. Armitage was minister of the congregation from 1772 until his death, March 26, 1794, aged 56.

84. "Peitches" are the small wagons in which the coal is brought up from the pits.

85. The Rev. Samuel Ecking, born at Shrewsbury in 1757; settled in Chester in 1783, where he remained until his death (Feb. 5, 1785) at the age of 27. He was buried in the Dissenters' Graveyard, Wrexham, where his wife, a daughter, and three grandchildren also lie. He was the author of "Three Essays on Grace, Faith, and Experience," published in 1784 at Chester.

In 1799 are the following :—

> Paid 1 years Interest to Dr. Joseph Jenkins on
> £50, being money laid out by him on the
> large house in Chester Street..   ..   .. 2 10 0
> Paid Cash to Mr. Roberts, the minister   .. 5 19 7½

On June 1, 1806, at a church meeting it was resolved (see ch.
IV, note 29) that there should be recorded as owing to Mr.
Wm. F. Jenkins in respect of moneys disbursed, during the years
1803-1806, for the repair of the Chapel and Chapel-House, the
sum of £30 19s. 6d. This sum included, among other items, the
following :—

1801-1804.	To Pool for colouring the Meeting	£1 0 6
	Balance of Pallisades in front of Meeting ..	1 15 5
1805.	For repairing of the pump	10 15 0
1806.	Expenses at R. Price's ordination (see ch. IV., sec. 44)	3 8 0

Among those who contributed to meet these charges were :—
John Ratcliffe, Anna Jenkins, W. F. Jenkins, 25/- each ; R.
Price, £1 1s. 0d. ; S. Roberts, 5/- ; Isaac Matthews (see ch. IV.,
note 25a), 5/- ; Elizth. Griffiths, 10/6.

I now resume the regular course of the extracts :—

Dec.	1805.	Half year's salary to Mr. Price..	25 0 0
May	3, 1806.	Filling the baptistry	1 0
Dec.	6, „	To Cash pd repairing Burying ground Wall ..	1 1 8
		paid to the [Baptist] Fund	0 18 0
Aug.	10, 1807.	To Price (Collection for Fund)..	1 0 8
Dec.	14 „	To Mr. Price for Letters	2 0
		Years Salary paid to R. Price	60 0 0
	1808.	Filling Baptistry	4 6
		Hay and Corn a ministers Horse	4 6
		3 sets Briefs	7 0
1809, 1st Jany. to 1st Sunday in July, Cash to Mr. Price			30 6 0
Sept.	1809.	To do to Mr. Barraclough (see ch. IV. sec. 45) for supplying	7 7 0
„	„	To cash towards Mr. Barraclough's journey ..	1 1 0
		Briefs	4 8
		„ to Mr. Shepard [Rev. Shepherd, of Byrom St. Chapel, Liverpool, for supplying]	12 0
		Briefs to Mr. Pryce [for supplying] ..	1 5 0
Oct.	8, 1809.	To Miss Jenkins to two weeks board, Mr. Price	1 4 0
		carriage of Barraclough's Box and Pack ..	19 1
	16 „	To Mr. Barraclough for Expenses of Journey	6 0 0
Dec.	21 „	To Cash to Barraclough	4 4 0
		To Baptizing gown	14 11
Jany.	10, 1810.	To Conveyance for Pryce to Oswestry in part of road home	6 0
Feb.		To Expenses of Provision, &c., at the ordination [of Mr. Barraclough]	2 2 0
May	1810.	To Miss Jenkins [interest of] £60 on Cottage, 9 months..	2 2 0

			£	s.	d.
Nov.	„	To Owens, Carpenter, for repairs and troughs for Baptistry and altering Pulpit	9	2	8
		To Davies for painting Trough and Meeting ..	2	5	0
		„ Briefs		3	0
June	3, 1811.	To Davies for supplying and horse		8	6
	20, „	To Mrs. Barraclough		2	6
		„ Sundry Expenses at the funeral of Mr. Barraclough and shroud	2	18	6
		„ part of Stokes Bill for the Alteration of the House by Mr. Barraclough	5	4	9
	[Other charges for the alteration of the house amounting to £13 0s. 10d.]				
July	18, 1811.	Cash to Mrs. Barraclough	4	4	8
	22, „	Funeral Cake, 7lbs. at 2s.		14	0
Feb.	1812.	To Mr. Pryce for supplying	1	1	0
		½ year's rent of house at Gresford	1	1	0
		To Cash Mr. Pain for supplying twice ..	1	10	6
		To two Horses, Hay, corn, and Ostler.. ..		10	6

II. Receipts :—

[Before]	1708.	Rec[d.] from Mr. Hignetts Executor's the sume of 150		0	0
[Before]	1722.	Rec[d.] from a Legacy left by Mrs. Ann Parry of Ruall	9	4	6
Aug.	30, 1725.	Rec[d.] then of Mr. Jno Jones, Taylor, one half-year's rent for the croft due and ending Midsummer Last past, 1725[86]		18	9
Oct.	31, 1725.	Rec[d.] of John Clubb[6] for the hay of the new churchyard for 1725[87]		10	0
July	17, 1727.	Rec[d.] of Mr. Benjamin from Mr. Hugh Lloyd of London for ye minister, which Mr. Lloyd gave 2 guineas	2	2	0
June	25, 1728.	Rec[d.] from Mr. Samuell Zackary[83] for the minnister's use		10	0
[Dec.	1728.	£20 spoken of as received from Rhual]			
Jany.	11, 172[9].	Rec[d.] of Mr. Ratcliffe, skinner (see ch. III, sec. 18) the sum of two pounds being Mrs. Roberts his Legacy to our Meeting	2	0	0
June	26, 1729.	Rec[d.] of Mr. Nathania Griffiths[80] for the Interest of 40 pounds being forty shillings for one years Interest due the 15th day of february last past, 1728			
June	28, 1729.	Rec[d.] of Mr. Zackary forty shillings in part for Mr. [John] Phillips his diet (see ch. IV, sec. 12)	2	0	0
		Rec[d.] more from Mr. Zackary which was lent Mr. Whilliams Newmarket (see ch. IV, note 7)	1	0	0

86. This was Hugh Burton's croft—The Garden Field—now an open space, nearly opposite the Rhosddu Burying Ground, which was mortgaged to the Old Meeting to secure the money lent to Mr. Burton.

87. The Dissenters' Graveyard in Rhosddu Lane was at first commonly called "The New Churchyard," or "The New Burying Ground."

88. I believe Mr. Samuel Zackary, who was a prominent member of the congregation, to have lived in the parish of Gresford.

80. Probably Mr. Nathaniel Griffith, brother of Mr. Thomas Griffith, of Rhual (see ch. II., note 15.)

[1729. Collections are now mentioned for first time: "collections for the poor at the door" seldom at this time realized more than 2s., nor "at the ordinances" more than 8s.]

Aprell 9th day	1730.	Recd. from Mr. Zackary. In part for a years diet which came from Ruall	2	0	0
June the 24th day	1730.	Recd. then more from Mr. Zackary, more towards diet from Robert Ellise from Ruall	2	3	6
June	6, 1730.	Recd. from Cousin John Kenrick (see note 57) paid Mr. Phillips for Mrs. Roberts Allowance to the Ould Meeting ending Lady Day, 1732	2	10	0
Jany.	20, $173\frac{0}{1}$.	Recd. from Mr. Hugh Lloyd for the use of the Congregation for the supplies of ministers..	1	10	0
Dec.	16, 1732.	Recd. from Mary Burton, widow, [of Hugh Burton, Stansty], Executress to the will of Jannet Davies, the sum of 2lb. 0s. 0d. Left by her to the poor of the Congregation of the Ould Meeting she belong to			
		Recd. of Colections at the Door when Mr. Edmon Jones (see ch. IV. sec. 12), cam the second time			
Mch.	12, $173\frac{4}{5}$.	fro: Nancy Edwards		6	0
"	21, "	two pounds fro Peter Fenna[61] fro Rhuall, being one year's Interest for Mr. Edmund Jones Diet, for the yeare 1733			

[The "Collection at the door" after 1734 seldom reached 1/6, except once a month on Sacrament Sunday when it averaged 3/-.]

Sept.	14, 1735.	1st Sabath Mr. [Morgan] Harry [see chap IV. sec. 12] cam ye second time. Recd ..			10
"	27 "	1st Saboth: Mr. Hry (see before) cam. Recd ..			9
Oct.	31 "	1st Saboth. Mr. Hary Cam (see before) ..			10½
Jany.	23, $173\frac{6}{7}$.	1st Sabath. Mr. D. Jenkins cam		1	2¾
"	26 "	Recd. then a legacy left by Joseph Jones, son of Jno Jones of Cay Mawr to the poor of the Congrä of the ould Meeting and Distributed		10	0
Mch.	3, $173\frac{6}{7}$.	Sould to Jno Clubb (see note 60) of Bordes fro: the new yeard[87] 200 fo[ot] of Sickimor Bords at $\frac{4}{3}$ p. fo:		18	11
		for too Side Trees..		1	0
May	20, 1739.	Recd. at the Door of Colection towards the Building of a new Meeting house at Lanbrinmaire[90] the sum of seventeen shillings			
Sept.	23, 1740.	1st Sabott. Mr. Jenkins came this time ..		1	2
Jany.	9, $174\frac{1}{2}$.	Mary Davies of the Tabot [Talbot] Put her Corne in the Loft belonging to the meeting the Rent is 10s.			
"	11 "	Recd. from Benjamin Jones one pound 8/-. Interest Due fro Hugh Burton and one shilling fro: Joseph Wittycar			

90. The congregation at Llanbrynmair being expelled from Ty Mawr, a farmhouse in which they had long worshipped, were now building the chapel which was enlarged in 1778, and rebuilt in 1821. The pastor of the Llanbrynmair church at this time was the Rev. Lewis Rees, the father of the well-known Dr. Abraham Rees.

Jany.	14, 174$\frac{3}{4}$.	Rec^d then from Mary Williams [of the Talbot] the sum of ten Shillings for one whole year's Rent for the Loft belong to the meeting. [This entry often recurs, but will not be again quoted].			
June	6, 1742.	Rec^d at ye Door for ye Chaing of ye Peeter peny			7
	13, ,,	Rec^d at the new meeting			8
July	30, 1743.	Rec^d of Hannah Club (see note 60)	2	13	1$\frac{3}{4}$
		,, of Simon Jones for the butt of a tree		7	0
June	8, 1746.	Rec fourteen shillings being the od mony of what was Rec at Rhyall		14	0
July	7, 1747.	Rec^d of Mary Burton twenty shillings Interest [of £20 for 1 year]	1	0	0
July	11, 1749.	Rec^d Hannah Dutton's rent [for half-year] ^{1}..	4	10$\frac{1}{2}$	
Sept.	26, 1749.	Rec^d Mr. Daniel Leonard's Half years rent^{91}	9	9	
June	1, 1759.	Rec from Mr. Wright 5/- for ye Mares graseing in ye Burying yard		5	0
Sept.	16, 1764.	Collection was given to ye Brifs (see note 75)			
	30, ,,	Collection was for Mr. Waine's meeting			
Mch.	24, 1765.	Collected for the parish of Gwenddwr [Brecknockshire] for a meeting which was paid to that purpose			
July	10, 1770.	Recev^d of Mr. Hugh Burton junior the Sum of Eight pounds, being interest due for £20 wich was lent his father upon Bond and wich Interest is due since the 5 of November 1761 Exclusive of what is not paid before, Received by me for the Benefit of the Poor of this Congregation as witness my hand THOS. JONES.			
		We the underwriten members acknowledge that the said sum was paid with no vew but to secure the princapile and that it was Returned to Hugh Burton junior to enable him to support his father in his illness as witness our hands, Richard Roberts, John Matthews, Benjn Jones, Robert Thomas his mark, John Hughes.			
Aug.	14, 1774.	Collected for Mr. John Hughes^{92}			
Oct.	2, ,,	Collected for Christopher Seaman a Refugee from Poland.			
		N.B.—This was an impostor and afterwards imprisoned.			
May	5, 1776.	Collected for Mr. Hartleys Case	4	10	0
Aug.	18, ,,	,, ,, ,, The [Baptist] Fund		18	0

[This collection recurs every year : it amounted at this time to 15/- a year on an average.]

May	28, 1786.	For the thorns in Burying ground		8	6
		grazing three horses in Burying ground		9	0

91. These are the rents of the two houses in Chester Street, belonging to the Chapel Trustees.

92. The Rev. John Hughes had formerly been minister of the church at Glyn Ceiriog, but having been obliged to depart thence [see App. IV., 3 (6)], came to Wrexham, where he doubtless suffered much from poverty: he afterwards became minister of the little church at Brassey Green (see ch. IV., note 16), where his income must have been very small, and where he died Dec. 25, 1783, aged 38, "leaving this Testimony, the result of six years' confinement by a . . . palsey, 'I know, O Lord, Thy judgments are right.'" He was buried in the Dissenters' Graveyard, Wrexham, where his tombstone may still be seen.

IV.

Old Church Book belonging to the Baptist Chapel.

1. The book begins with the following solemn confession and and declaration of faith :—

We, the Underwritten, Members of the *Baptist Independent Church* in *Wrexham*, professing the Belief of the Doctrines of free, sovereign, and efficacious Grace, do acknowledge the Riches of that Grace of God in providing a savior for us *wretched sinners*, even the *Lord Jesus Christ :* His goodness in sending the Gospel to us at the ends of the earth ; giving us the experience of the power of that Gospel in our souls (thro' the said operations of His Holy Spirit), humbling, comforting, changing, renewing us ; calling us to be a part of His church in this world ; and fixing a pastor over us ; and we *Do Now* in the *Name* and in the *Fear* of *God*, give up ourselves to the Lord and to one another by the Will of God ; desiring to walk together in *Church Fellowship* according to the Rules of the Gospel, that is to say—conscientiously to sanctify the Lord's Day ; to attend on the publick preaching of the word and the administration of the *Ordinances of Christ*, Church-meetings and meetings of prayer, unless some *Unavoidable* Hindrance prevent ; to walk with and watch over one another in love ; endeavouring in the strength of divine grace to *Maintain the Unity of the Spirit* in the Bond of peace, to keep up the life of Religion in our own souls, the exercise of daily prayer in private and in our Families (not forgetting, at such seasons, the peace and prosperity of Zion, and of our own church and pastor in particular) ; and to walk uprightly and circumspectly in our own Families and before the world, That others may see our good works, and glorify our Father who is in Heaven. *Amen.*

Signed by the church present this *Fourteenth Day of September* in the year of our Lord, 1773, By Joseph Jenkins (Pastor).

Men.	*Women.*
Richard Roberts [died Aug. 20, 1777, aged 69.	Sarah Lewis[94]
Benjn. Jones (see ch. IV., note 12)	mark of Anne Roberts
John Matthews (see ch. IV., note 21)	„ „ Eliz. Roberts
mark of Robert Roberts[93]	Frances Jones [junior, expelled]
Wm. Lloyd (see ch. IV., note 22)	Mary Jenkins [widow of Rev. Evan Jenkins]
Daniel Roberts (see ch. IV., note 23)	Elizabeth Jones [afterwards Parnel, dismissed to London]
John Williams	mark of Jane Davies
Jno. Wright	„ „ Anne Jones [dismissed to Glyn Ceiriog, 1776]
John Hughes [Deacon; of Newbridge, farmer] ‡	Anne Roberts ‡
mark of Hugh Davies ‡	mark of Mary Price
„ „ Edward Jones	Elizabeth Hughes [wife of John Hughes, see note 92]

93. Robert Roberts, often called "Robert Roberts *Thomas*": he was a deacon of the church and by trade a shoemaker; died June 3rd, 1787, and was buried in the Rhosddu Road Graveyard.

94. Miss Lewis, daughter of Mr. Arthur Lewis, of Brymbo (see ch. IV., note 13); died Aug. 22 1777, aged 69, and was buried in the Rhosddu Road Graveyard.

„ „ Robert Parry   Lydia Price[95]
Samuel Jones [farmer, of Erddig]
mark of Richard Richards ‡
John Hughes (late pastor of the church
    in Glyn Ceiriog, dismissed Nov.
    10, 1774) [see note 92]

2. Members subsequently admitted to the church signed in addition to the foregoing covenant the following declaration :—

We, the Underwritten, having been (at our request, with a view to the
glory of God, and the comfort and edification of our own souls), proposed and
admitted *Members* of the Christian Church; and having had recited to us
the *Covenant* within agreed to, *do hereby* testify our hearty and unfeigned
assent to the *Solemn Profession of Faith* and experience therein made,
earnestly desiring in the strength of Divine Grace to give ourselves up to
this church in the Lord, to conform ourselves to the several regulations
therein laid down from the word of God, and to walk with the other Members
in Christian Fellowship, according to the rules of the Gospel. Amen.

Men.

Joseph Baumer (cut off)
Edward Davies ‡

James Maddock

Joseph Jones 1774

John Price ‡
Willm. Dixe [see sec. 3 (8)] 1776
John Mellor (see Ch. IV., note 24) † 1777
John Davies
mark of John Charles ‡ 1778
Robert Roberts 1779

Thos. Crane [of Chester] † 1781

Wm. Baugh [farmer of Wrexham,
    see App. I., 176] 1785
Wm. Ridge, of Welshpool
mark of John Edward
    „ „ Rob. Humphreys

Women.

Mary Jenkins, junior) [Sisters of the
Anna Jenkins   ·Rev. Dr. Jen-
)   kins.]

Hannah Jones [wife of Mr. Benjn
    Jones]

mark of Mary Perry [died March 10,
    1785, at Bury, Lanc.] 1771
Ellinr Hughes 1774
mark of Jane Hughes
    „ „ Anne Wynne
    „ „ Deborah Roberts
Est. Elizth. Dixe [see sec. 3 (8)] 1776
Mary Mellor [wife of Mr. John
    Mellor] † 1777
Hannah Jones [daughter of Mr.
    Benjn. Jones?]
mark of Anne Roberts 1778

    „ „ Mary Bickerton 1779
Hannah Langford 1781
Jane Price †
mark of Catherine Hughes
Elln. Chalner
Mary Walley [of Road Street,
    Cheshire] †
mark of Anne Davies [wife of John
    Davies] ‡ 1782
mark of Anne Jones 1785
    „ „ Frances Jones, senior
    „ „ Julian Thomas

95. This Lydia Price was of Newbridge, in the parish of Ruabon, where she died March
15, 1786, aged 90. In connection with her name the following remarkable extract from the
parish registers of Ruabon may be given :—"10br 18, 1725, John, Anne, and Edward, children
of John and Lydia Price, Anabaptists 'Baptized'." It is impossible not to believe that
these children were baptized against their parents' will.

3. After these lists[96] follow the "Minutes and Resolutions" (1773-1787), of the church, headed by the quotation "Let all things be done decently and in order."

(1). At a Church-Meeting, Sept. 14th, [1773] (being the first after the settlement and ordination of our brother Joseph Jenkins as our Pastor), it was *Agreed*, after prayer to the Lord for direction,
That our Brethren, Robert Roberts Thomas, John Hughes, and Daniel Roberts, be put on Trial for the Approbation of the Church in order to be set apart to the office of Deacons in this Church, after the order of the Gospel.

(2). At a Church-Meeting, Lord's Day, November 7th, 1773, Edward Davies, Joseph Baumer, James Maddock, Mary Perry, Mary Jenkins, Anna Jenkins, and Hannah Jones (having been severally at different church-meetings examined as to their faith and experience; submitted to the ordinance of Baptism last Friday, Nov. 5; and signed the church-covenant) were all this day received into the church, and admitted to communion.

[Entries similar to this last frequently occur].

(3). Church-Meeting, Lord's Day, Dec. 5th, 1773, Agreed,
That it is highly proper and may be for the glory of God and the good of this church, that a day be appointed for solemn prayer and fasting, to humble ourselves before God, and seek his presence and blessing upon us as a church of Christ.
Agreed also, That the 25th day of December, as a day of leisure, is proper to be improved for this purpose, and that all the members be entreated to attend here then, at 10 o'clock exactly, if possible.
Agreed, That the Lord's Supper be, during the Winter Season, administered here the Lord's Day that is next to the full moon, for the convenience of the country members, and that this be a regulation in future winters.

(4). December 25th [1773]. At a church meeting of Fasting and Prayer to humble ourselves before God, and seek his presence, direction, and blessing as a Church of Christ after Prayer, it was Agreed,
That every Friday evening from 7 to 8 o'clock be appointed as a weekly meeting of prayer, and that the members will, as often as possible, attend for this purpose.
Agreed, That this be also occasionally a meeting for Conversation on the frame of our own souls and the affairs of the Church.

(5) At a Church-meeting for prayer, held April 14th, 1774,
Information was given that through too great indulgence and neglect for some years past, several abuses have been introduced respecting the Interment of Persons in the Burying ground. It was therefore *resolved unanimously*, that it is highly proper and necessary to remedy the above grievances, and
b Agreed, That none but professed and declared Dissenters from the Church of England shall be buried in our Burying-ground without leave from this Church in a Church-meeting first obtained ; And that for every such person allowed this privilege shall be paid the sum of five shillings, part of which shall be given to our Brother who takes care of the Burying-ground, and the remainder is to be disposed of by the Church.
c Agreed also, That any Persons professedly or declaredly dissenting from the Church of England, and asking leave of the Minister or Deacons of this Church, or either of the Trustees of this place for the time being, shall be

96. Those names to which † is attached are the names of those subsequently dismissed to form the Baptist church in Chester, while those to which ‡ is attached are the names of those dismissed to form the Baptist church at Cefn Bychan. And here it may be proper to add that in Congregational language to "dismiss" is merely to recommend a member of one church to the membership of another.

M

admitted to bury their dead in the said Burying-ground on complying with the payment of the necessary expences, of which no more than 3ᵈ., nor less than 2ᵈ., shall be demanded.

d Agreed also, That our Brother, William Lloyd [see ch. IV., note 22] (being appointed and continued by the Church, keeper of the said Burying-ground), shall have, under the direction of this church, the appointment of places for the interment of the dead, the nomination of the grave digger, and other matters ; That none be admitted to dig a grave there, unless approved of by him, and that, in all cases of difficulty, he appeal to the Church.

e It is desired also, That our Brother, William Lloyd, may have a Copy of the above Resolutions, which he is to produce, if needful, to persons soliciting the Interment of their dead in the Burying-ground.

f And it farther recommended, That, if possible, there be no Funerals on the Lord's day, as it is very inconvenient.

g At this Church Meeting, Intimation was given also, of the Death of our Brother, Samuel Jones [of Erddig], who died in London, March the 8th ; and it was desired that this and the like Providences be inserted in the Church Book, as a motive to the surviving members to be earnest with God, to add more to the Church of such as shall be saved, and to supply the places of those that are taken from us.

(6). At a Church-Meeting, Lord's Day, Feb. 5, 1775, the Revd. John Hughes, late pastor of the church of Glynn, with his wife, Elizabeth Hughes, having been separated from that church by the unkindness of the people, were, in consequence of their dismission to us, and on signing the Church-Covenant, this day admitted members of our Church.

(7). At a church-meeting for fasting and prayer, April 18th [1775] our Brethren Robert Roberts Thomas (see note 93) and John Hughes (of New Bridge), were solemnly recommended to the blessing of God by prayer with imposition of hands, being set apart to the office of Deacons in this Church,—Daniel Roberts having declined the office [sec. 3 (1) above].

(8). At a Church-Meeting, Lord's day, April 21, 1776, it was agreed,

a. That this Church having been for many years on the plan of *open* or *mixt-Communion*, proposes still to continue it, and not alter the original constitution by which Independents (believing the baptism of infants), but agreeing with us in other respects, were admitted to the Lord's Table and other privileges of this Church. Nevertheless, in order to preserve the due ballance between the privileges of the Independents and the Baptists, it is judged proper that such Independents as may for the future enter into this Church do sign the following covenant or agreement, which is ordered to be inserted in our Church Book for that purpose, and a space left for the names of those that may sign it :—

[Then follows the Declaration] :—

We the underwritten, being Independents believing the *baptism of infants*, yet entertaining a Christian affection for our Brethren who believe *adult baptism* only, and being desirous of communicating with them at the table of the Lord, do hereby declare (at our entrance into this Church) that it shall, thro' grace, be our prayer and our endeavour to walk with them in *Brotherly love* and *Christian fellowship*, maintaining the *unity of the spirit* in the *bond of peace* ; and in case of the removal of the present or any future Pastor, this Church should become vacant; that then we will consent to the settlement of a minister of the Baptist persuasion over it, and by no means seek to prevent or disturb such settlement ; and this we think but reasonable, considering that there is a Pædobaptist congregation in this town, the minister of which may admit the infants of such as desire it to what we think their priviliege ; and that it would not be equitable to deprive our Baptist Brethren of a minister who may administer the ordinance of

Baptism to them in the way that they think most agreeable to the word of God.

Willm. Dix [of Chester.]   Est. Eliz. Dix [Spinster.]

[No other signatures are attached to this declaration.]

(9) At a Church Meeting, January 1st, 1779,
Our Brother and Sister, John and Mary Mellor, having intimated by our Pastor their desire of being dismissed in order that with others they might be formed into a Baptist Church in Common Hall Lane, Chester, the Independent Church which lately met there having built another Meeting House, It was unanimously Agreed, That they be dismissed for the above purpose ; and that we will consider that Church, when settled agreeably to the order of the Gospel, as a Church of Jesus Christ, and take pleasure in being helpful to its comfort and advancement.

(10) [Feb. 10 and July 14, 1779, were observed as days of fasting and prayer, the first " by public authority," the second " in Association by the Baptist Churches throughout Wales." Mr. Jenkins' sermon on the first occasion is included in his " Discourses on Select Passages of the Scripture History."]

(11) At a Church Meeting, Sept. 1st, 1779 . . . .
It was intimated that the Presbyterian congregation in this Town have made a disturbance, and threatened us with law concerning the exclusive property of this church in the Burying ground; whereupon it was unanimously Agreed, That this Church consider it as their duty to maintain, as far as in them lies, their sole right to the said Burying Place, together with the disposal of the key, the appointment of the grave-digger, and the settlement of the rates of burial, and that no other congregation or church can with justice infringe on this right, tho' this Church admits Dissenters in general to bury their dead there upon paying the dues required.

Agreed also, That our brethren, Joseph Jenkins, William Lloyd [ch. IV., note 22], John Mellor [see ch. IV., note 24], Joseph Jones [mason], and John Hughes, of New Bridge, be appointed to watch over the concerns of the said Burying Place, and take such measures as shall be necessary for defending our right to the said Place.

Agreed also, That they have power to call in the assistance of any other of the members if necessary.

Whereas a Resolution was entered into by this Church, April 14, 1774, That none but professed and declared Dissenters from the Church of England shall be buried in our Burying Ground without leave from this Church in a Church-Meeting first obtained; And whereas in particular cases, it has been found inconvenient and impossible to preserve the corpses until such leave can be readily procured, it was Agreed, That the Pastor or Deacons of the Church may give such liberty ; but that this power be only admitted of in cases of immediate and absolute necessity, and that the said Pastor and Deacons do insist upon the latter clause of the said agreement of April 14, 1774, respecting the dues to be paid by such persons not declared Dissenters.

(12). At a Church-Meeting, Nov. 27, 1780, It having been recommended to us that for our own satisfaction and for the sake of posterity, a true state of our Right and Title to the *Burying Ground* should be drawn up and inserted in the Church-Book; the same was read by our Pastor, and is as followeth :—

(*a*). That in the days of Oliver Cromwell, on (as it appears from authentic proof) as far off as 1656, there was a congregational church in Wrexham, dissenting from all national establishments of religion, even when the worship of the Parish Church was Presbyterian.

(*b*). That of the Dissenters who composed this Church, we are, as a Church, the regular successors.

(*c*). That these Dissenters purchased a Burying place for themselves and their successors, which was always considered as the joint property of the said Congregational Church.

(d). That after the Restoration of King Charles the Second, Mr. Ambrose Mostyn was ejected from the Parish Church for nonconformity to the rites and ceremonies of the Church of England, and with his people met, as often as the times permitted, in part of an house now turned into an Inn, and known by the name of the *Red Lion*.

(e). That when the Revolution took place (upon the coming in of King William in 1688), and Dissenters had more liberty, both the above congregations met for some years in an house commonly called the *Old Meeting*; but still were always considered as two distinct Churches, though having one Minister; the old Dissenters consisted of Antipœdobaptists (more commonly called *Baptists*) and Independents under the pastoral care of the Rev. Mr. John Evans; the others were Presbyterians, to whom a minister came occasionally to administer the Lord's Supper.

(f). That, upon a doctrinal dispute some years afterwards, the congregation divided, the Presbyterians betaking themselves to another place of worship, and procuring a minister of their own, by which means arose the *New Meeting* in distinction from the *Old Meeting*.

(g). That till very lately it was never disputed that the property of the Burying-ground was solely in the Old Meeting, as it had been before the Presbyterians came to hear with them.

(h). That but very few of the Presbyterians, till of late years,[97] desired to be buried in the Burying-ground; on the contrary, their principal people and some of their ministers (Mr. Long, for instance), were buried in the Parish Churchyard; nor were any of their ministers buried in the Dissenting Burying-ground till the year 1744, when the Rev. John Kenrick was interred there by permission of the *Old Meeting*.

(i). That the Old Meeting congregation always have buried in their own Burying-ground, and five of their pastors lie there, to wit, Morgan Lloyd, John Evans, Jenkyn Thomas [?], John Williams, and Evan Jenkins.

(j). That the Old Meeting congregation have always kept the key of the said Burying ground without the smallest interruption, settled the rates of burial, and appointed the gravedigger, who was always one of their own members.

(k) That it appears from an ancient Book of Accounts belonging to the congregation, that the wall, doors, hedges, etc., of the said Burial Ground were repaired entirely at the expense of the Old Meeting; nor did the New Meeting ever interfere in these concerns, or ever contribute anything towards the said repairs.

(l) That from the said Book, it appears also that the Old Meeting congregation have cut down trees which grew in the said Burying ground, sawed them into boards, paid for the sawing, and sold the said boards, without the interference of the New Meeting or the least pretence to a power of interrupting them.

(m) That the congregation which formerly met in the Old Meeting-House, resolving to build that Meeting House in which we now assemble for divine worship, cut down trees in the said Burying ground for the use of the said Meeting House without any interruption.

(n) That from the congregation-book above mentioned it further appears that the said Burying Ground was let out by the Old Meeting congregation,

97. This statement is not correct. The earlier Presbyterians, it is true, still hoping to be included in the Established Church, were generally buried in the churchyard, but as soon as they came definitely to regard themselves as Dissenters, few of them were buried there. In 1746 the Presbyterian minister began to keep a regular register of the burials which he conducted in what he calls "The Meeting Yard," and these burials were then very numerous, and doubtless had been numerous for some time before.

and that they sold the grass and hay which grew upon it (sometimes even to members of the New Meeting) the money for which is accounted for in the said Book, and receipts drawn.

(o)   That an abuse having been introduced and practised for some years of permitting others besides Dissenters to bury in the said Burying Ground, it was found necessary to be stopped ; but no one pretended to a power of rectifying this abuse till it was done by an agreement of this Church entered into April the 4th, 1774.

(p)   That the aforegoing particulars having been laid by our Pastor before Council learned in the laws of this country, it is the unanimous opinion of the said Council that our long and uninterrupted possession of the said Burying Ground secures to this Church an exclusive property therein ; and it is strongly recommended that, as in former times, no one be permittted to bury therein without paying an acknowledgment for the favour, which acknowledgment ought to be paid to this Church, or to some one by them appointed to the custody of the said Burying Ground.

(13)   At a Church-Meeting, April 29, 1782,

Application having been made to us by our Brethren and Sisters, John and Mary Mellor, Thomas Crane, Mary Walley, and Jane Price for a letter of dismission from this Church for the purpose of joining with others to form a Particular Baptist Church in Common Hall Lane, Chester, the same was agreed to, and that a letter be drawn up for that purpose.

(14).   December 28th, 1783, our Brother John Hughes, formerly Pastor of the Church in Glynn Ceiriog, having departed this life Dec. 25th, after a confinement of six years, by a stroke of the Palsy ; his funeral sermon was preached this afternoon from Psalm 119th, 75th, *I know, O Lord, that thy judgments are right, and that thou in faithfulness hast afflicted me.*

(15).   At a Church-Meeting, Lord's Day, April 4th, 1784 (our country brethren being present), it was agreed,

That Daniel Roberts did causelessly rent himself from the Communion of this Church about May or June, 1776, hath ever since been out of Communion, and hath discovered a temper of mind in which the Church could not consider him as a member of it.

That the said Daniel Roberts having cut himself off from the privileges of a member of this Church, and being still unconvinced of his error, the Church does, on its part with prayer to God formally continue [so] from communion till it shall please God to restore him by repentance.

(16).   1785. At a Church-Meeting, March 30th, it was reported, etc. . .

. . . .

Whereas, also, our Pastor did at the Assizes in March, 1779, levy a Fine upon the Burying-ground belonging to this church, and put the said ground into the hands of Trustees for the sole use and benefit of us and the succeeding members of the Church, which Fine has passed the legal term unclaimed, it was agreed unanimously,

That the Church doth heartily approve of the conduct of the Pastor in regard to the said Fine and Deed of Trust, and that they do consent to any measures he may take for its further security.

And whereas the Presbyterian Congregation in this Town have frequently pretended a claim to a share in the said ground, which claim, however, they never attempted to make out, and which pretended claim, with all others, is now cut off by the said Fine, it was agreed, That this Church doth deny that the said Presbyterian Congregation ever had any right to demand Burial in the said ground, or ever did bury there but by permission. And this Church doth recommend the utmost caution against such mistaken notions and encroachments for the future, and is particularly of opinion, warranted by the behaviour of the said Congregation, that the making any concessions of any kind to the said Presbyterian Congregation, respecting the burial of their dead in future, in the said ground is utterly improper, and all requests of that nature, however artfully worded, are ensnaring, and put with a view to enveigle the Church into some Measure that may hereafter be improved into a claim to the right of burial in the said Ground.

And whereas a certain Congregation of Methodists hath of late years started up in this town,[98] calling itself by the name of an Independent Church, and which congregation hath explicitly avowed itself inimical to our Church ; hath by false pretences obtained the Independent Fund Exhibition of £5 p. ann. which had for fifty years been given to this Church ; and hath, by several of its members, declared a design of disputing with us in Law, the property of the said Ground, or on a right of burial thereon, It was agreed unanimously, That this Church (out of a regard for its own safety), will never admit any of the members of the said Congregation to be buried in the said Ground ; and that if any person or persons do separate from either of the two ancient Congregations of Dissenters in this Town to join the said Congregation, or attend there statedly, such person or persons shall not, or their families, be buried in the said ground. And that the present or any future minister of, or connected with, the said congregation, shall never be permitted to speak over a grave in the said ground. And that the Church hath come to these resolutions, not out of enmity, or a desire of returning evil for evil, but as steps necessary for the preservation of their own property.

(17). At a Church-Meeting August 7th, 1785 . . . .

The same day in the evening came before the Church Frances Jones, Senr., of Wrexham, who was examined touching her Faith and Experience, when it was considered by the Church, That the said Frances Jones having for several years solicitted to become a member of this Church, and still persisting notwithstanding many discouragements from our people, and allurements from other quarters, the Church does charitably hope that her knowledge and belief of the truth is genuine, tho' her inability of reading and incapacity of utterance prevent her expressing it to others, and therefore agrees, that she with William Baugh be baptized in this place to-morrow evening, the 8th Instant.

(18). At a Church-Meeting, Wednesday, March 1st, 1786,

Information was given the Church that William Lloyd, a member of this Church, into whose custody the Burying-ground had been put, died the 23rd of February in this year ; and the keys of the said Ground being laid before us at this Meeting, the question was put before us for deliberation, into whose hands the said Burying-ground should now be put? When it was agreed,

· That the said Burying-ground be put under the care of our present Pastor, who shall also take to himself the profits thereof.

Intimation being given also at this Meeting, That the Presbyterians in this Town have repeatedly refused to pay the dues for burial, and the Stamp-duty which by an Act of the last Session of Parliament became payable to Government—from Oct. 1st, 1785, It was agreed, That the said stamp-duty of threepence for registering every burial, and the other dues for interment, be for the future paid by the said Presbyterian Congregation previous to their obtaining any Grave in the said Burying Ground.

(19) At a Church Meeting, Sept. 3, 1786,

Our Brethren and Sisters, John Hughes, Hugh Davies, John Price, Edward Davies, John Charles, Richard Richards, Anne Roberts, and Jane Davies, having desired their dismission from this church, in order to unite with others in forming a Baptist Church at New Bridge under the pastoral care of Mr. Jenkin Davies, the said dismission was read to the church, and signed by the Brethren then present.

---

98. The congregation above indicated is that represented by the present Independent church meeting at Pen-y-bryn. It was from the beginning in form and fact Independent and not Methodist.

(20) June 3rd, 1787. Died, our aged Brother and Deacon, Robert Thomas, who was buried the 6th instant, and his Funeral Sermon preached Lord's day the 10th Inst., by our Pastor from John 11th 11th—*Our friend Lazarus sleepeth.*

4. The above is the last entry in the " Church Book" in the handwriting of Dr. Jenkins; nor do other entries of any kind occur in it until Sept. 25, 1805, when the following record appears in the handwriting of Mr. W. F. Jenkins :—

Wrexham, 25th September, 1805. We the underwritten having been this day baptized by immersion on profession of faith, and about to be formed into a Church, intend, in the strength of divine grace, to abide by the following particulars, namely, To maintain the doctrines of free, sovereign and efficacious grace, acknowledging the riches of that grace of God in providing a Saviour for us wretched sinners, even the Lord Jesus Christ, his goodness in sending the gospel to us, giving us some experience of the power of that gospel in our souls through the sacred operation of His Holy Spirit, and calling us to be a part of His church in this world. And we do now, in the name and fear of God, give up ourselves to the Lord and to one another by the will of God, desiring to walk together in Church-fellowship, according to the rules of the gospel, attending on the means of grace regularly, and endeavouring in all things to adorn the Doctrines of God our Saviour.

W. F. Jenkins (see ch. IV. note 29)
Isaac Matthews (see ch. IV. note 25a)
Hannah Jenkins (wife of Mr. W. F. Jenkins)
Elizth. Griffiths
Sarah Roberts
} Baptized 25th day of Sept. by John Palmer, and formed into a church.

John Ratcliffe (see chap IV. note 25)
Mary Ratcliffe
} By dismission from the Baptist church at Manchester.

Richard Price [see ch. IV., sec. 44 & 45] By dismission from Newtown.
Hannah Griffiths[99]
Anna Jenkins
} Received as members of the Old Church.

Ann Matthews — By dismission from Cefn Bychan.

5. Then comes the following record :—

" 1805, Nov. 20. Our brother, Richard Pryce, was called to the Pastoral office by the Church and regularly ordained. The ministers present were— Mr. Webster, Liverpool ; Palmer, Shrewsbury ; Thomas, Broseley ; and Jones, Glynn Ceiriog. And at the same time our brother John Ratcliffe was called by the Church to the office of Deacon."

6. This is followed by a list of persons baptised in the year 1806, the last entry in the book :—

John Jones
Elizabeth Jones
} Baptised by our Pastor, 2nd day of February, 1806.

John Walley [farmer, of Farndon]
Thomas Walley [farmer, of Utkinton, Cheshire]
Edward Hurler [?]
Phœbe Walley [wife of Thos. Walley, see above]
Martha Walley [wife of John Walley, see above]
Elizabeth Robinson
} Baptised by our minister, 6th April, 1806.

99. Wife of Mr. Richard Griffiths, of Oswestry (see ch. IV., sec. 49), and I suppose the Hannah Jones mentioned in the second list of members in Appendix IV.; a member at Wrexham because there was as yet no Baptist church at Oswestry

Edward Parry Gwen Parry [wife of Edw. Parry] William Baugh	Baptised by our minister, 4th May, 1806.
Thomas Sudlow [see ch. IV., note 31]	By dismission, Baptist Church at Salop.
Sarah Davies	Baptised by our minister, 6th July.
Edward Edwards Sarah Edwards	Baptised by our minister, 3rd August.

V.

The Dissenters' Burial Ground, Wrexham.

1. The Dissenters' Burial Ground, Rhosddu Road, Wrexham, may with truth be called *The Bunhill Fields* of North Eastern Wales and of the parts of Cheshire adjoining. The bodies of thousands lie within it and make its dust sacred, who in their lives cherished high thoughts, withstood temptation, and wrought righteousness. And desolate and neglected as it now is, the place seldom fails to affect me, kindling within me as I pass it the memory of those whose dust it holds.

2. This graveyard is of ancient date. It is generally believed that it was laid out during the period of the Commonwealth, and that Morgan Lloyd was buried in it. Both these statements were made, as matters of common knowledge, in the year 1780 [App. IV., sec. 3 (12)] ; and, though I am bound to say, that neither of them can be regarded as absolutely proved, there are various considerations which incline me to think that they are both of them probably true.

3. In support of the Præ-Restoration origin of the graveyard may be mentioned, first of all, a statement made by the late Mr. Isaac Matthews (see ch. IV., note 25a), that on the 14th of March, 1820, he found a gravestone in the ground bearing the date 1656. This stone cannot now anywhere be found, and it is therefore impossible to subject Mr. Matthews' reading of it to criticism, but there is no reason to suppose that he was mistaken. Next must be mentioned the tradition that Morgan Lloyd, who died in 1659, was buried within this graveyard. This tradition is clear and definite, and the stone which was supposed to mark the great mystic's grave (with no more than the letters M.L. upon it), was still in existence within the memory of many now living.

4. " But," it may be asked, " what could have been the reasons which moved the Puritans of the Commonwealth time, who already had control of the churchyard, to establish another burial ground in the town ? " It would be difficult to give a satisfactory answer to this question, but it should be said that the Puritans of

that time were divided into Independents and Presbyterians, and that for some years before the Restoration it was the Presbyterians who were predominant in the town, while the graveyard in question is supposed to have been laid out by the Independents. The members of the Old Meeting have no papers to show how the burial ground came into their possession, and their title to it before 1779 rested solely upon prescription. But there is no doubt that full rights of ownership were exercised within this burying place by the Old Meeting at the beginning of the 18th century, and I find it described in 1697 as belonging to the Dissenters, or, at any rate, as used by them. It is pretty certain, from the form of the graveyard, that it was originally a quillet enclosed out of the Common Fields of Wrexham, probably out of the field called " Talar-y-geifr."

5. In view of the large number of notable people that have been buried in the Rhosddu Road graveyard, it is very much to be regretted that no complete registers exist of the burials that have taken place in it. What makes matters worse is the wicked havoc made here among the memorials of the dead about forty years ago when, on the night of Wrexham races, all the brasses in it, save one, were sacrilegiously torn from the tombs and carried away, the memorials of many families being thus destroyed.

6. In the year 1857 the hedge around the graveyard was replaced by a wall; in 1883 a portion of it was surrendered, in order to widen Rhosddu Road; and this year (1888) the graveyard has been, by an order in Council, finally closed.

ADDENDUM.

I have learned, since the third chapter was written, that Sarah Kenrick (see page 76), who married Ralph Eddowes, died at Philadelphia, U.S.A., July 30th, 1815, at the age of 61. and was therefore born in 1754. In the paragraph on page 76 in which Sarah Kenrick is mentioned there occurs a misprint which has unfortunately escaped correction, Ralph Eddowes being stated to have died in 1883 instead of in 1833.

Corrections

Since my *History of the Parish Church of Wrexham* was issued, I have accumulated quite a mass of additional matter, which, should that work ever come to a second edition, will be incorporated with it. Additional matter can wait, but I am anxious to seize the first opportunity of correcting any mistakes I have made in writing the book.

Page 11.—It appears that Browne Willis, whom in this matter I followed, was mistaken in assigning the 1st of October to St. Silin. The feast of St. Silin was on September 1st, on the same day as the feast of St. Giles. It is easy to see, therefore, how the one saint became confounded with the other, and the strongest argument against the former dedication of the church to St. Silin is thus disposed of.

Referring to note 36, page 26, the shield on the third corbel on the north side of the clerestory was not meant to be represented as blank, but only (as presenting some difficulty in its charges), to be left undescribed.

In sec. 48, page 28, I have followed the transcriber of the deed quoted, and written "*John* Sontley," but I strongly suspect that for "*John* Sontley " we should read "*Robert* Sontley."

In sec. 65, page 33, I have wrongly explained the phrase " pair of organs." A " pair of organs " had only a single set of keys.

As to the offerings at funerals, in what I said in sec. 85b, page 44, I had forgotten an earlier passage in the Wrexham Parish Register to the following effect: — [Buried] Dec. 17, 1718, Thomas Povah, Taylor, then ye offerings began there." So that it appears that offerings at funerals were begun here in 1718, *diverted* in 1730 to the use of the curate of Minera, and afterwards resumed by the Vicar of the parish, for it is certain that in the time of Canon Cunliffe, the latter and not the curate of Minera, received the offerings.

Although I followed the parish register in stating (note 23, page 80), that the father of Mary Rogers was John Rogers, of *Bersham*, I have since had reason to believe that he was John Rogers, of the Chapel Farm, *Broughton*.

In note 152, page 98, probably by the omission of a line in my manuscript, I have given a wrong account of the transmission of Mr. Morgan's estate. The facts are these :—Mr. Morgan's daughter Elizabeth married (September 13, 1756), Mr. John Dymock (see note 181). The estates in Stansty, Brymbo, and Broughton, which belonged to Mr. Morgan, and which Mrs. Jane Eyton [see App. V. sec. 5a (17)] had formerly owned, passed thus ultimately, with the rest of the property of the Dymocks of Stansty, into the possession of the Wynnes, of Garthewin.

I shall be glad also if the reader will make with his pen the following corrections :—

Page 48, note 55, last line, for "1869" read "1868."

„ 68, „ 13, „ for "Bodelwyddan" read "Bodrhyddan."

„ 76, 3rd line from top, for "Perth-y-bi, Erlys" read "Erlys Hall."

„ 87, note 16, 7th line from top, for "30" read "30b."

„ 100, 4th line from top, for "Henry Carstairs" read "Richard Puleston."

„ 101, note 180, 2nd line from top, for "William Jones, of Wrexham, wine merchant," read "Rev. William Jones, formerly curate of Wrexham, see page 77."

„ 108, note 276, 2nd line from top, for "Acton" read "Gourton."

„ 118, note 315, 2nd line from top, for "32" read "35."

„ 115, „ 341, 1st „ „ for "27" read 25."

„ 115, „ 349, 2nd „ „ for "Jessie" read "Ann."

„ 116, note 360, 2nd line from top, for "24" read "34a" and for "1808" read "1858."

„ 122, 5th line from top, for "1876" read "1886."

„ 141, note 39, 1st line, cross out "Sir," and for "Kt." read "Esq."

„ 150, note 58, last line, for "1745" read "1744."

„ 166, „ 83, 3rd line from top, for "short" read "shoot."

„ 174, „ 105, „ „ insert "Briscoe" after "Bostock."

„ 186, in sec. 6 (2) and note 5, for "Standy" read "Stanney."

„ 197, line 13 from top, for "represented in the accompanying illustration," read "figured as a tailpiece to this appendix."

„ 210, 5th line from top, for "176$\frac{1}{2}$" read "167$\frac{1}{2}$."

„ 211, 18th line from top, after "Dni" insert "MDCLXXIII" and in line 19 erase "MDCLXXIII" and write "75"

„ 217, note 27, for "Pate" read "Manning."

„ 225, line 20, for "Treen" read "Green," and for "Green" read "Treen."

LIST OF SUBSCRIBERS.

Allmand, Ernest, Wrexham.
Acton, T. Bennion, Grove Road, Wrexham.
Ashley, W. J., M.A., University College, Toronto, Canada.
Alexander, Wm., 6, Hill Street, Wrexham.
Allmand, Frank, Wrexham.
Allbright, Arthur, Mariemount, Edgbaston, Birmingham.

Baugh, S. T., Plas-pen-y-ddol, Wrexham.
Bates, Thomas, Tenter's Square, Wrexham.
Bate, George, White House, Wrexham.
Brown, Frank A., St. John's Lodge, Harborne, Birmingham.
Bennett, Edgar, 2, Court Ash, Yeovil.
Brown, Rev. F. B., Coed Efa, near Wrexham.
Boult, Peter S., Mosley Hill, Liverpool.
Boult Joseph, D17, Exchange Buildings, Liverpool.
Bithell, Wm., Rise Park, Hull.
Barnes, Lieut-Col., Jas. R., Brookside, near Chirk.
Bury, John, Hilbury, Wrexham.
Beirne, John, Plas Derwen, Wrexham.
Barton, Theo. B., Wrexham.
Boothey, Henry, 17, Stanley Street, Wrexham.
Brown, Alfred W., Coxwold House, Worcestershire.
Broad, Wm., 20, Penybryn, Wrexham.
Bird, S. H., Brooklands, Wrexham.
Barnes, Wm., 30, Cunliffe Street, Wrexham.
Beakbane, Thos., Llai Place, near Wrexham.
Blackwell, Henry, Woodside, Long Island, New York (6 Copies).

Caldecott, Geoffrey, 12, Regent Street, Wrexham.
Coleman, T. H., L.D.S., Bryn Edwyn, Regent Street, Wrexham.
Corporation of London Library, Guildhall, London, E.C.
Cudworth, J., 9, Osborne Terrace, Talbot Road, Wrexham.
Clark, E. S. Pen Llwyn, Chester Road, Wrexham.
Chadwick, J. A., Percy Road, Wrexham.
Crompton, J. G., 4, Mostyn Terrace, Wrexham.

Darby, Alfred, Wren's Nest, Rhosddu, Wrexham (2 Copies).
Davies, John, 2, Hope Street, Wrexham.
Davies, Howell, Bodhowel, Wrexham.
Dodd, Charles, Clovelley Cottage, Wrexham.

Davies, Llewelyn, Eirianfa, Chester Road, Wrexham.
Davies, Dr. Edwd., Plas Darland, Wrexham.
Dobie, Alex., 28, Lambpit Street, Wrexham.
Davies, C., 58, Hope Street, Wrexham.
Darby, Wm., 18, Mount Pleasant, Oxton, Birkenhead.
Dodd, Simon, Chestnut Villa, Gwersyllt, Wrexham.
Davies, James, 10, Percy Road, Wrexham.
Davies, Rev. J. E., Llangelynin Rectory, Llwyngwril, Merioneth.
Davies, Wm., Old Vicarage, Wrexham.
Done, R. H., Town Hill, Wrexham.

Edwards, Rev. T. C., M.A., Principal of University College,
    Aberystwyth.
Egerton, Sir R. E., Coedyglyn, Wrexham.
Ellis, Wm., Claremont Cottage, Rhosddu, Wrexham.
Edwards, E , 39, Cunliffe Street, Wrexham.
Evans, E. B., Oxford House, Wrexham.
Evans, Edwd., Thorndale, Urmston, Manchester.
Evans, Edwd., Bronwylfa, near Wrexham.
Evans, W. R., 29, Chester Street, Wrexham.
Evans, E. D., 31, Regent Street, Wrexham.
Edwards, J. P., Guardian Office, Wrexham.
Edwards, Jno., Old Vicarage, Wrexham.
Evans, John, M.A., Salop School, Oswestry.
Edwards, James Alfred, Oswestry.

Fraser, James, Queen Street, Wrexham.
Francis, John, Nythfa, Grosvenor Road, Wrexham (2 Copies).
Fernley, T. R., 17, Hope Street, Wrexham.

Gordon, Rev. Alex., M.A., 9, Upper Crescent, Belfast.
Gummow, M. J., 1, Hill Street, Wrexham.
Griffiths, Llewelyn, Market Hall, Wrexham.
Glascodine, Chas., Ruthin Road, Wrexham.

Howell, Rev. Canon D., B.D., The Vicarage, Wrexham.
Hughes, A. Ll., Brynhyfryd, Wrexham.
Houghton, Wm., 4, Salisbury Road, Wrexham.
Heyward, Wm., 30, Chester Street, Wrexham.
Holland, Mrs. C. M., Bryn-y-grôg, near Wrexham.
Humphreys-Owen, A. C., J.P., Glansevern, Garthmyl, Mont
                                                    (2 copies).
Ingham, Thos., Percy Road, Wrexham.

Jones, A. Seymour, 20, Grosvenor Road, Wrexham (4 Copies).
Jones, R. Meredith, North and South Wales Bank, Liverpool
Jones, Simon, Wrexham.   4 Copies.

Jones, Thomas, 57, Hope Street, Wrexham.
Jones, E. M., J.P., Timber Merchant, Wrexham.
Jones, J., J.P., St. John's, Wrexham.
Jones, Hugh, Lion Stores, Hope Street, Wrexham.
Jones, William, Old Bank Buildings, High Street, Wrexham.
Jones, A. Rhys, 1, Hope Street, Wrexham.
Jones, Wm., 42, Cambrian Terrace, Wrexham.
Jones, Edwd., Architect and Diocesan Surveyor, 12, Temple
    Row, Wrexham.
Jones, T. C., Leeswood House, Wrexham.
Jones, Wm., Woodland View, Gwersyllt, Wrexham.
James, T. Reginald, Brynyffynon, Wrexham.
Jerman, Rev. Edwd., Holly Bank, Wrexham.
Jones, Henry A., Poplar Road, Wrexham.
Jones, Richd., 21, Henblas Street, Wrexham.
Jones, Chas., 8, Lambpit Street, Wrexham.
Jones, F. M., Henfryn, Wrexham.
Jones, C. D., 35, Chester Street, Wrexham.
Jones, Ll. Hugh, The Caeau, Wrexham.
Jones, Peleg. J., Eirianfa, Broughton, Wrexham.
Jones, Rev. J. Evans, 32, Erddig Road, Wrexham.
Jones, Samuel, 28, Gwynfa Terrace, Wrexham.
Jones, D., 92, Willow Street, Oswestry.
Jones, J. Parry, Town Clerk, Oswestry.
Jones, Miss Bertha, Holly Bush House, Canal Street, Chester.

Kenrick, J. Arthur, Berrow Court, Edgbaston, Birmingham.
                                                    [6 Copies.
Kenrick, Llewelyn, Wynn Hall, Ruabon.
Kenrick, Geo. H., Whetstone, Somerset Road, Edgbaston,
    Birmingham.
Kenrick, William, M.P., The Grove, Harborne, Birmingham
Kendrick R. J., Solicitor, Wrexham.   (2 Copies).

Lloyd, E. Ll., Heathfield, Sale, Cheshire.
Lewis, J., Beechley, Wrexham.
Lewis, J. Herbert, Vaynol, Ivanhoe Road, Sefton Park, Liverpool.
Lancashire Independent College, Whalley Range, Manchester.
Lewis, John, 7, Trevor Street, Wrexham.

Minshall, T. E., 13, Lawn Road, Hampstead, N.W.
Martin, T., 52, Hope Street, Wrexham.
Myddelton, W. M., 12, Albion Grove, Stoke Newington, N.
Manchester Public Free Reference Library, King St., Manchester.
Morgan, J. T., Mount, Gresford.
Mundella, A. J., M.P., 16, Elvaston Place, London, S.W.

Mudd, Albert Edward, 13, Regent Street, Wrexham.
Morris, Evan, J.P., Roseneath, Wrexham.
Mason, Edmund, Beaconsfield, Wrexham.
Myers, Edward, The Parsonage, Shrewsbury.

Norris, Wm. J., Coalbrookdale, Shropshire (2 Copies).
New, Joseph P., 9, Regis Place, Wrexham.

Odgers, Rev. J. Edwin, M.A., Horton, Bowdon, Cheshire.
Oliver, Rev. Wm., M.A., 8, King Street, Wrexham.
Owen, Alfred, Wood Hey, Wrexham.
Owens, Edwin, 18, Town Hill, Wrexham.
Odgers, J., 34, Cunliffe Street, Wrexham.
Owen, Griffith, 2, Greenfield Terrace, Wrexham.
Overton, Wm., Irvon House, Wrexham.
Owen, Benjamin, Penybryn, Wrexham.
Owen, Edwd., India Office, Whitehall, London, S.W.

Parry, S. P., Willow Street, Oswestry.
Poole, Edwin, *County Times*, Brecon.
Pierce, J. Hopley, Solicitor, Regent St., Wrexham.
Palin, H. V., Crescent House, Wrexham.
Phennah, Thos., 11, Trevor Street, Wrexham.
Price, Isaac, 6, Earl Street, Wrexham.
Prichard, Wm , J.P., 7, King Street, Wrexham.
Powell, R. J., Irvon Villa, Grosvenor Road, Wrexham.
Powell, Evan, Broomcliffe, Llanidloes.
Phœnix, James, 15, Holt Street, Wrexham.
Pierce, Mrs. Jane, Sherbourne House, Leamington.
Powell, Ellison, 86, St George's House, Eastcheap, London.
Pierce, Wm., Bridge Street, Wrexham,
Prichard, John, Longfields, Wrexham.
Powell, J. E., Grosvenor Road, Wrexham.
Potter, W., High Street, Wrexham.
Powell, Benjamin, Queen Street, Wrexham.
Price, Noah, 18, Queen Street, Wrexham.
Powell, Mrs. Mary, Irvon Villa, Grosvenor Road, Wrexham.
Phennah, James, Temple Row, Wrexham.
Pierce, D. D., Hope Street, Wrexham.
Parry-Jones, Dr. W. R., Penybryn, Wrexham.
Parkins, W. Trevor, Glasfryn, Gresford, Wrexham.
Phennah, R., Woodlands, Chester Road, Wrexham.
Phillips, Wm., 14, King Street, Wrexham.

Rocke, Geo., 81, South Hill Park, Hampstead, London, N.W.
Roberts, David, D.D., 2, Garfield Villas, Wrexham.
Rawlins, F. L., Rhosddu, Wrexham.

Russell, W. J., B.A., Grove Park School, Wrexham.
Rogers, M., 2, Henblas Street, Wrexham.
Rowlands, Jno., 39, High Street, Wrexham.
Roberts, R., M.R.C.V.S., 80, Bridge Street, Wrexham.
Roberts, H. R., Roderick Terrace, Wrexham.
Roberts, E., Bryncoch, Brymbo, Wrexham.
Rees, Rev. Wm., Berse, Wrexham.
Roberts, D., 53, Willow Street, Oswestry.

Sturge, F. A., Coed Efa, Wrexham.
Seebohm, Frederick, The Hermitage, Hitchin, Herts. (2 Copies).
Shone, Isaac, Wrexham.
Smith, Edwin, 83, Wheeley's Road, Birmingham.
Smallwood, R. H., Wrexham.
Stobo, Robert, Lambpit Street, Wrexham.
Stanford, J., Central Temperance Hotel, Wrexham.
Sayce, Benjamin J., Parkfield, New Ferry, Birkenhead.
Sudlow, John, 6, Hope Street, Wrexham.
Samuel, W. E., Stratford House, Wrexham.
Storr, Frederick, 5, Charles Street, Wrexham.
Snowden, Joseph, 21, York Street, Wrexham.
Stokes, Wm., 13, Penybryn, Wrexham.

Thomas, Thomas, Tynywern, Pontypridd.
Taylor, William, London House, Abbott Street, Wrexham.
Thomas, Wm., Bron Llwyn, Wrexham.
Thomas, Wm., 42, Hope Street, Wrexham.
Thomas, J. E., 47, Talbot Road, Wrexham.

Vaughan-Jones, Rev. W., 7, Stanley Street, Wrexham.

Williams, W. H., Hope Street, Wrexham.
Williams, W. Harrison, Regent Street, Wrexham.
Williams, Dr. Edwd., Holt Street House, Wrexham.
Williams, Rev. W. H. Barrow, 19, King Street, Wrexham.
Williams, Rev. Griffith, Chester Street, Wrexham.
Wakeford, J. B., 43, Chester Street, Wrexham.
Williams, Wm. P., Upper Bangor, Carn.
Williams, Wm. H., 5, King Street, Wrexham.
Williams, W. J., Fairfield House, Wrexham.
Walmsley, Gilbert G., 50, Lord Street, Liverpool.
Wallis, C., Queen's Square, Wrexham.
Williams' Library, Dr. Daniel, Grafton Street, Gower St., London.
Williams, Humphrey, M.D., Plas Darland, Wrexham.

Young, Andrew, Park Lodge, Wrexham.
Yorke, Simon, J.P., Erddig, Wrexham.